R. VALENTINE

REVENANT

Copyright © 2012-2024 R. Valentine
Editing by Nina Fiegl, 2024
Proofing by Nina Fiegl, 2024
Cover art by Beauxif Graphics
Formatting by NVPLLC
Published by © Night Vision Publishing LLC (C1319203)

ISBN: PB: 978-1-963336-00-9
ISBN: 978 1 963336 12 2

Introduction

This Adult Fantasy Paranormal Romance series is intended for mature audiences and unsuitable for young readers. This book contains violence, gore, explicit language, and detailed intimate scenes.

The War of Blood and Roses Series challenges conventional themes and explores visionary concepts, innovative technologies, and ideologies that invite readers to embrace open-mindedness, inclusivity, and sustainable living in a futuristic, post-apocalyptic fantasy setting.

This book series has darker themes and tropes that may not be suited for some readers. Caution is recommended.

A full list of content and trigger warnings is located at the back of the book.

This book will end on a cliffhanger.

R. VALENTINE

REVENANT

To the me reading this: You're doing amazing.

It took nearly two decades to finally get it right—well, mostly. Is it perfect? Not even close. But I love it anyway.

Here's to chasing dreams, one awkward, stumbling step at a time.

And to all you fellow dream-chasers out there, keep reaching for the stars.

I'm proud of us.

Contents

Chapter One

Running was an essential part of living these days. I ran because I liked it, and I ran to stay alive. Outrunning a carcass was literally a do-or-die kind of thing ... and a great motivator for daily exercise.

It was a crisp morning in Thompson Falls; the air was cool enough that I could see my breath with each exhale yet warm enough to be without a jacket. The small compound I called home was still mostly asleep as I made a lap around the perimeter, keeping close to the steel fence and guarded walls while I jogged. The uneven, beaten-down path of dirt and grass was a familiar comfort as I tried to ignore the world around me.

In the distance, just beyond the border walls, I could hear the gnarl and shuffle of a *kook* straggler as it made its way closer to town. Only for a moment, the desperate cries of hunger escaped the dead's lips before being cut off by the click, pull, and a bang from one of the tower watchmen.

"Morning, Abby," Jerry hollered down to me once he lowered his weapon.

I gave him a brief wave but kept moving. The surrounding wilderness was quiet for a moment—my heavy breath a loud echo in the stillness of the early light—but soon the forest was happily chatting again, proving that even the creatures of this world were used to this way of life.

Nobody knew the exact time or day. Even the year it happened was lost and forgotten—as time did when it slipped by unnoticed—but the end of the world had come and gone, leaving in its wake a path of death and destruction.

The population had grown at an alarming rate and, as a result, the human populace forced the world into rapid climate change, compelling the planet to turn on itself. Weather and natural disasters killed off humans faster than they could get rid of each other. Coastlines grew while islands disappeared. Earthquakes and tsunamis had taken out entire countries, leaving extreme temperatures to take care of the weak and frail; starvation, dehydration, and heat exhaustion were major players for Team Earth. The apocalypse warned and foretold about for centuries had finally happened, and millions perished under the force of rock, water, and flame. Those who survived fled to major cities, seeking safety on higher ground, while others went to smaller, underpopulated towns and untouched lands. Where there were once billions of souls, now only millions remained, and if the estimations were right, the dead outnumbered the breathing twenty to one. As a result, humanity spread thin across the world to survive, but life was hard and living wasn't easy.

As I rounded the last corner of my lap, the O Motel came into view and, with it, the first signs of life. The light in my mother's room was on.

When we first came to Thompson Falls, the O Motel had just been fixed and was the temporary housing that new arrivals stayed in until something permanent became available. But Mom and I liked it, so instead of leaving, we'd made it our home. I remembered feeling comforted by the constant flux of visitors, in and out all day, and feeling safe by having so many people around. It was nice after being alone for so long.

Thompson Falls was a small town near the border of what used to be Montana. The area had been colonized specifically because of its location and its uncontaminated condition, which was mostly unheard of. Thompson Falls was nestled next to a brimming river and surrounded by vast, open lands. Its proximity to the mountains and the abundant life that lived in them made it perfect for safety and security, and ideal for growing crops, foraging, hunting, and fishing when necessary. It was also a great location because it put us far away enough from the bigger infected areas, but not so far that we couldn't travel for supplies.

As I made my way in through the front door of the O, the bell dinged with my entrance and the old, heavy door made a hollow thud when I pushed it shut. I took off my running jacket and hung it on the coat rack near the entrance, then headed into the dining room, following my nose to the smell of the morning's first pot of fresh brew.

"Coffee's ready," my mother told me as she passed from the kitchen through the double swinging doors. Its parchment-colored paint was rubbed and worn, and exposed old pine beneath. The squeak of the small door's hinges reminded me it needed oiling again.

The rest of the O, however, was nearly immaculate in its old-world charm. It was bright considering the floor, tables, and countertops were all medium- to dark-toned wood. Long, wide fat planks lined the floors throughout the restaurant, bar, and gaming room. The serving counter area and the back of the kitchen were concrete-poured for a more functional space and industrial look. The gray and tan stone accent walls in the public area helped with the lightness of the room, almost as much as the large pane-glass windows around the entire space. Long, pale curtains hung to the floor from the ceiling at each window, though they were rarely used. The setup was like that of an old bar and grill. There was a long countertop bar with stools, tables and chairs throughout the middle, and booths lined the edges of the room.

We had a menu with daily specials and served breakfast, lunch, and dinner. We also had what constituted a full bar in this day and age, serving beer, wine, and liquor. The kitchen usually closed after dinner but always offered snacks and leftovers when we had them. The O became popular with the town locals after my mother and I decided to stay and run the place. At the time, it'd been the only spot offering or serving food and drink like an old restaurant. Now, it was one of several in town but still a favorite for the locals.

With roughly thirty functioning motel rooms, The O offered guests comfortable lodging complete with beds, full bathrooms, sitting areas, and kitchenettes, along with a row of small cabins that lined the back of the property. In addition to the guest rooms, there were several larger spaces we used for various reasons and utility rooms to keep the place up and running. My mother and I each occupied two double rooms that were remodeled and turned into private living quarters.

The O also had a slew of volunteer staff members for everything, from cooking to cleaning, serving, and bartending. We did what we could for our town and community, offering a place to relax with food and drink, and a bed to sleep on if you needed it.

"Thanks," I said to Mom and headed to the sink, grabbing a glass and filling it with water, then pouring a cup of coffee. "If you give me a few minutes to clean up, I can make you something to eat before you go." I chugged the rest of the cool tap water from my glass.

"That's sweet, Abby, but you don't need to do that. Besides, I wanted to be early at the clinic today, and I'm already running late." She dumped the rest of her coffee into the sink then rinsed her chipped, over-sized mug and set it on the rack upside down to dry. The cursive *Don't talk until empty* was nearly smudged off from use. Normally, she took it to work with her, but the pot was already half empty before I'd poured my cup, so I silently approved of her wastefulness this morning.

"So, you're running late for being early?" I cocked a brow at her.

"Ha ha, Abby. Very funny." She smirked at me.

My mother, Olivia, was shorter than me by only an inch or two, putting her at around 5'5", and we looked nothing alike, other than our smiles. Her shoulder-length, dishwater-blonde hair had a natural wave when dry and would curl when wet. Her dark blue eyes were almond-shaped and framed with light brown lashes and brows. Faint freckles covered her body, and her skin was pale with pink undertones and highlights, which blushed easily. She was soft and gentle in all manner, and her smell reminded me of the snowdrop flowers she always grew outside in the summer.

My mother's appearance was in complete contrast to my long and stark, straight dark brown hair that hung to the middle of my back. Dark lashes and brows that matched my tanned skin framed my green eyes. My shape was more angular, harder in muscle—due to my profession—and I rarely smelled of sunshine and flowers.

Mom and I had first come to live here in Thompson Falls when I was eight. Commander Hendricks and his team found us after we'd been on the run for several weeks, having lost almost all of the people in our group. Hendricks was still putting the town together when he'd come across us and brought us to the Falls. At the time, the small town had only around a hundred or so people living in it. It wasn't long after our arrival, though, that my mother became something of a paragon and was quickly in high demand. Hendricks was more than just the leader; he was also the resident doctor—the only one until the point of our arrival.

Mom was midway through her general medicine studies when the plague surfaced. As a result of the pandemic, she underwent a crash course as a field medic. She quickly learned in the aftermath and had since become a skilled practitioner.

Years of continued disaster had left the planet's surface and the life on it forever changed. Buildings were ransacked, towns destroyed, and highways and streets were littered with abandoned vehicles. God and country had been replaced with fear and self-preservation—it was Martial Law and then every man for himself. Yet this was only the beginning of Earth's demise, with a forecast a barometer couldn't have predicted. The worst had yet to come, and it was then—during the quiet—that the eye of the storm finally showed its face.

The plague wasn't transmitted like in the old Hollywood movies. There'd been no neat epidemic maps or calculations, and soon there was no Army, Navy, Marines, or Air Force left to guide us with direction and show us the way. The infection hadn't spread like rolling waves or wildfire—there weren't enough people left for that—but it was strong and spread quickly in the first days, taking with it thousands of the remaining few.

Life on our planet was dying and both species wanted to survive, so when the vampires offered humans a solution, we readily and greedily signed on the proverbial dotted line—neither party aware of the oversight we were making.

A world without humans meant a world without blood, so while they created "I-M", we formed the receiving lines. For a time, blood became the new currency. It wasn't mandatory, but thousands lined up anyway.

Ageless immortality had been neatly packaged into a little vial. It kept the humans human and the vampires fed. The serum made humans stronger, healthier, and close to immortal, without changing the person into one of the vampires. For some, immortality had seemed a small price to pay to ensure the survival of the human race. So in exchange, a regular blood donation was traded indefinitely, which gave both species the opportunity to live to see another day.

It had given us humans an infinite amount of time to rebuild and learn from our mistakes, and with enhanced health, strength, and durability to survive Mother Nature, we were less subjective to the power and force of her will. We would no longer die because of human frailty and disease. Sickness would no longer affect those who had taken the vaccine, and our wounds would more easily heal.

The vampires' gain was that of the sun, and with the creation of "I-M", they were no longer left to live in the shadows. Our blood was the key to their survival, so when our population dwindled, so did their food supply. The inoculation was an antidote for death—it meant they would never starve, and we wouldn't perish. It wasn't until it was too late that we understood what that would mean and that we had made a terrible mistake.

Everything dies, and when it does, it stays dead—or so we thought.

Those who died with "I-M" in their system hadn't stayed that way for long. When they came back, they came back hungry, and the virus spread quickly. It was soon discovered that there was nothing to be done once you were bitten or infected, and that the only cure for this disease was a bullet to the brain or some other form of gray-matter destruction. Not even separation between head and chest was enough to stop this contagion.

I'd found I was proficient at the former but lacked the required upper body strength to be any good at the latter, which didn't bother me all that much—getting up close and personal with any zombie was something everyone strived to avoid.

"Will you be here when I get back later?" Mom asked as she gathered her things to leave for the care center, where she was now one of the dozens of doctors and nurses who worked there.

"Should be. We're still waiting for Rick's team to come in." I swirled the coffee in my cup instead of looking at her when I said this.

When I was old enough to look over a gurney and into a person's mouth, Mom taught me basic care and first aid, in the hope I would follow in her footsteps so I could work in the care center. But the job wasn't for me, and after two years, I'd thrown in the towel. I didn't have it in me to stitch a person back together or hold a puke bucket for someone else to get sick in. I'd learned a lot over those two years, but I couldn't imagine myself taking care of people in that setting for the rest of my life.

I knew she was disappointed—so was Hendricks—but neither of them had said too much. They'd both known what I wanted to do. I guess I was more comfortable with the dead and killing them, rather than trying to save someone from it. Eventually, as the town grew, more doctors and nurses came, and my guilt over the disappointment became less and less.

Once I decided I would not work in the care center, I began "slingin' hash"—as Hendricks called it—here in the kitchen at the O, and serving drinks to the townspeople when I wasn't on rotation. When I wasn't working at the restaurant and bar, I went out with the rest of the vanguard to collect supplies and gather essentials we couldn't make or produce for ourselves here. Most cities still standing, after the natural disasters stopped beating us down, later became infected with the dead. They were crawling with *grave mutants*, the remains of which they refused to be, but were also loaded with product, food, and supplies that would last us and generations for years.

Thousands of cities and towns across what was left of the United States, Canada, and the world were full of leftover commodities, and it was our job to retrieve these items while disposing and clearing the zombie-filled streets. Every time someone left the protective guard of the gates, they were risking their life—and death—but there were things left within the old cities' walls worth going after.

We rotated our raids in shifts, but several teams were usually out in the *Morgue*—the land outside the gates where the dead roamed—searching for, gathering, and rescuing lost treasure at all times. When I wasn't out there, I worked here at the O and fed the locals, but either way, I was in the business of service.

"How long have they been overdue?" Mom asked about Rick's team, trying to keep her voice even.

"Two days, but it's not a big deal, so please don't worry about it."

"Uh-huh." She came over to hug me. "And Zach? Have you heard anything else?"

"No. Hendricks hasn't said anything since they radioed a few weeks ago. I'm sure if he heard anything new, Mom, you and I would be the first to know." I smiled at her.

"You're right." She nodded in agreement.

Zach was with Mom and me when we'd been rescued to the Falls. He and his family had been part of our group, and he had no one else when we lost them, so my mother had taken him in. He was my best friend, like a brother to me and a son to her. She worried about him as much as she did about me and Hendricks when we were out in the *Morgue*. Zach's team had been gone for several weeks, and we didn't know when to expect them back. Which wasn't a problem until we'd lost contact with them, but even though we'd expected it, it still made us uneasy.

"Bye. Love you," I told her as she gathered her things and headed to the front door to leave.

"I love you too." She smiled back at me over her shoulder.

We were able to keep in contact with the town when out on assignment by using satellite phones, CBs, and radio waves—provided we had charged batteries and weren't too far away from a signal. I didn't understand all the mechanics behind our ability to talk over long distances or how we still had utilities most of the time, but I was thankful for it. That's not to say it didn't fail us often because it did, and it wasn't an uncommon thing to lose contact with someone outside the gates, if for no other reason than a battery going dead or a wire getting crossed. Still, it made us anxious and—for my mom, in particular—it was cause for alarm. She treated a lot of injuries, and saw and heard things that made it hard for her whenever the people she loved were out in the *Morgue*. Because of this, little things like a simple miscommunication made life all that much harder for me.

The town itself was powered with solar, wind, and water power plants' energy, left over from PEI—Pure Energy Initiative, enacted to combat climate change. Add that to our own minor production, and we had close to a functioning civilization. It was another thing Hollywood had done wrong in the old movies too; we hadn't lost all our technology or electricity, and we still had running water—usually.

Once mom had left for her shift, I went back to my room to get showered and cleaned up for the day, and I passed the rest of the morning prepping for the lunch rush. Breakfast was cooked to order, but lunch needed to be prepared since it was our busiest service of the day. A few regulars came in and helped in both the restaurant and the bar, and several part-timers liked to come in for the latest gossip or some other reason. Either way, I hardly ever found myself overworked or asking for help to run the place.

The vanguard hung out here a lot when they weren't out on rotation, and often stopped by for a drink before heading home when they got back into town, so the O usually got the best booze and found goods—if there were any—when they returned.

"Hey, Gigi," I greeted the little woman through the order window as she approached the serving counter. "I didn't know you were coming in today," I told her once she was next to me in the back.

I bent down and gave her a kiss on the cheek. She was soft, warm, and smelled like my childhood.

"Sure did. It's Friday, honey. This is when I make all my big tips," she said with a wink and a subtle drawl to her words.

The world differed greatly from how it used to be. One thing we didn't miss was money. Currency, mostly, was null and void. We didn't get paychecks, have banks, savings accounts, or credit cards—we all just worked in kind, exchanging in trade or barter, and did what we could to help each other out and provide a service in exchange for services provided. The life we lived now was beyond monetary gain or what we possessed.

Being alive was the most valuable of all things, and everything else was less than secondary. So, we took what we needed and had no desire to compete with each other. The items that used to be important or high-end had little meaning in this new world. It all looked the same after it'd been stained with blood, guts, and rotting flesh.

“What’s on the menu today?” Gigi came into the kitchen and wrapped an apron around her soft waist. Today, she’d chosen one that had a vintage look, with various kitchen items patterned on the material—she made them herself from fabric brought back from raids. This apron had deep pockets in the front, looped around her neck to cover her white short-sleeved shirt, and the strap wrapped twice around her waist before she tied it at her back.

Gigi was a tiny thing, only about five feet tall and a buck twenty soaking wet. Her head was full of thick stark-white hair that she curled and usually wore in a bun. She had vibrant blue eyes and smooth, youthful-looking skin for her age—you wouldn’t know she was in her late seventies. She was a spitfire of a lady. *Whatever Gigi says, goes.*

“Fish and chips,” I told her. “Grady’s out back cleaning up the rest of his catch, and Charlie’s cutting potatoes.”

“And you’re making a mess with the batter.” She shook her head at me. “Go clean yourself up and get out in the front.” She took the filet I was getting ready to batter out of my hand and gently bumped me out of the way with the side of her body. “I don’t know what I’m going to do with you, kid.”

This was Gigi’s way of helping—taking my place and doing my work as a way for her to “earn her keep”, as she had once said. The O was one of a handful of places in town she could work at, and it was only because it gave her purpose and pride that I “allowed” her to do anything. Gigi being alive and breathing, and one hundred percent human in this day and age, was a blessing she didn’t need to earn. But like I’d said... *What Gigi says, goes.*

“Yes, ma’am.” I hung my hands limp over the counter so I didn’t make a mess on the floor before heading over to the sink.

“I see you got in trouble again, Abby,” Charlie teased. She was cutting the potatoes into thin raw slices down the mandolin and then soaking them in salt water. Later, they'd be drained and fried for the fresh chips set for today's menu.

"Yeah, I wasn't doing it right." I smirked.

"You never do." She laughed and then looked up at me. "*Kid.*"

Snorting, I rolled my eyes at her and went to work in the front of the house—just as I'd been told—not bothering to respond to Charlie's "kid" remark. I stacked plates and rolled silverware, pulled the overturned chairs off the tables and set them back on the floor, and made sure everything was clean and ready for when the lunch crowd showed up.

Gigi didn't talk about the zombies much, and she didn't use our terms when she did. If she ever spoke about them at all, she called them "the dead" and nothing more. I thought it was hard for her, knowing what was going on outside the safety of the walls, and she tried to forget by not talking about it in casual conversation, unlike everyone else.

Kooks, grave mutants, flesh monsters, munchers, or any other term we could come up with applied to the original dead. They were the people who had received the "I-M" injection from the vampires—which was supposed to allow them to live indefinitely—but then they had accidentally died from heart failure, brain injury, or something else that couldn't be fixed with the rapid healing. After they died, they'd come back as a walking, biting, infection-spreading animated corpse. They'd been the first, the plague starters, that set this new world in motion.

Kids, evos, ankle-biters, etcetera, were what we called their children. *Kook spawn* were smarter than their predecessors, stronger, faster, and liked to hunt in groups. Essentially, they were the leftovers that got away. They were moving and mutilated body chunks on a mission to find blood and flesh. These zombies had been turned by the originals and somehow escaped while infected—sometimes with just one bite, other times by not being completely consumed. They were more intelligent through some sort of mutant evolution and had proven to be the more dangerous of the two, even if uglier and sometimes with fewer parts to them. The *kids'* parents were slow, dumb, and weak in comparison.

Gigi wouldn't know the difference—she'd never seen a *kid* and never would. It was only several years ago that we realized ourselves the *kooks* had changed into something else. Most people who stayed in town had never seen one and wouldn't know what to look for as far as differences went. Unless you spent a lot of time hunting zombies, you didn't pay too close attention to the breed of *flesh-eater* charging after you to munch on your face. You just killed it.

Plus, Gigi wouldn't use our terms to insult me. Charlie was just an ass like that.

Surprisingly, no one came in for breakfast, which left us plenty of undisturbed time to prep for lunch. Grady finished cleaning the rest of his fish, Gigi battered it all and put it in the fridge to pull out when needed, and Charlie cleaned up her mess after slicing all the potatoes before the first lunch-goer came through the door. The next couple of hours were a steady service of orders, drinks, and clean-up.

"Abby!" Hendricks yelled a few hours later as the door chimed with his entrance. It had just quieted down, and the restaurant was empty for the first time since lunch started.

"Yeah?" I called back to him from the serving counter. I'd been bent down when he walked in, pulling fresh ketchup bottles from the shelves to place on the tables.

Commander Lane Hendricks, MD—master of all trades—was the big guy around town. He'd started this colony many years ago and was the man in charge ever since. He was the go-to guy for anything important, but mostly, for everything directly related to the security of Thompson Falls. He was also the man who saved my and my mother's lives.

"Hey, peanut." He sat at the counter across from me, dressed in his usual garb: a T-shirt, cargo pants, and boots. Today's color choice was tan. Classic. "You have any of that lunch I've been hearing about all afternoon?" He removed his cap, which exposed dark gray hair that wasn't age-related but simply his color. He must have gone to see Jess recently too since his hair was freshly trimmed and buzzed.

"Grady's fresh catch of the day?" I teased. "I sure do."

"I'll take two."

"Sure. Two fish 'n' chips, please!" I hollered through the service window to give Gigi the order.

"You don't have to yell. I'm standing right here." She surprised me as she dropped the fillets in the fryer.

"Sorry, Gigi! I didn't see you."

"Well, honey, there's only the five of us in here. I could've heard the good doctor's order from way in the back," she continued to chide me as she put down the sliced potatoes. "Even if you didn't see me, I'm not deaf."

I apologized through a stifled laugh and faced Hendricks again.

He was smiling too as he greeted his mother. "Now, Ma, you be nice to Abby or she'll fire you." He winked.

"She could sure try," she tittered to herself. "But I'd just keep coming back."

"Oh, I know." I poured Hendricks a cup of coffee. I knew from firsthand experience she'd keep coming back—I'd already tried that once.

She *tsk*ed me from the kitchen as she kept with her work.

"I need a favor." Hendricks took a sip from his mug. "And I need you to keep it quiet." He lifted his brows, which piqued my interest.

"What is it?" I'd been off rotation for a couple of weeks now, and I was itching to do anything that didn't involve plates and beer.

"I need you to cover for me with your mother. I have to run over to Outpost Six and get rid of some *neckers* that haven't heard we don't work with their kind here."

"*Neckers*" was a slang term for the vampires people used. Hendricks had a strong dislike for them too.

"I'm sure they're just passing through." I crossed my arms and leaned against the counter. I didn't like when he used derogatory terms like that, and he knew it.

"This is the second time they've come this way. The guys at the post say they insist on aiding," he told me with a sneer.

Hendricks had no use for vampires, and that was putting it mildly. When he first put this outpost together, he'd made sure that everyone knew it was an all-human camp—no *blood-drinkers* allowed. When he traveled, made contact, and allied with other communities, he'd clarify he would deal with them but not their vampire counterparts. Most colonies were fine with this exception, but for a few, it was a deal-breaker. The protection of vampires was readily sought after in most communities. I couldn't blame them—they were stronger and faster, and we all had to look out for ourselves and the ones we loved any way we could. If it wasn't for Commander Hendricks bringing us to the Falls, I'm sure Mom and I would have done the same thing had the opportunity presented itself.

"They're people too, Lane," Gigi chided him from behind the wall. "They're probably tired and hungry. You should offer them food and rest," she drawled as she shuffled around. The bubbling of the fryers in the background didn't cover the swishing sound of her hands as she wiped them against her apron.

"They're not people, Ma," he said through clenched teeth. "And they aren't welcome here. I will not have a bunch of *vamps* sucking the life out of my people for protection we don't need. We can take care of ourselves, and they can move on."

Gigi came out of the kitchen and stood in the doorway while she waited for her son to finish speaking. She continued to dust her hands off on her apron and then folded them across her chest. Standing silently, she stared at him with brows barely raised and gave him a look only a mother could. "You didn't always feel that way. It's best you don't forget." Without another word, she went back to work.

I wasn't surprised by their exchange. Gigi and Hendricks butted heads about this subject and most others, but it was enough to remind me to not get on her bad side. She might be in her seventies, but I was positive her wit alone would take me down without a fight.

No *vamps*. That was the one rule in Thompson Falls, and because of this, the outposts, towers, and entry gates were constantly running off "tourist vamps"—the ones without any real purpose, just looking for a warm meal in the form of a positive or negative blood type. It was a rarity we had any vampires come this way who actually wanted to stay and help. Most were just passing through, and it was pretty easy to spot the difference. They looked transient, just like the humans who lived nomadically.

It didn't matter if they were *tourist vamps* or members of the VIG—Vampire Increment Guard. Hendricks blamed all vampires for our situation, stating it was their fault we had to protect ourselves from the dead and that we wouldn't be living this way if it wasn't for the "I-M" vaccine.

I didn't agree with him. After all, our human need and want to survive was half to blame. Neither party could have known the outcome of the choices they were making, and as far as I was concerned, it didn't all start with "I-M" and *kooks*. If we had taken better care of the planet to begin with, there wouldn't have been a need for an eternal vaccine to save the human race in the first place.

But this was his town and his rules—*the* rule—and we all followed it. He was reasonable and listened in every other way, open to suggestions, often making the townspeople take the lead on decisions, as long as they hurt no one else. Thompson Falls was one of the safest and best places to live. If we needed to follow the rule to stay, so be it.

"Abby, please?" he asked again after a few minutes and a refill of his mug.

"Alright," I agreed to his request. "What would you have me do? I can be ready to go in five minutes," I told him, guessing he wanted me to ride with him.

"No, no. I need you to cover for me with your mom, remember? I can handle the *neckers* by myself."

"You mean *actually* cover with Mom? Why would she care?" Now, I was skeptical and concerned that he wasn't telling me the whole truth. There's no reason he would need to hide what he was doing from her. This was our life, and it was his job. She understood that, even if she didn't like it half the time.

"We were supposed to have lunch today." He held up his hands after seeing the look on my face. "After that, we're scheduled to do a minor surgery together. I won't be able to make either since I'm going to the outpost. You're my buffer."

"Why wouldn't you just tell her? I'm sure she would have understood." I squinted my eyes at him.

"She was busy. I couldn't bother her when I got the call." He shrugged and then rested his chin in his left palm, wrapping his right hand around his warm mug of coffee.

I still wasn't convinced he was telling me the whole truth, but Gigi had his order up in the window, so I took the time to distract myself by putting it in to-go containers rather than analyzing his motives.

"Fine. But take your lunch." I sat the two containers on the counter in front of him. "I'll put down more fish to go over there with."

He smiled at me as he stood, leaned his long body over the counter, and kissed the top of my head before putting his cap back on. "What do you think these are for?" he said with a wink. "You know I don't like fish."

"How was lunch with your mom?" Charlie asked when I came back later that afternoon. She had obviously been home to change since I was here last. Now, she was in pleather pants, boots that looked like they had socks over them at the ankle, a belt made of gears, coins, and a chain, and a part-corset shirt. Her hair was rolled up in a messy bun and braids, and her lips were the deepest shade of burgundy I'd ever seen.

"Remind me not to do any favors for Hendricks anymore." I grabbed a stack of dirty dishes and stomped off to the back, where I vigorously washed them.

Lying by omission was still lying, and I wasn't too impressed with the good doctor or his favor this afternoon. He'd left out the part about the" minor surgery" they had scheduled together being a cesarean section and that it was my mother's first one solo. Pregnancies weren't all that common given the state of the world, and cesarean sections were even more rare because of that. She had not only freaked out about the whole thing but—as a punishment for my part—made me scrub in and assist the other nurses. Of course, she was fine. She's an amazing physician and other doctors were in the care center to assist if she needed them, but she was still upset, and I didn't blame her. So, no. I was not very happy with Hendricks.

On the plus side, after my initial shock and reluctance to even be in the operating room, we'd delivered a healthy baby boy and added another member to our growing community. On the downside, we'd added another member to our growing community. It made my job of keeping the town and its residents safe all that more important and worth doing, but it also added the *tiniest* bit more pressure and about seven and a half more pounds of stress.

The dinner rush had come and gone by the time I sat again to take a break. Gigi left after lunch, so Grady had taken over in the kitchen since it was his fish fry. Charlie and I continued to serve, with the help of a few others who had come in after I'd left for lunch with my mom. Dinner wasn't as busy as lunch—most people liked to spend the evening and their dinner meal with their family—but we still fed a few of them and, sometimes, those families as well.

Fridays were busy nights for the bar, though, so we opened the patio and pulled back the sliding walls, where the pool tables and extra chairs and tables were. Most people came in to blow off steam from the work week and get all the latest gossip and news from any vanguard that had returned, while others liked to come in because they didn't want to drink alone. There was something normal about gathering around other people, even if you were just going to ignore them.

The door clanged with the entrance bell as Don and John walked in.

"Abby." Each brother greeted me with a nod as they went to the back corner to their favorite table.

They were definitely brothers, looking very similar in the face. Don was a little taller than John and John was a little bulkier with muscle, but they both wore work boots, overalls, and T-shirts. They had dark brown hair, olive skin, and straight white teeth. Don had green eyes, and John's were brown. The brothers were quiet and well-mannered, and their accent reminded me of those old cowboy movies Hendricks liked to watch.

"Hi, boys," I greeted, then grabbed a bucket and some beer.

Grady was in the back, cleaning up the fryer mess and closing down the kitchen.

"Are you staying tonight?" I asked through the order window.

"Nah, not tonight. I've got some old computers Hendricks wants me to put together, see what I can come up with."

"Computers from where?"

"One of the old military bases. Neko's and Boris's teams brought back two trailers full, said there was plenty more to go back and retrieve too. Weapons, vehicles—all kinds of stuff. They'd grabbed a couple of computers that looked important."

"That is definitely something you would be excited about, Grady." I chuckled at him, filled a bucket with ice, and shoved in several bottles of barley to keep them cool.

Grady fixed the ice machine earlier this week, so we were all excited about cold stuff again.

Grady was our go-to guy for all things techy. Actually, he was a genius. He worked magic on old computers and programs, and helped keep the town organized for Hendricks. I understood nothing of what he did, but I knew he'd had a hand in getting us connected with the other colonies through radio waves or some other magic form of communication. He'd also made it possible for us to keep in contact with the town while we were out on a job. Smarter than all the other knuckleheads who served in the guard, he naturally took a lot of flak from them about being a nerd—or what they assumed a nerd was based on ancient gossip magazines, TV shows, and books.

Grady was older than me, but he had such a baby face that he sometimes looked younger than I was. He was tall and wore his golden-brown hair in such a way that I was never sure if it was on purpose or if that's just how he'd woken up. He always wore the same thing every day: a blue or gray T-shirt, jeans, and sneakers. Sometimes he wore glasses, either brown or black. The only time he was in something different was when we were out in the *Morgue* and he was in his vanguard uniform.

"Thanks for helping today," I told him before going over to deliver the beer to Don and John. "How are my two favorite ranchers this evening?" I sat their bucket on the table. "I hear I'll be getting some corn soon."

"Yes, ma'am. Crops lookin' real nice. Shouldn't be more than a couple weeks er better, and we'll get ya the best pickin' of the bunch," John drawled after taking a long swig off his cold beer.

I beamed. "That's good to hear. We haven't had any fresh since last season, so it'll go quick here. It's not the same out of a can." I wrinkled my nose.

"No, it's not. And how you doin', Abby? Them boys been treating you right outside the gates?" Don asked with serious eyes. It was a standard question from him, and he always gave me a certain look when he asked.

"Oh, of course!" I waved a hand in front of me as if to knock the question out of the air. "Not one of those boys is dumb enough to mess with me, Don. They know they'd have a world of hurt coming to them once they came back. Plus, I carry a gun." I winked at him.

"Well, if you ever need anything..."

"You'll be the first to know," I promised. "Holler when you need a refill. There's plenty more where that came from." I smiled at them again before turning back to the bar.

Don and John were two of the farmers who worked over in the town fields, both big boys with fists and hearts the size of my head. The two brothers worked hard and rarely came in, so when they did, I tried to keep them happy.

The farm itself was located furthest from the main part of town, with the biggest designated part of open land. The farm had a slew of animals, a couple of cows, chickens, pigs, turkeys, ducks, goats, rabbits, sheep, and several more that were kept for fertilizer for the farm, pest control, and their byproduct. The farm grew a lot of food for the town and housed the animals, but it wasn't a place of slaughter. Since we were a mostly plant-based species these days, the animals were kept alive, and only if they died would they be used for food and leather. We didn't waste resources, so feeding them just to kill them for taste wasn't customary.

Today's fish fry was an exception to that rule, but that too only happened a handful of times a year, and it was more out of necessity than anything else.

In addition to the farm, with everything the vanguard brought in from the *Morgue* raids, what we gathered in the wild or grew ourselves in personal gardens, and the rare hunt or fishing expedition, we kept well-fed around here.

By the time I went back to the front, a small group of people had come in. Since Charlie quit helping after dinner, Harper wasn't here yet, and the others had gone home after cleaning up, I was all alone—besides Blaise, who had come in to bartend.

We had a decent amount of liquor to choose from, and we never ran out of beer. We didn't always get the "brand name" stuff left on the old supermarkets and liquor stores' shelves, but we had a few people around town who had taken up brewing and distilling their own, so we kept the bottles and served their private stock here when ready.

I couldn't mix a drink to save my life, so unless the customer knew what was in it, they were shit out of luck. Blaise was the bartender or "mixologist", as he liked to call himself. He was a chemical engineer with all forms of liquid. During the day, he made ethanol and biodiesel for the trucks and cars to run on—for the ones that used it instead of or in addition to electric. He made reserves that powered the town for when—or if—our PEI equipment went down. And to get a break from it all and do something "fun", he came in on the weekends and mixed drinks here at the bar.

It was also nice to have him around when someone let the booze get the best of them and got rowdy. He looked mean, even though he was as gentle as a teddy bear. His rich umber skin looked warm to the touch, as if it had soaked up the setting sun's heat on a summer night, but not soft since it was stretched over hard muscle. Blaise was about 6'5" and 280 pounds of brawn and bulk—a brick shithouse nobody messed with. His dark brown eyes, thick brows, and long lashes matched the black hair he wore in a ponytail at the base of his head. Down the length, an elastic wrapped around the thick locks' every inch to keep the hair bound tightly together, like a rope resting against his back. Legend had it that someone had once picked a fight with him and ended up in a coma for a month after Blaise punched him in the head a single time. Blaise was a great guy, and even though the boys liked to talk shit, none were stupid enough to try and debunk the rumor.

By the time Harper showed up, Blaise had been there for a full hour and the bar was packed. She went straight to work after she'd apologized and given Charlie the stink eye—those two had a thing for getting on each other's nerves. I'd told them it was because they were a lot alike, but neither agreed. *Shocking.*

I was stocking the cooler in the back when Hendricks opened the door and stood there, waiting for me. I was still pissed at him for what he'd pulled on me earlier, but I knew it was nothing compared to what was waiting for him with my mom. Still, I gave him the silent treatment while I finished what I was doing.

After I was done with the cooler, I started boxing up some of the empty bottles that had been cleaned and sterilized to send over to Summer's garage, where she could fill them up again with her newest barley brew.

Hendricks was a patient man, so instead of pushing me to speak to him, he helped me with my work and waited for me.

I lasted about eight minutes before I broke. "She made me scrub in." I tried to sound as angry as I was, but the truth was that it'd been an amazing experience and I was glad to have been a part of it. I wished it would have been my choice, however, and that I hadn't been tricked into doing it, but after I got over my initial reaction, I'd been able to step back and allow myself to enjoy the experience. There weren't too many people who could say that they'd gone on break as a waitress and instead of lunch delivered a baby.

"She was really mad, then?"

I looked at him like he was crazy and raised my brows at the ridiculous question. "Yeah."

"I should probably get home."

"You should probably go into hiding and change your name."

He stopped what he was doing and turned to me. "She'd find me."

"I have no doubt." I faced him as he had done me, then gave him a smile to let him know all was forgiven.

"I wasn't completely honest with you today, Abby, and I apologize. I should have warned you about what you were walking in on. To be fair, I knew she would be fine and that your mother just needed to be pushed, but it was wrong of me to use you as my poker. So, I am sorry."

I shrugged it off, knowing he hadn't meant any harm. "You're forgiven, but just so we're clear, I won't be doing any more favors for you ... at least, not for a while."

Hendricks could be trusted completely—that wasn't in question. His full disclosure, or lack thereof, was what got the best of him sometimes. When he was doing something he thought would be beneficial but didn't want to tell anyone all the details in case it fell through, he would dance around the information. The fact that what he did usually *was* beneficial wasn't the point either. He needed to learn that people could be trusted and that he could share his burdens.

"So, should I get her chocolates or flowers?" he asked in light of the situation.

"Well, since we don't have either, I'd go with something more useful. Say, a nice bottle of red from the back and a foot massage."

"Right," he responded solemnly as if I'd just told him he would need a bone set without pain meds.

"And unless you're looking to be scolded in front of a bar full of people, I would find her before she finds you," I added as I started for the door.

"Abby?"

"Yeah?"

"Thanks."

I nodded and made my way back behind the bar out front.

"Everything okay?" Blaise asked as I washed glasses.

I looked around for empties and those who needed refills. "Yep, everything's great. How's it going out here?"

"Usual stuff. Charlie's in the back, shooing away bar flies and hanging with some friends. The winos are getting ready to leave with a couple of bottles of pinot. The boozers broke two beer bottles and a glass, knocking over a table on the patio, and Jeff just showed up, informing me Holden and the rest of the guys were on their way."

"So, same shit, different day, huh?"

"You got it."

"Hey, Abby, are there any more peanuts or popcorn in the back?" Harper asked as she came up to the bar with another tray of dirties for me. She was short, so I had to help her get it on the counter and then slide it away from her the rest of the way. "The farmer boys are looking for a snack," she finished saying once her tiny fingers were freed from the tray.

"Hmm, I think we have some popcorn but not peanuts. Do you want to check or should I?"

"I got it." Her coral lips pushed up into a smile, creating deep laughter lines from years of happiness around her mouth and cheeks. The wrinkles of sadness by her eyes were the only indication she hadn't lived a completely charmed life.

"Hey, are they hungry or just snacky?" I asked as she made her way around the bar toward the double swinging doors to the back. The ankle of her jeans drug slightly over the back of her boots and onto the floor as she walked.

"Snacky?" She looked at me with an odd expression, her light blonde eyebrows quizzically stitching together. "Really, Abby?"

"What? That's a word."

"No, it's not." She rolled her eyes at me and flipped her blonde ponytail as she headed for the back. "And I didn't ask. I'll just get the popcorn and let you ask if they want anything more. I'm not opening that can of worms."

Harper was sweet and non-confrontational—except with Charlie—so if there was even a hint of drama, she pulled herself out of the situation as fast as she could. She had gone through some major changes over the last couple of years and was trying to live the most basic life she could—her words. So I wasn't surprised when she passed the buck to me to avoid an encounter.

"Hey, guys, did you want something more to eat than just popcorn? I can whip you up a couple of sandwiches real quick?" I asked the two brothers just after Harper had come back with the popcorn.

"Thanks, Abby, but we ain't wantin' to cause no fuss. This here popcorn will do us just fine," Don answered me and then took another pull off his beer.

"Nonsense. I'll be right back with two sandwiches and some chips." I walked away before they could argue any further. They provided our community with the majority of fresh food, so the least I could do was make it for them when they were hungry.

"I'll take a sandwich too. Since you're going back there," Holden quipped rudely as I walked by. He and the rest of his crew had shown up and sat down while I was talking to the ranchers about getting them something to eat.

"Kitchen's closed, Holden, but we start serving breakfast at seven." I kept walking past him without batting an eye. "It's going to be one of those nights, Blaise. I hope you're ready," I told my bartender as I pushed through the double swinging doors into the kitchen to make sandwiches for two of the handful of men in the bar that I liked.

A few minutes later, I walked back over with two stuffed veggies on rye with spinach, red onion, tomato, carrot, cabbage, and watercress, a whipped olive oil and Dijon mustard spread, extra pickles, and homemade chips from this afternoon's lunch. "Here you go, and if you need anything else, don't be afraid to ask." I sat two plates full of food down on the table and handed them each a napkin before turning to leave them to their meal.

"I'll take a refill." Holden pushed his empty bottle into my stomach when I walked by.

I yanked the bottle from him and slapped his hand away. "It's a little early for you to be acting like an asshole, Holden. Maybe you should call it a night."

"I just got here, Abby."

"And you're already finished with your second beer."

"Well, I wanted a sandwich, but you wouldn't give me one of those, so I guess I'll just drink my dinner."

"Holden." I clenched my teeth and took a deep breath before continuing to speak. "You and I both know damn well that you don't want a sandwich. Why do you do this?" I paused for a moment until his cocky grin formed. "You know what? I don't care. Do you guys want another round too?" I faced the rest of the table.

Without bothering to get an answer from them, I left Holden to make his smart-ass comments behind my back and went to the bar.

"I don't understand why you keep letting him come back in here, Abby," Blaise commented as he filled up two buckets with ice while I grabbed the beer. "You don't owe him anything, and putting up with his shit isn't healthy."

I didn't reply, just shook my head in answer to his question. Sometimes, I wondered the same thing.

"Hey, why don't I take his table for the night. You know, to make up for me being late today," Harper suggested as she cleared off her tray. "He's nice to me." She gave me a partial shrug as if she was embarrassed by the fact.

"Deal." I stuck my hand out to shake on it. "No takebacks."

"Promise." She shook my hand and crossed her heart with a finger, then grabbed the beer to take it back to Holden's table.

The next several hours went by smoothly, and by the time ten o'clock came around, most of the patrons had gone home, leaving only the heavy drinkers for the rest of the night.

Harper was good at containing Holden. She'd even convinced him to leave before midnight, which meant we could close early. Cleanup was quick, and an hour later, I shut down all the lights, locked up the doors, and headed to my room for a much-needed shower.

I was snuggled deep under my blankets and was almost asleep when the night bell in my room chimed. I thought I might be dreaming, so I ignored it the first time, but when it rang again, I knew sleep would evade me this night.

With a groan, I threw back the heavy comforter and climbed out of my warm bed. I slid on my fuzzy slippers and dragged my feet over the carpet, out of my room, and down the long hallway toward the front door as I tied my oversized, beat-up robe around my waist.

The metal sliding and releasing from the door's latch echoed loudly in the motel's empty lobby. I would have treasured the sound if I had known it would be the last bit of quiet for a long time.

Chapter Two

Several steps needed to be taken before entering the city limits was permitted—for everyone, every time. It could be a tedious process and was guaranteed to get on your nerves, but it kept the town clean of infection and the people in it safe. It's why Thompson Falls was one of the larger settlements to never have an outbreak.

Two main entryways, connected by an old highway that ran through Thompson Falls, allowed people to come and go from the town. They each included three separate fenced-off security checkpoints, each with tracked mesh security gates to pass through before you made it to the final entrance letting you into the town.

The first guarded gate allowed you in based on who you were and what you were doing—the obvious requirement to process through this gate was that you displayed no visible signs of infection or had no hostile intentions.

Once you passed through, you were in the decontamination zone. A medical outpost in this guarded section was a mandatory checkpoint for all breathers, including animals. This was also where weapons, clothing, and any outside items were inspected and cleaned before eventually being reissued, destroyed, or shipped to the town.

Most clothing items contaminated with blood went to the incinerator. Weapons were cleaned and sterilized along with our protective gear. Food items were inspected, and if there were any signs of contamination, they were also disposed of via incineration. Food was not known to be a carrier of the disease, and the only time it was contaminated was within range of blood spatter. It was rare for any member of the vanguard teams to ever bring back something with the potential of infection, but it had happened and nothing was left to chance.

Animals were not carriers of the virus either, so putting any animal through the medical bay was mostly cautionary and humane. Animals of all kinds would die from a bite but they didn't spread it, and thankfully, they didn't come back after death either. If an animal had a bite, it would be euthanized instead of allowing it to suffer before its eventual death.

Any breathers who made it to the medical bay were stripped of all weapons and clothing, and then showered. After you had been cleaned, you were provided with a hospital gown, and a member of the medical team would examine you for any bite marks or wounds. The last inspection before clearance was the blood test—a finger prick, where a smear of blood was placed on a slide brushed with mercury. If the blood was contaminated with the virus, it would react with the mercury immediately upon contact.

It had been discovered, with the help of vampires, that mercury had a deadly effect on zombies because of its known poisoning effect on blood. Since blood was their diet and consumed the reanimated in every way, its effect on them was exponential. Even in humans, mercury in high doses would cause sepsis, which could lead to death. Vampires had a high allergic reaction to it, but not as severe as the *kooks*. The mercury blood test was the only test really needed, but in the past, it had proven not to be foolproof, which was why the physical examination was still necessary.

If you were cleared from the medical bay, you were given something to wear and processed through to the next gate. If you did not pass the exam or the blood test, you were taken to a holding cell within the decon-zone. What happened there varied from person to person.

The last checkpoint section was an overflow space leading to the main gate. There was nothing but time in this section, and it acted as a buffer in case of an outbreak from the medical bay. The last defense in this section before the town was like that of an old castle, connected to the outer brick wall that surrounded the entire compound.

The main gate, as it was called, had two towers that acted as an anchor for our last line of defense. The entrance had two separate gates that could be opened manually or with controls, on both sides of the wall. The first was a cantilever sliding gate with infill and rotating serrated edge spikes at the top. It slid across the entire roadway, which allowed vehicles and groups of all sizes in and out before securely locking behind you. This gate was closed at all times. The second was a crash-resistant, solid-sheet-infill sliding barrier, closed only during emergencies. Fully staffed, armed vanguard patrolled each separate gate section at all times. The gate towers also had a guard sitting as a gunner at the gun turret positioned at the top of each tower.

A large brick barrier wall surrounding the entire town connected to the towers. It was roughly fifteen feet high and wide enough to have a walkabout. In addition to the gate towers at the main gate, guard towers were positioned every hundred feet around the town, each equipped with its own alarm, CB radio, armed guard, and spotlight.

On the inner side of the brick wall and guard towers was the last line of defense for the town—the large steel fence that bordered my running track. The steel fencing had been retrieved from old prisons, airports, and any other high-security facility incapable of being an outpost or community. The fence was a high-quality galvanized steel measuring approximately sixteen and a half feet tall, topped with coiled razor wire, which added between one and a half to two feet of additional height. The fence in most areas was anti-climb, with no toe or finger holes, giving it a flat profile and making it nearly impossible to scale.

Once you were inside the gates of Thompson Falls, you found what a small town used to look like before the "end of the world" happened. The cozy town and all the buildings had been rebuilt or repaired and left almost exactly as they were originally. With some new buildings, roads, and housing we'd put in ourselves, the only things noticeably different were the extra wind turbines and solar panels. Everything else probably looked like it had when all the original inhabitants lived here.

Thompson Falls ran alongside the Clark Fork River. It was our primary water source and we used it for everything, including the energy we collected from the water turbines. Unfortunately, the town walls blocked out most of the river view, so you could only hear the river water as it flew by. Only if you were higher up than ground level could you see the beauty around us. We took pride in keeping our small home beautiful and safe, and tried to make it as comfortable as possible given the circumstances. Gardens, plants, trees, or flowers filled every yard of space to make up for the comforting but dreary view of our border wall.

Everyone in town had had to pass through the same security measures before being allowed into our little community. It could make you feel separated from the rest of the world sometimes, but what was waiting for you on the outside made these precautions necessary to keep you safe here on the inside.

The soft scrape of my slippers as I moved sluggishly across the floor was a quiet echo as I took the last few steps toward the entrance door of the motel. I could make out a few shadows through the window curtain with the light provided by the full moon. The white beam illuminated a glow of direction in the otherwise pitch-black darkness of the O, and outlined a figure I recognized immediately.

I grabbed the cool round doorknob once the lock had unlatched and opened the heavy wood barrier. The edges of the door scraped softly against the frame, and when it was open, I found Hendricks and two guards standing on the large porch.

"Hey, Abby, sorry to wake you." Hendricks took off his hat and stepped in through the entryway after I'd moved aside.

"It's alright. Sleep's overrated," I croaked with a yawn and a lazy smile. "What do we have?" I looked from him to the others standing as a group outside the door.

"Rick's team. He brought back a small group, five adults and three children." He waved his hand at the people as an indication they should come in.

Three men walked in first, each with a small child in their arms, followed by two women and a couple of vanguard members that Hendricks had brought along as support.

"How many rooms?" I asked no one in particular as I looked at the ragged group in front of me. The smell of burnt wood lingered around them despite their obvious showered state and clean clothes.

"Four," Hendricks answered for them after a moment of silence.

He was good at studying the information the people provided at the gate—he liked for them to know he was paying attention just as much as he liked knowing who was in his town. I'd never met anyone who could remember names or details about a person as he could.

"This is Ryan and his son, Connor." Hendricks introduced me to a man standing immediately to his left. "They'll need a room."

Ryan was a taller, slim guy in his thirties. He had dark hair, dark eyes, and a short dark beard. The boy he was holding, Connor, was just the opposite, with light skin and blond hair. He was sleeping, but I guessed his eyes were probably blue.

"Alright." I went around the front desk to retrieve keys that hung in a locked box inset into the wall, handing them out after each introduction Hendricks made.

"This is Lucas, and the little one he's holding is Lexie. They will need a key," Hendricks indicated to the next two.

Lucas was about my height—5'7"-ish—with extra weight around his waist. He wore round glasses, and had shaggy dirty blond hair and a kind smile. The little girl, Lexie, was awake. She gave me a shy grin and wave while she halfway hid her eyes behind her dad's face. Her curly, strawberry-blonde hair complimented her tiny figure and highlighted her blush lips and cream skin.

"Here is Lucas's brother, Owen; Owen's wife, Emily; and their daughter, Madelyn," Hendricks continued.

Owen looked like his brother, maybe shorter and slightly more overweight. He also had curly blond hair and light eyes, and was probably in his late thirties. Emily was a little taller than her husband, with a slimmer figure and lackluster light brown hair. Wide-eyed and worried, she stood protectively by her husband and smoothed her sleeping daughter's dark hair as she slept comfortably on the man's shoulder.

"And finally, this here is Paige. She'll need her own room," Hendricks introduced me to the last person in their group.

Paige looked my age, maybe a year or two younger. Her shoulder-length hair was pulled back in a messy ponytail with long, loose bangs that lay flat and almost in her eyes. The color of her hair was hard to gauge in the muted light of the desk lamp, but if I had to guess, it looked auburn. She had long lashes and full dark lips that matched her tawny skin, and she was pretty. I could tell that much, even though she was obviously exhausted and anxious, like the rest of the group.

"Welcome to Thompson Falls." I smiled at each of them as I handed over the keys. "I'm Abby."

Quiet and tired murmurs of thanks were followed by polite refusals of the sandwiches I offered before I showed each of them to their rooms. Once they were settled, I went back to where Hendricks and his two guards were waiting for me. He'd made a pot of coffee and was pouring himself a cup while the other two leaned against a wall. The smell was strong in the room, and I guessed he'd made it extra stout for his long night ahead.

"How are they?" He blew over the black coffee before taking a cautionary sip of the hot beverage. As he moved to sit on one of the stools, he sloshed some of the liquid over the cup and onto the counter

"They didn't say too much, but they all looked really happy to see the beds in the rooms." I grabbed a towel to wipe up the spill as he wiped his hands down the front of the tan cargo pants he was still wearing. The only additions to his earlier uniform were his gun belt and the weapon he wore securely around his waist.

"You look beat, girl. You should get some rest," Malik, one of the guards, said as I flopped myself down in a chair. He was dressed almost identically to Hendricks, but his stocky, darker frame and long black dreads gave the garments on him a more defined look.

Josh, the other guard, was close to the exact opposite of Malik. His white skin and bald head were in contrast to his dark gray cargo pants and a black T-shirt. Both men were attractive, in their mid-twenties, and were rarely seen without the other—on or off duty. Once the two started dating, Hendricks had allowed them to continue and work together only because they had been work partners for so long beforehand. Otherwise, it was something that wasn't generally allowed.

"Oh, I'm only here in physical form." I stifled a yawn and tucked my legs under myself. "The rest of me is still passed out in my bed."

"Why don't you go back and rest," Hendricks told me. "I'll clean up here after I finish my coffee. There's no need for you to be sleep-deprived."

I shook my head and shrugged at him. "What's the story with Rick's team? And where was this group found?"

While Malik and Josh held back snorts and laughter, Hendricks gave me the stink eye at my silent refusal of his request before telling me what I wanted to know. "Rick's team had been over in the Dakotas, gathering medical supplies. They were circling around and heading back through the northern part of Wyoming when they found this group coming from the Honor Camp near Newcastle; they say the place was overrun with *kooks*."

"And the eight of them were the only ones that escaped?" It was surprising because Honor was a large settlement with numbers close to our own, plus it had once been a prison of sorts, so its security was good too.

"They don't know for sure." He nodded toward the rooms. "They each said it all happened so fast that when they saw an opportunity to escape, they took it. They don't know how many, or if anyone else, escaped at all. The two brothers, Lucas and Owen, and their families had been together when they fled. They came across Paige and Ryan soon after, but no one else as they ran away."

"Wasn't Honor under vampire protection?"

"Yeah." Hendricks picked up his coffee to sip at it again.

"Their facility was almost as secure as Thompson Falls. Add that with the vampires..." I wasn't sure of how to continue.

"That's where the details get a little strange." Hendricks's tone aligned with my confusion. "From the sound of it, they were *kook spawn* and not your regular *munchers*, but the *neckers* should have been more than capable of running them off." He shook his head in frustration as he relayed to me what had been told to him. "They said everything was fine, normal as always. It was in the middle of the night when they heard an explosion, and the first screams and shots being fired. Fires broke out all over town in a matter of minutes, and *kooks* were everywhere, they said. The vamps were nowhere in sight."

The reason vampire protection was so sought after was that, in theory, they didn't lose. They were stronger and faster, and their senses were better than humans'. Even if it had been a large group of *evos* attacking Honor, they should have heard them way before they reached the town, and should have been able to handle the problem and not lose anyone, let alone an entire community.

"Are we sure about them?" I indicated with my eyes that I meant our new sleeping guests. "Or their story?"

"No." He didn't hesitate. "But for now, we have nothing that says otherwise. It seems unlikely that a group of *kooks* could overrun a town under the protection of vamps, wipe out over three hundred people, and leave only a handful of escapees to tell the tale, but until we know for sure, that's what the story is."

Hendricks downed the rest of what was left in his mug, then went to the coffee pot to pour the remainder into a thermos. He took his time and rinsed out the carafe, wiped up his spills on the counter, and then rinsed out the washcloth before screwing the lid to his thermos back on.

"What's the plan, then?" I knew he wouldn't just let this go, and once Rick's team was debriefed and he had time to consider all the information, we would learn more and get answers of our own.

"The plan right now is for you to get some sleep." He scowled at me. "Then, and only after you don't look like roadkill, we'll talk more about what to do."

"Fine. But if it's beauty sleep you're after, then we're all screwed." I raised my hands in mock horror, which drew another round of quiet chuckles from Malik and Josh.

Hendricks shook his head at me and jutted out his chin toward the two men. "I'm leaving these two here for the night."

"You guys know the drill," I said to them as I walked down the hall. "Just make sure I have enough food left to feed the locals in the morning."

"If there aren't any other questions about the rescue trip to Honor, let's get home and get some rest. We'll need all the sleep we can get," Hendricks announced to the vanguard group assigned to the rescue operation.

For the last hour and a half, we had been sitting around in the school gym, going over everything that Rick and the group from Honor had told Hendricks. Everything was repeated today for the rest of the guard, along with the specifics of our mission. The plan was to make a run down to Honor, hoping to rescue other survivors and offer our help if there was anyone to offer it to. If the worst had happened, and Ryan and the others from the group were the only ones who had survived, then we would try to piecemeal information together to figure out what had gone wrong.

Generally, vanguard teams explored the *Morgue* alone, or with one or maybe two other units, depending on the mission. We tried not to travel in squads bigger than three for various reasons. One, we made more ground by spreading out our teams across the country for retrieval. Two, the larger the group, the more attention it drew. If we ran into trouble, it was easier to escape with a smaller company than with a large one. It was also easier to keep track of our people and stay organized when there weren't as many.

This time, however, we would travel with a larger crew. It was a long trip, and if we found a horde of *kooks* or *evos*, we would need all the hands and guns we could get. In all, there would be five teams going, equaling thirty-six people.

"Alright, then. Get some rest." Hendricks dismissed us from the gym when there weren't any more questions about the plan and trip. "We'll leave first thing in the morning."

By the time I got back to the O, the dinner rush was dying down, and the staff was cleaning up and closing the kitchen to get ready for the bar crowd. Gigi, Charlie, and Harper were running the place with a couple of regular helpers, along with several extras on the floor. Word must have gotten out that we would need help around here for a couple of days.

"Hey, lady, how goes it?" Charlie asked as I made my way up to the counter. Today, she was wearing her short hair in spiky ponytails on either side of her head, and her makeup was dark to match her clothes—a short tight skirt, tank top, and knee-high boots. She looked like a cartoon character.

"We leave in the morning." I sat on the stool, grabbed her drink, and took a big gulp out of the glass. I immediately regretted it and had to force the thick, grassy-tasting liquid down my throat. Charlie was very "earthy" in her diet. She mostly ate raw fruits and vegetables, which was great, but the drinks she would mix up were gross, and that was putting it mildly.

"Good, right?" She smiled at my disgust. "It's a detoxifying super green smoothie."

"Oh, yeah." I swallowed thickly and grabbed the glass of water she had sat in front of me. "It's frickin great," I grunted.

"It's good for you too."

"Are your taste buds broken or something?" I chugged half of the water she had given me. "That tastes like lawn clippings."

"And how would you know what lawn clippings taste like, Abby?"

I tapped the side of my nose. "I can imagine based on what I smell, Charlie."

"You know how you like to shoot bad guys and I don't? I like to taste my food how nature intended."

"And I like food to taste good. So, yeah, I get it. Totally the same thing."

"So, you don't want one of these, then?" She smiled at me mischievously and took a big drink of her glass full of grass.

No, thank you. I'll get something and take it to my room. What did you guys make, anyway?" I instantly felt sorry for the patrons in here tonight, and after having just tasted her "drink", it made sense that the place was already empty.

Usually, Gigi or I came up with lunch and dinner menus, but since neither of us had tonight, we'd left it up to Charlie and Harper to decide what to make. I hoped it wasn't so bad that people chose not to come back.

Charlie scowled at me as if she knew what I was thinking and then smiled, obviously proud of herself, before telling me, "We made pizza."

"Pizza? How did you do that?" I would have expected something like salads or sandwiches that didn't need to be cooked.

"It was easy, and we wanted something easy." She shrugged. "First, we had Gigi show us how to make some dough before she left since neither Harper nor I knew how. Then, we used some of the canned tomatoes and fresh herbs from the garden to make the sauce, chopped up some veggies, threw on fresh basil, and drizzled cashew cheese on top. Voilà! Pizza!"

"Wow, good for you two. I'm glad you're able to bond over food." I stood to go hunt down some of their pizza, ignoring her eye roll and attempt to whip me with her towel.

The leftover pizza was cooling on the counter before they could put it away, so I grabbed two of the remaining few slices and hollered to Charlie through the serving window that I was going to bed. "Will you be here in the morning before I leave?"

"Yes." She was out on the floor and had cleaned off a couple of the tables while I'd helped myself to some dinner.

I ducked out through the back of the kitchen and hurried to my room to enjoy the comforts of civilization before I found myself out in the open, without the luxury of a good night's sleep on a soft bed with cozy blankets.

Once in my room, I settled on a stool at my small kitchen counter with a glass of water and a napkin. After enjoying the surprisingly good pizza, I kicked off my shoes into the closet and headed to the bathroom for a long, hot bath. It was a ritual, a going-away gift to myself that I indulged in the night before a mission—provided we had hot and running water.

I filled the tub up as high as it would go and as hot as I could comfortably stand it, and soaked until it got cold. When I got out, my hands and feet were wrinkled, my skin sticky, and every fiber of my being was excited to crawl into bed and fall fast and deeply asleep, which was exactly what I did.

By the time my alarm went off the next morning, I had been lying in bed awake for close to an hour. I was a mix of nervous energy and excitement. The adrenaline rush and constant on-alert anxiety you experienced when out in the M*orgue* tended to keep you wired. It usually started the night before for me, which was why I did the hot bath routine—so I could get at least a few hours of sleep before a mission.

I put on a pair of jeans and a T-shirt, and slid on some sandals. Since my feet would be trapped inside heavy steel-toed boots for the next couple of days, I wanted them to be free for as long as possible. I grabbed my little travel pouch and locked up my room, then headed down the hall to the restaurant.

The smells of breakfast filled the air, and I found my mother pouring a cup of coffee for herself and then one for me when she caught sight of me coming through the door.

"Good morning. How did you sleep?" She handed me the white mug of hot coffee and stepped back into the kitchen to dish me a plate of breakfast from the stove.

Gigi was cooking, and Charlie and Harper were both running the floor. A few others were here for breakfast, but it was much quieter than normal, probably because the regulars were mostly vanguard and were getting ready to leave, just like I was.

"Good. How was your night?" I made my way over to sit next to Hendricks.

He raised a brow at my question, which made me smirk once I realized how loaded it actually was.

"Oh, fine, I guess." She looked at him and then back at me. "Someone surprised me with a bottle of red wine last night. I don't suppose you had anything to do with that?"

"Me? No." I shook my head and hid behind my cup of coffee. "Was it one of Clint's?" I asked her.

Clint made most of the wine here in Thompson Falls. He had a decent-sized garage he used to make his blends and a small bar you could sit at and drink. Twice a year, he would go out into old Idaho and Washington with a team to collect grapes from any of the old vineyards around us. One storehouse in town also had a decent collection of aged wines, but people rarely touched those for casual drinking. They were special, almost like lost artifacts found, so they were treated with a certain level of respect. The vintage wines were used for special occasions and shared with as many people as possible.

"It was." Mom smiled. "It was a Primitivo from a couple of years ago. It was really nice." Reaching over, she rested her hand on Hendricks's. "Are you ready to go?" She glanced up at me, then back down to her plate again. She was always more nervous about us going out into the *Morgue* than anyone else. I understood her concern—she had to watch two or three people she loved leave at once, never knowing if she would see them alive again or not, and if she did, if they would be hurt when they came home. I felt bad for leaving her, but it was the job.

"Yep. All ready to go." I patted my little pouch of essentials. "It'll just be for a couple of days."

"I know." She nodded.

Breakfast was quiet after that, much like it usually was before we went out on an assignment. We ate our pancakes, eggs, and fruit in companionable silence, and when we were finished, Hendricks and I both said our goodbyes to her and went to the Safe.

The Safe was exactly what it sounded like—a safe for our weapons, combat items, and a locker room of sorts where we got dressed and geared up. Over the years, people had learned quickly that T-shirts and jeans were not suitable clothes for protecting themselves from a *kook* bite, and they soon wore things more appropriate to withstand hungry teeth.

Our bite-proof suit was a requirement for all vanguard when out in the M*orgue*. We'd stockpiled hundreds of different clothing, cloth, and protective gear that had proven time and time again to be the second-best defense against a *kook* attack, the first of course being anything sharp or a bullet. All our gear comprised of one or a combination of several cut-proof cloths, shark chainmail, or Kevlar items.

The vanguard wore a uniform that started with cut-proof long underwear and a T-shirt, tank top, or long-sleeve turtleneck. It was lightweight and form-fitting, so it didn't get bunched up under our suits. Tina, our resident seamstress, had tailored them so they fit perfectly and didn't get in the way under everything else we wore. Our vanguard wore a black leatherette and Kevlar jumpsuit over the cut-proof undergarments. We had knee-high, bio-leather, steel-toed biker boots that zipped or laced up over the top of the suit to protect our feet, ankles, and calves, which were highly susceptible targets for *munchers*. Sewn on the front right breast and covering the back of the jumpsuit was a reflective red Japanese symbol that meant "human". It looked like a fancy upside-down Y that was a bright and reflective crimson color, and it acted as a silent signal to protect us from each other. We could be out in the *Morgue* for days or even weeks at a time, during all hours, and if we were moving around in the dark, it was easy to mistake a friend for a foe, so the reflective symbol was necessary. It'd saved a few people from being shot by teammates a few times, myself included.

We also had bullet-proof vests, gloves, body armor, tactical gear, ballistic thigh and shin guards, bicep and splint protectors, neck and collar shields, and helmets to choose from along with a slew of other protective and defensive items to layer on. The only things required for vanguard were the underwear, a jumpsuit, and boots. Everything else was optional, but most chose to safeguard themselves and layer on protective wear. It felt like a lot of equipment until you were hunted and chased by something dead and infectious. It was then you felt naked and exposed, and cursed yourself for not putting on more but were thankful when you had.

Once we were dressed, we grabbed our personal weapons and headed over to the Pit, where we loaded up our transport with extra weapons, food, water, and first aid supplies before heading to the gate.

The Pit was an enormous parking lot next to our upgrade station and repair shops, along with a storage garage for vehicles equipped with external defensive weapons that could accidentally cause harm if left out in the open. The Pit housed vehicles we used most regularly while the rest of our fleet was stored outside of Thompson Falls. The long-haul tractor trailers, for example, that we used for retrieving mass quantities of goods, were kept outside the gates along with building and construction equipment, and all other extra vehicles we didn't use routinely. The Safe and the Pit were both near the east gate along the northeast wall, for easy exit and entrance.

Hoping to find survivors and due to the uncertainty of what we were walking in on, we were taking a larger array of vehicles than we normally would—ranging from a blacked-out school bus with bars on the windows and spikes welded to the body and tires, to a caravan of trucks and military vehicles we'd found over the years and repurposed to suit our needs. Humvees, Army GILA, Armored Fighting trucks, and heavy-duty pickup trucks would all be in our convoy this time, each painted black and reinforced with various weapons, roll bars, road armor, spotlights, and grills standard for our fleet.

When we traveled, we stayed away from major roads as much as possible—aside from interstates and highways—besides avoiding major cities and big towns. The once heavily populated areas held the most danger for us still, from both the living and the dead, and unless absolutely necessary, we kept our distance.

Humanity had suffered in more than just the obvious ways. The climate pandemic and subsequent zombie apocalypse were disastrous for humans, nearly pushing us to the brink of extinction, but humanity had suffered beyond those global catastrophes. Although thousands of us still functioned on a basic human level, there were also those who had lost all their benevolence and morality. Groups of humans incapable of processing the traumatic events that ended the civilized world had resorted to a barbarous lifestyle, wherein they'd immersed themselves into a dystopic way of life filled with oppression, squalor, and suffering. They were ruthless, unprincipled degenerates who preyed on those unlike them and spoiled what wasn't already rotten. It was sad and unfortunate that the disease that had plagued the world wasn't enough to rid us all of our indecencies against each other.

For those of us interested in surviving this nightmare, it had strengthened and united us in ways we once only hoped for. Now, only one war was worth fighting, and that was against the dead. Battles over imaginary boundary lines were no longer fought. A person's skin color, race, or ethnicity should have never been used to marginalize people, but now especially, they had no place in our world. We no longer held prejudice or fear of one another based on antiquated beliefs, and people were free to live their lives how they saw fit, be who they wanted to be, and love who they wanted to love while being treated with equality and respect.

Of course, there was still hatred in the world—a minority would always exist—but most of us were all just happy to be alive.

"Stay close. We'll be drawing a lot of attention to ourselves traveling this way, and we can't afford for anyone to fall behind," Hendricks addressed us one last time as we stood around the gate, readying ourselves to leave. "Keep your radios tuned to Channel Four. Our first stop is Seeley Lake."

The three-hour drive to Seeley Lake was quiet and uneventful, save for the few wandering *kooks* we'd picked off in the fields or on the sides of the road. It was one of our traveling games, and we kept score. There was no prize unless you counted bragging rights. So far, I was in the lead.

Seeley Lake itself had been empty and cleared of infection for a while now, and we used it for ourselves since no one else wanted to make use of it. Its out-of-the-way location was ideal and close enough to Thompson Falls for our convenience. We stopped in the small town to fuel up, stretch our legs, switch drivers, and use the facilities to clean up.

We used Seeley Lake regularly, and took care and pride in what was left of the small town. We kept it stocked with supplies and frequently checked on the area to keep it in running condition. Most of the town had been burned long before we came here, but a few buildings were untouched and some cabins further in the hills were great for a safe shelter. We'd slowly been building a perimeter fence around the town so that we could use it more, but it wasn't a top priority, so we only passed through for now.

Eventually, Thompson Falls' population would grow beyond what the walls could accommodate, and Hendricks would like to have something ready to go as backup for when that happened. He also thought it would be nice to have a recreation town to escape to. Seeley Lake would be a perfect vacation spot if secure. Right now, we had several fishing boats we kept here for those who felt comfortable enough to use them and spend a day on the water, but since the town wasn't secure, it was a risk. *Kooks* couldn't swim, but they floated sometimes, and they didn't bloat and fall apart as quickly as one might think. So the possibility of coming across a floater was a fair consideration since the water inflow hadn't been secured.

The rest of the trip had lulls, and peaks of calm and commotion. Once we passed through the small wilderness section between Deer Lodge and Clancy, our trip through Townsend was accosted with gunfire. The small town was a hotspot for *stragglers* coming from the overrun capital, Helena, and as often as we'd tried to rid the town of the dead, the best we could do was clear the road of their remains for the next time we came through.

Once we had killed them all, it took us a couple of hours to clear the bodies off the street and surrounding area, and put them into a burn pile. We touched the infected as little as possible and never intentionally came into contact with them with our bare skin. We kept boxes of bio gloves, disposable face masks, and other protective gear on hand to safeguard ourselves during the cleanup. Instead of using our hands, we also had an array of shovels, meat hooks, and trash pickers to move the bodies and their parts. Even plows were attached to the fronts of most of our pickup trucks, in case there were just too many to move one by one. If we could avoid it, though, we didn't use the vehicles as weapons or cleanup tools. They were a pain in the ass to clean and could sometimes take weeks to be cleared for use again.

Scooping up a severed foot with my shovel, I saw Holden out of the corner of my eye. He had just whipped his favorite cleanup tool—the meat hook—through the air. Arcing it over his head, he slammed the point under a *kook's* jaw through its skull, until the tip popped through one of its eyes. Then he turned and pulled it toward the burn pile.

"What?" he said in his cocky tone as he noticed me watching him, then kept walking, dragging the dead body behind him, leaving a trail of mess and old blood in its wake.

"You're disgusting, that's what." I lifted the shovel up over my shoulder and threw the foot I had in it past him into the pile.

"You mean *efficient*."

I scoffed at him before heading to the other side of the road.

Blaise had just flung a bag full of parts over his back and was heading in our direction. "Just ignore him, Abby. You know how he is."

I bent down, grabbed a half-man by the ankles, and dragged him to the pile with the rest of the bodies. Blaise was right—it was better not to feed Holden's need for attention or let him know what he's doing was bothersome. It would just make it worse.

With cleanup done, we dumped a gallon of burn fuel on the carcass heap and set it on fire. When the lifeless mass was thoroughly burning and we were satisfied that it would continue to cremate the dead without help, we loaded back up and headed out before anything else found itself drawn to our location—and before the smell got any worse.

By the time we reached the abandoned airport hangar a few miles past the old Wyoming border, we had been on the road for over twelve hours. Travel at night could be far more dangerous than travel during the day, so after making sure the area was clear and secure, we parked our convoy and set up camp inside the large steel building.

"You should get some rest, Abby." Hendricks sat down next to me and the small fire we made.

"I will, after you. You're the one who drove all day. Besides, I've napped on and off for most of the way here." I shrugged.

Nodding in acknowledgment, he turned his focus on our guest. "Ryan, how you holding up?" He looked over to the man as he handed me a bag of fruit leather.

I reached in for a strip of the rubbery snack while he pulled off the tops of several soup cans and set them carefully around the fire. Ryan was one of the rescued from Honor who had come back with Rick's team. When he'd learned of our planned trip, he'd offered to be our guide into the town and helped with the devising of our mission.

I couldn't decide if he seemed better or worse after the few days he'd been with us in Thompson Falls. He still looked like a mess, his face hollow from stress and weight loss. He was jumpy and didn't seem like he was beginning to trust us. I could understand, sympathize even. He'd been through a lot the last couple of days.

"Thanks." Forcing a quick smile, he accepted the bag of dried fruit I'd passed to him. "I'm doing alright. A little anxious, to be honest," he answered Hendricks, then slid the chewy ration between his teeth, clamped down, and ripped the end from his mouth.

"Well, that's to be expected." Hendricks stretched out his legs. "We can't turn around or afford to send anyone back with you, but if you change your mind about going all the way there—at any time—we can find you a safe spot to wait until we're through."

"No." Ryan shook his head, his voice strong with conviction. "No, sir. I want to go. I need to know if anyone survived. There are people we left behind, our families and friends. We need to know what became of them."

Hendricks stared at him for a moment, gauging his response. "Understood." He nodded as if they had made some sort of pact or deal, then handed him one of the soup cans he'd been warming by the fire.

We didn't say anything to each other after that—the three of us—and instead sat in silence, eating our lukewarm potato soup and fruit leather. The quiet was only interrupted by the crackle of the fire. The wind howled and rustled the metal sheeting of the building, whistling through the seams of the structure and small cracks and fissures in the windows.

Outside, the night was bright with a clear sky full of twinkling stars and a full moon that shone in through the glass. The faint glow shimmered in through the windowpanes and danced in competition for attention with the blaze from the fire.

In this flimsy shelter, I felt eerily comfortable out here in the *Morgue.* Maybe it was the large group with me or the leisure of the night, but I was perfectly at ease in this place we had sought for protection. On a normal run, there were no relaxing meals by a fire, and quiet conversations and storytelling were an unlikely occurrence. We rarely found a true shelter to wait out the night and rest. Normally, our focus was strictly and soundlessly on the surrounding dark.

I watched the two men sitting on either side of me and contemplated the thoughts going through their heads as emotions played across their faces. I wouldn't want to be in either of their shoes. The unknown of what we were walking into was enough without the added pressure of being responsible for everyone here, or the fear of what you might find at home. I couldn't imagine what Ryan was going through, and I would never want to make the tough decisions that came with command.

We kept by the fire for a while longer before making our way over to the others in our group. After setting up a watch rotation, most of our party took to their vehicles or a quiet place to get some sleep. I volunteered, along with a couple of the others, to be on watch for the night, knowing we could sleep while we traveled throughout the day again tomorrow.

I went over to where I would spend my night and settled in with a watchful eye over the darkness of the *Morgue*. The window I was looking through was filthy, a layer of old dirt and grime looking like it had been collecting for years. Pulling my sleeve up over my wrist, I cleaned the glass the best I could with just the pressure of the cloth. Once I was satisfied and could see more clearly, I settled in and stared out into the night.

As the hours ticked by and my mind wandered, I couldn't help but think about what life must have been like before all of this—something I often fantasized about. I had an idea given the old magazines, newspapers, and movies, but it was the feeling of security that often eluded me. It was hard for me to imagine myself without the sense of caution I lived with daily, never fearing your own shadow and death. I envied those of the past, but as the night sky lightened into a blue and yellow hue, my reality settled back in and around me. Off in the distance was an old burn pile of torched bodies. All that remained were the blackened bones and a pile of ash around them, but it was enough to erase the mild night of daydreams and wishful thinking and get me back to the present.

The group began to wake and stir with the morning light, and the smell of coffee put on a small fire was strong in the air. My back was stiff as I made my way over for a cup of the black stuff. Cream and sugar were luxuries only to be found at the O, but I was thankful for the hot beverage anyway. After having our rationed breakfast of apples and bread, I stretched, brushed my teeth, and shook off the night, then went back to work.

Ryan showed us on a map the best way for us to enter Honor, and he and Hendricks went over everything again to make sure our plan was sound. Less than an hour later, we had reloaded and packed our caravan and were on the road again. It would be a couple more hours before we were close to our stopping point and reached our destination, so once en route, I settled into the backseat of the big truck I was riding in. I let myself be lulled to sleep by the hum of the engine and the gentle sway of the vehicle as it glided over the paved road.

Chapter Three

I was in a field by a quiet lake, the sun bright on my face as heat pierced my skin, the rays lighting up my closed eyelids as they blazed bright and gold from within. The sun soaked in my hair and warmed each strand, emanating from the crown tingling with perspiration as it rose to the surface. A dew of sweat pooled on the cap of my head and ran down the sides of my face. It wove through the fevered locks as it raced down my skull to the nape of my neck, leaving a wet trail that felt cool on my skin before drying with the small breeze.

The birds chirped happily around me as I waded in the warm water, my jeans rolled up to my knees. Their feather-light wings flapped and fluttered as the birds moved from tree to tree, rustling the leaves with the slight weight of their tiny bodies. As I stood in the cool tarn, I squashed the sand and mud between my toes and skimmed my hand over the rippling surface. The smell of fresh water, clean air, and wet sand filled my lungs and cleared my head.

"Abby..." a familiar voice called from behind.

I knew the sound. I was even comforted by it. When I turned from the watery view, the movement caused the ripples to lap up higher against my legs, dampening my jeans and leaving my flesh wet with its touch.

I wasn't surprised to see my father approaching me. My cheeks pulled up as a smile formed on my face.

"Abby..." he called again, his advance quickening with each step as he moved toward me.

I felt myself sinking into the mud and mire as I struggled to pull free of its grasp. My heels pushed into the soft earth first, followed by the balls of my feet as I sank in further with each shift of my weight. I tried to move toward him, but the pull of the water became heavy as the clay thickened around me. I was glad he was so close, so he might help me escape.

I reached out for him, his name a mumble on my lips as he trampled through the shoreline to get to me. He could see my struggle. His movements hurried as he splashed through the calm surface to catch up to me, each determined step bringing him closer as he walked unimpeded through the lake, until the liquid changed, and he struggled against the immersion too. His speed and stride slowed into dragging movements, and his face contorted from concern to desperation, to consuming with need.

I flinched away from him, bringing my outstretched hands against my chest protectively at his approach. I tried to move back from him and his progress, only to find myself still trapped by the mud, water, and the wind as it pushed against my back and held me by my feet, caging me and cornering me as if against a wall.

The world spun around me. Dizzy with despair, I looked into the hollow death on his face. His clothes were stained black with blood and dirt, ripped and torn as the threads tentatively held together. His jaw unhinged and skewed, as his broken, dirty teeth clapped and gnashed together in anticipation. His eyes were cloudy and bloodshot, sunken and purple.

I moved to get away from him, frantic now, but my body wouldn't co-operate. I was stuck, dumb and slow, feeling heavy and defeated with dismay.

"Abby!" The coherent word bellowed clearly through his rotten lips, just as his bony hand reached out and grasped my arm.

My panicked inhale, accompanied by the gentle rocking at my shoulder, woke me. Startling, my eyes flew open in alarm as I focused on my surroundings, biting down on my desire to cry tears of relief once I realized it had only been a dream.

"Are you alright?" Hendricks patted my leg before pulling his hand away from where he had shaken me.

I swallowed the lump in my throat, unsure if I could trust my voice not to break, and gave him the thumbs up. Rubbing my eyes to hide my face and rid myself of any remainders of sleep—or tears that might have escaped—I took a couple of deep breaths to calm my racing heart.

"We're about twenty miles out of town," he told me when I was upright and sitting. "You should get something to eat and drink. Wake up and stretch your legs before we leave again." He opened the doors for us to get out.

I did as I'd been told and walked off the remnants of the dream, letting the fresh air clear my head. It had been a long time since I'd had a dream like that, and I was glad the images had faded quickly. I couldn't remember my father's face awake, so thankfully, neither could my unconscious mind. What I saw was more of a blur of images combined and easily forgotten.

After getting something solid in my stomach and washing it down with a drink, I went over to where the rest of the group had gathered to talk while they waited for everyone else to refresh so we could get moving again.

The sky was clear, and the sun had already heated the pavement on the surrounding road, making me feel flush. I was glad I hadn't zipped up my suit yet because I was sure I'd be a hot, sweaty mess. There was a slight breeze, but the air was too warm to offer relief and instead only added to the swelter.

"Load up," Hendricks hollered at us a short while later. "I want everyone with their regular team members as we move in. I'll take the lead." He patted the hood of the truck he was driving. "Once we're at the border of the town, we'll see what we've got and go from there. Turn on your radio pieces and listen for Grady. Any questions?"

When no one said anything, he nodded to the group in approval, then looked over to Kat, his second.

"We'll be going in through the remains of Newcastle and circling back around to get to Honor," she explained, showing us on the map what she'd meant and how we would approach the town. Newcastle was the old city next to the Honor Camp. "There, we'll go in through the north side of the camp, which should put us on the main road that runs straight through the whole compound. Once we're in, we'll radio for you to follow if it's safe." She stepped back to let Hendricks finish.

"Alright, people, stay alert and stay alive." He put his cap back on. "Ryan, you're with me. Let's move out." He moved around the truck to get into the driver's side.

We followed his instructions and found our teams, then loaded up into our assigned vehicles. Brooks, my team leader, had been assigned to follow Hendricks and his group who would take the lead in an old military GILA armored vehicle while we followed behind in a military Humvee. Each of the lead vehicles had roof-mounted gun rings and turrets and had been chosen to go in first specifically for this reason. Behind us were Blaise and his team in the Ford F250, followed by Dan's team with the bus, and then Rick's in another Humvee taking up the back.

The twenty-minute drive felt faster than it was. As we passed through the ransacked and burned remains of Newcastle, I felt saddened at the thought that some of these people would have lost their homes twice. Newcastle itself had long ago been burned to clear out the infection, and the Honor facility was where they'd gone to start again.

As we approached the perimeter of Honor, it became obvious that whatever had happened was let in easily because most of the trauma done to the town was a result of them trying to get out. The broken border surrounding the camp expelled outward rather than in. The fence laid and pushed out at awkward angles while piles of brick and debris scattered around the barrier as repeated attempts had been made to flee. Small plumes of smoke rose from various places across the compound while other buildings blazed with the consumption of what was left.

We stopped outside the facility, as instructed, and waited as Hendricks went ahead and then signaled for us to follow. In our vehicle, Dawsen sat as gunner at the turret while the rest of us took aim through the open windows as we crept in and made our way to the middle of the town, stopping behind Hendricks and his team. Once we were all in and parked, we filtered out of our transports and waited for further direction.

The entire area looked as though it had been hit with a bomb. Save for the fresh blood, bodies, and fire, it seemed as though it had been abandoned long ago. Layers of ash covered all the surfaces while garbage and lost treasures littered the streets—burned, warped, and faded. A sad, howling, hollow wind whistled past broken windows and vacant buildings as it pushed the smell of smoke and pulled the scent of death throughout the area.

As we walked alongside the vehicles and moved closer to the front of the line, the sound of dirt crunching under our boots loudly echoed in the stillness, leaving our sole imprints in the dust of death. On the other side of the armored truck, a chorus of moaning and shuffling drew louder as it moved closer, before quiet pops from a silenced rifle cut it off. A hollow thud followed as the bodies fell to the ground.

"Abby," Lauren, one of my teammates, whispered intently and nodded toward the *kook* that had rounded the corner of a building to my right.

"Got it," I said to her before putting a bullet between what was left of its eyes. It staggered to a halt, falling first to its bony knees before face-planting to the earth.

We made it to the front of the GILA but not before a dozen other pops and thuds went off all around us. Earnest signals and quiet commands were the only discernible noises to be made out between the carrion and quiet. As everyone gathered around the lead vehicle, we formed a half-circle around the nose of the armored truck to cover all angles and directions.

Hendricks was in the center and had his hands wrapped around Ryan's face, locking him in place as he appealed to the man sharply. A frantic and desperate look played across his features as Ryan barely held it together. He shifted his weight from one foot to the other, clenching and unclenching both his fists and his jaw as his eyes darted around the space.

We were in the middle of the compound and could see almost everything around us. The little town was destroyed. These people had fought back—that much was clear—but ultimately, they had lost. Dozens of bodies littered the streets. Some were old, their death unmistakably long ago, but the new ones were obvious by the way the fresh blood soaked through their clothes.

Hendricks had calmed Ryan down enough for him to give specifics of where to look in town. Then, he relayed the message. "Search only the major buildings, stay in your groups, and keep your ears on," he radioed without moving his eyes from Ryan's face. "Team leaders need to stay in constant contact. We'll meet back here when all the buildings have been cleared and confirmed empty," he ordered while keeping a firm grip on Ryan's shoulders. "Blaise, I need you with me. Kat will take command of your team," Hendricks ordered.

The only reason Blaise and Kat would trade positions in a situation like this was if Ryan wasn't stable. Blaise had a special way of dealing with hysterics, and it usually involved quick reflexes and pressure points. They would also need his massive frame and upper body strength to carry Ryan if they put him out.

This didn't bode well for the rest of us or our efforts to process through this town with as little notice as possible. We hadn't been in a situation like this in years, and we didn't make it a habit of walking into a fresh den of the dead, so we could only hope that Ryan was in control enough to allow us to do our jobs and get us all out of here safely.

Brooks, my team leader, indicated to us to follow him. We headed in the opposite direction of Blaise, Ryan, and Hendricks, and went for one of the larger buildings we'd been told was used for storage. As we passed through the scarlet-painted streets and the bodies that lay on them, we made sure the dead would stay that way. We used hunting knives to pierce through the base of their skulls and temples when we could. Not wanting to deplete our ammo, we saved our bullets for those that had reanimated so we wouldn't need to get close.

The entire front and left side of the building we went to first had been burned away. Only smoking support columns, singed floors, parts of walls, and what was left of a partially collapsed roof remained. The basement was where we were headed, and after carefully making our way through the battered shelter, rubble, and debris, a stairwell led us to where Ryan had said people might have escaped to to hide.

With our gun lights on, we went down the uneven concrete stairs and into the basement. Only two directions could be taken once you reached the floor and they met up again, making a square route. We split off, half going one way, half the other, and then swept through the area, checking all the doors and rooms. When we met back up with the rest of the team, nothing had been found except for a stray cat that belted out in fear when the door to the room it had been hiding in opened. We made our way back through the basement and up the stairs into the light. Brooks—while holding the scared feline—radioed to the other team leaders that the building had been cleared and we would move on to another.

Brooks was a total badass. He was a general surgeon, a master in martial arts, and our vanguard tactician. When unexpected situations arose, he developed a plan and determined how best to respond to it. He was a respected "guy's guy" who didn't bullshit around, and he looked as fierce as he was. His skin was strewn with tattoos only a few shades darker than his carbon tone, which made him look intimidating. He had bulging muscle on top of muscle over his entire body, every cut defined and ripped under his taut skin, his veins thick and his pulse visible. Cropped black hair, a goatee, and full brows gave him a naturally powerful look, and when concentrating on something, he took on a menacing stare, his eyes and jaw tightening into a scowl as his lips sort of pursed together. But holding this scared, dirty, tiny little cat in his big arms was a clear glimpse into his soul and communicated everything you needed to know about him as a person. Brooks was generous beyond measure, loyal to a fault, and as gracious as they came.

We left the building with the cat in tow and searched through two more buildings to find only darkness, ransacked rooms, and disregarded items. With three other teams in Honor doing the same things, we cleared the city quickly, not vocalizing our distress over not finding anyone alive while remaining vigilant and watchful through our unease at the lack of bodies.

Hendricks's and Dan's teams were getting ready to head into the last building as the rest of us made our way back to the meeting place. A few minutes later, the two teams communicated that something was wrong, just as gunfire pelted the air and broke the near silence of the devastated town.

We ran the rest of the way, backtracking through ashen ground by following our remnant footprints, until we made it to our meeting place.

As we came into view, Hendricks ordered over our earpieces, "All teams, get out! Get out of here now!"

Next to our convoy of vehicles, Hendrick's and Dan's teams had taken cover as they fired on a group of *kooks* heading for them. Two team members had climbed inside the lead vehicles and were shooting at the oncoming horde, using the gun turret rings, while the others shot at the *kooks* from the ground. They were coming at them in troves, one after another, dodging fallen bodies and pushing their way past each other to get to the front.

"They're *evos*!" Brooks yelled into his radio, which resonated in surround sound for me as he relayed the information to the rest of the group.

Evos were the smart ones—the group hunters and the most dangerous of the zombie breeds. They weren't intellectually smart but had advanced enough in their viral evolution to give them a survival instinct and what appeared to be an ability to process enough information to persevere.

Our team was closing in to help the others when Kat noticed our approach. "Stay back!" she ordered while those with her continued to load into the two lead vehicles. Most of the team members with her piled into the GILA and positioned themselves out the row of windows to fire at the *kooks*, while the remaining few went to the Humvee.

My team moved back and took cover, following her direction, then watched as the two vehicles took off out of the area after throwing Hg-80 hand grenades into the cluster of the dead. When the shell casings hit the ground, the bluish-gray vapor from an engineered mercury smoke bomb plumed out, then exploded and dispersed the specialized poison into the air. Hg-80 was a canister-type grenade that first emitted a vaporized mercury substance, then exploded for maximum damage.

The *kooks* that weren't incinerated by the blast soon after faltered from the mercury smoke enveloping them. It attacked the blood cells and spread through their systems as it attached itself to the plasma and proteins, eating away their composition, and liquefying the fluid and anything it touched—blood vessels, muscle, and flesh. The affected were soon nothing more than a mound of melting and rotting body parts as the mercury ate its way through their systems, hissing and bubbling off blood and guts, leaving behind only dirty, ragged clothes and scarred, broken bones to simmer in the slimy mess.

Brooks ordered half of my team to back up Hendricks and his team, who were firing on a bunch of *kooks* off in the distance, as he and two others went for the three vehicles left from our convoy. Evan, Lauren, Joni, and I formed a loose circle around one another and drifted toward Hendricks and his team, while Brooks went with Dawsen to retrieve the F250, bus, and Humvee.

The *evos* seemed to pour into town, coming out of nowhere, and had us surrounded by the time we made it to Hendricks and part of his team. There were eight of us, but twenty of them and counting. As the horde grew and drew in on us, Ryan fell apart and began to prattle off names that meant nothing to any of us but something very real to him. He was inconsolable, and every time any of us tried to get him to focus, he would look back out to the gathering dead and see another face he recognized.

Ryan had insisted on being here when he found out we were coming to Honor, but bringing him had obviously been a mistake. We couldn't control him or calm him down, and whenever one of us shot one of them, he would scream, his frenzied panic starting all over again.

"Blaise!" Hendricks hollered after he'd failed to control Ryan's hysteria, then turned his attention back to the real danger and fired on the dead again.

It only took Blaise a few seconds to render Ryan unconscious once the command had been given, and shortly after, he had him draped over his shoulder to hang limp against his back. We tightened our circle around Blaise and the unconscious man, to protect them both since Blaise could no longer assist now that he had a dependent.

The F250 one of my teammates had retrieved plowed through a group of *kooks* coming at us and cleared a path as he ran them down, scraping them away with the attached plow. The Humvee followed closely behind and ran over the *kooks* the plow had missed, before coming to a stop at the bumper of the truck. The bus followed last. Its rotating blades welded to the rims of the tires turned into a blender of sorts as it sliced through a handful of *evos* before it came to a halt behind the Humvee. When the truck stopped, we formed a half-circle around it to provide cover fire while Blaise shoved Ryan in the back.

One minute, we were standing there surrounded by advancing *kooks* and their spawn, picking them off one at a time as fast as we could pull the triggers, and the next, we were surrounded by members of the Vampire Increment Guard and their long, sharp swords as they sliced through the dead alongside us.

"Get in your vehicles and leave," one of them ordered, then danced and decapitated the dead with blinding speed.

Aston and Lauren didn't hesitate and made their way into the Humvee. James hopped in the front seat of the truck next to Brooks after Blaise had shoved Ryan in and climbed into the back after him. Rick, Joni, and Evan went to the front door of the bus, where Dawsen had opened the double doors, and Holden unlatched and pushed open the back. Dan, being the closest, headed to the back door first, where Holden was waiting to pull him in.

Hendricks, Blaise, and I kept our formation and moved to the back of the bus, the vampires guarding our backs, when we heard a horrific scream as one of our people was taken down.

"Evan," Hendricks curse under his breath.

I couldn't afford to look away from where I was shooting and could only guess it was him who was lost.

We reached the back of the bus and Blaise bent down to boost me into the back, when two stragglers came from around the side, surprising both of us. I still had my rifle, but Blaise was fast. He stood up and shoved one of the dead away from us with one hand as he pulled his knife out with the other and rammed it through the *kook's* eye. I was about to put a bullet through the other one's skull when the zip of a stray round whipped past me and landed in Hendricks's left shoulder. The scream from the person holding the weapon as it took him down rang clear over the commotion, and the repeated crack from the gun he held was loud as the bullets discharged, lobbing off aimlessly in our direction. Hendricks caught another slug in his leg before he hit the ground. As quickly as I could, I shot the *kook* that Blaise had shoved into the dirt, and went to kneel beside Hendricks.

Several other *kooks* had followed the first two, so Blaise pulled out his pistol and took them down when a vampire appeared, finishing the small herd upon us. As soon as the small group had been taken care of, I turned my focus to Hendricks and his wounds.

I set my weapon down to access him when he yelled at me, "Goddamn it, Abby, get on the bus!"

I was about to protest when, out of the corner of my eye, I saw more of the dead approaching us. Picking up my weapon, I got ready to aim, but I was grabbed around the waist and thrust into the back of the bus. After I caught my bearings, I turned around, and found Blaise and a member of the Vampire Guard working together to protect Hendricks.

When only a few *kooks* remained around us, the vampire knelt and picked him up faster than I could track with my eyes, bringing him over and placing him on the floorboard.

"Grab under his arms and pull him in," the vampire instructed before he went off in another direction.

As gently as we could, we pulled Hendricks inside the bus, and he helped by pushing with his one good leg. When he was far enough inside, Blaise jumped in and slammed the door shut behind him. The team members already inside the bus were positioned in the seats, with their rifles aimed out of the windows as they shot at the massive horde. Blaise yelled at Dawsen that we were good to go, and he wasted no time to turn the bus back into a weapon—grinding our way through the mass of the dead as we drove through the streets, sawing and eviscerating the *kooks* in half, and leaving a river of blood, entrails, and loosely ground-up flesh in our wake.

Over the radio, the other teams confirmed they were clear of the town and heading back to the hangar to wait for us. The bus weaved its way through the town while the vanguard continued to fire out of the windows, killing off as many *kooks* as they could.

I was next to Hendricks, trying to stop the bleeding from his leg when we pulled out of the town. Once we were on the smooth pavement, I peered out the backdoor window to see what we were leaving behind and discovered, instead, *who* we were leaving behind.

"Stop the bus!" I yelled at Dawsen and moved to the back, readying myself to open the latched door.

"What the hell are you doing, Abby?" Holden snapped and pushed my hand away from the handle.

"We can't just leave them here! They'll get killed!" I pointed through the door window at the four vampires. Dozens of *kooks* and *evos* were closing in on them, and it didn't matter how fast they were—there were too many. They wouldn't survive if they stayed and tried to fight.

I shoved past Holden and again went for the handle. Dawsen had slowed down the bus, and I had just unlatched the door and swung it open to holler at them when Holden pulled me back, grabbed me around the waist, and clasped his hand over my mouth.

The vampires were *fast.* They had either heard what I'd said or noticed the bus had slowed and took advantage of it because they were up and inside the back of the bus before Holden had even taken us back two steps.

"Let her go," one of them said, his voice like ice as his words shivered through the air. The threat laced in that came with defiance and sent a chill down my spine.

"Or what?" Holden snapped at the tall, menacing vampire.

"Or I'll fucking kill you."

I froze.

Holden wasn't hurting me. In fact, he hardly had a grip on me at all. So when I elbowed him in the gut, he easily let me go and turned his full focus on the four vampires standing before us.

"Nice threat, bloodsucker. I wasn't hurting her. Now, get the fuck off the bus." He side-stepped and moved to stand in front of me, placing his enormous body between me and the hostile vampire.

"Holden!" I tried to shove him out of the way, but he was solid. If he'd noticed my attempt to move him at all, he didn't show it. "They helped us. We can give them a ride."

"No," he snarled at me.

The horde of the dead left behind was now coming at us quickly, their hungry sounds a loud chorus made audible by their numbers. The sight of them highlighted the smell of fresh blood in the air, which pulled me back into the now. Hendricks had already lost a lot of blood and was still bleeding. He needed medical attention.

"We don't have time for this!" I hissed and bent down to pick up where I'd left off, starting again to remove the sticky clothes away from Hendricks's blood-soaked skin.

"Commander?" Holden asked.

We didn't deal with vampires. That was the rule, and I had just broken it.

"Just drive," Hendricks garbled and then passed out.

Chapter Four

When I was sixteen, I'd watched a man die. It was the first time I had ever seen anyone die up close and from something other than a *kook* attack. It had been my first true death and would forever be in my memory.

His name was William, and he'd been thirty-six.

I was working in the care center when one of the vanguard teams came back unexpectedly. My mother had made me go with her to the decon-zone to help with the wounded, and it happened there in the medical bay. He had been shot several times by some spyders*—people who chose to live outside of humanity and thrived stealing from the rest of us. The* spyders *had tracked the vanguard coming back to town and attacked them before they could get here or call for help.*

William was barely alive by the time we got there and had lost a lot of blood—so much that I was sliding through it as I scrambled to the side of his bed. I slipped once and almost fell, and when I reached out to grab the side of the gurney, he grabbed my hand and pulled me back upright. His face was dirty and his eyes bloodshot, but they were the purest and brightest blue I had ever seen, like a clear summer sky glowing cerulean on a sunny afternoon.

His lips were cracked and chapped, his teeth stained red from the blood that leaked out from both sides of his mouth. It left wet trails that traveled from the corners of his lips, down the small expanse of his cheek to his jawline, and slipped down his neck, where it delicately dripped on the white sheet beneath him.

His breath stunk like metal, blood, and death, as he labored to pull in a gasping lungful. With it, I could hear a subtle rattle and rasp deep within his chest. When it expelled, it left as intensely, his lungs nearly collapsing with the force of evacuation. The hot vapid exhalation stuck to my face as it rushed at me, thick and heavy on my skin like hot humid air in the summer before a heavy rain. I longed for a wet washcloth to wipe across my face, but I desperately clamped down on my reflexive gag and desire to flee in order to help this dying man.

His hand clasped mine and kept me upright next to him. Under the layers of blood and grime were remnants of hard work that had scarred his skin and hands. His nails were dirty and black, and scars lined his knuckles with grease that had been stuck in the crevasses for years. His hand felt cold and rough against my soft skin, his calluses like sandpaper and his grip like steel bars, wrapping around my hand like a cage.

My mother had spared only enough time to look over his wounds and check his vitals before she moved on to the next patient. Before she went, she'd squeezed his hand and looked down at him. They nodded at the other in silent communication. She looked up at me with regret in her eyes before she turned and walked away. I knew then that he wouldn't make it and no other doctor would try to save him when there were so many others who could be helped.

He must have known that this was his fate and that he would die because when I looked back at him only seconds later, the resignation was in his eyes, the once unclouded blue now as bloodied and red as a sky on fire.

He tightened his grip around my hand and gave me a weak smile, whispering, "It's okay."

I felt panicked and angry that no one would help him, that they were leaving him to die without even trying. Though I knew in the back of my mind there was nothing to be done, it still felt wrong. Logically, I understood that if there had been any chance of saving him, they would have tried. Of course, they would have tried, but he couldn't be helped.

I attempted to compose myself and be strong for William. I was to be the last person he would see before his death, and he deserved kindness and strength. I knew that, rationally, but putting it into practice was a task I was not yet up for.

I realized at one point that I should help the others with the rest of the wounded. This man was a lost cause, after all, and I had skills that could be used elsewhere, even if very limited. But I couldn't leave him alone. If I could not save him, I could at least usher him into the next life with what little I had to offer.

I held on to William's hand, more tightly than even he had the strength to, and with my free hand, I ran a cool washcloth—that someone had kindly brought me—over his forehead. At one point, William reached up and wiped away a tear from my cheek. I hadn't realized I was crying. The movement was slow and jerky, and the effort it took him was evident by the determination on his face.

I kept up my ministrations, running the washcloth along the sides of his face and over his matted hair. When his features began to lax and the life slowly drained from his eyes, I continued to hold on to his hand as I whispered and mumbled an array of comforts, my eyes now blurry and my voice cracked.

His breathing became harsh as he drowned and choked on his blood, and when his last breath left and there was no more gasping, I had to remind myself to still breathe. My throat burned and hurt from my sobbing cries, my nose running wet and my body shaking with each hitching breath. Hot tears poured unimpeded down my face as I looked into his lifeless eyes.

It was sometime later that I pulled myself away and rested his hand against his chest. With shaky fingers, I closed his eyes and cleaned him up the best I could. I knew it was a wasted effort, but I couldn't leave him dirty in his death.

Once the morticians had been notified, they came after him. They snapped open a clean, crisp sheet to pull over his body and face before they wheeled him away. They spared me only a brief, sad look as I watched them go, leaving me to stand in the mess of his death and a half-dried pool of blood.

Hendricks's eyes were blue, and as we worked on getting his wounds to stop bleeding, I kept remembering William and the way he'd looked at me while I desperately tried not to make the comparison.

We made it back to the old airport hangar, running high on anxiety and adrenaline as we secured the area, worked on the wounded, and waited for news about Hendricks.

He hadn't woken back up since he'd passed out on the bus, which made it easier to work on him but harder for me to keep myself focused and in check. Brooks was a doctor and Lauren was a nurse, both working on him, while Joni, who was a medical assistant, and Kat, who had field medical training, fixed up and bandaged the other vanguard with wounds.

The first bullet Hendricks had caught was in his shoulder and had gone right through. It was the one in his leg that was giving them a hard time.

While we'd been on the bus and with the help of Blaise, I got the bleeding from his shoulder under control but was only able to apply pressure to the femoral artery with a tourniquet at his leg.

"I can help him if you'll let me," the vampire with the cool-toned voice said.

"No." I shook my head in denial at his request and continued to pack on bandages, applying pressure to the leg. "He would consider it an offense."

"An offense?" he copied my choice of words with disdain. "He would rather die than accept help from a vampire?"

"Yes." I spared only a few seconds to look at his face.

His eyes were the typical violet all vampires had, but I had never seen this shade before. They were clearer, deeper somehow, and brimming with secrets as they bore into me as if into my soul. In those brief seconds, a chill ran down my spine and my breath caught at the sight of him.

Thinking back now gave me a similar sensation, and I felt cool, even though my palms sweated. Vampires had always been a curiosity to me. They were courtly and ethereal, untouched by age while old with wisdom. I'd never been in a room with one long enough to explain my intrigue, so I shrugged it off to lack of exposure. I'd been around vampires and met them, but because I grew up in Thompson Falls where they weren't allowed, it had limited my experience.

Since our arrival, the vampire with the commanding voice and his team members had kept their distance. They appeared vigilant and maintained a watchful eye on both the inside and outside area of the hangar, but every so often, I'd feel eyes on me and whenever I turned, I'd find the one vampire watching me. We would hold each other's gazes until I looked away. I was sure I was making him and everyone else in the room uneasy and nervous with my constant pacing and incessant questioning.

We'd only been back for less than an hour, but it felt like days. Once we had gotten Hendricks off the bus and onto a working table, I wasn't allowed too close and only glimpsed his face with each pass I paced.

Everyone else had long since been bandaged, so I'd had nothing to do with my hands for some time now, except to wring them together and bite my nails. I could feel the blood as it pumped through my veins, the swoosh and pounding of it in my ears, my heart beating enthusiastically with adrenaline while coursing through the vessels. My neck and shoulders hurt from tension, and no matter how many times I rolled my head or stretched my back, they both continued to burn.

"Abby!" Brooks hollered at me. "We need your blood."

"Yep." I ran to him, unzipped my suit, and pulled my arms out of my sleeves. I had O-negative blood, so I was the easiest person to draw from. Sitting down on the chair next to Hendricks, I waited for Lauren to place the IV.

"What the hell are you doing?" the vampire demanded. Lauren was just about to place the tourniquet around my bicep when he'd come up behind her.

"He's lost a lot of blood. We're doing a transfusion." She gave him a side glance while she swabbed alcohol across my skin in prep for the needle.

"She could die," he snapped and stepped closer as if to put himself between us.

I looked up, surprised. "He could die."

He was angry, this stranger I had yet to meet. Furious. His brows pulled tight over squinted eyes, and his jaw clenched and contracted as he ground his teeth. His hands had balled into fists at his sides, the muscles in his forearms corded, and the veins bulged from the tension.

"So, you should both die to save one human's life?" He scoffed as our eyes locked.

"I'm not going to die," I roared back and pinched my face in confusion. "This is perfectly safe, and his life depends on it."

"There's no way to control the blood flow."

"He needs my blood. What does it matter to you?" I questioned.

He didn't respond. We were silent for a moment, each staring at the other with indignation and an unwillingness to concede. I couldn't understand why he would care, but I also didn't have the time to find out.

"Just do it, Lauren." I turned away from him and shoved my arm at her.

Lauren was good at her job, and barely a pinch later, red flowed from me through a tube and into Hendricks, all while the vampire stood furiously by.

"We won't bleed her dry. He just needs a bump until we can get him home." Brooks glanced over his shoulder at the irate vampire. "It's not ideal, but out here, we don't have a lot of options."

"You could take one of our blood," the vampire retorted, that same acidic tone he'd used on the bus clear in his words.

"True." Brooks pulled off his bio gloves. "But we've stopped the bleeding, and he only needs enough to keep him alive for the journey home. We aren't losing anyone today," he drawled and tossed his bunched-up gloves in a trash bin like a basketball through a hoop.

"I can ensure that better than you." The vampire glared at him.

"And I would rather take my chances," Hendricks croaked and then cleared his throat.

I grabbed his hand with my free one. My face flushed with relief, and my shoulders sagged with the release of tension. "How are you feeling?" I asked as Lauren flashed a little light back and forth between Hendricks's eyes.

"Like I was shot." His voice was hoarse.

"Weird." Brooks smirked, then read off his vitals and informed him of what they had done to the wounds he had suffered.

"How long has she been hooked up to me?" He turned his head toward me.

I squeezed his hand and gave him a reassuring smile. "Not very long."

"Almost two minutes now," the vampire talked over me. "They should remove her from the transfusion line. It's been long enough."

I tensed in the chair, and my back stiffened at the exchange. Somehow, it had escaped me during the commotion of the last hour that Hendricks may not appreciate the vampires still being here. As we'd readied ourselves to travel home, bandaged our people, and waited for him to wake up, we'd failed to mention to them that we didn't work with their kind. Hendricks had given the go-ahead for them to ride back with us, but that didn't mean he wanted them to stick around once they were safe.

The room went quiet. Everyone stopped what they were doing and waited for Hendricks's reaction.

"Agreed." He looked at Lauren taking his vitals. "Get her off the drain, and someone find her some OJ and cookies."

His agreement surprised me, then annoyed me. "No. You've lost a lot of blood, and I'm fine."

"Abby, this isn't up for debate, and I'm not arguing with you." He jerked his head. "Lauren."

She nodded and moved around the table to my side.

As if to prove both him and the vampire right, I stood up to protest but fainted. The world went fuzzy and black around the edges, the room turning. One minute I was upright, and the next I was falling to the floor, my vision blackening out. I expected the hard surface, but my descent stopped as I got swooped up into someone's arms.

Around me, I could hear a flutter of commotion as different voices argued, but I couldn't make out any of the words over the ringing in my ears. My slight consciousness obscured whatever was said, garbling into a mash of syllables that made no sense to my muddled brain.

Everything seemed to dim in and out for a while before it eventually came back into focus, and after a few minutes, I hung onto the present and what was happening around me. Though I was light-headed and queasy, I could make out that the arguing had stopped and it sounded as if everyone had gone back to work.

"You'll feel better in a few moments," a rich voice murmured when I blinked against the brightness in the room.

"Here is a cool washcloth," Lauren said, though I couldn't see her face.

"My hand is cooler than this." Warm wetness swiped across my arm. "She'll need a bandage," the hard voice demanded, and then a cool hand pressed against my forehead.

Involuntarily, I let out a comforting moan at the cool sensation against my brow and how it whisked away the nausea. It must be the vampire, his hand pressed against my forehead.

Minute by minute, my surroundings became clearer and clearer. Soon, I felt self-conscious about my proximity to this stranger. Cautiously, I moved and then realized I was on his lap. He must have been the one to break my fall. Mortified, I was confused as to why he was holding me.

I shifted around uncomfortably and, with his support, slowly sat up. When the room stopped spinning, he guided me off his lap, easing me onto the bench we sat on but keeping a hand on my back to hold me steady. I sat motionless for a moment to collect myself.

"Thank you," I conceded quietly. "I guess you were right."

"Usually." He stood and took a step to my side.

Lauren had come back with the bandage he had demanded and sat next to me, taking hold of my arm. "Sorry, Abby." She removed the warm cloth pressed against my inner arm, dried the skin, and placed the adhesive over the tiny hole at my inner elbow.

I watched her while she worked. She seemed tired and sort of scattered. Her normally neatly done hair was messy and held together loosely by a knotted bun at the back of her head. Dark blonde bangs fell in her eyes, wisps curling around her ears and shoulders. She had unzipped her suit to her waist, and her cut-proof undershirt was wet with sweat in a V-shape over her chest and half-circles under her arms. The garment was splattered with blood.

"Are you alright?" I asked her.

She stopped and looked at me, then shook her head. "You're ridiculous. Yes, I'm fine. Are *you* alright?"

"Yes."

"We should have been paying more attention."

"It's not your fault." I put a hand on her shoulder. "We don't know how much blood is being transferred when we use a direct line."

"I know, but we should have been paying more attention." She grabbed the can of soda and oranges she had found in our food storage and held them out to me.

Taking them, I set the items beside me. "This isn't your fault."

"Abby, if I shot you in the leg right now, you'd find a way to tell me it wasn't my fault. So, forgive me if I insist on taking some responsibility for you passing out." She rolled her eyes and patted my knee.

"Now, who's being ridiculous?" I griped as she stood to leave, then glanced around the room at everyone in the hangar as they packed up.

Now that Hendricks was safe enough to travel and his wounds had stopped bleeding, we would get back to Thompson Falls. There was still a chance of infection and the potential that the quick repair job Brooks had done wouldn't hold up, so we would move while Hendricks was stable.

The crack of a can and the release of the carbonation brought my focus back to where I was and the outstretched hand holding the beverage in front of me.

"Drink," the vampire demanded.

"Thanks." I accepted the can from him, tipped back a few sips of the fizzy sugar water, and mustered up the courage to really look at him for the first time.

He was very tall and muscular. Not nearly as large as Blaise, my bartender. And he wasn't corded and bulging like my team leader, Brooks, but he was toned and well-defined from what I could see. Dark hair was disheveled in a way that lay neatly on his head. It was several inches long and layered, the few strands that didn't stay in place with their style wisping out in odd directions at the back and sides of his head. His bangs fell and feathered over his forehead, hanging nearly into his eyes. The color was dark like mocha, the silky strands shiny, smooth, and probably soft.

His dark brows had sharp arches that dramatically crowned his piercing violet eyes, which were framed with long, black lashes. High cheekbones and a straight nose led to a set of full lips with a prominent V and a plush of softness, the top smaller than the pouty bottom. The color was a warm light maroon, and they parted just enough that I could see the sharp, white points of his fangs. Unshaven facial hair spread across a square chin and strong jawline, then continued down his neck to create a five o'clock shadow.

His clothes were like ours: heavy boots, leather pants, and a tight-fitted black shirt worn under a leather jacket. The major difference was that his belt held a long sword in addition to a gun.

"What's your name?" I asked him faintly as I traveled his body up and down with my eyes.

"Ethan." He lifted one side of his mouth. "Ethan Sterling," he repeated with a sly grin and a lift of his brow as he crouched down in front of me.

His swift movement took me a few seconds to catch up with; he was much faster than my eyes could track. A small breeze wafted across my face with the action, the cool, freshly scented air a far cry from the musty smell of the hangar. It reminded me of a summer sun shower in the woods on an early morning.

He held out his hand, so I responded by placing mine into his.

"It's nice to meet you. I'm Abby Rose." I gave him my full name since he'd given me his, which was strange, but whatever.

"It's nice to meet you, Abby." He inclined his head and gave my hand a quick squeeze before he flipped it over, placing two fingers on the pulse at my wrist.

"What are you doing?" I yelped, trying to pull my hand free.

"Checking your heart rate." He looked at me through heavy lashes.

His eyes were so striking it was hard to look away. His pupil wasn't black. Instead, it was the color of eggplant in its darkest shade and rich in depth. From there, the color drastically faded out into a thistle hue, which covered the entire iris and subtly rippled with indigo, a circle of dark lilac ringing around the edge against the porcelain white.

"Thanks." I tried to pull my hand free again. "But I'm perfectly fine. This isn't the first time I've been light-headed after giving blood, and I'm sure it won't be the last."

"I'm sure not." He let go of my hand to stand back up to his statuesque height.

"Abby! It's time to go," Holden bellowed as he walked up behind Ethan. "Say goodbye to your friend." He sneered, trying to get a rise out of one or both of us.

Holden had unzipped his suit, which seemed to be the trend among the vanguard at the moment, and let his arms hang loose at his sides, exposing his cut-proof undergarment. He was wearing a tank top version that put his arms and upper body strength in full view. Holden was light-skinned, tall, and ripped with so much muscle it looked uncomfortable. He spent all his extra time in the gym, and it showed. When he wasn't sleeping, eating, or drinking, he was punishing himself with weights and long workouts. Out on assignments, he'd find anything heavy to lift, and if there wasn't anything, he'd use his own weight against himself.

His hair was nearly bald on both sides above his ears, shaved to a point at the base of his skull but slightly longer on the top. He was scarred in various places across his whole body. Small ones dotted his head and face, with a few over his arms and chest, all noticeable by their slightly raised edges and pink color. A long, bulbous, and jagged scar sat higher on his left bicep, running from the top of the deltoid down to his elbow. He'd said to have gotten it from an ax-wielding *spyder* he'd fought before coming to Thompson Falls, but that was all anyone knew since it was a closely guarded secret on his part.

I stood from my chair but kept my attention on Ethan. "Ignore him. He's a jackass turned into a real boy by a drunken fairy."

"Funny. Now, let's go." Holden crossed his big arms over his chest, his face holding its permanent scowl. Deep-set lines between his brows bunched and furrowed together to let me know he wasn't amused.

Continuing to ignore Holden, I kept my focus on the tall vampire towering over me. "Ethan, thank you for everything."

"You're not serious about leaving tonight?" His tone was no longer the friendly, playful one it had been a moment ago.

"We need to get Hendricks back to our care center as soon as possible."

"It is nearly nightfall." He scowled at me and clipped out the words.

His entire demeanor had changed in an instant. His harsh tone was loud enough that it had drawn the attention of people around us, and the room quieted. Some vanguard stopped what they were doing and turned toward us, a couple of them even taking a few steps in our direction. The other vampires with him had also turned their focus on the three of us, no longer standing casually off in the distance.

"It's also not up to her bloodsucker. Now, back off." Holden jabbed a finger at Ethan, putting his roadblocked-sized body between me and the now hostile vampire. "Abby, get to the damn bus. Now," Holden clipped at me.

Holden wasn't technically my superior, but I listened to him anyway. He was a hardass with a poor attitude but also a man you wanted to have your back. Not that I was scared—Ethan's tone and change in demeanor hadn't triggered any of *my* alarms. But whatever had set Ethan off, now was not the time for Holden's and my normal banter. I walked away from them toward the bus, passing several large-bodied men moving toward Holden to take my place.

Blaise and Brooks were loading Hendricks in through the back door when I came upon them, evidently so engrossed in their own dilemma that they hadn't noticed what was going on behind them.

"We need to get him all the way in and then turn him so the stretcher will lay across two bench chairs," Brooks instructed Blaise.

"Can't we rip out a couple of these back seats first? Make it a little easier." Blaise sounded more than a little frustrated.

"We don't have the time—" Brooks said before being cut off.

"Commander Hendricks." The vexation in Ethan's voice marred his silent approach.

Blaise and Brooks set Hendricks and the stretcher he was strapped to back down on the table, and then looked at Ethan in confusion.

"What are you doing?" I hissed at him.

He stared down at me with a steely gaze for the briefest of moments, ignored my question, then walked closer to where Hendricks lay nearly unconscious and heavily medicated.

Hendricks seemed uncomfortable and less than pleased with his current condition. "Yes?" he croaked as though he had just woken from a deep sleep.

"You're aware your team is planning to travel back to Thompson Falls tonight?"

"Yes."

"You think that's wise?"

"Excuse me?"

"Traveling at night is a risk to the lives of all these people."

"Under normal circumstances, I would agree with your ... disapproval, but in this case, yes, I think it is wise," Hendricks returned the hostility, his voice stronger and louder with each word. "That mess we left back there is on its way here. I don't want my people anywhere near this tin can when they arrive, and we're running out of time."

Ethan stood quietly for a moment, his brow furrowed. "Then we will join you."

As soon as the words were out of his mouth, I knew this would not go over well.

"You will do no such thing," Hendricks practically snarled. "I think you've overstayed your usefulness as it is."

Ethan's expression was fierce, the muscles in his jaw and neck flexing in accord with his anger, his eyes drawn into narrow slits as he and Hendricks glared at each other.

"Very well. Then we will follow you," he stated defiantly as he walked away from Hendricks and his fiery protests.

We loaded and secured Hendricks in the bus, then made our way out of the hangar and into the first signs of trouble. The GILA and the military Humvee were leading the way when they stopped and opened fire into the vast darkness. We were barely out of the hangar, sandwiched between the two lead vehicles and the two rear, when we came to an abrupt stop.

Since I was on the bus with Hendricks instead of with my team in the Humvee, I didn't understand what was happening at first. I scrambled out of my bench seat next to Hendricks and pulled out *Walter*, my handgun, from the holster at my thigh, then moved to the front of the bus. The Walther P22 matte-black pistol with a laser sight and barrel compensator almost never left my side and had been my trusty sidekick for many years. Unless I was using a rifle, he was my go-to right-hand man for quick defense and protection.

After I'd pulled him out, I made my way to the front and listened for any response to Dan's request for information. He had radioed Kat and Dawsen in the two lead vehicles when we'd heard the first sounds of gunfire and hadn't heard back.

Dan put the bus in park, then locked the accordion-style door and secured it with a custom latch over the handle, rolling down the sliding shutter door to block the entrance. Sitting back in the driver's seat, he armed himself with a DPMS Panther rifle and turned to aim out of the window while we waited for feedback. I took up a position in the second seat on the opposite side of him and aimed out of my side through the window.

Brooks, with his pistol drawn, took a defensive position over a sleeping Hendricks, who had been medicated for the journey home. He tried to get a response from the forward teams over the radio but got nothing for feedback either, while Holden—also at the back of the bus with the Lee twins, Buck and Bush—split off to cover both sides of the metal tube.

Buck and Bush were identical twins and loved to prank people with their look-alike features. They were about my age and had come to Thompson Falls around the same time my mother and I had, so we knew each other well after growing up together. Buck and Bush were both formidable members of the vanguard and took their training so seriously that they taught it to new recruits and students at the school as part of the curriculum. Their combat techniques were a mix of martial arts, S.C.A.R.S., and the SPEAR system, which all focused on hand-to-hand combat for protection. Both were well-toned in muscle and skin color, and had a large-boned frame. Their facial structure especially set them apart. Sloping foreheads led to deep-set, almond-shaped eyes that held pine-green irises framed with black lashes and dark blonde brows. High cheekbones and wide noses sat atop prominent, almost triangular-shaped jaws that held straight, blocky white teeth behind thin lips. They were always clean-shaven, wore their hair in a buzzcut style, and smelled like soap.

The barrage of gunfire went quiet, but only for a few seconds before the turrets on the two lead vehicles fired. At the sound, the rear Humvee pulled ahead and joined in on the assault. With the three of them each blasting heavy artillery out into the darkness, along with personal shots from rifles, we could finally see what was headed for us.

In flash and strobe, a mass of *kooks* rambled and shuffled their way toward our location, and for every one that fell, another would take its place. It was hard to know exactly how big the horde was, but from the sea of bodies that rolled in toward us, they appeared to outnumber us three to one. It looked as though the entire town of Honor, and more, had been turned and were headed straight for us. They stretched out across both lanes of the highway, into the boulevard, and over the fields. The gunners at the turrets were doing a lot of damage, but the number of dead was too great. A few at a time, *kooks* slipped by and made their way into our space, closer to our vehicles.

"They're a distraction," I said in a breathy observation. Shots rang out behind us at almost the same time the thought left my mouth.

"What?" Holden hollered at me.

"They are a distraction!" I yelled and went from the front side of the bus to look out of the back toward the new gunfire.

"Shit!" Holden clipped and fired at a group of the dead that had come around the hangar to rush us.

These *kooks* were faster and moved with more skill than the ones on the road coming at us, which meant they were *evos* and not your ordinary *munchers*, so the pack mentality made sense. They were corralling us like wolves hunting prey.

Buck and Bush ran over to the middle of the bus. While one was opening and climbing through the roof hatch, the other was unloading a chest of weapons to hand up to his brother.

When the last weapon was passed up, I went over to Buck.

"Need a lift?" He bent down to give me a boost.

I put my booted foot into his waiting hands, and he hoisted me up through the top, where Bush grabbed me around the arms and pulled me through the rest of the way.

"Thanks." I holstered *Walter* to grab a rifle instead, then took my position.

The top of the bus had rails along the four sides that sat waist-high for fall protection, and were welded to the top and bolted down for extra security. The roof was painted with an anti-slip textured coating for situations exactly like this, so we could use the height of the bus as a vantage point without having to worry about falling or slipping off if we lost our footing.

On the roof, I could see better what was happening around and ahead of us. The two forward vehicles continued to fire at the original mass of dead still coming at us. They were taking a lot of them out, but not enough to slow down their progression and numbers. The Humvee that had pulled ahead had stopped firing from the gun mount, which had to either be jammed or out of ammo for it to stop its assault. Several vanguard moved to the top of the vehicle, fighting off the horde with their rifles, while the rest propped themselves out of the windows to shoot at the dead.

The vanguard members in the F250 parked behind the bus were doing much of the same thing. Someone stood behind each door, using it as a shield and firing at the hungry swarm closing in on them. The teamwork gave the rest who were with them time to jump in the truck's bed or climb up on the roof, where they provided cover fire. Seeing this, my team helped and fired at the *kooks* coming at both the Humvee and F250, so they could move up higher and faster.

All around the old hangar and on the street and fields that surrounded us were *kooks* in various degrees of rot and death. Dozens and dozens of them advanced on us from all directions in a near-constant flow. Orange burst of light from the muzzle flash was so steady and near non-stop that it bathed the area in a golden glow.

I put down fifteen or twenty *kook spawn* when I had to stop and reload my weapon, which was when I caught sight of the vampires. I couldn't make out their figures or individual shapes, but I could see the gleam of the moonlight and discharge fire as it glanced off their blades, catching light with each rise and fall of the metal weapons as they flew through the air. Each sword was in such constant motion that it left a light streak in its wake.

They seemed to be in the middle of all the chaos—surrounded by the dead and unaware that the horde was growing around them. I wanted to say something, deciding to try as soon as my weapon was ready, but before I could, someone yelled from one of the forward vehicles.

"*Bomb!*"

Panic spread through my body, and I stopped what I was doing to yell at them in warning. "It's mercury!" I shouted, but it was too late.

One of the mercury grenades blew up a short distance away from where they stood. The next few moments moved in slow motion, and I watched everything around me proceed at an exaggerated rate.

One of the other vampires—Sylis, I thought was his name—made his way to the bus and leaped to the top where I stood. He jumped through the latch hole in one swift motion, seconds after the Hg-80 had exploded. All the others soon followed, except Ethan.

The echo of the explosive had dulled all other noise and quieted the surrounding babble, which left the whoosh of my breath and the pound of my heart a loud throb in my ear. I searched into the darkness, watching for Ethan or the glint of his sword, but saw nothing to indicate he was okay. Another bomb blast followed only moments after the first, and it pulled my attention away from the darkness to the opposite side of the bus it had come from.

I couldn't see anything. My sight was partially hindered from the light of the explosion, and my pupils enlarged to adjust to the night blindness. But I could hear muted commands until those were also cut off by a piercing, keening shrill that split through the limited clamor.

I turned toward the sound, only to witness the dead pull Dave from the top of the F250. Several *kooks* had grabbed hold of him while his team members tried to pull him back, but it split their attention and the attempt to save his life had allowed another group of *kooks* to gain an advance on them. I shot at the encroaching mass and yelled at my team to help me lay cover fire, but the words were barely out of my mouth when Dave slipped through their hands and was dragged down by the mass. His screams echoed through the darkness, clear as a bell. The horrifying sound of his consumption reverberated and harmonized with the hungry horde and jealous cries of the envious *kooks* who had been left out.

A chill ran through me, but we kept shooting to take down as many as we could. The others were still surrounded, which left no room for shock or to mourn. We cleared a path, and the three that were left scrambled off the truck and ran to the bus, where they were lifted—one by one—into the back with someone's help.

Once they were safely inside, Ethan climbed up to the roof where I stood. We made eye contact briefly before he handed Holden a grenade pouch filled with Hg-80s. Then, he leaped down into the bus through the hatch. Holden hesitated only long enough to dig into the bag and pull the pins before he hurled them through the air into the largest of the groups. I saw the first one glint through the air and the beginnings of an explosion before the world around me shifted, my stomach rising as my feet fell. The next thing I knew, I was back on the bus, an oxygen mask shoved into my hands.

"Put it on!" Ethan yelled before he disappeared through the roof opening again, several more masks in his hands.

I did as I'd been told, then went over with another and put it on Hendricks, who was blissfully unaware thanks to the heavy sedation.

One by one, they all jumped back into the bus. Sylis, who had taken Dan's place behind the wheel, put the bus into drive and pulled away, the two lead vehicles close behind. Once we were on the open stretch of road, Ethan opened the back door and signaled the GILA and Humvee to move around us. When we came to a stop about one hundred yards away, he jumped up onto the roof again.

"Go!" he yelled when he came back down a moment later.

The bus lurched forward, faster this time. The unexpected speed jutted me forward and nearly out of my chair. I'd steadied myself against the speed and tried to turn and look, but Ethan surprised me again by pressing me down against the seat.

"Cover your head," he said as he shielded me with his body.

The explosion that followed was so loud that some windows shattered, and the bus jerked forward with the concussive force from the blast. We seesawed back and forth, the rubber tires screeching against the pavement as Sylis fought to get it under control. After the bus had straightened out, Ethan let me up from his protective cover. I finally looked behind us.

Coherent words failed me. The entire area was up in flames and circled in a ring of fire. A mushroom cloud of smoke was soaring up high, as bright as the sun, and billowed black and red with smog and flame. Everything in the circle and around it burned, including the Hanger and the F250 pickup we'd left behind. It engulfed groups of *kook* bodies while single targets flitted about before they fell to their last death. The black night was now ablaze with a bright and fiery glow as the ground burned, the carnage illuminating the sky.

Chapter Five

Several hours later we finally stopped in a small town about eight hours from Thompson Falls. We were in short supply of fuel and needed to find more before we could continue back home. Ethan had used up most of our fuel reserves when he created the fire that had allowed us all to escape the hangar alive.

Hendricks was still stable, and had slept through most of all the turmoil and the drive here. He was in pain and at risk for infection, but Brooks believed the worst was over and that he would make a full recovery with no lasting side effects if we could get him home quickly and safely.

The last twenty-four hours had been exhausting for everyone, and more than anything, we needed rest. We took turns driving. Some napped while the rest kept watch, either because of obligation or, like in my case, because we couldn't sleep. I wasn't concerned about our safety any longer; we had made it far away enough from the hangar that even if anything had survived, it couldn't have kept up with us.

I didn't recognize the town we stopped in, having never been here, but someone else called it Absarokee. I did, however, recognize the insignias on the sides of the buildings as our own. After we cleared and stripped a town of all its resources and usefulness, we tagged the buildings with the same red insignia we wore on our uniforms. It let other team members and vanguard that passed through know there was nothing left in the area and to not waste their time. Normally, this was great. We saw the insignia and moved on, but in this case, it was unwelcomed news. The entire town of Absarokee had been cleared and marked, which meant we would find nothing here, especially not the fuel we desperately needed. So, we would need to leave vehicles behind.

We emptied the tanks of the ones we would leave by siphoning the fuel out into the Humvee and the bus. Clearing out all our gear, weapons, and essentials, we loaded them on the top of the bus. We locked the doors on the ones we were leaving behind and flattened the tires of each—just in case someone found them—then covered them with branches and vegetation.

Replacement vehicles were a dime a dozen if you were brave enough to go into the bigger infected towns and cities to get them, but vehicles that ran and didn't need work were harder to come by. Not to mention all the upgrades, safety, and defense additions we added to our fleet. So, we liked to keep them, and since we'd already lost one today, we wanted to minimize the risk of losing another. Our ride home wouldn't be as comfortable as it'd been when we left, but we would save time and fuel by leaving them behind and carpooling.

"I'm going to wash my face," I whispered to Lauren while we waited for the fuel to be transferred from one vehicle to another. "Be right back."

She nodded at me.

The town was small enough that you could almost see the end while standing at the beginning. I wasn't concerned as I left the group to wander off by myself. Since we'd arrived, there had been no signs of *kooks*—or anything else, for that matter—so I thought it was fine.

We'd parked just past a bridge next to a river, and as soon as I saw the water, I immediately craved the fresh liquid on my face. I wasn't the only one who'd tested it. I just did it a little further away.

It was a short walk from where we'd parked, and I found a trail—probably worn down by animals—that led me to a small bank with slow, shallow water. It had been two days since I'd taken a shower, and I felt the filth of sweat and grime on my skin in layers. Unzipping my uniform to my waist, I pulled my long-sleeved undershirt off and knelt next to the edge.

The air felt cool on my warm skin. The suit always left my flesh feeling hot and tacky from wearing it, so the change of temperature was welcomed. I didn't hesitate to dunk my shirt in the cold water. The river was icy, and my hands turned red after a few minutes while I worked the fabric to get it wet. Once it was soaked, I used it as a towel to wipe over my entire upper body. I dipped the shirt again, then wrung out the excess water over my head, letting it trickle down. The spring melt-off was freezing, and it made my flesh prickle on contact, but it was clean and welcome after being trapped in my suit for so long. I wanted to strip down the rest of the way and dunk myself in it, imagining the icy flow as it swept across me, washing away the last two days. Instead, I settled for a few more splashes to the face.

I wrung out the remaining water from my shirt, snapped it open with a crack, and quickly put it back on. The fabric clung tighter to my skin than usual, sending a chill down my spine, but I was relieved to be clothed again as I reached for my gun, ready to face whoever—or whatever—was approaching.

Spinning, I balanced on one bent knee, my other planted firmly against the earth. Peering down the sight of *Walter*, with my finger next to the trigger, I met Ethan's unsurprised and amused gaze.

"I would scold you about letting down your defenses and leaving yourself so vulnerable," —he smirked— "but I can see that I would be wrong."

"What are you doing down here?" I stood from the hard ground and gritted my teeth against the cool sensation of my wet shirt as it shifted around on my skin.

"I will not hurt you, Abby." He gestured to *Walter*, which I still had pointed at his face.

"Are you following me?"

"Yes," he said matter-of-factly. Ethan stepped toward me, then pushed my gun down and away from both of us. "I wanted to make sure you were safe."

"Why?" I flipped the safety back on before I holstered *Walter* again.

He ignored my question and bent to run his hand through the river's stream. "It's peaceful here."

The sun sparkled against the rippling water, and the reflection lightened up his eyes as if they were aglow from the inside.

"Yes, it is." I crossed my arms over my chest. "But you didn't answer my question."

He stood, flicked the drops away with his fingers, and rubbed the remaining wetness between his hands. He'd turned toward me as he did this, each of us silently staring and assessing the other. It was hard not to look into his eyes; they were so striking. It felt familiar yet like nothing I had ever seen before. I was embarrassed after staring at him for what felt like too long, but I couldn't seem to pull away.

"Have we met?" I blurted. Maybe that's what was happening. Recognition.

"No. Trust me, I would remember if we had."

I raised my brows at him. "Trust is earned, and sneaking up on people is probably not the best way to start."

His answering chuckle turned his smirk into a full smile. "Have you finished here?" He gestured to the water.

"Yes."

"We should get back, then. They are ready to go."

As we walked back to the convoy, side by side, I grabbed the arms of my suit and tied them around my waist. We remained silent as we followed the trail back, and even though it wasn't awkward, the air felt charged.

When we arrived at the bus, most everyone was already loaded and ready to go.

"Thank you, Ethan, for sneaking up on me and escorting me back." I wasn't smiling, exactly, but my face felt as light as my tone.

He raised a brow at me. "It was my pleasure."

"Maybe we can do it again sometime."

"That would also be my pleasure."

That *did* make me smile, and when I reached for the railing of the bus, it surprised me to find a cool hand instead of the metal I'd been expecting. Ethan clasped my hand in support as I stepped onto the first stair through the door. I looked down at our joined hands, confused by the gesture, and then up at him. He held my gaze briefly, then informed Kat that he and the other VIGs would ride topside for the rest of the way home.

Since we'd left the hangar and after they'd saved us for the second time, no one questioned their continued presence and, instead, seemed to welcome it. I, for one, was part of the latter group, happy to have them along. We owed them several times over, and I felt safer having them with us.

After I'd climbed the last two stairs, I idly found myself next to Hendricks. I checked on his vitals, adjusted his blanket and pillow, and made sure he was comfortable. Sitting on the seat next to him, I gazed out the window at the scenery as it passed by, rubbing my hands together. They felt cool and tingled a little, and I tried to convince myself that it was from the cold water and not Ethan's touch.

I was curious why they didn't ride inside with us. At first, I'd thought it odd but then realized I knew nothing about them or their habits. I wondered if it was out of respect for Hendricks and his rules or for their comfort, how being around humans affected them, and if it was hard for them to be near us. I was interested in their diet and how often they needed blood to survive. Making a mental list of questions I wanted to ask, I wondered if I would ever have the opportunity. These were personal questions, and we had only just met. It was probably rude to drill them just to satisfy my curiosity. I didn't know if or when I'd ever spend this much time around vampires again, and for the first time, I was finding myself annoyed at Hendricks and his rule. Lost in thought, I hadn't realized we had driven the hour's distance from Absarokee to Big Timber, where we would search for more fuel.

The small town was often littered with the dead, so as we moved around it, we kept close together and found what we needed quickly. We'd parked a few blocks away from the main road, where we focused our attention and search. There were several options to choose from, and after testing the pumps at one of the old bio-pump stops, we radioed for the vehicles to pull ahead and fuel. It was much easier having the VIGs with us. Their quick movements and quiet weapon skills drew little attention to our presence, making our work faster. We were at the edge of town, where there weren't as many dead to deal with but enough still that it was necessary for us to be on guard. We let the VIGs take the lead since they were so much faster and quieter than our weapons, and we only used silenced gunfire when we absolutely had to. When the portable containers and vehicles' tanks were full, we loaded back up and went to Seeley Lake, which had enough stock to get us back home.

The rest of the journey was quiet and uneventful, and the three hours it took to reach the familiar gates of Thompson Falls went by quickly. It disappointed me that I couldn't ask all the burning questions I had on my mind and that I hadn't spent any more time with Ethan or the other vampires. As Brooks said his thanks and goodbyes to the VIGs, I was anxious at the thought of Ethan leaving and never seeing him again. It was such a bizarre yet visceral reaction to him. I didn't understand it or what it meant. Maybe nothing, but it set me on edge anyway. I knew this was the end of the line for them, but now that it was here, I was conflicted. *More* than conflicted. I didn't want them to leave.

"We really appreciate your help," Brooks said to him and his team while some others unloaded Hendricks out of the bus and onto a waiting gurney. "Thanks for escorting us back here too."

I listened to them exchange pleasantries while Hendricks was secured to the gurney, and then walked alongside him as they escorted him toward the medical bay. I wanted to thank them myself, but it didn't seem like enough.

It relieved me to see Kat at the medical bay entrance, and when Hendricks was safely inside, I went up to her. "Don't you think we should offer them a shower or a place to sleep?" I whispered intently.

She was second-in-command. With Hendricks hurt, in and out of consciousness thanks to the medicine Brooks kept pumping into him, I figured it was her decision to make.

"Yeah, I do." She nodded. "Blaise is over there right now to ask them to stay. I want to talk to Hendricks before deciding, though."

"Wait, you're actually going to ask them to stay?" It stunned me that she and I were on the same train of thought. That rarely happened. We liked each other and worked together well enough, but we had different approaches to most things. I was glad that wasn't the case this time.

"I want to know what they know, Abby. Aren't you at all curious why they were in Honor the same day we were?" She raised her brows at me.

"I wasn't until now." I looked over my shoulder to see Ethan nodding to Blaise, feeling foolish that the thought hadn't occurred to me. It seemed so obvious now that she'd said it out loud. "This is why you're good at your job and I'm just a lackey."

She rolled her eyes at me. "Why don't you get processed through and cleaned up. You're going to have a few extra guests tonight." She patted me on the shoulder, then headed off to talk to Hendricks.

We made it back to Thompson Falls late in the afternoon, and by the time I processed through the checkpoints and had been cleared to go home, it was early evening.

I felt anxious about my new guests who would arrive at any moment and was strangely worried if their presence would be welcomed or not in our town. Logic told me no, considering the rule, but I found myself hoping to be wrong. I flipped the *Yes, we're open* sign over to the *Sorry, we're closed* side as instructed. It was unusual. The team leads thought it would be best if no one else came in for the night or knew the vampires were here until talking to Hendricks.

I quickly waved at Charlie then hurried off to my room. Before the door closed, I had stripped off the clothes borrowed from the med-bay. I had cleaned up in the decon-zone, but I wanted to be in my own clothes before the VIGs came, so less than fifteen minutes later, I was back at the front entrance.

I felt out of breath but relieved to find that neither the vampires nor members of the vanguard were here yet. Most of the patrons had finished their meals and gone home, which left only a few to be on their way. After giving Charlie a knowing glance, I went to the check-in desk by the front door and found four room keys for the vampires, then met her behind the bar where she was cleaning glasses.

"What's going on?" She wiped her hands on the towel she had laced through her apron.

"We're closing early tonight," I whispered. "We have some ... guests that require privacy."

"Is everything alright?"

"Oh, yeah. Everything's fine." I grabbed a couple of the clean glasses from the drying tray and placed them on the shelf behind the bar.

"Okay." She didn't sound convinced, but she didn't press me since there were still patrons in the restaurant.

I helped her and the other servers with what they had left of the evening, all while trying to convey nonchalance. When the last of the diners finished and the extra staff had gone home for the night, I pulled Charlie back behind the bar to explain. Unfortunately, I wasn't able to say anything to her before the bell on the front door chimed. At the sound, my nerves spiked and a wave of titillation erupted in my belly.

Kat and a couple of vanguard that hadn't been on assignment with us walked through the door first, followed by Ethan and the three other vampires in his company.

"What the..." Charlie let her mouth hang open.

They were unmistakably vampires, carrying themselves in a way no human could, and even without seeing the violet in their eyes or the points of their teeth, you knew immediately that they were not human. Vampires were usually tall, but it was more than their height that set them apart—it was something about the *way* they held their bodies and walked with a graceful gait. The sheer size of them was generally an indication too. They were just *bigger* than most humans.

I flushed, my breath catching as I watched them walk in like in a slow-motion movie scene. They owned the space they were in. Cool, calm, and collected had never been attributed to a more deserving group.

Ethan was ... gorgeous. When he smirked at me, my heart fluttered in my chest. My stomach clenched, my back tingled, and I was embarrassed to admit that an ache settled between my thighs as his eyes raked over me.

"Abby." Kat raised her brow at me and eyed Charlie.

"There wasn't time." I gave her a nearly imperceptible shrug as she made her way to the restaurant bar, where Charlie and I stood.

She released a sigh as she moved further into the room. "Charlie, do you think you could listen to me this one time and go home while we settle some business?" She tilted her head at her daughter, but there was no hope in her eyes that what she'd asked would be answered.

"I'm not done working yet, and there's still so much for me to do." Charlie didn't bother hiding her smile.

"That's what I thought." Kat shook her head and turned her focus back to me. "Hendricks cleared them to stay, at least for the night." She sat at a stool and halfway faced the vanguard and vampires that had followed her into the room.

"I have room keys for each of you." I reached into my pocket and pulled out the keys. "I can show you the way if you'd like?"

"I'm sure we can manage," Sylis said and winked when I handed over the keys to him.

Sylis was taller than the other three vampires, but only slightly taller than Ethan. His features were stronger, boxier, and his shoulders were broader while his skin was bronze with almost burgundy undertones. He wore his black-as-coal hair pulled back into a low ponytail, where it fell straight down his back to rest between his shoulder blades. Thick umber brows, equally rounded and peaked, swooped down like wings over his wine-colored eyes and dark lashes. A straight, wide-brimmed nose led to rounded and thin lips that sat on a diamond-shaped face.

"I've assigned some guys to post up inside and out for the night." Kat's voice was stern. "I don't expect any problems, but it is a stipulation, you understand," she addressed the room.

I wasn't sure if she was informing me or telling them, so I nodded in agreement with the order.

"There won't be any problems, I assure you," Ethan seethed.

The temperature between him and Kat was less than warm, and since I didn't know what had transpired between them in the decon-zone after I'd left, I couldn't venture a guess why. We had been through a lot over the last couple of days, and the collaboration I thought we had established seemed less tolerant than only hours ago. That bothered me because, as far as I was concerned, we owed them for saving our lives.

Kat didn't respond to Ethan or his comment, and while he all but glared at her, she barely gave him a side glance before she turned to face me. "Do you need anything?"

"No, I don't think so." I tried to sound sincere through my slight irritation and confusion at the strange question. I understood the need for security, but I doubted it would be the same if they were humans instead of vampires. In fact, I knew it would be based on how the Honor group had been treated when they arrived.

"Great." She gave me a quick nod and stood up. "I'll check in with you tomorrow." She looked at each of the vampires before she motioned to the other men to follow her.

"Would any of you like something to eat?" I asked once Kat and the vanguard were in the other room, and instantly regretted it.

Charlie spun to gape at me, open-mouthed.

Facing her, I rolled my eyes. "Oh, for fuck's sake, Charlie, I meant chips or ... cookies."

The vampires chuckled.

"We had sandwiches in the medical bay while we waited for entrance." Ethan's voice drew my attention to him. He had a humored grin, and his eyes were bright with amusement.

"Abby, I need to talk to you for a second." Charlie grabbed my hand, pulling me through the double swinging doors into the kitchen.

I was so uncomfortable with the situation that I hadn't stopped her and was instead grateful for her antics at the moment.

"Rooms are down that hall. We serve breakfast at seven." She pointed them toward the rooms with her free hand.

Pulling me past the serving window once we reached the kitchen, she turned on me. "What is going on?" she all but yelled.

"Shh!" I clipped, put my hand over her mouth, and pushed her into the cooler.

Closing the door behind us, I waited for the fans to turn back on before saying anything to her. I could only hope the ventilation and walls were enough of a sound barrier to mask my voice as I gave Charlie a short version of what had happened over the last couple of days. As we stood in the cold, cramped room of the walk-in refrigerators, she accepted the information exactly as I'd thought she would—with excitement and glee.

"I don't expect them to be here for very long," I tried to suppress her. "You need to stay out of trouble and keep your distance."

I had no hope she was listening. Her eyes had already glazed over, and the corners of her mouth had pulled up into a mischievous grin.

"Charlie!" I snapped my fingers in front of her face.

"What?" She rolled her eyes at me. "Oh, fine. I'll be good."

I didn't believe her.

We went back out front to find that the vampires were no longer there and only a single guard left in the room.

"They went to bed, and Kat went home," Jo told Charlie, who was careening her head around the restaurant and bar looking for them.

"Did you volunteer or get chosen to babysit tonight?" I asked Jo as I walked around the counter to sit next to him at the bar.

"Both." He chuckled. "I don't have a problem with vampires. I worked with them back east before coming here." He shrugged.

Jo was middle-aged, slightly graying, and had wrinkles around the eyes. He was known for his patience, sound advice, and a good listening ear if you needed one.

"I think maybe I'll stay the night too." Charlie stretched her arms over her head as if to get limbered up before yoga or a run. "You know, to help keep an eye on the place." She twisted her body and bent at the waist to touch her toes.

"No." I shook my head.

"What? Why?" She jerked herself back in an upright position.

"We have enough help here as it is."

"Abby..."

"No way."

"So, you're what? Kicking me out?" She folded her arms over her chest.

"I mean, I guess. If that's how you want to take it," I sassed back.

"Kat said she expected you home, anyway," Jo told her. "She said, 'Tell her to hurry up about it too.'"

"Well, this is bullshit!" Charlie scoffed and dropped her arms. "I'm an adult."

"That's debatable." I laughed at her.

"Ass." She huffed and grabbed her bag from behind the counter where she'd stashed it. "I'll be here first thing in the morning!"

"Thanks for the warning."

She stuck her tongue out at me and bounded to the front door. I snickered at her and the mocking face she made.

When she was gone and the front door had closed with her exit, I turned to Jo. "You know, you really don't need to stay either, Jo. I'm sure everything will be fine." I stood up from the stool and moved around to the other side of the counter.

"I know, but you know I can't leave, Abby."

"It was worth a shot." I shrugged, then assembled the coffee and filters to make a fresh pot. "Do you want me to get you anything to eat? Or I can pull out some snacks for you since you're stuck here."

"Snacks are good." He stood up and put his cap back on. "Whatever is simple. Don't make anything—I'm not hungry, but I could chew on something later." He winked then indicated that he was headed to the restroom.

Back in the kitchen, I rummaged through the pantry and cupboards to find some snacks that would keep overnight and required no cooking. There weren't too many things to choose from since almost everything was made fresh, but I found some stuff that would keep a bored eater busy for a few hours. Chips, cookies, dried fruit, nuts, and even some old and probably stale packaged crackers might not be so bad with the fresh jar of jam I'd pulled from the stockpile.

Next to the check-in counter by the front door was a small room. It had an entertainment system, two small couches, a couple of chairs, and tables set up like a living room. Guests used it as a lounge and so did some patrons, but mostly it was used by a guard member assigned here on night duty. It didn't happen often but enough that we considered it the designated area.

I took the loot in and set it out on the table, with a frosty glass I had brought from the freezer. I couldn't remember what Jo liked to drink, so I grabbed a few beers and filled up a pitcher with some ice water. Normally, drinking on the job was a no-go, but in this case, I figured it would be fine. I didn't worry about getting anything for the guys Kat had posted outside. They would come in if they wanted or needed anything.

"It looks like Jo's going to have a good night."

Ethan's deep voice startled me. I sloshed some water from the pitcher and cursed quietly as I sat it down.

"Did I scare you?" he mused.

"You seem to have made a habit of sneaking up on me."

"I apologize." He inclined his head. "I will do my best to make myself noisier as I approach you in the future."

"Thank you." I smiled at him and secretly approved of his casual appearance.

Ethan and the other vampires would have gone through most of the same precautions and checkpoints before they were cleared to enter Thompson Falls. They would have been given a cursory check for injuries and bite marks, but because their blood naturally reacted to mercury, the swab test would have been skipped. When they first came to the O, it hadn't registered that they were all still dressed in their regular clothes, but now that he was standing in front of me with wet, dripping hair from an apparent shower, it should have been obvious.

Ethan's hair was soaked through and carelessly slicked back, as if he'd only run his hand through it instead of using a towel and a comb. At the ends, little droplets of water fell from the locks and trailed down his neck to soak into the collar, blooming out into the fabric and darkening the fibers with the moisture. The clothes the decon-zone had provided clearly worked in his favor. The dark colors contrasted handsomely against his olive skin and gave him a casual appearance. His chiseled arms and chest were on full display under the navy-blue cotton T-shirt, and the loose-fitted jeans hung nicely off his hips yet held firm in all the right places.

"How was your shower?" I remarked after appreciating his appearance.

"Hot." He ran a hand through his hair, exactly as I imagined he had earlier. "It was a pleasant surprise."

"We've been lucky. Our electricity hasn't gone down for a few months."

"A few months?"

"Not to brag or anything." I chuckled at the mockery. "How's your room? Do you need extra pillows?"

"No." He grinned. "The room is fine."

"Great." I folded my hands in front of me while I waited for him to say something else since I assumed he had come back here for a reason. "Can I get you something else?" I questioned after a moment. "Or you're welcome to help yourself to anything here." I cleared my throat, trying to hide the growing nervousness budding in the pit of my stomach, and wafted my hand out at the snacks behind me.

"Anything?" His already deep voice dropped an octave.

My breath audibly hitched as tension filled the room. He stepped further into the limited space, making the four walls feel even smaller.

My skin flushed as the seconds of thick silence noticeably ticked by while I struggled to think of anything to say. Ethan's hand twitched at his side as he searched my eyes, and just as he opened his mouth to say something, Jo rounded the corner.

"Whoa, hey there!" he blurted out after nearly walking into Ethan's back. Luckily, the near collision seemed to leave him blissfully unaware of the awkwardness he had just walked in on. "I didn't think anyone would still be up. I thought you were going to bed, Abby."

"I was. I am." I tucked a piece of hair behind my ear. "I was just getting you a few things to snack on when Ethan here surprised me." I kept my eyes on Ethan's face, who seemed just as content to keep his eyes on mine.

"Did you need something, Ethan?" Jo grabbed a beer and twisted the top off. "Anything I can help you with, so Abby here can get some sleep?"

"No, thank you." Ethan gave him a quick glance. "Good night, Abby." He inclined his head and then was gone, just as quietly and quickly as he had arrived.

My shoulders sagged as I released a breath. I had to blink a few times to wash away the dryness I felt from staring. My mouth suddenly felt arid, so I swallowed to get rid of the lump in my throat and wiped my hands on my pants—they felt clammy and tingly from the release of tension.

"Vampires." Jo shook his head and took another swig of his beer. "Go to bed, Abs. If I need anything, I'll let you know." He flopped down on the couch and kicked his feet up on the table.

"Okay, good night." I left in a hurry and walked down the hall to my room in a daze.

Overwrought and anxious, I was a little confused but excited by my brief encounter with Ethan. Sitting on my couch for more than a few minutes, I replayed the silent moments that had passed between us, but it didn't make it any clearer.

I needed to rid my head and thoughts of him. or I wouldn't get any sleep. I *needed* sleep. After the last couple of days, I was exhausted. If I didn't distract myself, I was likely to spend the night dwelling on him and what he would have said if Jo hadn't interrupted us.

I put on some music and readied myself for bed. The soulful sound of an old playlist quickly put my mind at ease and was exactly the distraction I had needed to wind down. The crisp sheets and cool pillows were a welcomed way to whisk away the tension, and soon, I drifted off.

The next morning, I woke more rested than I had in nearly a week, and I relished the crack in my bones with each shift and stretch. The music player I had put on shuffle still played on the dresser, so I turned it up and readied myself for the day. After a shower, I pulled my hair into a tight ponytail and dressed in a T-shirt and jeans. I brushed my teeth, slid on some shoes, and headed out the door.

It was a little after eight in the morning, and I could already hear the babble of conversation as I made my way toward the sounds and smells of breakfast. I was sure Charlie had kept her word and was already here, and I knew Gigi would be too. It surprised me, however, to see Gigi at a table full of vampires instead of in the kitchen like I'd expected. They were all crowded around, hunching over massive plates loaded with food. Steaming cups of coffee, juice, and pitchers of water surrounded them.

When I approached the table, Ethan stood to greet me, which caused Gigi to turn in my direction.

"Well, good morning, honey." She lifted her cheek to me.

"Morning, Gigi." I bent down and kissed her.

"Would you like something to eat?"

"No, not just yet, but thank you."

"Are you sure?" She giggled. "Charlie came in early, so I put her to work. She's been slaving away all morning, making this meal." She fanned her tiny hands out in presentation of all the food.

I grinned at that bit of information and looked through the kitchen window to find Charlie back there. She seemed more than a little flustered, which made me smile.

"Good morning, Abby," Ethan greeted.

"Good morning." I tried not to stare too obviously. "Did you all sleep well?"

"Yes, thank you."

The other vampires grunted and mumbled about how well they had slept too.

I smirked at them. "You all seem surprised."

"Well..." Sylis pulled the bite from his fork, tucked it into his cheek, and held out the utensil. "We don't usually get the best rooms when we're 'asked' to stay for work. So, the comfortable beds, separate rooms, and hot showers from an anti-vampire town were a surprise." He didn't say it with even a hint of disdain, only humor. "I expected a barn."

"We have a rather large farm with a nice barn on the other end of town. It's heated, and the roof is new as of last year. If you'd prefer to stay there, I'm sure Bess would be more than happy to share her hay. She likes hugs and pets behind the ear, so I'm certain she'd be fine with a cuddle."

A wide smile spread across his face as he chewed. "I like you. We're going to be great friends."

I snickered at him.

"What this idiot is trying to say is 'thank you'," Pike, one of the other vampires, cut in. "We aren't treated like barn animals, and the hospitality was unexpected but appreciated."

"Food's good too," Seivor, the other vampire, added then raised his glass of juice to me.

I jeered at them. "You all are entirely too grateful for basic necessities, but I'm glad you were comfortable. I'm sure Charlie will be over the moon to know you enjoyed her breakfast."

"She'll be something alright," Gigi chortled.

"Speaking of, I think I'll go check on our early bird. Excuse me." I walked to the kitchen.

I grabbed a glass of water before I passed through the swinging doors, where Charlie was busy at work. Leaning up against the counter. I watched her struggle as I sipped my drink.

"This isn't why I came in here this morning," she grumbled and dusted her hands off on the apron wrapped around her waist.

"You should have known that Gigi would be here and would put you to work." I tried to hide my smirk behind the glass.

"Well, I didn't."

"It could be worse." I reached out and grabbed a pancake off the grill. "It could be the entire town here for breakfast instead of just the guests. You're lucky I flipped over the *Open* sign to *Closed*."

"Do you have any idea what a pain in the ass it is to make pancakes from scratch?" she whined.

"Oh, but they taste so much better than those old, stale boxed-up versions, don't you think?" I flopped the pancake around in the air and then took a huge bite out of it.

Charlie rolled her eyes, turned away from me, and went back to work. It's not as if eggs, hash browns, and pancakes were all that hard or complicated to make. Even from scratch. Charlie just didn't like to do anything that wasn't her idea.

"Are you going to ignore me now?"

"If you're not on my side, you are now an enemy of the state and I have nothing to say to you." Her voice was high with feigned indignation.

"Fine," I taunted, grabbed another small pancake, and went back out to the front to get a cup of coffee.

I picked up the sugar when the front door chimed, so I stepped around the corner, worried someone hadn't read the sign. I wasn't prepared for an awkward conversation with a hungry townsperson—I hadn't even had caffeine yet.

Luckily, Kat came in, with Ryan close behind her. Their faces were drawn down with tension, grim and tired. A small flash of relief passed over Kat's face when she saw us all in the restaurant. Instead of continuing forward and down the hall to where I guessed they were headed to talk to the Honor rescues, they both came into the restaurant.

"Morning." Kat nodded to the table, then came over to the coffee pot and poured two cups—one for her and one for Ryan. "Gigi put Charlie to work, huh?" She grinned behind her mug.

"Yeah." I beamed.

She snorted and looked through the order window. "Hey there, kiddo, why don't you ever make me and your mom breakfast?" Kat hollered at her.

Charlie ignored her, as she had me, which made us both laugh a little harder.

Kat and her team had found Charlie out in the *Morgue*—scared, alone, and on the run when they'd happened across her. She was only a few years younger than me, and even though she didn't act like it most of the time, she'd grown up fast and dealt with a lot in her younger years. When they first brought her here, she'd stayed at the O, but that had only lasted a day or two. Kat had bonded with her and Charlie had latched on to her too, so Kat and her wife, Lisa, had taken her into their home and they became a family.

"Have you been to see Hendricks yet this morning?" I asked Kat as she took another careful sip from her cup.

"Yeah. He's okay." She sat down next to me at the counter and wrapped both of her hands around the mug. "Not great, but okay." She then turned her attention to the VIGs. "It looks like you guys will stay another night. Commander Hendricks isn't in any condition to meet with you today. Maybe tomorrow." The way she made it sound was as if they didn't have a choice. I was sure that's what she was hoping to imply, but everyone knew that if the vampires wanted to, they would go and nothing could stop them.

Ethan put his glass down and turned in his chair to face her. "We'd be happy to accept your invitation and stay another night. If Abby will have us, that is."

Heat flushed my skin, and I felt several degrees warmer. "Yes, of course," I all but stuttered on the words and hoped no one noticed. I wasn't in any position to grant or deny something like that.

"Then we will stay and meet with your Commander as soon as he is able." Ethan stared Kat down, who I was sure was doing the same to him. They clearly did not like each other.

"You'll stay closed again for the night. We don't need any more to deal with," she said to me over her shoulder.

"Of course."

"I don't want to tell you to stay holed up here in the motel all day, and it's not as if there's a whole hell of a lot to look at in town, but it would be best if you stay out of sight while you're here," Kat addressed them again. "To get some fresh air, there are trails and a few places out back you can go, but I would avoid the rest."

It was an awkward thing to suggest, and I felt uncomfortable about it, but they didn't seem bothered by the condition. They all nodded and ignored the undertone of it, instead making plans to go for a walk after breakfast.

I volunteered Charlie for a job I knew she would be happy to do. "I'm sure Charlie would love to take you on some hiking trails out back and down by the river." I lifted my coffee to take a drink and looked at the swinging doors as I whispered a countdown to Kat.

She smiled, knowing full well what her daughter's answer would be.

"One ... two ... three ... fou—"

"Yes!" Charlie barreled through the kitchen, the swaying wood barriers crashing and bouncing off the walls from the force, and ripped off her apron in one fell swoop. She tossed the flour-dusted fabric into the sink and then smoothed back her hair. "I can totally do that! Just let me get cleaned up, and we can go."

The table behind me snickered at her over-the-top enthusiasm over a simple walk.

"Oh, child." Gigi scooched her chair out and stood up. "You're nothing if not subtle." She patted her on the back as she walked past her into the kitchen.

Kat laughed at her daughter before she addressed the vampires again. "If there's anything else you need that Abby or *Charlie* can't get you, let me know."

She hesitated for a moment, then with a resigned sigh, she and Ryan went back to where the rest of the Honor survivors were.

Charlie nearly bounced out of her skin with excitement as she explained to the vampires where they would go and how long she'd need before she was ready. "I'll just use Abby's room to get cleaned up." She didn't ask for permission.

I'd need to visit Vickie's shop to replace whatever she took since I knew she wouldn't give it back. Not because she'd like it enough to keep it, but because she hated my clothes and would take the opportunity to throw them away.

As Charlie scurried off to my room, I grabbed a bussing bin and went over to clean the breakfast table. I cleared the mess of all the plates of food, glasses, and mugs empty of drink as the vampires chatted.

"Will you join us?" Ethan picked up plates to set in the bussing bin.

"No. I'll stay back and help Gigi in the kitchen."

He was quiet for a moment. "May I join you?"

"Wouldn't you rather spend the day outside with the others?" I scrunched my brows.

"No."

"You're a guest. I couldn't put you to work." I shook my head. "And I'm sure it would bore you."

"My *anya* kept a bakery once," he countered.

"Your *anya*?"

"My mother." The smile that followed reached his eyes. "I think you'll find me quite useful in the kitchen. She did." He winked.

I smiled at his adoration of his mother. It was hard not to.

"I'll take you up on that offer." Gigi had a wet towel and cleaning spray with her. "I have a few dozen pies to bake today, and I would be happy for the help."

"It's settled then." He took the bin from me, so I took the towel from Gigi and wiped the table.

She tilted her head at me for taking away her work, but said nothing. Ethan followed her back into the kitchen, where she promptly put him to work.

Sylis came up to me after I'd finished wiping the table. "His *anya* made the best pies. You'll see."

Chapter Six

"This is your mother's recipe?" I shoved another heaping bite of warm apple pie into my mouth.

"Yes." Ethan chuckled at me.

"And you have it memorized?" I covered my full mouth and asked him around the gooey goodness. "Or are you in the habit of making delicious pies for everyone you meet?"

He chortled at my question but thoughtfully chewed his bite, then took a sip of water before he answered me, "Eidetic memory, and no, it's not something I'm in the habit of."

"That's lucky."

"Not really. It's a condition of my biology."

"All vampires have perfect memories?"

"Perfect may be a bit of a stretch, but near total recall is accurate," he said as if we were talking about hair growth. "Our biologists assume it's an evolutionary advantage because of our longevity. We're less likely to keep making the same mistakes if we can remember them. Do you not have total recall yourself?"

"No," I snickered. "I have a decent memory and can hold a grudge, but nothing close to total recall. That's not a common thing for humans."

He nodded thoughtfully and then pointed to his head. "Of course, I knew that."

I laughed at him.

It was early afternoon when we finished making all the pies Gigi wanted, plus a few extras for the O. The morning went a lot smoother than I'd expected, and the three of us fell into a simple rhythm of work and conversation.

Ethan hadn't been joking about being useful in the kitchen either. Gigi found him more helpful to her than me, which wasn't saying a lot. His knowledge alone was a benefit, but his quick movements and skill made the work faster. The mixing and chopping were done in half the time, and more often than not, it was the oven that held us up.

"Alright, kids." Gigi balanced a pie between her palms and came out of the kitchen. "I have the pies cooling on the counter, except for this one." She held up the covered dish. "I'm off to look in on my son and feed him some of this wonderful pie. Thank you both for your help, and thank you, Ethan, for parting with your *anya*'s recipe."

Ethan walked her to the front door. "It was my pleasure. I hope Commander Hendricks recovers quickly."

"Oh, he'll be fine! He's too stubborn not to be." She cackled. "Now, when your friends get back, you share that *one* and keep out of the others."

"Yes, ma'am." He opened the front door for her then came back to the table, staring down at his plate.

"Is everything alright?" I asked.

"Yes." His brows were still furrowed.

"You look confused."

Another quiet pause. "Is Commander Hendricks your father?" He tilted his head to one side and sat back in his chair, his arms outstretched and resting on his thighs.

"What? No." I shook my head.

"Gigi is his mother?"

"Yes."

"She's your grandmother, though."

"She is."

"Then, yes, I am confused."

I laughed and cleared our plates. The day spent with Ethan had been so effortless and comfortable, it was easy to forget that we were relative strangers and he knew me as little as I did him. Which was virtually nothing.

"Gigi is Hendricks's mother, yes. But no, he is not my father. Not biologically," I explained as I cleaned up what little mess was left of the day. "He and my mother have been dating for years—actually, they've been together for as long as I can remember—so I consider him my father, even though I don't call him that."

"I understand. He's like your stepfather."

"Yes, exactly."

He smiled. "Your Gigi is lovely."

"She is." I beamed.

"What do the Gs stand for?"

It was my turn to look at him, confused, before I realized what he was asking. "Actually, her name is Gigha. When I was young, it was such a mouthful to call her Grandma Gigha that I started calling her Gigi, based on the spelling of her name and not the letters themselves."

"That makes more sense." He smirked as though embarrassed.

"Your way would work too."

"Gigha like the island, then?"

"Yes, exactly." I was excited that he knew it. "She said her parents came from there and named her after their home because it was beautiful and they loved it, which I thought was sweet."

"It's a lovely island. Well, it was before all of this." He sort of wafted his hand in the air to indicate the world and the state of it. "I haven't been for years. Not since before."

"She told me stories about her visits when I was growing up. I always wanted to see for myself. I've seen pictures, and it looked nice."

"Maybe you'll get there one day."

"Maybe. If it's still there." I wrinkled my nose. "Oof, that was super dark."

He chuckled. "Valid, though. It might not be there, for all we know."

"I'd rather pretend it's as perfect as her pictures."

"I'll pretend with you, then." He grinned.

"So, is your *anya*..."

"Safe and alive, yes," he finished my thought as I washed and he dried the dishes. "She's in a safe place. I get to see her several times a year if I'm able."

"She must be far away, then?"

"Far enough that it makes it difficult." His answer was vague and a little stiff. Then he changed the subject, so I didn't ask anything more.

We finished the dishes, and when we were back at the table, he continued his questioning. "What is the Commander's reason for not working with vampires?"

"I honestly don't know." I shook my head. "He's never said. Not really, anyway, and whenever anyone asks or brings it up, he ignores the question. All I can say for sure is that he didn't always dislike vampires or working with them. At least, that's the impression Gigi gives, but there is something there from his past. I just don't know what that something is."

"No vampires have ever lived here?"

"There've been no vampires living within the gates since I've been here, only humans. I can't say for sure, but as far as I know, your group is the only to ever be let in Thompson Falls." I shifted in my seat, uncomfortable about that fact.

"Really?"

My face scrunched at that embarrassing fact.

"You've had no interaction with vampires?"

"Very little. We've met some on the road. I've been with Hendricks when he's made deals with other outposts and vampires have been there, but for the most part, no. That's a really weird thing to admit." I shifted in my chair again. "You must think we're totally bizarre."

"No. It's not as uncommon as you might think. Thompson Falls is well-known for its stance. I would venture a guess that you're constantly turning away our civilians."

"We do." I tilted my head. "Why would you assume that?"

"Most of the civilians that roam free aren't known for propriety. They would no doubt want to push the issue to see how far they'd get. I'm sure your interaction with VIGs has been limited too."

"Yes. Very limited."

He nodded. "There are rules, and we follow them. If our help isn't required or asked for, we stay away. Our civilians do not hold themselves to the same code."

"Required as in how you helped us in Honor?"

"Yes. I fully expected us to be turned away at the gate when we got here. I'm glad I was wrong." He looked at me intensely when he said this.

"Me too."

He smiled at that, then changed the subject again. "Has anyone ever died and come back within the walls?"

"Not that I am aware of. The process you went through to get here is what everyone has to go through every time they come through the gates."

"Every time?" He lifted his brows. "I guess that makes sense, actually."

"It's annoying sometimes, but we haven't had any outbreaks because of it."

"What about 'I-M'? Has anyone revived from that?"

"I don't think so. I don't know for sure. If there are people here living with 'I-M', I don't know about it."

"It would be unusual for there not to be anyone here with it but not impossible." He lifted his drink and took a sip. "Where is your biological father?"

"Whoa." I held up my hands. "That was a big leap."

"I apologize. I didn't mean to pry." He looked at me sheepishly, though I didn't think he was actually sorry.

"No. It's fine. I have questions too," I admitted.

"What questions do you have?" His face seemed to brighten at my admission. He even sat up a little straighter as he waited for me to ask him something.

He looked too eager, and all my curiosities seemed way more personal now that we were alone than they had before. So, instead, I answered his question. "My father died when I was little. He was killed by a pack of *kooks*, along with Zach's family and a few of the others in our group."

"Zach?" He pinched his eyes at the mention of him.

"Sorry…" I huffed at myself. "I forget sometimes that we just met and you have no idea who I'm talking about."

His lips lifted, and his eyes softened. "I've caught myself thinking the same thing."

My stomach erupted in tingles and the air felt heavy, but I pushed through. "Zach's family. His team is out on a run. We don't know when they'll be back, so I doubt you'll meet him." I shrugged. "Anyway, my father died when I was very young."

I didn't like talking about him or his death. I didn't remember very much and only had second-hand stories to tell about him, which made me uncomfortable since I had nothing of my own to say. It felt wrong.

Ethan reached out and took my hand in his. The movement was so fast it made my breath catch. "I am sorry to hear about your father. I know how difficult it is to lose a parent."

"I don't really remember. I was only six."

"You don't remember him at all, then?"

"I do. Just very little. The memories are fuzzy, like a dream." I laughed. "Not that you know what an unclear memory looks like."

"No." He smiled with me. "But I understand what you mean. I am sorry to hear about his death, though. I also lost my father."

"Vampires can die?" I blurted out and then immediately regretted it. "I am so sorry. That was rude and insensitive."

In response, he squeezed my hand, scooting his chair closer to mine. "It's alright, don't apologize. It was a very long time ago for me as well. But yes, to answer your question. We can die. Nothing is truly immortal, not even vampires."

His thumb absently drew circles on the top of my hand, and the tingling in my stomach met the electric chills that went up my arm. My heart grew heavier in my chest, and my temperature raised. His hand felt cooler as mine warmed, and I became acutely aware of everything Ethan—his smell, his eyes, his touch. He was all that was in this room, and I was surrounded by nothing but him.

He reached up and brushed the hair from my brow, my breath catching at the touch. It took effort not to lean into his hand when he ran a cool finger down the profile of my face. All I could do was stare into his eyes and try to breathe normally.

"Abby." His voice was deeper than it had been, and the way he said my name felt like he'd caressed it on its way off his tongue. His eyes dropped as his thumb swept over my lower lip, which parted open at the touch.

Suddenly, I had a sharp vision and desire to suck his thumb in my mouth. The thought surprised me, but the idea of it shot tingles to my stomach, up my spine, and down between my thighs, where they settled into an ache.

His voice lowered again. "Is there someone—" He stopped mid-sentence and turned his head toward the back of the room.

His shoulders dropped with his hand, and a moment later, the back entrance scraped open. The warped wood was loud in the quiet, heated room as it rubbed against metal, and the hinges whined with overuse. Charlie, Sylis, Pike, and Seivor bustled through the door seconds later. Their bolstering conversation and laughter broke the tension like a crack of thunder from the sky.

Ethan and I both seemed reluctant to pull away. He held my gaze intensely as we stood together, then we turned our focus on our friends who had interrupted us.

"Hey!" Charlie beamed.

"Hey, yourself. How was your walk?"

"It was great! Wasn't it?" She turned back to face the others.

"Yes, it was nice," Seivor agreed. "It's really beautiful up here. You two should have come with us."

"Is this your *anya's* pie?" Sylis threw his leg over a chair and reached for the dish.

"It looks like they had a busy day themselves." Pike slapped Ethan on the back and gave me a wink. "Maybe they can pry themselves away and come with us next time. Is this all the pie that's left?" he whined and sat next to Sylis, then grabbed a slice from the dish, not bothering to put it on the plate and instead held it like a sturdy slice of pizza.

"No, but it's all you get right now." Ethan shook his head at his friends.

The three vampires were practically inhaling the pie through grunts of appreciation and approval.

"What's for lunch?" Charlie served herself the last sliver of what they'd left of the sweet treat, then sat back and looked at me expectantly.

"Lunch?" Glancing at the clock, I was surprised to find that it was so late.

"Yes, lunch. Did you lose track of time?"

"They were busy." Sylis raised his brows up and down suggestively.

"Sylis," Ethan clipped, to which his friend only snorted.

"Are you making anything? What about the other guests?" Charlie took another small bite of the pie. It surprised me she was even eating it—it wasn't normally on her "approved food" list.

"The other guests are using the kitchenette and cooking for themselves. They've had a rough couple of days. I doubt very much they want to be around a bunch of strangers."

"That's true. Alright, well, I guess I'll make me and the fellas something to eat, then." She sauntered off into the kitchen with her plate.

I followed her. "You are so dramatic." When I was at the swinging doors, I figured I'd ask the vampires if anything was off-limits. Normally, there were options to choose from but if there was nothing you wanted, then you didn't eat here that day. We rarely made anything special to order. "Are you picky eaters or..."

They all cut me off with a resounding, "No".

"Okay, then." I pushed through into the kitchen.

The doors hadn't closed or even finished swinging when I heard Sylis, Seivor, and Pike tease Ethan with smooching sounds. If they were trying to be quiet, they hadn't succeeded. I pretended not to notice anyway.

Charlie was digging through the refrigerator with a scowl on her face. "Ugh, why is there so much bleeding animal carcass in here? Where are all the veggies?"

"Grady's new water net didn't work as expected, and he accidentally snagged a bunch of cutthroat." I scrunched my nose too.

Right before the town border, a heavy-duty net of sorts was supposed to let fish and small debris through while trapping the *kooks* so they didn't accidentally wash up near the border wall in town. Grady's recent design had flaws, so we had a ton of trout.

"That's why we've been serving so much the last couple of days and most of the veggies are still in the garden. We haven't picked them. What are you looking for?"

"After that pie? Anything to make a salad." She grabbed arms full of the fresh produce in there.

"Let's do some of these filets too, so it doesn't go to waste."

"Fine, but I'm not touching it." She stared down at the wrapped brown packages with disdain. "I'll make the salad."

Charlie didn't eat meat at all, no exceptions, or anything with a face—as she liked to say. She liked all-natural foods, from the garden, a bush, or a tree.

We didn't consume much meat in general. The meat industry's impact on the planet had been significant, and we recognized the need for more sustainable practices. As a species, we aimed to rebuild and learn from past mistakes rather than repeat them.

Everything we needed nutritionally, we got from plants, and any meat we consumed was for various reasons. The fish we ate helped keep the population down. When we were out in the *Morgue*, we sometimes had to hunt for food, and in town, we used everything so as not to be wasteful. So if an animal died and we noticed soon enough, it was butchered and used. We occasionally milked the cows and goats to make cheese, and used the eggs from chickens because if we didn't, they'd rot and stink up the town.

As Charlie and I made lunch, we talked about our day. I told her how many pies we'd made and what kinds, and she talked about the trails they'd taken and where they'd gone on their walk.

The vampires would join in and add to our conversation from the dining room. At first, it'd been a little strange and had taken us both off guard, but as the conversations continued, it became less and less awkward. Our easy chatter proceeded through lunch and never felt forced. Like with Ethan, it was easy to forget we'd all just met. We became fast friends.

It was mid-afternoon when we finished with lunch. I felt anxious that I hadn't visited Hendricks yet, so when Charlie opened the back room and everyone was distracted with games of darts and pool, I decided it was a good time for me to get away.

Littered with flour and dough, I hurried off to my room to change into clean clothes. I should be presentable since I was going to the care center for a visit. I changed both my shirt and my jeans, brushed through my hair again and put it back up in a ponytail, then squawked in surprise when I pulled the door open to leave and found Ethan there with his hand up as if to knock.

"Oh!" I covered my mouth. "I thought we talked about this."

He laughed. "I'm working on it."

"We should get you a bell," I grumbled and pulled the door closed.

"You're leaving?" He noted my clean clothes.

"To visit Hendricks. He'll hate it, but I'm going anyway."

"Let's play a game of pool when you get back, then."

"Sure. That'll give you plenty of time to practice so you don't lose in front of all your friends."

"Oh, really? You sure are confident for someone who sneaked away."

"I wasn't sneaking! I waved to Charlie."

"And she's the only one you thought to say goodbye to? Did our time together mean nothing to you?" he bantered, but there was an undertone to the words, and my pulse jumped.

"Today was the only time I've ever enjoyed making so many pies, and you were in the middle of a conversation. I didn't want to interrupt."

"Next time, please do. You're never an interruption." He reached out and opened the front entrance for me. The movement brought his face right next to mine, so close that I could feel the temperature of his skin.

His proximity sparked a tickle in my stomach.

"How long will you be?" His voice was low again, and his cool breath washed over my face.

"Not long." Neither of us bothered to move away from the other. "Then, we'll play."

"Looking forward to it." He raised his brows and smirked at me.

"So, they aren't giving you any problems?" Hendricks asked for the third time since I'd been there.

"No. They are fine," I told him——again. "They aren't tourist vamps. They're VIGs. I really believe they just want to help."

"I still don't like it."

"I know."

"Kat better get some fantastic information for keeping them here," he grumbled.

"It's not as if they don't deserve our hospitality. They helped save your life," I reminded him.

"We would have been just fine without them."

"Maybe. But I'm glad they were there."

"As am I," my mother spoke up. She'd sat quietly next to me for the last half hour while Hendricks had gone over everything that happened since we came back home.

I squeezed her hand. She seemed tired, and even though we all knew Hendricks would be fine, she still worried and had stayed with him since he arrived.

"Will you be getting out of here tomorrow?" I asked.

"Yes. I shouldn't have been down this long, but we laced the bullets with mercury and the doctors wanted to make sure there wasn't any latent poisoning," he told me.

I knew they were worried about him getting an infection, but I hadn't realized it was because of the bullets.

"Mercury bullets?" I squinted my eyes.

"It's something we are trying out. It never occurred to us that one of us could get hit and poisoned too." He shook his head. "Stupid oversight, and I can't believe we didn't think of it. It's a good weapon design, though. What happened to me was a fluke."

"You should have told us you were trying out a new weapon." I was angry with him.

"It wouldn't have changed what happened."

"That's hardly the point," I argued. "It could have been helpful information. Since when do you test weapons in the field without testing them in training first? And not tell us?" Okay, maybe I was a little more than angry with him. He almost died, for crying out loud.

"I've already heard all this," he argued back. "It was a bad call. I know that."

"It was dangerous."

"Alright, you two, that's enough," Mom interjected and stretched her back. "What are you making for dinner tonight?"

I released an annoyed breath and tamped down my irritation. "I haven't put too much thought into it, to be honest. We're closed while the VIGs are in town, and the Honor guests are cooking for themselves."

"Well, you still have to feed yourself, don't you? I'm sure they'd like something to eat too," she chided me.

"Yes, Mother." I smiled at her, knowing what she was really getting at. "What would you like for dinner?"

She took a deep breath and straightened her spine. "Well, now that you mention it, Lane has been talking about a burger all day long. Do you have anything like that?"

"I have giant portobello caps that need to be used. We could grill those."

"That sounds perfect!" She clasped her hands together and looked at Hendricks. "What do you think?"

"Sounds good to me." He reached out his hand so she came over to sit by his side. "With steak fries." He pointed a finger at me as if to enunciate the addition.

"Pfft. What am I, new?" I scoffed and stood to leave. "If I can't bring it up myself, I'll send it with one of the guys you have 'secretly' stationed outside."

He laughed. "They're not doing a good job if you know they're there."

"Charlie would have been less obvious."

"Tell the vamps I'll be there first thing in the morning." He furrowed his brows. "And if you can have the Honor group out of the O for the day too, that would be helpful. Whatever the VIGs have to say, it might be best if they don't hear it."

"I'll figure something out." I told them bye and pulled the door shut behind me.

I wasn't surprised to find the VIGs and Charlie still in the back when I returned to the O. I *was* surprised to find a couple of vanguard in here with them, though.

"Abby!" Sylis hollered when he saw me round the corner. "You're back! Now, we can watch you kick Ethan's ass in pool!" he cheered.

"Are you drunk?" I raised my brows and smiled.

"Yes, and I heard you tell Ethan that he would lose if you played him, so I asked Charlie and these guys here." He nodded toward Malik and Josh. "They both agree that you are worth your weight in salt." He gave me a mischievous smile and took another swig of whatever he was drinking.

"I don't know about all that." I shook my head at him. "I wasn't gone that long. How much have you had to drink?"

"You'll find that Sylis likes his alcohol and is a champion at the sport of drinking. And we were told that you're the one to beat in this town." Ethan walked over to me with a pool cue in his hand.

"Obviously, someone was exaggerating." I peeked my head around Ethan to Charlie.

"Don't look at me!" She held up her arms. "It was these two." She pointed at Malik and Josh.

"We're just making sure our guests here are taken care of." Josh laughed. "Besides, you're the one who told Ethan to practice."

He got me there.

"But, more importantly, we wouldn't want anyone to feel like they were being taken advantage of, Abby." Malik grinned. "It's part of our job."

I laughed. "Don't you two still owe me a night's worth of work in the kitchen?"

"No." He shook his head foolishly.

"No. I'm pretty sure we don't," Josh agreed, feigning innocence.

They looked at each other and shrugged as if they had no idea what I was talking about.

"Yeah, I think you do."

"So, what do you say?" Ethan ducked and put his face in my line of vision. "Want to play?"

Yes. The sensation that erupted in my stomach was becoming a familiar reaction to him.

I took the cue from his hand. "Are you racking or am I?"

In truth, I was good at the game. It helped that I had pool tables where I lived, and sometimes when I had time to kill, I'd hit the balls around by myself. What I didn't account for were his superior vampire senses. It almost wasn't a fair match-up if you took that into consideration.

I'd won the first couple of games but was convinced it'd been just a test of my ability since, after that, I had to concentrate and really focus. I only won a few more times between being crushed. It was fun, but Malik and Josh enjoyed it a little too much, so as punishment, I called in their debt and made them grill, cut, and fry the potatoes, then help clean up after dinner.

"Totally worth it." Malik fist-bumped Josh when they sat at the table with the rest of us after the dishes were done.

Night had fallen, and we all sat around and conversed after the games had played themselves out. We talked around the table for a long time, laughed over drinks, and joked over apple pie.

I was surprised when hours had passed and only noticed because someone knocked on the door. At first, it was just regular knocking so I didn't hurry toward the front, but when I was halfway across the room, whoever it was banged on the wood so hard the window next to it rattled.

"Just a minute!" I hollered out in irritation.

"Open the door!" the angry voice yelled back at me.

Ethan appeared in front of me just as I had reached the front desk, with Pike to my left. I startled a bit, but I was getting so used to being snuck up on that the scare went away just as quickly as it'd come.

"Open the ... damn door!" the voice yelled through the curtained window.

"It's just Holden. He's drunk." I reached for the doorknob.

"Are you sure you want to let him in?" Ethan put his hand over mine.

"If I don't, he'll stand here and bang on the door until I do. He probably wants more beer or something. I'll see what he wants, and then have Malik and Josh take him home."

Ethan stepped back to my other side so I could open the door to a visibly and highly intoxicated Holden.

"It's ... about fuck'n ... time!" He pushed himself inside. The door crashed against the wall as his huge drunken body banged into the wood and glass. He busted through the opening and all but fell inside.

I took several steps away from his uncoordinated entrance and crossed my arms over my chest, watching him catch himself on the door and attempt to right himself. He squinted against the bright lights of the O and looked around as if confused about where he was.

"We aren't open, Holden."

He ignored me, stumbling his way past the three of us into the dining room. He hit a couple of chairs and pushed a table as he clobbered further into the room. The stench of old booze and sweat left a heavy scent behind him, so strong it was nearly nauseating. I had to cover my nose and mouth.

"Is there something I can get you before you go back home?" My voice sounded like I had a plugged nose. I talked louder so I wouldn't have to move my hand.

"I don't need 'nything from you." He sneered. "And I know you're closed... Hiding these bloodsuckers 'n here ... keeping the town out."

"Hey, man, why don't you let us take you home?" Josh stood from his chair, with Malik beside him, and met Holden before he reached the table we had been sitting at.

"No, no, no." Holden slurred and waved his hand in the air. "I'm here to help... Watch 'nd make sure they don't eat 'nybody." He pointed with a jab to each of the VIG members, squinting one eye and looking down his finger toward them one by one as if they were in a gunsight.

"Come on, man, you're drunk." Malik was obviously annoyed.

"Let us take you home." Josh tried to grab him by the arm.

"No!" Holden yelled and jerked his arm out of the way. He was holding a bottle of booze and must have only remembered he had it after it sloshed out onto the floor. Looking down at his hand as if confused by it, he then brought the glass up to his mouth and took another long pull from the bottle. "I came to make sure every ... thing ... is on the up 'nd up." He wiped the dribble from his mouth and stumbled back.

Malik and Josh both stepped forward to catch him, but Holden righted himself and laughed. Ethan and Pike beside me had both taken a half-step forward, not impressed or amused at the drunkard in front of us. Sylis and Seivor stood from the table too.

"Everything here is fine, Holden." I dropped my hand from my face and chided him.

"You don't talk!" He whipped his head around and spun his body toward me, pointing a finger. "I'm not here for you ... so sh't 'p! I'm here 'cause it's my job!" He jabbed at the air and fell forward a step from the movement.

Ethan put himself in front of me and blocked my view of Holden, the same way Holden had done to block Ethan from me on the bus. His voice dropped to that same acidic tone it had been that day too. "You have said enough, and now you will go," Ethan seethed.

"D'n't tell me what to do ... suck'r," Holden yelled back as best he could. "You don't b'long here." His voice dropped as he tried to speak with authority, but it only made him sound drunker.

"Holden, you need to go home. You're just looking for a fight," I tried to reason with him, but that was a mistake.

He yelled at me again and tried to push past Ethan. Pike stepped next to Ethan, as did Sylis and Seivor, and the four of them formed a wall in front of me. The way Holden was acting would have caused anyone to think the worst, and I was sure it looked to them as though he was trying to come at me, but I had dealt with him and his erratic behavior a lot over the last year and knew better. Holden was all talk. He would never hurt me, but Ethan and the VIGs didn't know that. So when Holden tried to push past them a second time as if to charge at me, they grabbed him and had him face down on the floor, with both of his arms wrenched up behind his back, his legs locked in place before any of us thought to blink.

"Oh, wait. Don't hurt him," I pleaded with them as Holden dimmed out of consciousness.

"He was trying to hurt you, Abby." Ethan gritted his teeth.

"No." I explained to him in a calm voice, "He wouldn't hurt me. I know this looks bad, but he wouldn't hurt me." I squatted down next to Holden and watched with my peripheral as his eyes rolled to the back of his head.

The murderous glare on Ethan's face made my breath catch. His eyes had darkened to the deepest shade of purple I had ever seen—crimson mixed with violet—and the rage in them was a certain warning of death. His fangs seemed to glisten with venom as every visible muscle in his body coiled and was taut with bane.

"Please," I said in a careful tone.

It took several tense moments and what felt like an endlessly quiet plea, but finally, he released his stranglehold on Holden. Sylis let go of his shared hold, and Ethan grabbed Holden around the collar of his shirt, jerked him up from the floor, and sat him in a chair at a table.

Holden, for all intents and purposes, was now passed out. His head lolled from side to side as he fought to stay awake and upright while he mumbled a meaningless slur of words.

Malik and Josh each grabbed an arm and propped him up to haul him out of the bar and home.

"We'll stay with him awhile and make sure he stays asleep before we head back over," Josh said.

"Take your time. We're all fine here," I told him but kept my eyes on Ethan.

"Uh, speak for yourself!" Charlie quipped. "I need a drink after all that!" She sashayed over to the bar.

"Make that two." Pike clapped Ethan on the back and followed.

"Three." Sylis smiled and hop-skipped behind Pike.

Ethan didn't acknowledge the group, nor the suggestion, so I indicated my head toward the back door. "Go for a walk with me?"

Walks always seemed to cool Zach down when he got all worked up. I hoped it would do the same for Ethan.

He turned for the back, so I fell in step next to him until we reached the door, where he stopped and opened it to let me out first.

The night air was warm, and the slight breeze rustling through the trees held the smell of fresh pine and wilderness. In the distance, the babble of the nocturnal insects and animals accompanied the sound of the river as it rushed downstream. The sky was clear, the moon full and bright, and the stars twinkled against the near-black backdrop of the outer void. The path ahead of us was easy enough to see, thanks to the lunar shine bathing our surroundings in a silvery glow. It was calming.

We walked together in silence for a while, and when the O was far out of sight, I peeked up at him. "Are you still angry?"

His face relaxed, and his eyes had returned to their normal thistle hue. "Not with you. Holden is a different matter."

"He's not a bad guy. He just has a drinking problem."

"He wasn't drunk the first time I met him."

"True." I thought back to the bus where Ethan and Holden had exchanged heated words, and then again at the hangar. "He's been going through some personal issues," I rephrased my excuse for Holden's behavior.

"That affects you somehow," he stated.

"It's complicated. I know that's not a good explanation, but he's been through a lot."

"So, he gets a pass? You all act as though that was normal and acceptable behavior from him," he bristled.

"It may not be acceptable and it shouldn't be normal, but for now, we put up with it. As I said, it's complicated."

"You may think so, Abby, but I disagree. You may want to believe he would never hurt you, but the man I saw tonight would very much like to prove you wrong. Given time, he will."

I still didn't believe Holden would hurt me—not physically, anyway—but his actions had gotten more and more hysterical as the year went on. His antics had ballooned over the last few weeks too. I wasn't sure what to do about it, though, so I stopped talking about Holden and what happened, and instead went back to walking quietly.

We remained silent as we went and kept on the trails for as long as there was one to follow. When there wasn't one, we continued to walk along the wall through the flat, short brush. It was dried out and mostly dirt, but we crunched our way down the entire length of the river wall until we had to come to a stop.

"Stay here for a moment." Before I could respond or ask Ethan what he was doing, he jumped up and out of my sight, then reappeared a few moments later with a thud behind me.

As he stood back up to his full height, I was relieved to see a carefree look on his face.

"If I ask you to come with me, will you trust me and know that I will keep you safe?" He searched my eyes.

"Yes." I didn't even question it and wasn't surprised by my quick answer. I'd go with him anywhere.

"We will climb this tree, jump the fence, and then the wall. Get on my back and hold on tightly. Close your eyes if you must, but you'll be fine."

"Really?"

"You'll be fine. I promise," he affirmed.

"I'm not worried about my safety with you."

His smile was wide at my statement. "Then what are you questioning?" He stepped forward and dropped his voice.

"The reason for jumping the fence. We could just as easily go back to the O and then through the gate." I had to look up at him, he'd moved so close to me.

"Yes, but what fun is that?" he teased and bent down to the ground. "Grab on."

With childish laughter, I wrapped my legs and arms around his upper body, pressed myself to his back, and held on as tightly as I could without choking him.

He scaled the tree and then found a thick branch to walk along, using it like a balance beam to inch us closer to the top of the wall. When we were close enough, he jumped from the branch and launched us over the razor wire fence, where we gently landed on the ground between the steel barrier and brick wall.

"You okay?" He adjusted my weight against him.

"Yeah," I breathed excitedly.

"Then hold on." He took several quick steps and used our momentum to scale the bricks. Once on top, he ran down the length of the walkway toward the river.

Ethan leaped off the corner edge, then pitched us up over a small group of trees and across a small expanse of water to land on an open bed of exposed rock in the middle of the river.

I laughed like an idiot as my adrenaline junkie cheered.

"That didn't scare you?" His eyes were as bright as mine felt.

"Not even a little."

My arms were around his shoulders, my hands tight against his chest, and he held me firmly to him with his arms circled under my knees pressed snug against my thighs. My legs were encased around his stomach—my whole body wound around his—and our faces were only inches apart. The tension between us was unmistakable, and the growing excitement between our connected bodies was nearly tangible.

In an instant, the friendly mood between us had changed. His hands tightened around my thighs imperceptibly, but the touch made my breath catch and his eyes flash with heat. Ethan spun me around, and when my feet were on the ground, he threaded his fingers through my hair and crushed his mouth to mine.

I mewled at the contact and threw my arms around his waist, greedily pulling myself closer to him. A deep hum rumbled in his throat as he swept his tongue against mine. His lips were soft yet firm, and the kiss was fueled and burning with desire.

His hands slid down my neck, his thumb gently pressing over the front of my throat, where he left it. His other hand slid down my side, where he gripped my hip before pressing his palm over the small of my back and down my backside to squeeze me. I moved my hands from his back around to the front of him and up his chest. When I threaded my hands into his hair, tracing his jaw and neck with my fingers, he responded with a deep purr and pulled me tighter against him again.

My heart was beating wildly in my chest, and warmth pooled between my legs. I whimpered when he curled his fingers around the plump cheek of my backside—so close to where I ached for him I was sure he could feel the damp heat.

He released my mouth with a pull on my lower lip, then kissed and licked along my jaw, down my neck, and back up again until he was pressed against the sensitive spot next to my ear.

"If we don't stop, I'm going to take you right here on these rocks." His breath was hot, his voice low and full of promise.

What came out of my mouth was a cross between a giggle and a groan, and he crushed his mouth to mine again in response. I let him own my mouth for a while longer but then eased away.

I was plenty ready for him and all too willing for the taking, but I didn't think a river bed of rocks was the best choice for either of our naked bodies.

"I've wanted to do that for days," he mumbled against my lips.

"We've only known each other for two."

"I know."

When he pulled back to look at me, he had that small smirk on his face that clenched my stomach every time I saw it. His breathing was as excited as mine.

"I don't know how I'll be able to keep my hands off you now." His eyes were burning, as piercing as they were serious.

"Then don't try."

He crushed his mouth to mine again. "You say that now, but you don't know what you're agreeing to. Or how possessive I can be."

"I'll just add it to the list of things we don't know about each other."

He hummed, rested his forehead against mine, and held me there for a moment as we shared breath. Lifting his head, he looked behind him at the forest, then bent down next to my face and pointed toward the trees. "Over there."

At first, I couldn't see anything. The edge of the forest in the direction he'd pointed was dense with trees and vegetation. So much so that barely any of the moon's light made it through the branches in reach of the ground. But as I continued to look, my eyes adjusted, and I saw what he'd pointed out.

At the edge of the forest was a mother bear and her three cubs drinking and playing in the water. The mother bear stood next to the river and took laps of the cool liquid, watching on as the young cubs splashed around and play-fought at the shore. Their dark figures were only visible against the black expanse of the forest from the slight reflection of the moon on their fur. Their little growls and grunts as they attacked each other made me chuckle as I watched. The smaller one of the three ran around in circles, splashed through the water, and charged the bigger cubs to knock them both down into the river. They took turns as they pounced on one another. They bit, pawed, swiped, and bear-hugged as they played and practiced their technique. After a while, the mother bear joined in on the fun but eventually broke them apart, walking them back into the forest.

"I rarely get to see wildlife so carefree," I whispered as we watched them ramble off into the woods.

"They should be safe if they stay deep in the forests and away from town." He looked back at Thompson Falls. "Your people do a good job of keeping the dead away. That should help."

I turned back at Thompson Falls too and saw a view of my home I had never seen before. From where we were standing, I could get an almost complete panoramic view of the small compound. In the distance, at the two entrance gates, were the only areas brightly lit. The guard towers around the perimeter were darker than I'd imagined, and throughout the rest of the town, very few outside lights polluted the scenery. Thompson Falls was a shaded, walled-off fortress in the middle of tall trees in a dense forest and just barely visible against the ebony night. The twinkling sky was a magnificent backdrop, and the moonlit river in the foreground made for a breathtaking scene.

"It's really beautiful, isn't it?"

"Yes," he agreed. "Beautiful."

I found him looking down at me. "Smooth," I quipped, which drew up a smile on his face, and another kiss followed.

"Do you want to go back?"

"Not unless you do." It was so peaceful, and the evening air was comfortable. I didn't want to leave unless we had to.

We were protected, surrounded by a fast river on the virtually inaccessible island. It was nice being outside the wall, not on alert or concerned with looking over my shoulder.

"We can stay as long as you want." He tucked me into his side, where I mostly stayed for the rest of the evening.

Chapter Seven

We spent hours together, talking and not talking. We stayed on the island for a little while longer, then he jumped us back to walk the trails for a bit before going to the O. Everyone had gone to bed by the time we returned, and no guards had been assigned after my visit with Hendricks, so we went into the room by the check-in counter and talked more there.

I was embarrassed to admit I knew nothing about vampires, save for the rumors and stories I'd been told all my life—mostly by people with prejudices against them. Ethan was more than understanding and graciously answered my questions in between kissing me until I couldn't breathe.

I knew the most basic and obvious things about their species: violet eyes, enhanced senses and abilities, fangs, and blood-drinking. The development and distribution of "I-M", the Vampire Increment Guard (VIG), and last, the partnerships they had with some human outposts rounded out my knowledge. I braved through the list of questions I had compiled and finally learned the answers to my curiosities.

I was most surprised to learn that Ethan hadn't been turned but born a vampire. Vampire births were rare among the species, and their scientists suspected it was due to some cosmic and evolutionary balance to their life expectancy. When he talked about his mother, I'd assumed that she'd been turned like him or that he wasn't that old and she was still alive. That was *not* the case. Vampires could be born to one another and were a natural, evolved species on Earth as much as any other—but they could also turn humans into one of them.

"That's where the lore comes from." He smirked at me.

The ability to turn someone was a biological condition or anomaly specific to their species, but not so dissimilar to humans passing a virus or a bacterial infection. True, one irrevocably changed its host while the other merely caused mild discomfort and annoyance.

"So, if you were to bite me..."

I smiled at him when he brought my wrist up to his mouth to nibble on it.

"It's not as simple as that." He kissed and raked his fangs up my arm. "If that were the case, then every time we took from someone's vein, they would turn."

"If they die with your blood in their system?"

"Lore," he whispered against my neck. "Turning someone is a deliberate process and something that cannot be done accidentally. Think of our fangs like those of a snake. The venom must be consciously delivered through a bite, then the vampirism process begins. It works much as an antidote would. The venom is injected into a recipient, essentially 'curing' the host of being human. The change can be an uncomfortable and lengthy process. All vampires can change a human and all humans can be turned, but there's no guarantee they will live. The process can be painful, and sometimes the body can't handle it. Turning someone isn't as common as it is in lore either. If it's done at all, it's to save their life, and we try not to do it unless the person wants it."

"Have you ever turned someone?"

He regarded me before answering, running his fingers down my face. "Only once, and it was a hard decision but one I am exceedingly grateful to have made."

"No regrets?"

"Not anymore." He kissed me then, in the possessive and demanding way I was quickly becoming accustomed to.

Asking him about blood and their feeding was the most uncomfortable question I had but the one I was most curious about. I wasn't awkward about it for long, though, when I realized it wasn't any different from talking about tacos and pizza. He explained a vampire's relationship to it the best he knew how. Sensing or smelling blood wasn't exactly right, but those were the words he used to describe how it attracted them.

"It's like hunger but not quite the same," he said.

Every human's blood was different, its flavor specific to the person. Blood types, heritage, gender, and diet all slightly changed the flavor. He likened it to meat and how differently cow, deer, and elk tasted compared to chicken, lamb, or fish. A person's diet and life experiences also factored in, each very distinct and dissimilar. Vampires consumed blood regularly, like anything else for nutrients and survival.

They could take from each other, but it didn't fully satiate their needs, which was why they still needed human blood. Humans required water much the same as vampires required blood. However, they could live exceedingly longer without it, unlike humans without water. Again, not exactly the same, but it was the analogy he used to compare. Feeding more often was for enjoyment—once a month or so was standard for sustenance, but he didn't elaborate on how long they could go without it or what would happen if they did. He was uncomfortable talking about it, so I didn't press.

For most of history, vampires quietly lived among humans and were only thought to be of creation written about in fiction. I wasn't surprised to discover that, across the board, most of the lore was unequivocally false but that in almost every case something true had been accidentally written. It wasn't any different from the stories humans wrote and dreamed up of our own species. Like Spiderman or X-Men.

"Sun?"

"Obviously not. We met in the middle of the day."

"Holy water?"

"All the religious aspects are nonsense." He rolled his eyes, which made me chortle.

"Stake to the heart?"

"Would kill anybody. That's such a ridiculous myth. Of course it would kill someone, but turning to ash? No." He chuckled. "That's just silliness."

"Invitation? And before you laugh, remember, you didn't get on the bus until I invited you. Plus, they invited you inside the gates and, by proxy, the O."

"Why does it not surprise me you broke that down? No, I do not require an invitation to cross a threshold." His face was a mask of humor, which made my crazy, nosy questions easier somehow. "I can also cross a water barrier. As you know, since we jumped the river last night."

My eyes lit up. "I didn't even think of that one!"

"Consecrated ground and temples are also accessible to us. Some of my favorite places are considered holy. The Sistine Chapel, for instance, was a place I visited whenever I was in Rome. It's beautiful."

"Is it still there?"

"Yes, thankfully." He smiled. "Maybe I'll take you some time."

"That would be a neat trick. I'm scared of deep water, so good luck getting me on a boat. And unless you can fly a plane…"

"I can." He looked at me smugly.

"Of course you can."

What he couldn't do at this point would surprise me more than what he *could* do. With such a long life span, it would be wasteful not to learn all you could.

"Now, quit distracting me. We already established you can eat garlic at lunch."

He chuckled again.

"Can you compel people?" I raised my brows.

"No." He squinted his eyes. "Although, it would be nice sometimes. I also can't read minds or predict the future or anything. But sometimes, we can sense emotions. Again, we think it's biological—a defensive ability we developed for survival. No superpowers, though."

"So, you're just super fast, super strong, and super hot? So boring."

"Super hot, huh?" He pulled me across his lap and ducked his head to kiss at my neck.

"I also said super strong."

"There are other things I'm super good at too," he murmured against my skin, then licked up my neck to nibble on my jaw.

"Not subtlety, though."

He confirmed, "No, not subtlety."

His mouth was on mine then, and we didn't talk again for a while.

Vampires worked and lived alongside humans in many instances throughout history but mostly kept to themselves. High-ranking officials and world leaders knew of their existence but respected their desire to remain private, since they didn't involve themselves in human relations unless it affected them. It helped a great deal that humans were not a threat to vampires either. Their technology was years beyond anything humans were capable of, as was their cohesion as a race. Socioeconomic status, religion, borders, and their physicality were not a hindrance to the vampire race, which allowed them to evolve and move forward more quickly as a species. Unlike the humans, who unknowingly lived among them and hated each other for the sake of hating each other.

"A world within a world," Ethan said. "It's easy to hide something from someone who doesn't see."

He was right—humans were a self-involved, narcissistic species. All you had to do was look around and read their history to know that. The "take first, regret later" mentality was all around us.

When I was done drilling him with my questions, he went to work asking me his. We exchanged stories about families and friends, our similarities and differences, things we had in common, and things we didn't. We spent a fair amount of time sharing our stories of battling the dead. He didn't appear to like how long or how often I'd been killing zombies, but seemed to relax when I told him about our training.

He was older than me—much older—so I teased him about his age, and he returned my jabs by calling me an infant. By the time I was ready to call it a night, I was so tired he nearly had to carry me to bed like a child.

My head was chalked full of new information about Ethan and the others, and as a result, I was excited to see them, so I quickened my pace down the hallway once I left my room the next morning.

When I rounded the corner, I wasn't surprised to see everyone around a large cluster of tables filled with plates of food, cups of coffee, and glasses of water. The scene was much the same as it had been yesterday, the only difference being Charlie and Harper sitting with the group rather than with Gigi.

Paige from the Honor group was there too. In her lap, she held the small black cat that Brooks had found while we were looking for survivors at her home.

"Good morning," I greeted everyone after getting myself a cup of coffee.

Ethan pulled out the chair next to him for me when I approached the table. As soon as I sat, he put a hand on my leg as if it were the most normal and expected thing to do. I supposed it was since that's how it felt.

Malik and Josh were there too, and if the empty plates in front of them were any indication, they had full bellies and coffee breath like the rest of the table's occupants. If they were still under orders and on duty to watch the vampires, they could have fooled me.

I asked them about Holden and pretended not to notice Ethan's jaw clench at the mention of his name. They told me what they knew, and then we let the topic drop since the table tensed.

"How are you doing, Paige?"

"I'm okay." She was quiet and didn't look up from the black cat that sat purring on her lap. "I'm so glad you found the little guy." She stroked the soft coat and smiled at the sleeping furball.

"Does he have a name?" I asked.

Brooks had hung on to the cat during the attack and had brought him here safely. When Ryan had asked Brooks what he would do with him, Brooks offered the cat to him. Instead, Ryan had brought the cat back here to give to Paige. She didn't have anyone, not anymore, and he'd thought she would benefit the most from the company. He'd been right.

"I don't know what his name was," she said sadly. "But I'm going to call him Wicket." She explained, "My little brother had a stuffed animal that he called Wicket. I think he read the name in a book somewhere. I always thought it was a weird name until now." Her eyes swam with tears.

"Ah, Wicket." Sylis kneeled next to her to pet the cat. "A fitting name for this little warrior." His voice morphed into old English and deepened as if he were narrating a story.

"You know the name?" Paige wiped away a tear from her cheek and looked at the vampire next to her.

"Of course!" he guffawed. "No self-respecting Jedi wouldn't know the great Wicket!"

The table laughed at him.

Sylis always seemed to know when to swoop in, be it for comedic relief or comfort. He told her the story of Wicket and where the name came from. She and several others seemed captivated by his performance, and the story was interesting enough that we all listened on. When he finished, everyone clapped and he bowed.

It was totally bizarre, and if my conversations with Ethan last night hadn't changed my idea of their species, this one interaction would have. They were definitely not the blood-sucking psychos I'd been told to believe.

Paige excused herself when he'd finished with his story. She had a smile, but her eyes were swimming with tears, so she took her new little warrior—still comfortably asleep in her arms—back to her room.

"That was nice," I told Sylis once she was out of the room.

"Ah, well." He sat down in her now vacant seat. "Poor kid has been through a lot."

Everyone nodded solemnly in agreement.

"So, what other stories do you know?" Charlie leaned against the table, rested her head in her hand, and looked at him expectantly. She batted her eyes, and I shook my head at her.

"Well…" He perked up, leaned forward, and changed his voice again.

I turned to Ethan instead of listening to the story. "Did you sleep well?"

"I did. Did you?"

"Yes."

"Me too." Pike stretched his long body. "Not that anybody cared to ask." He gave us a side glance and a grin.

I smirked. "How rude of me. How was your evening, Pike?"

"Good. We played games, drank a bunch of your booze, and when we tired of waiting for you two to come back, we called it a night."

"Those two drank a bunch of your booze." Seivor pointed at Pike and Sylis. "Charlie and I only had a couple."

"Why you throwing me under like that?" Pike threw his hands up. "It's not like we have to pay."

"Who said you don't have to pay?" I raised my brows at him.

"We're guests."

"All my guests earn their keep." I smiled. "You look like you know your way around a dishwasher."

Ethan, Seivor, and Harper laughed.

Pike nodded. "Alright, I see what's going on here."

"And what's that?"

"I drew the short stick. Sylis has stories, Seivor is a teacher's pet, and I'm not as super hot as Ethan."

"Pike." Ethan's voice didn't hold an ounce of humor.

"Oh, eavesdropping too? For shame." I tsked at him. "That'll earn you extra chores."

If he was trying to embarrass me, it didn't work. Men outnumbered me in my job three to one. I was used to their remarks.

Pike nodded in approval. "How about I'm in charge of dinner tonight, and I don't have to do dishes or clean toilets?"

"Can he cook?" I looked at Ethan, who was staring at me.

"Don't trust me?" Pike's voice raised like he was offended.

"No."

Ethan chuckled. "He knows his way around a kitchen."

"Deal." I leaned over to shake Pike's hand. "But if you make a tossed salad and call it dinner, you're mopping floors too."

He shook my hand. "I wouldn't dream of it."

The morning continued like that, and we all fell into a familiar rhythm while we waited for Hendricks to show up for the meeting he'd planned with the vampires. We moved to the backroom for some rematches of pool games and darts to pass the time. Even though we joked and made plans for dinner, it was on everyone's mind that this might be the last day we spent together and that Hendricks would more than likely ask them to leave. I knew for myself it was weighing heavily on my shoulders. Ethan and I hadn't talked about what would happen once they were asked to leave. Everything was happening so fast. It shouldn't be something I worried about since I'd only known him for four days, but it was.

As promised, he didn't bother keeping his hands off me and found creative ways to keep us in contact when not being blatantly obvious about it. He always sat next to me. When we were behind a table, he had his hand on my leg. If we weren't shielded by anything, he draped his arms over the back of my chair. When we were standing, his hand was on the small of my back, and when no one was looking, he'd sneak a quick kiss.

Ethan pressed himself up against me for a standing lesson on how to throw a dart, putting his hands on my hips to show me how to hold my body and the importance of follow-through. After that, I don't think we were fooling anybody.

It was just before noon when the front door dinged with the entrance bell. We all quieted for a beat but kept doing what we were doing. Maybe if we ignored it, time would stop, and whoever was coming toward us would go away.

The thudding of heavy boots pounded through the dining room and echoed off the walls until the sound came to a stop by the back room, where we all were. We turned together as a group, almost in sync, to look at who had arrived. I expected to find Hendricks and the other team leaders, but Kat, Dan, and Blaise stood there with two other vanguard members and no Hendricks.

"What is it? Is he alright?"

"He's alive," she said in a hurry and moved herself to stand in front of me, putting her hands on my shoulders. "He's not great, but he is alive."

The quick rise of panic and then a crash of relief made me catch my breath. "What happened?"

"He tested positive again this morning for high levels of mercury, and the infection in his leg is still spreading. They thought he was doing well enough to be released today, but the mercury is making it harder for him to heal. Overnight, he worsened instead of getting better. They are making him stay, and they don't know how long it will be."

"They don't know how long? He seemed fine yesterday."

"And he may have been when you last saw him. The mercury that was unintentionally put into his system is not your average poisoning, Abby. This is all new to us and the doctors."

"What do you mean? I thought the bullets were laced with mercury. As in, a coating or something?" I piqued, annoyed again at the fact that we hadn't been told about this new weapon.

"They were mercury-tipped, not coated." She raised her brows. "Don't look at me like that. I didn't know either, so I'm just as pissed about it as you are. Apparently, they concentrated doses of the liquid that shatters and releases the poison when a target is hit. The mercury in the system attacks the blood, exactly like the Hg-80s. It's the same technology, just on a smaller scale."

My face flushed as anger coursed through my veins. "He could have died!"

"I know." She crossed her arms over her chest, looking as angry as I felt, and it made me wonder if Hendricks had told anyone about the new weapon. "If the first bullet hadn't passed all the way through and if the second one hadn't bled so much, he probably would have."

"What is wrong with regular run-of-the-mill bullets? What is the need to use something so dangerous? It's unnecessary."

"It is necessary, Abby," she defended the new weapon. "We need better weapons. Not all of us can hit our targets in the head as accurately as a few of you. This will be a huge advantage to us out in the *Morgue*. In theory, we could hit the *kooks* once—anywhere on their bodies—and move on to the next, knowing that the mercury tips would finish the job. It would be a game-changer. Think about how this would have helped us in Honor if we had all been using these. We might not have lost anybody that day."

I understood her point, but I was still so mad I couldn't say anything to her, so I crossed my arms over my chest and gritted my teeth.

"It was a stupid oversight on his part not to think one of us would be on the receiving end of an HGB. It will be taken into consideration." She paused for a moment, then continued, "Regardless, that is why Hendricks is still down. He needs a few more days to clean out his blood and get some rest. He will be okay, though."

I shifted my weight from one foot to the other, focused on my feet. I still had nothing positive to say about this, and she couldn't guarantee Hendricks would be okay, so I thought it best to just keep my mouth shut for now.

"What would you have us do?" Ethan asked her.

"Hendricks has temporarily left me in charge and, if you are willing, I think it would be beneficial for you and your team to stay here in Thompson Falls," she said to him.

"He has agreed to this?"

"He's not exactly in any position to argue with me, but yes, he has reluctantly agreed to this." She sounded annoyed with Ethan and his question.

"You want them to stay in hiding?" Charlie asked. The look she received from Kat made her shrink back and put her hands up in the air. "Sorry." She cringed and sat down in a corner chair. "I was just wondering," she whispered.

"Yes, in hiding," Kat answered in a tight voice. "We think it would still be best if you stayed out of public view since Commander Hendricks isn't in any condition to deal with more right now."

"How long?" Ethan asked.

"Until he recovers. We don't know for sure, but they are optimistic he will make a full recovery in a week."

"A week!" I shrieked. "We can't expect them to stay hidden in town for a week! That's ridiculous. They're not prisoners."

"I know it's not ideal." She kept her eyes on Ethan. "But it's where we're at. I think we can help each other, but nothing will move forward without Hendricks. Are these acceptable terms?" she asked him bluntly and not very kindly, considering if they agreed, they would be doing us a favor—again.

"It shouldn't be an issue." He crossed his arms over his chest.

"Excellent." She turned to leave. "I'll let the Commander know."

She had taken a few steps when Ethan said, "Understand, though, that this is a favor to you." His voice boomed and transitioned from an annoyed, conversational tone to a commanding one. "We will stay hidden from the people of your town for now, but we will not hide. There is a difference. We will come and go through the main gate—or over it—as we please. We are not your subjects, and we do not answer to you. We will report anything that is necessary for the safety of your town and its people. Nothing more. We're happy to accept your hospitality as a favor to you. But if that changes, we will end our arrangement. Are these acceptable terms?" he reiterated her choice of words.

Kat stopped walking and stared forward as Ethan spoke, her posture was rigid. She didn't move until, finally, after what was too long of a pause, she turned her upper body just barely and looked over her shoulder. "It shouldn't be an issue," she repeated his words back like a volley, then walked unhurriedly out of the door.

The tension in the room lifted like a fog, and everyone exhaled a sigh of relief. Comments were made, and we exchanged nervous laughter through edgy smiles.

I went to the bar.

"I didn't take you as a stress-drinker," Ethan stated after he sat down on a barstool in front of me.

I had gone behind the counter and poured myself a drink, then took a huge gulp of it. "I'm not," I said in a tight voice and clamped down on the burn. I huffed out a hot breath. "And I don't really like this stuff."

"Then why are you drinking it?" he questioned with a squint of his eye and a humorous tone.

"I thought it was called for." I shrugged.

"Something a cup of tea could have accomplished perhaps?" He lifted an eyebrow.

"Totally." Almost as if to defy him, I finished what I'd left in my glass in one fell swoop. "But sometimes, this is better," I said hoarsely through the burn in my throat again.

"Don't let him get your goad, Abby." Pike peeked his head around the corner. "He's drunk plenty of his fair share of sorrows and trouble."

I poured another glass and sat it in front of Ethan. "Drink up, hypocrite," I teased and put the bottle back on the shelf.

He kept his eyes focused on mine, picked up the glass, dumped it down his throat, and then sat it back down with a clack. "Wow. That is disgusting." He pushed the shot glass forward. "What is that?"

"I have no idea." I grabbed the glass. "Summer makes it and brings it over. I usually just pour it, but it does its job, whatever it is."

"And then some, I'd say." He stood from the stool and waited for me to walk around the counter. Then he tucked me into his side and we walked together back to the group, where we fell easily into our earlier rhythm.

I really wanted to go visit Hendricks, but I didn't want to interrupt or barge in just yet. He did not like visitors when he was down, even if that visitor was me, and I knew logically that if it became serious, someone would come get me. So, I'd wait and talk to my mom first, and then visit him if he were up to it.

When we finished the games we had been playing before Kat showed up, we all felt cooped up, so we escaped outdoors to stretch and get some much-needed fresh air. We walked along one trail behind the O that took us further away from town. If anyone were out for a walk like we were, there were plenty of trees to get lost in so the vampires wouldn't be discovered. I was more annoyed about it than they were, so I tried to let it go.

We were deep in the trees and halfway along the trail when Ethan squeezed my hand. "The others and I will need to go out tomorrow."

"Oh?"

He stopped and tugged me into him, taking us away from the group and down an offshoot of the trail we were on. It led closer to the river wall and then connected again further up. I could hear the others and their conversation easily enough, even though Ethan and I had put a significant distance between us and them. Their voices carried in the forest's stillness, and I smiled to myself as I listened. Seivor and Pike made jokes and wisecracks back and forth at each other, which had Harper and Charlie in a fit of laughter. Sylis, Malik, and Josh were in a heated debate about what was better—cake or pie. It was all very entertaining.

Ethan walked us a little way further before we stopped in a thick of grass next to a large ponderosa pine. The tree sap and scent from the pine needles were so strong it made me feel like we were in the middle of the forest, way up in the mountains where everything was fresh and new to bloom. All that was missing was the crisp morning air, warm coffee, and a cool-tipped nose.

"Mmm. I love this smell." I tilted my head back and pulled in a deep breath through my nose.

Ethan pressed himself to my front and towered over me, wrapping his hands around my face. "It's a close third." He dipped his head down and pressed his lips to mine.

"A close third to what?"

"Rain."

"Mmm, I love the smell of rain," I mumbled against his lips. "And the sound of thunder."

"Mh-hmm."

"What's first?"

"You."

The next thing I knew, I was against the tree, encased by him, his body pressed to me. I wrapped my legs around his waist, his hands spread wide on the back of my thighs, and he'd split my mouth open to sweep his tongue in a tangle with mine. I yelped in surprise when he lifted me, but even to my own ears it was an erotic moan, and he responded in kind. A deep purr rumbled from his chest. Whether or not he'd meant to, his hips rolled into me as he increased the pressure between our bodies. He slid his hand up under my shirt to palm my breast and thumb over my nipple, and another moan slipped through my mouth. My hands instinctively tightened in his hair and my legs locked, pulling him into me. I could feel his excitement between my legs, and heat pooled at my center.

He took his mouth away with a growl and nipped at my neck. "Why do you always have so many clothes on?" he complained huskily as he dragged his fangs up my throat.

"Why do you always attack me in the wilderness?"

"Good point." He kissed me again, but without the raging fire and desire to consume. "This is not why I brought you over here," he hummed.

"It's not?"

"No." He pressed his lips up and down, over and across my neck and shoulders. "You're just so damn distracting."

I wrapped my hands around his face and lifted his head to look at me. "Why did you bring me here other than to ravage me against a tree?"

I laughed when he grunted and crushed his mouth to mine again.

When he pulled away, he kept his eyes on my mouth as he smoothed his thumb over my bottom lip. "We've been here for nearly a week, and the four of us will need to feed soon. We have a pre-arranged meeting for tomorrow that we will leave for."

"How long will you be gone?"

"Less than two days."

"Two days?" I squawked. "Are you eating the whole cow?" I laughed in embarrassment, and my face flushed. "You know what I mean."

He pressed his lips against mine again, then set me down and tucked me into his side as we walked. "I did say *less* than two days." He kissed my head. "It's the travel time that will make the trip so long."

"Where will you go?"

"We have donors nearby that will meet us in Glacier National Park."

"There's an outpost in Glacier?"

"Only for VIG members' use."

"No one lives there?"

"Humans used to a long time ago, but no, not anymore. And we usually only use it for a meeting place. Would you like to join us? It's really beautiful. I think you would enjoy yourself."

"Really?" I questioned him, unsure. "That wouldn't be—" I stopped mid-sentence because I wasn't sure what I was trying to say.

"What?" he prompted. By the look on his face, he was curious about what I would say.

"Well, I don't know… Awkward? Weird?" I shrugged.

"No." He tightened his hold on me. "I'm not suggesting you join us during our feeding. That *would* be awkward and weird. Beyond that, it wouldn't be any different from what we're doing now. I really believe you would enjoy yourself. All of us can go," he said of our little group.

I thought about it for a minute. "I would have to clear it with both Kat and Hendricks."

"As I expected."

"They may not agree." I raised my brow at him.

"Are you a prisoner here?" He grinned at me, using my exact words from earlier against me.

"No."

"Then I'm sure we will all go," he said with confidence.

"You want to go where?" Kat asked, a little befuddled. She sat back in her chair and steepled her hands together.

"Glacier," I told her again. "The VIGs need to feed, and I thought we could tag along."

"So, let me get this straight," she said in an ironic tone. "You want to travel over three hours in rough terrain, through *kook* valley, to join a bunch of vampires while they feed on other humans?" The look on her face was a mixture of speculation, curiosity, and mockery, and it made me squirm in my chair.

"Well, when you put it like that, it does sound crazy."

"And explain to me why this is such a good idea?"

"You want to keep tabs on them, right?"

"Right," she agreed with me while I paused.

"They need to feed," I stated the obvious. "And feeding inside of Thompson Falls is a no-go. Right?"

"Absolutely."

"If we go, it'll just ensure that they come back."

"You don't trust them to come back on their own?" She leaned forward in her chair and rested her arms on the edge of her desk.

"No! They'd come back, of course. I just mean that they would come back sooner and maybe they won't be gone as long. So that when Hendricks is well enough to talk to them, they are here and ready."

"Okay." She didn't sound nearly as convinced as I'd hoped she would.

I exhaled a deep breath and dropped my head to my chest. "Look, we just want to go. I've never been to Glacier. None of us have. We all get along well. Ethan invited us, and I thought it would be fun."

Kat rolled her eyes at me with exasperation. "Why didn't you just say that?"

"I don't know." I shrugged. "You don't seem to like them very much, and since you're in charge right now…"

"I don't have a problem with them. It's my job to be skeptical. That's all. And you know that you—and anyone else—can go wherever you want, provided you're taking safety precautions. You're not prisoners here." She squinted her eyes at me, and I regretted using the words since it'd backfired on me twice now.

"That's what Ethan said."

She gave me a smug smile. "I think you should go."

"Really?"

"Yes. But do you think it's wise to take Charlie?"

"She'll be fine."

"If you say so." She pulled herself closer to her desk as if to get back to work. "This little adventure will need to be more than just recreational, though. You can decide what vehicles you want to take, but it needs to be productive in more ways than 'to keep an eye on our new friends'. For one, you'll need the cover if anyone asks where you were."

"I thought about that." I sat forward, regaining some of my courage and excitement about getting out of town as I pulled out my tablet from my back pocket. "The route they told me we would take is close to a food distribution center we haven't cleared all the way. There is at least a truckful of canned goods, dried beans, and grains we could get. It wouldn't be a gratuitous trip if we loaded up and brought all that back with us."

"Perfect." She seemed to brighten at the idea. "It's a deal, then."

"Great, thank you." I clicked off the digital map and shoved it in my pocket again.

"One more thing before you go."

"Sure, what is it?"

"Holden will go with you," she said matter-of-factly.

"What? Why?" I squawked.

"You are more than capable of taking care of yourself. Malik and Josh are also excellent guards, and the VIGs are lethal. I'm sure they will provide you with superior protection. I'm not worried about your safety. But I want someone with you who will be a voice of reason should you need one. Someone who isn't so ... easily won over," she said after she'd thought about her last couple of words.

"What is that supposed to mean?" I bristled.

"It doesn't mean anything. I only meant that the five of you are quite comfortable with the four of them. As you've already stated, you get along really well. You may not see certain situations as objectively as someone like Holden. I trust him and his judgment as if I were there with you myself."

"But you don't trust me?" I crossed my arms over my chest.

"That's not what I said and meant. Please understand that this is out of protection for you and our people, not a punishment."

"Then why does it feel like one?" I was not happy, and I knew she could see that by the look on my face if not by my words.

I didn't have a problem going out to the *Morgue* with Holden. He was an asset, for sure. But Ethan and he did not get along, and I knew this wouldn't go over well.

"I'm sorry you feel that way, Abby. But I insist." She sat back in her chair again.

I didn't argue and I couldn't do anything, so I gave her a quick nod and left.

"I agree with her, Abby." Hendricks sat up against a pile of pillows on his bed in the care center. "I would have told you no, so this seems like an agreeable compromise if you ask me." His voice was raspy and worn, and he looked paler than yesterday, chalky even. He had dark circles under his eyes, his lips lackluster and chapped, and he had thinned in the face. It was amazing what twenty-four hours could do to a person.

He wouldn't want to be treated like a patient, and everyone was already walking around on eggshells with him. I rolled my eyes at him and his statement. Besides, I knew he would be fine, so I treated him like I would have normally.

"Well. Then I'm glad to have Holden come along." I smiled in mock glee. I knew he was serious. Which made me grateful that Kat was in charge and he wasn't at the moment.

"The good news is that by the time you get back, I'll be out of here," he said. "In fact, I will be released at the end of the week. I don't suppose they can wait to leave for another day or two?" he asked hopefully.

"I don't think so. Ethan said it was pre-arranged. But I'm glad to hear you are doing so well," I changed the subject.

"Finally. It's stupid how long I've been here."

"Better here than in the grave." I raised my brows at him, still not over the fact that he'd kept the new HGBs from us.

"True. We will definitely tweak the potency level of our new bullets, and we'll do some careful field tests before we put them into use again. Something more controlled," he promised.

"That would be a really good idea," I agreed, smug and fully sarcastic.

"Yes, a good idea indeed." He looked up at me through his lashes and itched his arm around the tape, tubes, and wires.

"You know, we could round up some *kooks* down in Deer Lodge and test out the bullets there. We haven't been in a while anyway—we should make sure it's still ours," I suggested.

The old prison town was battered beyond repair, but it worked well for testing out new weapons and training new recruits.

"That's a great idea. We will definitely do that as soon as I'm all patched up." He shifted around in his bed for the third time since I'd been here and was stretching his arms overhead again.

"You're stir-crazy."

"No, not at all!" he replied with fake enthusiasm. "I love it here!"

"Well, what's not to love?" I joined in jest. "Four walls, a bed, and three squares a day. It sounds wonderful. I'm actually a little jealous."

"Don't forget the best part," he said with mock elation. "The twenty-four-hour service to attend to my every need."

"It sounds dreamy." I laughed at him.

He hated it here, and I was sure everyone knew it. Hendricks was a private man with his personal life, and except for the work he intentionally put himself in the middle of, he didn't like anyone knowing his business. So, this was a bona fide nightmare.

"You better live it up. You have a full plate when you get out of here." I approached his bed.

"And I'm ready to dig in."

"Bye." I bent down and kissed him on the cheek, his stubble slightly pricking my lips and cheek with the pressure.

"Be safe, Abs," he told me sternly. "Take *Walter* with you."

"I always do," I reassured him.

Chapter Eight

"Where is this place that we will stop for supplies?" Ethan's tone was tight and reserved. He was still not happy and obviously annoyed that Holden was coming with us on our trip to Glacier.

Ethan was irritated when I'd told him last night the stipulation that Kat had made for us to go. He was pissed that there would even *be* a stipulation, and that it was Holden of all people who she'd chosen. He'd been moody for the rest of the night, and I'd hoped he would be over it by now, but I'd been wrong.

"Outside of Missoula. It will add about an hour to the trip each way, not including loading time," I told him.

"Show me." He walked closer to the table I had sat my tablet on, so I pulled up the 3D image. Before, he'd refused to even look at it while he'd paced and brooded around the room, so this was an improvement.

"Here." I pointed with my finger. The image was a simple grid and not detailed, then I changed it so he could see the landscape.

He studied the map, then called the other VIGs over to look at the route with him. "There are back roads we can take to get us around Kalispell from there." He pointed at the map.

"We haven't been there before," Sylis said. "But this area here is overrun. It's not close, but we should still be cautious." He pointed to a different area on the image than the one Ethan had as they talked back and forth, working through a way to navigate our new mission with their own.

"These back roads are overgrown," Seivor pointed out. "They're covered in vegetation. We'd need to move slower through this area as well," he said of another road.

"It shouldn't be a problem." Pike looked up at me. "You said we can take any vehicle we want?"

"Yes, whatever we need, we can take."

"Anything with a plow big enough to fit ten?"

"We have two different options," Josh spoke up, and I was thankful he was here because I had no idea. "We have a couple of Bear MRAP that would hold all of us after we drop off the delivery truck. One has a plow, and another has a train bull bumper. They are each armed with gun turrets."

"Those would more than work." Pike and Ethan nodded at each other.

"Tell me about the shipping truck," Ethan said.

"They have minor modifications, truck grilles, window bars, and razor wire along the sides. They're all like that, so they're not weighed down and can carry more. It's usually never a problem since they don't travel alone."

"Good enough." Sylis shrugged, and the other VIGs nodded in agreement.

"When can everyone be ready to go?" Ethan asked the group. "Someone will need to inform Holden."

"We're always ready, just need to grab our bags," Malik said of him and Josh. "We'll take care of Holden too."

"I'll need an hour," Charlie said.

"An hour?" Malik repeated. "Girl, we're not going on vacation!"

"You may not be!" she bristled. "But I haven't been outside of these walls in almost a year. If I'm going, I'm going to look good doing it."

"Then you better take a couple of days and rethink your whole style." He cocked up an eyebrow. Sometimes, Malik got a little sassy.

"Now, play nice, girls," Sylis mocked.

"She started it." Malik snaked his head back and forth at Charlie.

"You're just jealous—"

"Alright." I put my hands up and stepped between the two of them. We didn't have time for a pretend fight. "It won't matter what you bring, Charlie," I told her in the kindest way possible. "We'll be out in the *Morgue*—you're going to have to suit up, like the rest of us."

"What?" she squawked. "Then why do those two get to take a bag?" She jerked her head toward Malik and Josh, the play in her voice gone and replaced with a whine.

"All that will be in our bag is some underwear, hygiene products, and a few personals," Josh said to her.

"Well, what the hell?!" She pouted and put her hands on her hips.

"So then ... under an hour?" Seivor asked her skeptically.

"Yes, under an hour." She folded her arms over her chest. "Like, twenty minutes."

"I'm ready as well. I just need to grab my bag," I told the group.

"We'll get our things and Holden, and meet you at the Pit in ... say, thirty?" Malik asked.

"That'll be great." Ethan went back to looking at the map.

"We'll see you in two shakes of a leg!" Josh announced through the door.

"I guess I'll be right back." Charlie sullenly followed the two men.

When they were almost at the exit, Malik and Charlie started in on each other again, taking stabs at the other for various things. Josh dropped his head as they continued to make fun of each other out on the porch. I swear I heard him sigh as he pulled the door closed behind him, which made me chuckle.

"Do you need to grab some things, Harper?" Sylis moved to the counter where she sat.

"No. I won't go this time. I'll stay here and keep an eye on the O."

"I bet Gigi would be perfectly happy to do that for you."

Harper was wringing her hands together and glanced over at me.

"I'm sure Gigi would be more than happy to do it," I said playfully. "And that's exactly why someone else needs to be here. To make sure she goes home. She can't run this place all day and night, and she would try if someone wasn't here to tell her no."

"I have other things I need to do, anyway," Harper said more convincingly. "Plus, I don't mind staying."

"No?" Sylis double-checked.

"No." She gave me a side glance. "You can tell me all about it when you get back."

"Absolutely." Sylis lightly bumped his shoulder into her. "I'll bring you back a souvenir."

She chuckled. "Okay."

It was obvious Harper didn't want to go and even more obvious that she didn't want to explain why. Luckily, Sylis had caught on quickly and made light of it, then dropped the subject altogether.

"I'll go grab my things," I told them.

Harper moved next to me. "Me too, so I can stay here while you're gone. I'll see you in a couple of days?"

"Yep." I hugged her. "We'll be back in two shakes of a leg!"

She sighed and then squeezed me tighter. "Stay safe out there."

"Always," I assured her as we let go of each other.

"This thing fits me like a glove!" Charlie turned in a full circle to look at her reflection again.

"They're supposed to," I grunted and sat back up after I'd laced my boots.

There were several styles of suits that people wore out in the *Morgue*. The uniforms the vanguard wore were tighter and made to be like a second skin, while the others were more like a loose-fitted jumpsuit over their clothes. If you were going to be out for an entire day or several days, you wore a vanguard suit, but if you were only going out for a short-term assignment, then you only wore the jumpsuit. People who weren't in the guard almost always wore jumpsuits.

"I'm not going back to them ugly-ass things you guys give out us 'commoners'. Next time, I want one of these!" she declared and looked at me pointedly, as if I had sole control over what uniforms they handed out and deliberately kept them from her all this time.

"I'll let the uniform police know," I mocked her and zipped up my suit the rest of the way.

When she finished checking herself over, Charlie and I left the Safe and headed over to the Pit, where everyone else was, deciding who would take what vehicle.

"Josh and I will drive the delivery truck," Malik told me. "You and Holden will take the big guy." He patted the Bear MRAP on its side like you would a horse.

"Okay."

"Unless you would rather one of us—"

"No." I cut him off. "No. I'm good." If Holden wanted to ride with someone else, then he could make that decision for himself. "Charlie, you're with me, right?"

"Yep."

"The VIGs are waiting for us just outside of town," I told them. It was the middle of the day, so there was no way they could have come to the Pit and stayed unnoticed.

"Are we ready then?" Josh asked, and we all nodded.

"I'm driving," Holden said brazenly as he brushed past us, threw his bag in the back, and proceeded around to the driver's side. He'd been off away from everyone while we talked but within earshot, so he'd heard everything we said.

"Well, this ought to be fun." Charlie scrunched her face.

"It'll be fine." I wrapped my arm around her shoulder and pulled her against me. "We'll play *I Spy*."

"Where you guys headed off to?" the gate guard asked. There were no restrictions for our leaving, and we didn't have official papers or clearance we needed to present before we left. He was just being polite to make conversation while the gate opened.

"Supply run," Holden said to him socially. "Why? You need somethin'?"

"Let me get you my list," the guard gibed.

"Ya, sure, we'll wait. We've got all day."

"Ha ha. Alright, man, you guys be safe out there." The guard patted the door like Malik had earlier and waved us through.

"Take it easy." Holden fist-bumped him out the window, then rolled us through slowly, one gate at a time.

We passed through the last without pause, and when we stopped to pick up the VIGs, I unbuckled my seatbelt to move back with the others so Pike could have the front as requested.

"Sorry," Holden said solemnly. He kept his eyes forward and chewed the inside of his cheek anxiously as he increased our speed.

This was as good of an apology as I would get.

"Thanks for driving," I responded and went to the back.

I sat down next to Ethan, facing Charlie, and buckled myself in. She gave me an inquisitive look that I responded to with a head shake. She understood and patted my leg three times before she sat back.

"Abby said we'd play *I Spy*."

"Ooh, and then after, *Never Have I Ever*." Sylis rubbed his hands together.

"*Kiss, Marry, Fight, Kill*?" Charlie raised her brows and looked up at him.

"Nope." I shook my head.

"Oh, come on, Abby! What's a road trip without awkward car games?" Sylis wiggled his brows up and down.

"We could play the quiet game?" Ethan suggested next to me.

"I like that. Let's do that one." I nodded.

"You two are lame." Sylis rolled his eyes.

"Yeah, laaaameee," Charlie sing-songed, and then they laughed like idiots.

Those two were way too excited about this road trip, and we'd only been in the car for twenty minutes. It was going to be a long drive.

"I spy something ... green." Charlie careened her head around.

"We're in the mountains." Seivor shook his head at her.

"Fine, I spy something white."

"Cloud," Sylis announced. "My turn. I spy..."

And that's how that game was played for the next four and a half minutes.

Nearly three hours later, we'd gone through the *Alphabet Game* twice, played *Twenty Questions* each, tried to *I Spy* again, and done one round of *Kiss, Marry, Fight, or Kill*.

"Sorry, Sylis." I held my hand up to my throat and slid my thumb across it like I was cutting it.

"Ouch! Fine, then I'm killing you too."

"Fine. I'll marry Charlie, fight Seivor, and kiss Ethan."

"Shocking." He scanned the group. "I'll do the same."

"No, you won't." Ethan shook his head.

"There aren't any other options."

"You can kiss Seivor and fight me."

"What?" Seivor balked.

Sylis turned to Seivor, looking him up and down. "Okay."

"What the fuck? No." Seivor protested. "This game is stupid."

"You're getting all worked up over nothing. We *could* be playing *Kiss, Marry, Fuck, or Kill,*" Charlie announced with a shrug.

"No," Seivor repeated.

Sylis perked up, and Ethan turned to me with a mischievous smile.

"Now that you mention it..." he said.

"No," I said sternly.

"You all are taking this game too seriously. I like it." Charlie bounced in her seat. "I'm kissing Abby, killing Ethan—sorry. I'll fight Seivor, and I'll marry you." She pointed at Sylis.

"Abby gets all the kisses," Sylis complained. "Let's play something else."

"You can do what Ethan suggested earlier and play the quiet game," Pike grumbled from the passenger seat.

"If you wanted to be included in the games, you should be back here," Sylis told him flippantly.

"Someone's got to be working. Holden can't be expected to keep watch and drive, you jackass."

"Hmph." Sylis waved dismissively. "Whatever. I'd kill you anyway."

"You're an idiot."

Ethan cut them off and suggested we play *Name That Tune*, but before we could guess the song he was humming, Holden told us we were at our first stop.

The old, run-down town of Victor was so small that if you blinked, you'd miss it, and it didn't have much to offer other than what we had come for. It had probably been a cute little town back in the day, but when the plague hit, people quickly abandoned little towns like this—much like Thompson Falls—and left them to nature and ruin.

When we were on a salvage mission, we went through everything in a town. Each building, every house, all the cupboards and drawers—everything. Victor had a large storage depot when we'd stumbled on it, and almost nothing else. It was in a fenced area with several steel buildings and was jam-packed with useful things. The other buildings were marked with our insignia and had already been cleared from previous trips. But there was a good portion left in the storage depot, and that was what we would come back for after we finished at Glacier.

"I'll pull into that last building there, and we can shut it in," Josh said of the delivery truck.

The building was mostly still a gray color, but parts of it had rusted and oxidized. The heavy doors made a terrible screeching sound as they opened and closed, and the rust on the door tracks flaked down on us when we moved them.

When it was locked up, we all piled in the bear and hit the road again. A short while later, we passed through West Glacier to get to the old national park entrance.

Ethan had been right. It was stunning, even with the buildings run down and destroyed. Overgrowth and vegetation covered the roadway, and though there was a general lifelessness to the small, empty town, it was still breathtaking. And this was only the beginning.

As we continued through the park entrance gates, we followed the road deeper into the forest and onto a scenic drive that ran along a large lake. Sylis drove us carefully over the unkept and overgrown road, snaking us through the two-lane cut-out in the trees until, suddenly, the pavement cleared. We picked up speed once we were through the hazardous disguise and sailed smoothly over the new-like pavement until we reached our destination.

The old rustic lodge and surrounding cabins looked out of place after seeing the state of the town, and the other homes and buildings. The lodge was perfectly intact and well kept, the grounds around the entire estate manicured artfully. The trees were trimmed, the grass mowed, and the blooming flowers potted beautifully. It was like a dream. The apocalypse that plagued the Earth was not visible here.

"Whoa." Charlie turned around in a full circle to take in the view when we were out of the vehicle.

"This is remarkable," I copied her in awe. I couldn't take it all in fast enough. It was like I had stepped into a painting.

"I knew you would enjoy it." Ethan had a big grin on his face.

"It's so beautiful. How do you keep this place a secret?" I stared across the giant lake, unable to tear my eyes away from the view.

The water was near perfectly still and reflected the mountain across the surface like a mirror, the sky crystal clear and a blue so bright it nearly hurt your eyes.

"The area is patrolled, and we have security surveillance," he told me. "But to be honest, there hasn't been a lot of human curiosity. It was left abandoned, so we took it over. If anyone comes this way, they are usually lost and looking for a home, not this place specifically. So, we find them one."

"It's so amazing. I've seen a lot of beautiful things as I've traveled, but nothing like this."

Across the glass-like surface of the water were sloping hills of green, brown, and tan layered up along the mountain. I knew it was far, but the lake was calm and smooth, and the mountain tops so large they looked deceivingly close. Further in the distance, snow-capped mountains varied in shades of gray, blue, and purple. Sheets of irregular layers and size stacked on top of the other, like rings of tree growth but of earth and rock instead of bark.

"Do you want to go inside?"

"Not really." I smiled at him. "But sure."

"We'll come back out."

"And drive around and hike the trails?"

"And boat on the water if you'd like."

"Yes!"

We walked to the front door to meet up with the others.

The inside of the lodge was just as enchanting as the exterior. The entry opened into an open space with vaulted ceilings three stories high, large dark logs serving as beams and frames for the structure. Pendant lights hung from the ceiling at different lengths, big and bright. They reminded me of hot air balloons floating in the sky. Massive fireplaces and oversized furniture crowded the large space, warm and inviting. Huge picture windows lined the walls and let in tons of natural light, which made the space feel open but still warm and cozy.

Balcony walks bordered the second and third floor, which led to huge rooms with more oversized furniture and comfortable beds. Fresh flowers were on the coffee table, and each of the bedrooms we picked had exterior balconies facing the lake. The rooms were more modern, having been updated and expanded from their original layout. They were more like studio apartments than a hotel room, similar to my room back at the O. But even with all the updates, the room still held an old-world charm that was inviting and made me want to stay—forever.

The lodge was more than just comfortable furniture, though, and had tons to offer for every personality imaginable. There were speed boats and pontoons, dirt bikes and ATVs, canoes, paddleboards, and rafts. Scooters, bicycles, tricycles, skates, and skis—for both water and snow. Basketball, volleyball, and tennis courts. Horseshoes, croquet, bocce, and corn-hole, plus more. Everything you could think of to play, entertain, or explore was ready and available for use at the lodge.

We decided on four-wheelers and dirt bikes, and found trails to explore that took us down and up, deep into the mountains of Glacier. Since safety was still a major concern, we had our weapons strapped to us, with a few extras bungeed on the backs of our rides, along with snacks and drinks.

Ethan assured us the surrounding land was patrolled constantly and anything that shouldn't be in the vicinity was rid of. A perimeter fence and other measures kept the area clean and secure, but nothing was foolproof, and it was always better to be safe than sorry. Even the waterways that led into the great Lake McDonald had metal net mesh screens keeping everything but fresh water from entering or exiting the lake.

After lunch, the land activities eventually gave way to water sports, and we spent the rest of the afternoon boating, water skiing, and tubing up and down the lake. The views were spectacular, the fun plenitude, and the company welcome. When our bodies were physically spent from the water aerobics, we lazed in the sun on rafts floating in the water until evening and the temperature dropped. We coasted back to the dock and cleaned ourselves up for dinner.

Holden took part as much as Holden-ly possible, and although he hadn't joined the water fun, he'd had a hand in catching our dinner. When Pike and Josh hadn't been doing flips off the boat or daring Sylis and Malik to various contests, they'd fished and caught lake trout too. Keeping an immense lake like this free of *kooks* was impressive, but the fish population had exploded because of it, so they encouraged us to fish to help with population control and water quality.

To my amazement, there were fruits and vegetables in a fenced garden and a greenhouse full of almost everything you could think of. It led me to believe they used this place more often than not. There was a pantry stocked with grains, beans, and canned goods, and a refrigerator full of everything else. We put together a proper meal much easier than it should have been away from home, but it was a welcomed treat for sure, and soon our bellies were full of campfire grilled fish, salad, and a variety of crisp, ripe vegetables.

When the sun started to set, a small cluster of armored trucks and extended Humvees came into view as they approached the lodge. We were all around a small fire, enjoying the approaching night, when the feeders and their vampire escorts stepped out of their vehicles, which looked out of place next to the beauty of the park. The vampire escorts were outfitted much like Ethan and the other VIGs in our group: black leather from head to toe, heavy boots, swords, and a comely presence. The humans seemed at ease and comfortable with their surroundings. They wore similar protective clothing, minus the sword, but they had weapons too. Smiling, they took in the views and laughed with each other at something I was too far away to hear. Their vampire escorts engaged with them comfortably and conversationally, and even though they looked as if this was all business, they also seemed like old friends.

"Excuse me." Ethan disappeared to the new arrivals almost instantly.

At his approach, they inclined their heads to him and talked for a few minutes, then he reached out and shook hands with two of the humans, clapping one of the males on the back as if they were old friends. He indicated with his hand toward the lodge, and together, the nine of them walked inside as they chatted happily.

Less than five minutes later, Ethan stepped out of the door closest to us and called for Sylis, Pike, and Seivor, and the three excused themselves. The rest of us fidgeted in our seats and tried not to make a normal, necessary situation weird and uncomfortable.

I caught Ethan's eye as he waited for the other three to pass through. We smiled at each other, and it reassured me. I instantly felt better by his small gesture.

When he stepped back inside and disappeared up to one of the many bedrooms where a feeding companion waited for him, the only emotion I felt was pure and unadulterated jealousy.

Chapter Nine

The feeding didn't last nearly as long as I'd imagined. Ethan and the VIGs were gone for maybe twenty minutes. *Maybe.*

It didn't, however, stop me or my vivid imagination from spinning a web of scenarios in my mind. Some of which included Ethan running off with the human he was feeding on, never to be seen or heard from again. That, of course, led me to imagine the innocent female turning into a flesh-eating zombie, wherein I became the hero who saved the day. My reward was winning the heart of the dashing vampire. Which was completely stupid for a number of reasons, least of all that *I* would ever rescue *him*—more than likely, it would be the other way. Nevertheless, my fantasies continued, and in the end, I was always rewarded. Handsomely.

I had also managed to chew down both of my thumbnails and was getting ready to start on my fingers when Sylis and Seivor bounded out the door, jumped over the rail, and sat back in their seats as if they had never left.

"See, that wasn't so bad, now was it?" Sylis smiled at me with a wink. Ethan and Pike followed only moments later, and then we were all back around the warm fire like nothing had changed. The feeders and their escorts disappeared soon after, just as quickly and quietly as they had arrived.

We picked up our previous conversations, told ghost stories, roasted marshmallows, made s'mores, gazed up at the night sky, and marveled at the magnificent expanse. A couple of hours later, when the fire had died down, the others individually excused themselves up to bed or off to do their own nighttime activity. It was dark this high in the mountains but still early.

"Are you ready for bed?" Ethan asked me after Charlie had left us for the warmth of a heavy blanket.

"No. Are you?"

"No. There are some trails on the other side of the lake we didn't get to earlier. How do you feel about a night ride?"

"Sounds cold. I'll go get my hoodie."

I hurried up to my room, taking the opportunity to clean myself up. I brushed my teeth, combed through my hair, and dressed in warmer clothes with the addition of a hoodie. Then, I left my warm room ready for a cool night ride.

We were on a trail, cruising in the dark over dirt and gravel at breakneck speeds, on one of the biggest 4-wheelers I had ever seen in my life. It was so big it was like riding in a car, and the seat was so comfortable it might as well have been a sofa. The wind was icy on my face, and my eyes watered from the rush of the crisp mountain air, but the rest of me was comfortably warm and cozy. I had my hoodie pulled up and cinched tight around my head while my feet were wrapped in warm socks and stuffed in my boots. The seat was heated, and the engine blew warm air over us. I was certain that the coziness I felt was because of the luxurious 4-wheeler and beauty of the night ride, and not because I was pressed tightly against Ethan's back with hands around his waist. Absolutely certain.

We rode up and down big hills as we pushed deeper into the wilderness, over rocks and small streams, through the forest, and past the canopy of trees as we climbed higher and higher up a sizable bluff. When we finally reached the top, we found ourselves perched near a cliff, in a small clearing bare of everything but trampled dry grass that gave way to a breathtaking scene of the expanse all around.

From our high position, we could see an insanely beautiful view. The sky was so clear and big it looked as though it went on forever, and as far as the eye could see were mountains of all sizes, shapes, and colors. Some were snowcapped while others were green with trees or brown and gray with jagged, rocky edges. Large and clear lakes reflected their surroundings and the night above like a mirror. Smaller versions dotted at the base of the forest floor like stepping stones, echoing the surrounding colors like gemstones.

The Milky Way arched across the sky in spectacular clarity. A long-stretched cluster of bright white, purples, and shades of blue nestled together to form an imperfect line. All around the main vein of the galaxy were millions of stars, sprinkled across the navy black expanse like white sugar on a dark floor. Periodically, streaks of light from shooting stars wisped past the ether and through our glimpse of the cosmos.

The view of the star system high above made me feel both alone and connected—bigger than life but insignificantly small. I felt homesick for the unknown and longed for the ability to be among the stars, yet content with wonder beneath the protective blanket of the atmosphere. Under the powerful cluster of light, I was but a glimpse in time, yet I felt hopeful to have so much of it ahead of me. Mostly, though, I was grateful that the problems of this earth were only here and that the plague that had wrecked my home wasn't infecting anything out there.

"It's so beautiful," I murmured.

"Look there." Ethan pointed a finger toward the sky. "That's Sagittarius."

With a little help and redirection, I saw what he was looking at. "Amazing." I let my hand fall from his grip to land lightly on my thigh next to his. "It's so awesome up here."

"Next time, we'll bring a telescope."

"Next time?"

"Yes, and we'll find a trail that takes us up higher too."

"Okay."

I was pressed tightly against him, and our eyes locked. The mood changed almost instantly, and our connected bodies seemed to increase the pull of energy we shared.

Ethan turned his body and simultaneously wrapped his arm around my waist and thigh, then spun me around until I was on his lap, encased by his arms and pressed against the front of him. Our eyes stayed connected for the briefest of moments, then his mouth pressed against mine—soft cool lips against the flame and heat of my own. His deep, throaty groan made me mew upon contact.

I moved my hands from around his neck and threaded my fingers through his thick hair. It was just as cool as his skin and soft as silk. He loosened the grip he had around my thighs, wrapped one arm around the small of my back, and pulled me closer to him as his other hand slid up my spine, settling at the base of my neck.

I didn't know how much time had slipped by. It could have been minutes, seconds, or hours, and I wouldn't have known. I was so lost in him.

His hands roamed my clothed body while my fingertips explored his face. When my hands traveled down to his chest and arms, he drifted up the side of my neck, where he wove his fingers through my hair. He moved his mouth from mine and kissed my jaw, then buried his face in my neck and wrapped his hands around my waist, pushing himself up into me. I moaned at his silent suggestion, and he crushed his mouth to mine again. The circle of his arms around me tightened.

"Stay with me tonight."

"Where?"

"I took a cabin instead of a room."

I smiled against his lips. "Subtle."

He hummed and sealed our mouths together again.

We didn't stay on the mountain for long after that, and when I was pressed against his back again, he took us down the trail through the dark forest. At the lodge, he dropped me off at the door and took the 4-wheeler back to wherever it was stored.

I hurried up to my room and changed out of my heavy boots and clothes into jammies. Then I cleaned up, packed all my things, and left the room.

He was waiting for me in the lobby, took my bag, and tucked me into him when I was close. Several cabins of varying sizes were scattered around the estate, and the one he took me to was sized in the middle, like a small home. There was a tiny living room, a kitchenette, a bathroom, and a bedroom.

He locked the door behind us, dropped my bag next to his, and shut off the lights in the living room as I pulled off my hoodie and kicked off my shoes. When his shoes were off, he reached out for me, lifting me to him, wherein I wrapped my legs around his waist. My arms went around the top of his shoulders, and I kissed him as he walked us into the room kicking the door closed behind him.

I was tingling all over—my stomach clenched, my skin flushed, my heart rate spiked—and I throbbed for him in anticipation. The attraction that normally pulsated between us was an inferno now that we were alone in a bedroom, no interruptions in sight. It blazed hot, and the charged air all but hissed with our flame. There was going to be nothing slow or romantic about our joining. We were both too excited, too pent up from the tension that had steadily risen between us since almost the moment we met. I didn't care about anything else right now. I just wanted him inside me, and by his urgency, he was clearly of the same mind.

We didn't pull away from each other while we stripped off our clothes. I ripped my shirt off. He tossed his to the floor, and as he worked getting his jeans off, I slipped my pajama bottoms down with ease. I yanked my socks off at the same time he did his and went to work on my bra as soon as my hands were free. When his boxers were gone, he helped pull the straps off my shoulders as we backed up together toward the bed, and when he ripped off the blankets, all I had left on me were my panties. He dropped and pressed his face to my stomach as he tugged them off. Then he was kissing me again and lifting me to the bed in the next instant. He had all my weight, so I wrapped my legs around him, and no sooner than I was flat on my back, he had his mouth sealed with mine again and was pushing himself into me.

I released his mouth and moaned at the size of him as he worked himself in, stretching me gently around his thickness. He dropped his head to my shoulder with a groan and kissed my neck, his pants catching in his throat with his retraction and re-entry. It didn't take long for my body to accommodate him; I was so ready. When he'd gone as far as he could go, he pulled his length in and out of me easily before increasing his speed, reigniting the fire. He wrapped one of his arms under my shoulder and held me at my hip with his other as I rolled myself under him. I fisted his hair, latched onto him with my mouth, and ran my free hand down his back to drag my nails over his skin.

Ethan sailed himself into me, positioning his body over mine exactly right so that every push and pull hit the nerve cluster at my core. His eager thrusts urged me forward, swelling me with a need to release so quickly it gave me chills that curled my toes and perked my nipples. His groans became grunts, and his hand tightened around my hip. His kisses on my neck turned to hot breath as his lips hovered over my skin, too concentrated on the building pleasure to keep his focus.

It was loud in the room and hot. Neither of us held back. My pitched exhales and soft cries of encouragement mixed with his strained grunts and strangled curses. We pawed, squeezed, licked, and bit each other as our skin dampened and the room turned musky. The bed rocked against the wall. When I clawed at his shoulders, he slammed into me and I surged under him. My back arched as the swell that had been building spilled over in a sudden rush of pleasure, enveloping my core and shooting up through my spine. I pulsed around him, my body clenching with the spasms and gripping him tighter.

Ethan's speed increased with my release until his loud groans became low, heavy shudders as he found his own climax and panted over me harshly. He tightened his hold and partially rested his weight on me as we caught our breaths. Then he plastered my neck and shoulder with kisses again, and I languorously ran my fingers up and down his back.

"There's no hope of me ever keeping my hands off of you now." He dragged his tongue over my jaw.

"Good thing I like your hands on me." I sucked his tongue into my mouth with his groan.

"I hope you didn't plan on sleeping tonight."

"Sleep is overrated." I pulled his lip between my teeth, then he pushed his mouth onto mine.

"I've wanted to have you since the moment I laid eyes on you."

His cool breath washed over my face as our foreheads rested together. My heart still pounded heavily in my chest, and we were both breathing hard.

"That's what you said about kissing me."

"I know."

"You first saw me in the middle of a zombie attack," I reminded him.

"So?"

"Maybe it was in the hangar, after the attack?" I offered. "When you rescued me from the floor as I fainted."

"No." His chest rumbled under me. "It was in Honor." He kissed me along my jawline. "There was a moment, just after we jumped on the bus, when I saw you—"

"I felt it too," I cut him off.

He rolled us onto our sides so he could look at me now, almost as if studying me. I gazed at him as I thought of the first time I stared up into his eyes. It had felt like a chill running down my spine. I felt it again now, but different as it settled in my soul.

"What did it feel like?" he asked.

"Like light." It was the only way I could describe it.

He smiled. "A warm glow."

"It gave me chills."

"Down your back?" He ran his hand down mine.

"Yes." I sighed as he grazed my skin.

"Spreading through your nerves." He trailed his fingers down my arm, where he clasped my hand and brought it up to his mouth to kiss my knuckles.

"More like my whole body." I ran my fingers over his face when he released my hand.

We stayed in that moment of confessed excitement and desire for each other well into the night, learning and exploring how we moved and fit together. We dozed on and off, but he was insatiable and kept his word about no sleep.

"Does this seem fast?" I was sprawled across his chest as he lazily ran his fingers over my body.

"Not for me. Time and everything humans measure by it works differently for our species. When you have an infinite amount of it, everything isn't as easily defined by it," he said. "Age, for example, which is just another form of measuring time... We don't get too caught up in it. If we did, we would limit ourselves to a very small existence."

"Because you and I wouldn't be here like this."

"Exactly." He kissed the tip of my nose. "There are ethical and moral restrictions. A child is a child, and age is indisputably recognized for the young. Those who violate and take innocence are abominations in all species and are dealt with swiftly. Consent and age consent are the law. There is no other way."

"Obviously."

"However, when a person is age-appropriate—emotionally, mentally, and physically—then the numbers aren't taken too literally. Twenty-five, eighty, or two hundred are all relative in that case. I have met three-hundred-year-old vampires who act like seventeen-year-old children," he joked. "You've met Sylis, so you know what I mean."

"He's two hundred?" I looked at him in surprise.

"No. He's older."

"Really?"

"By a dozen decades, yes."

"That's so ... bizarre." I rested my head back down on him and stared off as I tried to wrap my mind around being alive for that long.

"Does that help you understand? That time shouldn't factor in? What works for someone in a week can take a year or five for someone else."

"Yes. I wouldn't have let it, anyway, but it makes more sense now." I kissed his chest. "I'd known Sylis was immature before you alluded to how old he was."

"In a playful way, yes, completely immature." His chest and deep voice rumbled in my ear. "He's otherwise one of the kindest, wisest, and most reliable males I've ever known. Definitely someone you want watching your back."

"I believe you." I thought back to how Sylis had known exactly what to say to Paige at breakfast as she held the tiny kitten, Wicket. "I mean, you do give him weapons, so..."

"True." He laughed with me.

"Are there other outposts like this one?" I drew circles on his shoulder and arm. "It seems strange that this was here the whole time and we had no idea," I mused. This place was so spectacular it was hard to believe we'd missed it all this time.

"Keeping secret locations like this is not without effort. But humans are easily detoured. Roadblocks, intentional herding of the undead, destruction as camouflage, basic subliminal manipulation, and regular patrols keep out what we don't want in."

"Tricky."

"Necessary," he corrected. "Safe places like this are essential to our survival and to most of the other species' on this planet. There should be a reprieve from what's happening, and these types of locations should be safeguarded. Some human colonies, like Thompson Falls, do their best, but we can't live this life forever. We can't continue in this existence and never have something to return to. When the last *kook* has been killed, we'll need to rebuild. When the cure has been found, we'll need to move forward. Outposts like this protect things worth saving."

"So, they're not all just recreational and feeding outposts or secret vampire towns?"

"No. Although, there are a lot of those." He smiled. "Vampires worked with humans for years to save and protect what we could before it was all destroyed. Even now. While some of us are tasked with dealing with the dead, like you and me, we also have others out there who scour the Earth in search of Earth culture. We need to save what we can—art and history, for example. We have teams whose sole purpose is to collect everything they can find. You've only ever known this life, so I'm sure it's hard for you to picture, but there's much more to this world. More than you can even imagine."

"A world within a world," I used the words he had said.

"There's so much I want to show you." He rolled us over and kissed me. "But for now, I'll settle for this," he whispered against my lips and pushed himself into me again.

I couldn't imagine a time when I wouldn't moan or gasp at his entry. Feeling every thick velvety inch of him stretching me was a pleasure of its own. His smell in my nose, the taste of him on my tongue, and the feel of his naked body against mine were familiar even though it was new and exciting. I didn't want the night to end.

The next morning, we got up early, showered together, and loaded our things in the bear before going back to the lodge for coffee and breakfast. We weren't hiding us, not really. That would be impossible with the others anyway, but we were both relieved to find that Holden wasn't awake and downstairs yet. We were alone with our coffee but not long until Sylis and Pike were with us.

"You two are up early." Pike lifted his mug to his mouth. "Did the construction keep you up too?"

I scowled at him.

"All that banging around last night was loud." Sylis stretched. "Why would they be doing renovations up here in the middle of the night? Seems strange."

"That's enough." Ethan's tone was flat.

They feigned innocence.

"It's not our fault the crew was noisily redecorating all night." Sylis mocked.

"Well, you know what they say." I lifted my coffee to my mouth. "The bigger the hammer, the louder it pounds."

Ethan dropped his head as the other two howled and whooped like idiots. "Don't encourage them, or they'll never stop." He leaned over and kissed my head.

"Aww, did we go public and I missed it?" Seivor walked in and went for the coffee.

"Yeah, Abby's one of us now." Sylis winked at me.

"Yep, she moved all the way to the top of the food chain, and she doesn't even know it." Pike smirked.

Ethan shot him a look. "Seriously, that's enough."

"Alright, calm down." Pike held up his hands. "We're just voicing our approval."

I snorted and sipped on my coffee.

"I didn't ask." Ethan didn't find any humor in this conversation at all.

I didn't mind, liking they were comfortable enough to joke like this around me.

"I must have missed something good," Seivor commented but didn't press it like the other two.

"Our newest charge here can hold her own. She bites back." Sylis said. "We like Abby."

"You guys are idiots." They laughed as I stood. "Now, move. Unless you're going to make breakfast?"

Sylis and Seivor practically ran out of the kitchen to get out of the way.

Pike refilled his coffee. "I'll help make breakfast. What are we making?"

"Cut-up fruit."

"Fruit?" He crinkled his eyes. "That's not breakfast."

"And eggs."

"And you run a restaurant? No wonder Gigi's in charge of the menu."

I laughed at him. "But I'm really good at stacking plates and bossing people around."

He assembled the ingredients to make French toast with the bread in the refrigerator and scrambled eggs, while I washed and cut up fruit.

Holden and Charlie came down not long after we'd started, and while Charlie engaged in conversation with the others, Holden seemed to sulk in the corner, keeping to himself. Malik and Josh were the last to emerge from their room, and after breakfast, they cleaned up while the rest of us readied ourselves to go.

We left Glacier the same way we'd come, and several hours later, we were back at the storage facility to load up the dried and canned goods we'd promised Kat we'd bring back with us.

The vanguard hadn't been in the area for a while, and even though it'd been cleared of *kooks* the last time we were here, it didn't mean it was still a safe zone. So first, we retrieved the hauling truck from the building we had parked it in, just outside of the abandoned small town that was nothing more than a stretch of road with several brick and steel buildings. Any homes that were here, along with anything other but the brick and steel, had crumbled into decay.

We retrieved the hauling truck from the garage of what looked like an old fire department and drove to the food storage near the end of the town. The buildings there were surrounded by a steel fence and entry but had been left unlocked and wide open. It didn't seem likely any of our teams would have left the passageway unsecured, so we needed to safeguard the area before we could load up the food.

The space was a decent size, with several buildings and pavement inside the fence. Josh drove the hauling truck in first, then Holden backed the bear in, and Sylis and Seivor pulled the two ends of the gate closed around the front of the vehicle. The metal barrier was heavy and rolled on tires. If *kooks* happened upon us outside the fence, they couldn't get in since they didn't know how to roll open an access point, but the bear was left running and the doors open in case we needed to escape in a hurry.

Charlie wasn't good with a weapon, so instead of her tripping us up, we left her with a radio and binoculars to keep watch on top of the vehicle. Then, we split up into groups and went in opposite directions to clear our location of any dead that may have wandered in here.

"I see something over there," Charlie whispered into her radio a few minutes later.

"Over where?" Josh asked from the opposite side of the abandoned yard, where Holden, Sylis, Ethan, and I were.

"Can you be more specific?" Holden griped at her.

"Sorry! Holden, to your left, behind that red van," she said back after a few seconds of flustered shuffling and button-pushing on the radio.

Holden let his head drop forward, shaking it back and forth, while we waited for her direction. I pressed my lips together to hold back whatever might have escaped them. He was in his usual foul mood as it was, but he also didn't like being out in the *Morgue* with anyone who didn't know what they were doing. Laughing at Charlie would only piss him off further.

We moved in the direction she'd indicated. Where she was sending us to, there were two parked vehicles that weren't ours and weren't aged or caked over with grime, which could mean that someone was—or had been—here and was now in some other state of upright.

"We have a couple of shiners over here," Holden told the other team.

Zach and some of the other motor-heads in town had coined the term a while ago. Vehicles still in use weren't usually "dirty"; they were "shiny" compared to their apocalyptically abandoned counterparts. The term had evolved from there into a one-word warning that meant you should be on the lookout for breathers or newly turned *kooks* in the area.

"Copy," Malik responded.

"I hear something." Ethan moved forward ahead of us a little faster. He'd made it around the van and had his sword raised when he stopped, lowering his weapon. Holden and I came around the corner, with Sylis right behind us.

A stray dog was guarding a deer carcass, its mouth latched around one leg as it pulled with all its strength to drag it away. The dog was growling at us once in its sights, but the poor thing was too hungry to even let the deer go long enough to properly warn us off. We backed away, not necessarily out of fear but as a sign to the animal that we were not a threat to it or its meal.

I would have liked to save the little guy from the horrors of this world and what it must live through each day, but stray animals were feral. The older they were, the harder it was to tame them out of the wild. The world had changed them. Pets weren't as common as they used to be.

Most of them—cats and dogs, especially—had regressed to their primal nature when the world ended. Humans stopped bringing them home to feed and instead began to feed *on* them. Their innate natural instincts had kicked in, and to survive, they had become wild again. Now, they were too used to fighting for meals and defending their prey from dead versions of us to ever be fully trusted, and they passed on that fear to their offspring. It would take generations of breeding to domesticate them again.

"We have something over here." Josh's radio screeched and pierced through the air.

The sound scared the dog enough that it finally let go of the deer's leg to bark and growl at us.

"Go," Ethan indicated to us with the jerk of his head. "I'll keep the dog from following."

The three of us ran toward the other team. When we reached the opposite side of the building, Pike was taking down the last of two *kooks* while the others stood guard and watched for more.

"Just the two?" Sylis asked.

"No." Pike tipped his head toward the building, moans and banging from inside punctuating his answer. "These were the two that got out."

"How many?" Ethan surprised me from behind.

I hadn't heard him approach, even though we stood on loose gravel and busted-up pavement. It's no wonder vampires existed around humans without notice for eons. They could literally walk right past you, and you would have had no idea unless they wanted you to.

"Six," Seivor told him. "And a *litla*."

"What's a *litla*?" I asked when none of them explained the term.

"It means 'little'." Ethan looked down at me. "It is the term we used to describe the little ones that have been turned."

"Little ones?" I was confused, but ignorance only lasted a second, and then I realized what he meant. "Oh."

Everyone was quiet for a moment, the only noise from the *kooks* hitting against the door and walls as they crashed around to get to us.

"Uh, guys?" Charlie's voice cracked over the speakers of our radio and broke the silence. "Is everything alright?"

"Yeah, we're good," I responded without mentioning what we were about to do. "We'll be finished here in a few. Be on the lookout while we clean up."

"Why don't you go keep watch with her." Holden nodded toward the truck. His voice wasn't sharp, and he sounded like the old him. Even Ethan noticed his change in demeanor. "We've got this."

"I'll just cover from back here." I shook my head.

"Seriously, Abby." He raised his brows in a plea. "Go."

Ethan was confused by the exchange, but I squared my shoulders and armed myself with *Walter*. I aimed down at the ground until everyone else was in ready form, nodding to Holden one last time before he turned around and raised his weapon.

Pike stood next to the door with his hand on the knob, and when we were all in position, he turned the handle. The heavy steel door swung open with a grinding creak, the rusted hinges scraping together in a sinister wail of metal on metal, then crashed against the side of the building. It screeched, swaying back and forth a few times until it stayed fully open. Then, it was eerily quiet for a stretch of time ... until it wasn't.

Pike moved back and faced the door with Ethan, Sylis, and Seivor, each with their swords drawn. Together, they made a half-circle around the exit door while the rest of us positioned ourselves behind and between them to cover anything that they might miss.

Two *kooks* closest to the door pushed against each other to escape and fell face-first into the dirt. The others in the room then trampled out and over their fallen inert kin. One tripped and fell to land on top of the other two, who had started to drag themselves up from the ground toward us. Two more followed, made it over the grounders, and without pause continued forward with throaty cries toward the group of us.

Ethan and Seivor made quick work with their swords, *the kooks'* heads rolling off toward Malik and Josh, who each finished one with a bullet to the brain.

The remaining *kooks* in the building continued to stumble out of the door and over their smelly friends, but tripped and fell, landing on the grounders as they repeatedly tried to move, eventually piling into a snare of bodies a few feet from the door. The position the dead had put themselves in was a benefit to us, and the VIGs easily finished them, piercing their swords through each of their heads while standing just out of reach of their grasping hands.

The *litla* was the last and slowly made its way out. Tiny fingers wrapped around the jamb of the door as little feet trudged around and through the frame. As she stumbled forward with baby steps—one foot dirty and bare, the other covered with a filthy sock and shoe—it was hard to tell whether the un-coordination was from death or young age. Her arms stretched out in front of her either in reach for flesh or balance, her little hands and fingers opening and closing as she clasped out in hungry greed.

She couldn't have been older than two years of age when she was turned; she was barely the height of my knee. She wore faded pink shorts and a tee that had flowers and butterflies stitched onto the fabric, each article of clothing smeared with blood that had long ago turned black. Dirt and filth covered the parts of her clothes that hadn't been sullied with blood. Teeth marks and nips of missing flesh lined her tiny arms and legs, and a chunk of hair and skin was missing from her scalp. Her cries were barely audible, however familiar in sound as those of the dead, the tenor only quieter, smaller. Ghostly.

How she had stayed this whole and intact was curious to me, and I idly wondered about her story—another thing to add to the long list of questions I would never know the answers to.

I knew I was staring in awe and complete shock—the little ones were always surprising. I understood the nature of reproduction, but I couldn't understand the desire to bring a child into a world such as this. To risk the life of the very thing people claimed to love so much seemed incredibly selfish to me, and I knew I was looking at the only birth control method I would ever need to use.

As she continued to stumble forward, everyone was briefly stock-still. I wasn't the only one horrified by what had to happen next.

Ethan stepped in front of me just as Pike moved forward to put her to rest. The view he could cut off, but the sound of a blade as it silenced through flesh and interrupted snuffling cries couldn't be prevented.

The small burn pile was nearly out, the child's body hidden at the bottom. We were finally loaded up and ready to leave the storage facility.

Holden and Sylis argued for a few minutes over who would drive the bear while the rest of the group talked about the *litla* and how horrible and sad it was. Everyone except for Holden and me.

Sylis eventually won the argument after he'd reminded Holden of a bet they had made and he'd lost while we were in Glacier. Holden conceded by calling Sylis names and folding his big arms over his chest like a pouty child, but when he moved toward the passenger side of the bear, Malik laughed then tossed him the keys to the haul truck. Holden sauntered off with a smile on his face, flipping Sylis off with one hand while jingling the keys with his other.

By the time we were on the road, Charlie segued from what had just happened with the *litla* to something similar from the past. I looked out the window as the conversation continued, wishing I had ridden with Holden instead of having to listen to this and think back on a day I would soon rather forget than ever talk about again.

Chapter Ten

One year ago

It was in a city in old Oregon, close to the new Pacific coast where California used to be. We made our way through the city, dredging through building after building, looking for anything salvageable. It'd been pouring rain all day. We were wet, cold, and tired—from exhaustion and of each other. We hadn't been working with our regular teams, and everyone was running on a short fuse.

We'd been scouring the streets for a few days, hoping to find some running vehicles or usable parts. The other teams, on a mission for food and much-needed medical supplies, were at least finding what they were looking for, but us coming up empty-handed was getting on our nerves.

We eventually came across a large concrete building that had once been a parking garage, hoping we had finally found something. The stench of rot and death took our breath away it was so strong, and the weather only seemed to make it worse as if the rain and cold temperature kept the stench grounded. It hovered and clung to the building rather than dispersing out into the open air.

Inside, it was obvious where the smell was coming from. The mess of blood, guts, and everything in between stained the floor and parts of the walls. The sodden floor caused us to slip in some areas while the spillage had dried and turned black in others. We followed the path of end trails and blood to a large group of *kooks* in a corner that led to the second-floor ramp. If the noise was any indication, once we finished dispatching of this group, there would be an equal amount of dead waiting for us up there too.

We approached quietly, but the discharge of our silenced rifles made enough sound to draw their attention, so we positioned ourselves as comfortably close as possible to exterminate them. We used massive pillars and old vehicles as cover, then opened fire, knowing we couldn't stop once we started and that when this group was finished, we needed to move on to the next as quickly as possible so we didn't get overrun.

The *evos* came after us first, the rest of them soon following. There were too many to count, but we did our best to keep up with them. We backed away as they made ground against us, quickly pulling toward the exit when it looked like the entire horde would overtake us. Once the *evos* were killed off, though, the rest of the *kooks* tripped over them, which slowed them down enough that we gained control of the situation and cleared the first floor.

We paused long enough to check our weapons and then moved up the ramp to the second floor. Our shots had stirred the pot enough that the carrion on there had become a low hum of shuffling feet and a grumble of eagerness. We eliminated a handful of *evos* at the top of the ramp, then cautiously walked up the remaining distance with our backs against the wall, where we finished the last of the *kooks*. There weren't as many as we had originally thought, and because the rest were regular run-of-the-mill *munchers*, they were easy targets from our position.

We cleared the remaining two floors quickly. The rest were random *stragglers* throughout the building, so it didn't take long. When we were sure we had taken care of the major threats, we broke off into teams to look for anything useful.

I was coming from the other side of the third floor when I noticed Harper' standing next to a car in a far corner. I could see the profile of her body as she faced the walls but not her face. Her gun was hanging in front of her against her waist at an odd angle, her shoulders slumped and her head tilted down. I hollered after her a couple of times to get her attention. At first, I didn't move toward her, but I got worried when she didn't answer. She looked dead, or like the dead when they didn't move. My heart sank into my stomach, and adrenaline immediately coursed through my veins. We couldn't have missed anything. So I knew she was fine—she had to be fine.

"Harper!" I yelled again, in a dead run toward her with *Walter* drawn and ready in my hand.

It was later, when it was all over, that I admitted to myself I had believed she had turned, and that I had been prepared to kill her. The thought broke my heart.

As I approached her, I slowed my steps and wrapped my free hand around my right that held the gun. Keeping my aim pointed at the floor, I took another step toward her and said her name again, then once more when she didn't answer me.

It was the strangest sound.

Indescribable.

I took another step forward and stopped mid-step, stunned once I saw what was in front of her.

In the corner, where one wall met the other, was a heaping mess of what had once been a whole person. The body was sprawled, laid out as if it were some macabre form of horror art or a gruesome sacrificial arrangement for a demonic god gone wrong.

The left leg was pulled from the joint socket at the hip, and the bones of the femur, tibia, and fibula were chewed clean. What was left of the limb, including the foot and ankle, lay tossed aside and away from the rest of the body, shoe still attached. The right leg was turned up at an odd angle, broken at the knee and bent outward, the foot facing away from the body in the same way an arm would were it still there. Stringy leftovers of tendons, ligaments, and connective tissue were the only things left hanging on the bones.

At the left shoulder, an arm untouched from the elbow up was all that remained, other than the pool of blood that had spilled from the severed artery. The breast tissue, neck, and face were chewed off. Hollow holes where the eyes and nose had been left the back of the skull exposed, revealing blood and chewed remains that pooled at the base like a bowl of discarded food.

Snarled clumps of blonde hair matted in blood, and ears attached to what was left of the scalp, precariously held onto the back of the head. A gold earring pierced through the left lobe dangled and swayed from the slight breeze, the sunlight lighting up flecks of gold embedded deep inside the gemstone, sparkling cheerfully in contradiction to the grisly surroundings.

It was a gruesome mess. The concrete was stained with various shades of blood—black, brown, and even red in some areas—like paint that had poured all over the floor, then was left to dry. The palette color of death.

The kill itself was fresh—maybe only a day, two at the most. The same could be said for some of the bodies downstairs. The smell was the primary indicator it was still new—the tin of blood and decomposition was strong. An odor from rot and decay so sharp you could feel it coat the inside of your nose and taste it on the back of your tongue, whereas your eyes and nose automatically pinched, scowling at the offensive scent, and your hand moved to your face as if to shield you from the stench. My body coughed in rejection to the tainted air with each shallow breath I tried not to take, choking back bile and clamping down on the gag reflex because I knew that if I let it go once, I would definitely lose my lunch.

Still, this was nothing unfamiliar. We saw these sorts of forgotten meals all the time, smelled this vile part of life almost everywhere we went. That wasn't the part that was so disturbing, not what was astonishing. It wasn't why I remembered it so vividly, or why it had stuck with me as the saddest, sickest, and most haunting thing I'd ever seen.

The protruding belly of the female corpse initially caught my eye. It was almost perfectly intact, slightly round and full, which was weird and why it immediately drew my attention. When the dead got you down, they usually went for the belly first. There was a lot of surface area, and it was soft and easy to tear into, like the buffet section of the human body. Highly unusual to be left alone, but there it was—unharmed and nearly flawless.

Still, that wasn't what caught me off guard. It was the infant that lay next to the body in a pool of dried blood that was so horrifying. Just barely out of the birth canal; the umbilical cord was still attached to its belly and connected to what was left of its mother. Its little limbs jerked and thrashed about, making that strange sound.

It was tiny. A little girl, sort of purple and wrinkly with loose, papery skin. Its arms and legs kicked out, waving erratically in the air. Its head rolled from side to side, its baby jaw quivering with each whimper and cry of hunger.

It was not human. Not anymore. That much was obvious.

So innocent. So deadly. Yet somehow seemingly harmless.

Harper and I moved closer to the infant's body, almost as if drawn in at the same time by some unseen force. Standing over it, we both looked down at the tiny creature in horrified wonder. Harper's face and the posture of her body seemed to match my own.

"It's just a baby," she whispered, her voice shaking slightly on the words, more breath than sound.

She was right—it had once been just a baby. A brand-new baby. Or at least, it would have been if not for its death and current condition.

A million things ran through my mind and yet nothing at the same time. I didn't know what to do, what to say, what to think. It was just another *kook* ... but it was a baby, an infant. We had all seen zombie children before. It was horrible, heartbreaking, and inconceivable, but we had never seen a baby.

A brand-new baby, fresh from the womb? Alive but dead? I'd never even considered it.

After a few minutes of us staring at the little creature, Harper handed me her gun, and I took it from her out of reflex. It wasn't until after she'd bent down, cut the umbilical cord, and wrapped the newborn in a piece of blood-stained cloth from the dirty floor, that I realized I was running on autopilot—and that she was running on something else.

"Whaaat the hell are you doing, Harper?" I asked in horror as I pulled myself together.

"It's just a baby," she murmured, staring down at it in a daze.

It was still making that sound. Up close, it was even clearer what it had become. Purple lips, ashy translucent skin, and clouded, bloodshot, lifeless eyes all sat in a tiny, starved cherub face. Matted, curly black hair held firm in its place by its mother's blood, dried afterbirth.

"Shh..." Harper shushed as she shifted and swayed it around in her arms.

"Harper?"

"What are we going to do?" She looked at me expectantly. Her face had taken on a manic serenity I'd never seen. She was calm and peaceful as if in a state of bliss, but her eyes were wide and wild.

Worried for her instantly, I didn't want to say the wrong thing to my friend and partner who was clearly not okay. So, instead of answering her question, I carefully unloaded the gun she had given me, holstering it in my belt.

Harper tucked the cloth around the reanimated infant a little tighter and then rocked back and forth, shifting her weight on one foot then the other as she hummed a sweet lullaby. She smiled down at the lost soul and stroked the top of its head and its temple, wrapping its teeny fingers around her thumb. "Shh..."

I knew she wasn't mentally ill, but something wasn't right. I didn't know what that something *was* exactly, not at first. So I didn't know how to help her since she was suddenly in the midst of a psychotic break. I was way out of my depth here.

"I need help," I said over the radio. It was vague and not explanatory, but I didn't want to say too much and alarm Harper or push her further down the rabbit hole.

"Abby? Where are you?" Holden answered me immediately.

"Second floor."

"Are you alright?"

"No."

"What's the matter?"

"I don't know."

"What do you mean you don't know?" he yelled at me, but I could hear through the connection that he was already running.

"Abby! What the hell is going on?" Hendricks roared over the radio next. He was running too. The echo of his footsteps and other voices bounced off the walls, so I knew they couldn't be far.

"I just need help," I repeated.

I didn't know what else to say, feeling so stupid. I didn't want to say too much or reveal to Harper that I was asking for help for her.

Hendricks, Holden, and Brooks were there only a few moments later, Kat shortly after that. They had their guns ready as they approached. I couldn't see them—my back was facing their direction, but I didn't turn to look at them either. My view was fixed on Harper and what she was holding. I couldn't take my eyes off her for fear she might disappear for good. The way she held the undead newborn against her, stroking and cooing as she tried to soothe it, was as clear a sign as any that she needed help. She needed a face she trusted to tether to when she finally realized it was her we were concerned about, not the *kook* baby.

"Abby?" Hendricks inched forward, his tone and the way he said my name a sign he wanted more information.

I still couldn't think of anything that would explain the situation without distressing Harper, so I signaled him forward with my hand.

"Harper?" He moved around me, coming into full view.

"It's just a baby," her hollow voice repeated. She had just shushed it with a small, sad smile as she stroked its face.

The infant *kook* turned its head toward her finger each time she touched its cheek, letting out that sound with the rooting reflex. Its eyes were wide and unfocused, ashy gray from death, and its tiny jaw quivered as it sucked and smacked at the empty air.

"I see." Hendricks straightened himself, switched on the safety of his handheld, then holstered it before he waved his hand at the rest of the group to do the same.

A rattle of metal followed as they each shifted and lowered their guns. Then it was quiet again, except for that strange sound coming from the corpse baby. I wished it would stop making that sound.

"What are we going to do?" Harper twisted to face Hendricks, the look on her face now even more crazed than her side profile had displayed. Her eyes were so dilated only a thin ring of blue was visible, and her brows were so high up that her forehead wrinkled with layers of deep lines. Her face was pale, her lips were dry and chapped like she'd had nothing to drink for days.

"It's okay." Hendricks raised his hands, palms facing her, as he took a careful step forward. "We'll figure it out," he said to her encouragingly.

As Hendricks continued forward, Kat walked around me, getting her first real look at the situation. "Fucking hell," she exhaled with a grimace.

"She's so little," Harper whispered. She looked down at it again, took its purple hand in hers, and wrapped its fingers around her thumb.

"Give it here, Harper." Hendricks was right in front of her now and had his hands extended toward her.

"Why?" She pulled the small bundle closer to her breast, shielding its head.

"Let me take care of it," Hendricks said a little sterner.

"What are you going to do?"

"I'll take care of it while you go wash up and get some air."

"What?" She questioned, confused. "It's just a baby."

"Harper, give it to me," he repeated gently. "Please."

"B-but… It's not hurting anything. It's just a baby."

"Harper, it's dangerous," Kat told her kindly. "Let Commander Hendricks take care of it."

"No." She pulled it closer to her protectively.

"It's already gone," Hendricks told her.

"It's just a baby," she repeated, tears filling her eyes.

"It's already gone," Kat echoed quietly, inching forward.

If Harper didn't give it up soon, we would have to take it from her by force.

"I know." She hiccupped. "But it's just a baby."

"I know."

"It's not hurting anything. It can't." Her lips trembled.

"Harper," I relented. "It's not fair. You have to let it go."

She looked over at me now. Tears streamed down her face like a sluice, covering her cheeks and dripping off her chin. Mine followed. Big, hot, messy tears blurred my vision, made my throat hurt and my nose run. I knew at that moment it was Harper's baby, the one she had lost not so long ago, that she was projecting in this situation. Her innocent child who had died shortly after birth which she was seeing as the bundle in her arms. It had been too soon for her to come back to work, too soon to go out on a mission. What terrible luck that it had been her to find this horrible reminder of the precious life she had lost.

"It's just a baby," she cried through broken breath. Her entire body jerked with pain as she convulsed in mourning.

I closed the distance between us, pulled her and the tiny bundle she was holding against me, and wrapped my arms around her shoulders.

Resting her head against mine, she looked down at what she held in her arms, and we cried together for a while—she for what she had lost, and I for both that and my broken friend.

I was aware of the people around us as I stood there and held her to me. There would not be any judgment about her reaction—we had all suffered with her and her loss. But as they quietly discussed what would happen next, I ran my hands over her back and whispered in her ear a deluge of comforts to drown out the group behind us.

Some time had gone by—not too much, not too little—before she handed the baby over to Hendricks. It was still making that sound as Harper shifted it around and placed it in Hendricks's arms. Once it was out of her hands, Harper turned back to me and wrapped her arms around my waist, tucking her chin and hiding her face in my shoulder. I held her as she cried.

Hendricks and Brooks quietly took the little thing far away from where the rest of us were. Kat and Holden stepped away and gave us room.

I didn't know exactly what they'd done. No one had ever bothered to ask. We just knew it had finally been put to rest.

They were gone long enough, though, that it gave Harper time to collect herself as best as she could. I needed time too. The whole situation was a shitshow.

Harper washed her hands and face with water from a bottle I poured out for her. We both wiped over our clothes with several disinfecting towels, and when we were back at our vehicles, she cleaned herself again with what we had on hand. I rebounded, but Harper was visibly shaken and stayed that way for the rest of our mission.

As much as we all wanted to take her home as soon as possible, it just wasn't feasible. We had a job to do, and we were such a long distance from home that we had to stay and finish. We needed what we'd come for, and if we left now, all our weeks of travel and recovery would be wasted.

Keeping her with us and not taking her home had its own set of drawbacks. She was so out of sorts that she was now a liability. She couldn't be trusted with a weapon, and even if she could be, we would never ask. Instead, we were short-staffed by two people. She needed to be kept under constant watch, for both her mental state and signs of infection since she had held and touched the infant with her bare hands.

All of that would have been bad enough. It *was* bad enough. But before she calmed down, before we got her out of the parking garage and back to the truck, before Hendricks and Brooks reappeared, the infant's sibling had stumbled from around a hidden corner near the mess.

We'd missed it somehow. It moved so quietly it didn't make a sound. It couldn't. The lower half of its face and part of its throat were missing. It didn't stop the instinct to consume, though, and even though it was slow, it came directly toward us.

It touched my leg before I noticed it. Its little hands grabbed onto my thigh, and it was bringing its face down as if to take a bite.

I reacted on instinct. I jerked us both back, pulled out *Walter*, and shot it before I fully realized what it was or what was happening.

Harper screamed.

I stared at it in shock.

"What the fuck?!" Holden was up to us in the next instant, but by then, the threat was already gone. "Son of a bitch." He clenched his teeth.

He looked concerned. Probably waiting for me to lose my shit like Harper.

I didn't know what to say. I stared at him blank-faced.

"I'm fine," I whispered to him, then pulled Harper in my arms again as Kat relayed what had happened over the radio.

I must have zoned out a little while after Charlie had finished telling the story about Harper and me.

My attention was brought back to the group only when Ethan, sitting beside me, patted me gently on the knee while saying my name. "Abby…"

"Hmm?" I murmured.

His smile was sweet, but his eyes were guarded. "Are you alright?"

"Yes, I'm fine," I assured him as I rested my head on his shoulder and placed my hand on his leg.

It was a good thing we were so close to Thompson Falls because it was dark out. We were driving slower and more cautiously, but I was happy to see the lights from the guard towers off in the distance. I was more than ready to be done with this little trip.

"That's why Holden wanted you to leave," he whispered into my hair, almost as if to himself.

I nodded.

"Is that why Harper didn't want to come with us?" Seivor asked.

"She hasn't been out of the gates since," Charlie told them.

"I feel like a giant asshole now for trying to get her to come with us." Sylis sat back heavily against his seat, his head resting against the wall of the truck and his arms crossed over his chest. His furrowed brows pulled tightly together in a scowl that wrinkled his forehead in frustration.

"You didn't know," I brushed off his self-imposed guilt. "She's better now, anyway. She just doesn't like to talk about it or leave the gates if she doesn't have to."

We processed through the gate, and when we were back at the O, Ethan walked me to my room.

"I have some things to go over with the others, or I'd impose myself on you again." His hands wrapped around my face, and he pressed his lips to mine. "You need rest. You look tired."

"I wonder why."

He chuckled and kissed me again. "I'll see you in the morning."

I went inside and purged the memories with a good cry in the shower, then passed out.

CHAPTER ELEVEN

I woke early the next morning to go for a run. Feeling sluggish even though I was wide awake, I hoped the exercise would clear my head. It finally worked after the first lap around the town, when the sky lightened. With the surge of energy and the familiar, engaging burn in my muscles, I picked up speed and pushed myself until I was out of breath.

My legs were shaky and felt like jelly when I made it back to the O, and I had to hold on to the rail as I climbed the stairs, my muscles so fatigued. I all but stumbled through the door and held onto the walls for balance as I made my way into the restaurant.

"Morning," I panted and went to the sink for a glass of water.

"Good morning." Pike eyed me over his coffee mug.

"You're up early." I guzzled most of the water in my glass, letting the rest fall over the sides of my mouth, down my neck, and into my sweat-drenched shirt.

"You too."

"Couldn't sleep." I bent over the sink to catch my breath and then put my neck under the running water, letting it run over down the front of my collar to help cool me off.

"Me neither. I've been restless since we returned. Do you do this often?" He indicated my running attire.

"Every morning if I can. It keeps me sane." I turned to look at him, the tap still flowing.

"Yeah, you look totally sane." He smirked at me, and I laughed. "Maybe I'll join you sometime."

"Ha! I'll try to keep up." I shut the faucet off, grabbed a clean towel to pat-dry my face, and let the rest of the water run down my back.

"Not possible." He grinned. "But I'll keep pace with you."

"Keep pace with what?" Sylis rounded the corner, lifting his long leg over the top of the stool to sit next to Pike. Reaching over the counter to the shelf underneath, he grabbed a mug and poured himself what was left of the hot liquid from the table carafe.

"Help yourself." Pike shook his head at his friend.

"Thanks." Sylis cheered Pike's mug on the counter then took a big gulp from the steaming liquid. "So, what are we keeping pace with?"

"Running with Abby."

"Wouldn't that be more like *walking* with Abby?" He exaggerated the word, swaying his upper body as if walking slowly and lumbered.

"Rude." I swatted him with my wet towel as I passed him to go get cleaned up. It wouldn't be long before everyone else would be up and hungry.

Showered and dressed, I returned to the front where everyone was, just as I'd suspected. While Harper did the serving, Gigi was cooking breakfast for my new regular group. Along with Charlie, they all sat around what was quickly becoming "their" table. Except for Ethan, who was in the kitchen helping Gigi cut biscuits.

I smiled at him through the window, poured myself a cup of coffee, then took the pot to the table to fill everyone's mugs before making a fresh pot. Shortly after, Gigi and Ethan started cranking out plates full of food. I helped Harper carry out the breakfast trays the group had ordered while simultaneously removing the piles of empty dishes that had once been full of fruit, muffins, and toast.

I had just done another round of coffee refills and was headed back with a pitcher of water when my mom came in, Malik and Josh in tow.

"Hi." I pressed my cheek to hers in place of a hug.

"I'm happy you're home and safe," she whispered in my ear and kissed me on the cheek.

"Always." I moved around the table to fill glasses.

"Hello, Olivia." Sylis stood to greet her.

"Good morning." Her warmth faltered as she replied to him with a guarded smile. "Hendricks will be on his way in a few hours. He is being released and wanted me to let you all know he'll be over as soon as he is out of the care center." She scanned the room before landing on the service window, where Gigi and Ethan were.

My mother and Ethan locked eyes for the briefest of moments. His face froze in an unreadable mask, then he nodded at her once and flicked his eyes to me for a second. He turned away from the order window and went back to work, but not before I saw his jaw clench.

Neither of them had said anything about the other to me, but I knew my mom had been there with Kat that first night the VIGs came to Thompson Falls. I would bet anything she'd backed Kat with whatever she said that night. Mom probably had a few things to add herself.

She was opinionated when it came to the protection and safety of Thompson Falls, and was strict with the rules, expecting them to be followed. Not that the VIGs had done anything to break them. She was just leery of newcomers—always had been—and would often be the last person to warm up to and trust new people. So, I assumed her and Ethan's cold regard for each other was because of that first night, much like it was between Ethan and Kat—they were all three stubborn.

"He's better?" I followed her to a different table and asked once she sat down.

"Yes. Finally." She smiled up at me as I poured her a glass of water from the pitcher.

She was noticeably relaxed by the good news, which made me relax as a weight lifted. I was still holding on to some stress and anxiety over his well-being.

"I'll be glad to sleep in my bed again." She sighed.

"I bet he feels the same way."

"What's for breakfast?"

"Biscuits and gravy, rough-cut hash browns, and fresh fruit. There are also a few sweet potato muffins left from yesterday."

"I had one of those. I'll just have breakfast and some coffee if you wouldn't mind?"

"Of course not. I haven't eaten yet, so I'll sit with you."

"Perfect."

After breakfast, Ethan and the VIGs excused themselves. Mom and I helped Harper with the cleanup, and Gigi went back to canning. She had mounds of early spring vegetables from the garden she'd been working on since before we left for Glacier. Good thing the root cellar had been expanded earlier this year since it looked like Gigi was going to take full advantage of it. Although, I doubted Grady was too thrilled because he had been tasked to haul everything down there for her.

"I'm going to grab a few things from my room if you two don't mind finishing up." Mom wiped down the front counter once she was done with the tables and chairs.

"We're good," Harper hollered at her over the running water as she rinsed the last of the dishes.

I nodded in acknowledgement as I stacked and put away the clean plates and mugs.

"Thanks, girls." She tossed the rag she was using into the laundry bin under the sink.

Mom and Hendricks split their time staying between here and his place—separately and together, but mostly the latter. I didn't keep track or try to figure out their schedule—it had no rhyme or reason, but they were either here or there most of the time. If I needed to find them beyond that, I usually could at the care center.

After all the dishes were put away, Harper started cleaning the pans. I grabbed a clean washcloth to wipe down the stove and countertops, and got flour all over myself.

"You have a hard time staying clean in here, dontcha, honey?" Gigi came around the corner with a fresh tray of empty jars.

"I guess so." I tried to wipe myself off, which only made it worse somehow.

The flour that had only been on my shirt at my waist ended up smeared down the front of my pants, to my knees, all over my shoes, and up to the middle of my shirt. Puffs of white dust rose with each pat of my hand and eventually went up my nose.

Ah-choo!

"Oh, great." I sneezed several more times into my elbow, getting the powder in my mouth.

"I don't understand how you get anything done in here." Harper laughed at me and the mess I'd made. "It's astonishing that this is even a functioning facility at all," she jabbed and took the towel from me.

"She has a lot of help," Gigi joined in.

I tucked my face in my elbow for another sneeze. "You guys are funny." I sniffed. "We should do a comedy night." I sounded nasally, and my voice was thick like I was speaking with a mouth full of cotton.

"That's a great idea." Gigi perked up. "I bet people would pay big money to come and watch you stumble around in here." She whipped her towel over her shoulder to screw the lids on her now full jars.

She'd accomplished more in the last three minutes than I had in ten, and the only thing that was working fast for me right now was my running nose.

"Ha. Ha." I grabbed a tissue and held it up to my face while I fought back another sneeze.

"It would be quite amusing," Harper agreed as she finished what I had been doing and then moved on to put the pans away.

"You're like Lucy and Ethel, wrapped up in one." Gigi laughed to herself.

"Who?" Harper and I said in unison.

"Way before your time, girls," Sylis said on the other side of the wall through the serving counter, surprising us all. "I agree with Gigi, though. You are a train-wreck here in the kitchen."

"I am not!"

"Sure you are, hun." Gigi came over while Sylis laughed at my expense. "But we love you all the same." She reached up with her tiny, wrinkled hand and gave my face a tender pat, pinching my cheek. "Now, go get cleaned up. Some of us have real work to do in here." She turned me toward the door and walked me out.

"We all have our faults." Sylis leaned against the counter as he ate an apple. "Except for me, obviously."

"Didn't you just eat?" I sneered at him, ready for someone else to be under the microscope.

"At least you're good with a gun." He quirked a smile at me and ignored my jab, taking half the apple off with one bite.

"Oh, shut up." I stomped away toward my room. I knew they were right, or I might have actually been offended.

I cleaned up and changed in a shorter amount of time than it had taken for me to get dirty, which made me laugh at how true everything they had said was. Letting my door close behind me, I rounded the corner to walk down the hallway but walked in on my mother and Ethan, who seemed to be in a very heated conversation.

"You promised."

I thought I heard, "Don't push me, Olivia."

But then they both stopped and looked at me.

"What's going on?"

"Nothing," my mother lied while Ethan stood there silently.

"It doesn't look like nothing." I stared at them. "Is there something I should know about?"

"No," she said quickly before giving me a tight smile.

"Olivia was just reminding me of our conversation from our first night in Thompson Falls. Of the agreements we all made," Ethan answered with a tight jaw.

"Why?" I bristled. "They have done nothing wrong."

"Of course not." She sighed, walked over, and took my hands in hers. "It's protocol. All for the safety of the town. That's all." She smiled. "Nothing to worry about."

"I've never heard about this 'protocol' before." I emphasized the word, my voice laced with disbelief.

"I'm not surprised you didn't know, Abby. It's not part of your job. These are also special circumstances." She didn't like being questioned, especially by me. "I'll see you later," she said, abruptly ending the conversation. She gave me a quick peck on the cheek, then brushed past me in a hurry for the door.

"Mom?" I questioned.

"Love you!" She half-turned and waved as she stepped through the door, the echo of the bell chime the only indication of her ever being there.

"Are you going to tell me what that was about?" I faced Ethan.

"She was reminding me of what we talked about," he said evasively.

"Then why were you so angry?"

"I don't like being cornered in and held to bullshit. I also don't like my character and motives being questioned."

"She can be worse than anyone about the rules and safety of the town. I'm sorry she's being difficult, though."

"Don't apologize for her or her behavior. That's not on you. I understand she's being protective, but I don't agree with how certain things are being handled." He ran his hand through his hair, clearly flustered.

More than ever, I wanted to know what had been said that first night they came here. I wouldn't ask, though, and it wasn't my business. Not really.

"Whatever it is, it will work out. Besides, Hendricks is more reasonable than Kat or my mom, and he's the boss. I wouldn't worry about anything until you've talked to him." I stepped into his arms and wrapped mine around his waist.

"I just don't want any of it to come between us." He bent down and kissed me, then rested his forehead on mine. "I don't want to lose this."

"We'll figure it out," I assured him. If Hendricks stuck to his "no vampire" rule, it would make it more difficult to see Ethan regularly, but not impossible.

"I think you're more optimistic than I am." He ran his fingers down the side of my face when he pulled back.

"All I just heard was that we bring balance to each other."

He bent down and kissed me through his smile. "You bring me much more than balance, Abby. But I'll cling to your optimism."

"Good." I pushed my lips to his one more time, then grabbed his hand and pulled him with me back to the O, where the others were waiting.

"All cleaned up, Abby?" Sylis removed the triangle from the rack of cue balls on the table.

"Still stating the obvious, Sylis?"

"Always." He handed me a pool cue. "You're up, buttercup."

"Déjà vu," Sylis remarked before he rammed the cue into the white ball and sent it crashing into the triangle of colored balls on the opposite end of the pool table.

It was true, though. Waiting around for Hendricks while we all played various bar games had become quite the habit for our little group.

We'd been at this for a couple of hours again. Each of us had won two games, and we were playing the tiebreaker. I felt a surge of anxiety at the sound of the door chime ringing and looked at Ethan as the heavy door thudded shut. Resting the cue stick against the wall, I tucked myself into him. He wrapped his arms around me, pulled me closer to him, and kissed the top of my head.

The others in the room remained quiet, except for Charlie, who had flopped herself on a stool near me, crossed her arms, and griped, "Well, this sucks."

Sylis moved to stand next to her, threw his arm over her shoulders, and rocked her against him, nodding minutely in agreement with her. "Totally. If we get kicked out today, I'll probably never have this much free time and booze again."

"Don't act like it's just the booze you're worried about." Charlie elbowed him playfully.

"Yeah, you're right." He grabbed his glass.

The heavy footfalls grew louder and louder with each step, seeming to thrum to the beat of my heart until they came to an abrupt stop. The excited greetings from Malik and Josh confused me for only a moment before I recognized the other voices from the group that had just come in.

"Zach?" I straightened and turned to see the familiar face matching the voice I more than recognized. "Zach."

The anxiety drained from my body at the sight of him, for multiple reasons. I unwrapped myself from around Ethan but grabbed his hand and pulled him with me across the room.

Zach looked at Ethan and our joined hands, confused for a moment, then a bright smile spread across his face. "Hey there, gorgeous!" He reached out, picked me up, and spun me around the room, pulling my hand from Ethan's. "Damn, I missed you!"

"When did you get back?"

He squeezed me to him. "Late last night—or early this morning, really, depending on how you want to look at it," he said with a big goofy grin on his face, then smashed his lips against my forehead before he set me down.

"Why didn't you come and wake me?" I pushed against him a little so he would release me and went back to stand next to Ethan.

"We were so tired that we spent the night in the decon zone."

Zach—my very best friend—and the rest of his team had been out in the *Morgue* for over twelve weeks, doing a long run-up into old Canada. His team had volunteered for the mission, knowing they would be gone and out of contact with Thompson Falls for much of the time. Hendricks hadn't expected them for at least a couple more weeks, so neither had I, but I was beyond relieved to have him home.

"You look good." He reached out and brushed my chin.

"So do you. Maybe a little thinned out." I pulled on his shirt.

"Twelve weeks is a long time to be away from Gigi's cooking!"

"I can't even imagine." I turned slightly. "This is Ethan. Ethan, this is Zach."

"Nice to meet you." Zach's voice was flat and deep as he extended his hand out to Ethan.

"And you." Ethan stuck his hand out, his voice a little hard.

I wasn't sure how tall Zach was, but he barely had to look up to meet Ethan's eyes. Zach was almost as bulky with muscle as Ethan, and as they contacted each other, both their demeanors changed, tension rolling off each. Zach's arm strained from the tight handshake, the tendons in his wrist popping out, muscles bunching and veins bulging with the extended grip. Ethan, for his part, didn't look uncomfortable at all.

"Welcome home."

"Thanks."

They released their handshake but continued to size the other up. Which made no sense to me since they weren't a threat to each other. But whatever.

"We heard about Honor. I'm glad you're okay." Zach turned his attention to me. "It's too bad about Evan, Clay, and Dave. That's a lot to lose in one run, Abs. How are you doing?" He reached out, ran his thumb down my cheek, and held my chin again.

"I'm okay." I batted his hand away. "We're having the memorial tomorrow. It's nice that you're home for it."

"Yeah." He nodded. "That's good timing. Not that I want to go to any of those things ever again, but I'm glad we're here." He then changed the subject. "Hendricks was getting ready to come over. We saw him as we headed this way. He said he'd only be a few minutes." He looked around the room as he relayed the message, then flicked his eyes up to Ethan for a second. "No offense, but what's with all the vamps?" He lifted an eyebrow.

"I thought you said you heard what happened in Honor?" I smacked him. "And don't be rude."

He guarded himself as if I could really hurt him. "I did. But I didn't expect you all to be hanging out together."

"Stop."

"Just looking out for my girl, is all." He winked at me. "I'm sure your friend Ethan here knows what it's like to want to protect someone they love."

"Zach!"

"It's alright." Ethan wrapped his arm around my shoulders and pulled me to him, kissing the top of my head. "I know exactly what that's like."

Zach glared. He had always been protective of me, ever since we were little. He was only a few years older than me, but he took on a lot at a young age, especially after his family and my father had been killed. From that day on, he'd appointed himself my protector. He was nine when my family had met his. They had been alone for over a month after losing the group they were with. It hadn't taken long for Zach to get comfortable with my family—he'd said he had always felt like a burden to his parents and the third wheel to his sister. My parents recognized this, and so my father had taken it upon himself to teach Zach survival and fighting skills. We'd all traveled together for over a year when we were attacked. Zach's parents and his sister were killed, along with my dad, who'd sacrificed himself so that the three of us had a chance to escape. Zach always said he felt like it was his responsibility to make sure I was safe after that, and he had.

When I'd started training for the vanguard, he was not happy. He'd tried everything to get me to quit or kicked out, and when that hadn't worked, he'd spent months pestering Hendricks to put me on his team or let him switch over to mine. Hendricks had finally had enough and told him that if he didn't like it, then he could leave, which shut Zach up about it but hadn't made it any better for him. When he'd finally accepted that he wouldn't beat the system or change my mind, he trained and worked with me, teaching me everything my dad had taught him.

Training was something I'd already been going through as part of the program to join the vanguard, but it hadn't been enough for Zach, so he kept pushing me to master the skills.

"At least you'll know what you're doing, and I'll have done everything I could to protect you," he'd said once.

Zach now smirked then looked down at me. "We have a lot of catching up to do." He booped my nose, ducked down to kiss my cheek, then went over to Malik and Josh. Picking up Charlie, he spun her around the same way he had me, before being introduced to the other vampires.

"Zach seems like a nice guy." Ethan smirked.

"I'm glad you noticed. You two are going to have to try harder to get along." I walked back over to the pool cue I'd set against the wall, then lined up and took my shot.

"You better do what the boss says." Pike leaned back in his stool with a mischievous look on his face. "Or you won't get to do any more construction."

"Pike," Ethan clipped.

But I just snorted.

"What about construction?" Charlie flopped back on her stool next to Sylis after Zach was done messing with her.

"Just that Abby likes to renovate," Sylis told her seriously.

Charlie wrinkled her face, looked at me, then back at him. "What? No, she doesn't. Why would you say that?"

Pike and Sylis laughed. Seivor hid his smile. Ethan huffed under his breath in irritation, and I scowled at them for involving her in their little inside joke.

"Wait, is this a euphemism for something?" She glared at Sylis, then wrinkled her nose. "Gross. Actually, I don't get it. Whatever." She swiveled her stool and hollered at Zach for something.

They let the topic drop after that.

A short while later, Hendricks, Kat, and Brooks walked in through the front door. We stopped what we were doing and moved to the bigger room in the restaurant, where they were standing in wait for us.

Ethan patted my hip where he'd rested his hand. The four of them walked to the front to exchange a few words with Hendricks. They moved as a group to the far side of the room, opposite everyone else, and stood stoically behind Hendricks as he whistled to get everyone's attention.

"Whoever doesn't need to be here, now is the time to leave." He looked pointedly at Charlie.

"Yeah, yeah. I'm going." She wafted her hand in the air before heading to the door, along with most of the guys who had come in with Zach. They had just gotten back and weren't on duty, and since they weren't required to be here, most seemed inclined to take the break they deserved—except for Zach, who showed no signs of leaving.

"The rest of you, grab a seat," Hendricks told us as the room filled with team leaders, vanguard, and key members of the town.

I grabbed a chair at one of the tables as a low hum filled the space. Zach sat down next to me, then rested his arm around the spine of my seat and tipped back to balance his weight on two legs of his chair. I'd seen him fall doing this, twice. I hoped he had his balance this time since there were a lot of extra people here to laugh at him today.

"Are you trying for three?" I raised my brows at him.

"Don't jinx me." He rocked.

"Just don't take me down with you."

"I'll protect you."

I rolled my eyes as he wobbled, then he laughed at himself after he'd regained control. When the room was full and quiet as they waited for Hendricks to begin, he looked up at me.

"Abby?" He tipped his head toward the rooms.

"They're all gone." I nodded, referring to the Honor group.

I'd asked Harper to distract them for the afternoon while we used the O for the meeting. I knew some of what she was going to do with them and wasn't worried they'd be back soon. Understanding the need for them to be gone, she'd planned a long afternoon to show them around Thompson Falls. She'd take them to Vickie's clothing store, for sure, so they knew where it was since they still had nothing. Then she'd give them a tour of the school in case they stayed and show them some housing options from the list of available properties. For lunch, she was excited to take them to the bowling alley, where they made candy and had loads of arcade games. It would be fun for the kids. After that, they would go to the food pantry, so they knew where to shop for their own groceries rather than loading up on the stock from the O's fridge. I didn't expect them back for at least several hours, which would be plenty of time for Hendricks to have his meeting.

"For starters..." Hendricks looked at the VIGs—or more specifically, Ethan. "I need some clarification from you guys. I've been told some things and want to hear it from you before we continue."

Ethan inclined his head but said nothing. Instead, he waited for Hendricks to continue, as impassively as when Zach had introduced himself.

"Can you explain to me and the rest of us how you ended up in Honor the same day we were there? Or are we to believe it was just a strange coincidence?"

"We knew there was going to be an attack," he said assertively. "But it was a coincidence to meet you there."

I was as stunned by this as everyone else. All the heads in the room turned to stare at Ethan and the VIGs in shock.

Zach sat up, his chair clapping loudly against the floor, and blurted out, "Whoa! What?"

Hendricks snapped his head in our direction. "Do you need to leave?" he bit out.

Zach put his hands up and eased back in his seat without saying another word. The look on Hendricks's face made it clear it was not the time for questions and that this was not a conversation.

If the room hadn't been quiet before, it certainly was now. I didn't think anyone was even breathing.

"So, you all knew the Honor facility was going to be attacked?" Hendricks turned back to the VIGs and sneered at Ethan.

Ethan's jaw clenched, and his eyes narrowed. "No. We didn't know that Honor, specifically, was going to be attacked. We knew there was going to be an attack, but we didn't know where or when," Ethan seethed, defending his team and their integrity once again. "We've been tracking similar incidents for a while now. We were in the area when we saw your group traveling in the direction we were already headed," he finished, gaining some control over his voice.

"You followed us, then?"

"We were already tracking in that direction. So, we continued and intercepted once we knew you were in trouble. We would not have interfered with your group unless there was a reason to. As unlikely as it may seem, it was a coincidence that we were both in the same place at the same time. The only difference being that you didn't know what you were walking into and we suspected what we would find."

Hendricks crossed his arms over his chest, waited a few seconds, then proceeded to ask his next question. "And what exactly is happening? What are you tracking that led you there?" His voice no longer held suspicion.

"We don't know who or what is attacking these towns, and as far as we can tell, they are doing it at random. All we know is that they have been moving west from across the Eastern Seaboard." Ethan sounded less than willing to be giving out the information. The Vampire Increment Guard was notoriously secretive about their agency. I wasn't surprised that Ethan wasn't offering to spill all they knew.

"How many times has this happened?"

"As of a week ago, twenty-eight," Ethan stated.

"Twenty-eight?!" someone yelped.

The entire room collectively gasped in horror. Some leaned closer as if to get a better look at the new information. Others' faces had gone from shock to anger, to concern.

"The recent attacks over the last several months—or more specifically, the last several weeks—have increased significantly, which has raised the number that high," Ethan continued. "We believe the first incidents happened between eight to twelve years ago."

"Eight to twelve years? You've been tracking this for that long?" Hendricks's voice was edging toward accusation again.

"No," Ethan asserted, his voice dropping. "Through our investigation into the recent events, we've been able to profile the attacks. This has led us to believe it may have been going on for years, the first potentially being twelve years ago. And eight years ago is very likely. My team has been following the trail for close to three years now."

"How many in the last month?"

"Four last week, including Honor," Ethan told him. "Eight total in the last month."

The room fell quiet as if all breathing had paused again, then a sliver of whispers swirled around as secrets and speculations were traded.

"There have been no survivors, human or vampire. Not until Honor," Ethan said over the undertone of the room.

"How are you tracking them across the country but are unable to know or warn what town they are hitting next?" Brooks asked with pure curiosity.

"The earliest attacks weren't on large groups; they were small. They grew in size over the years, and with it, the evidence. We've been one step behind them since we first picked up the trail. Whoever is behind this is smart, and they know our tactics." Ethan explained, "We are under the assumption that the trace evidence they leave for us now is as intentional as it is when it goes cold."

"Do you have a best guess what we're dealing with?" Hendricks asked.

"We have two," Ethan said hesitantly. "A *spyder* group using the dead as weapons."

The room grumbled at the first theory. *Spyders* were a nuisance we all hated to deal with as it was. The thought of them using *kooks* as a weapon was something we had considered and even seen in the past on a small scale. If the VIGs first theory was correct and they were using them to this degree, it would be abhorrent, even for them.

"The second?" Hendricks coaxed when Ethan didn't continue.

"Another mutation in the virus." Ethan was straight-faced.

This was unimaginable. Another mutation in the virus was the worst news we could have received. I could speak for everyone by saying we would have taken a hundred *spyder* groups using hordes of *kooks* as weapons over a mutation in the virus. Hands down, no questions asked. The last thing any of us wanted to hear was that the *kooks* and *evos* we fought were still evolving and getting smarter. That they weren't just going after the weak and frail or distracted anymore but were now taking on entire towns and colonies with intention, and succeeding.

It was easy to tell the *kooks* we had dealt with in Honor had been *evos*. I'd just assumed it was some sort of dumb luck in large quantity that had allowed them to take out an entire town. It had never even crossed my mind that they were working of their own volition.

"This makes things infinitely more difficult." Hendricks took off his hat and rubbed his forehead. "Have you ever engaged them before Honor?"

"No, not exactly." Ethan shifted his stance. He didn't seem as unwilling to share as he had been a few minutes ago. "We've come across ones left behind. Alone, they are functioning on autopilot, as we're used to. When there are two or more, they seem better coordinated than the regular *evos* but nothing formidable. We haven't come into contact with more than five at the same time, but observing the five work together was what led to the mutation theory. It appears they may have developed a type of hive mind."

"A hive has a queen," I noted.

All the heads in the room turned my way.

Ethan's eyes locked with mine. "For it to function properly, yes," he said resolutely.

The room all but erupted in alarmed chatter.

"Now, wait. Wait just a damn minute and calm down!" Hendricks patted down the air with his palms, his hat still in hand. "You said you've never actually seen whatever it is we're dealing with, right?" he asked Ethan over the drum of voices that still echoed around the room.

"Correct. We have not," Ethan confirmed, which quieted the room more than Hendricks's demand. "We've only seen what they are capable of by what they leave behind. Which is usually nothing more than mangled bodies and debris."

"Alright, let's cut the shit then and admit that it is some form of *kook*. Smarter, stronger, faster, and operating under a collective consciousness." Hendricks rammed his hat back on his head and dropped his hand to his hips. "And that it's not a group of *spyders*."

"Probably," Ethan relented.

"Most likely," Hendricks challenged Ethan to confirm his conclusion. When he didn't, Hendricks turned to the group that had quieted into a sea of expectant faces waiting for orders. "The VIGs are overly cautious. If it were *spyders*, they would have had contact. Those groups of people are not smart enough to evade VIGs for twelve years. It's a mutation in the virus. Wrap your head around it," he ordered us.

He was right, and we all knew it. Looking at Ethan and the others, they knew it too, but Hendricks was right—they wouldn't guess. They needed evidence.

When the room grew loud with conversation and Hendricks didn't seem inclined to stop it since he was lost in thought himself, Kat stepped forward. "Let's take a break. We can regroup in a couple of hours after everyone has had time to think."

Yeah. That's a good idea. Are you fellas okay to stick around for a while yet?" Hendricks looked back to the VIGs.

Ethan flicked his eyes in my direction. "Yes. We'll stay as long as we're welcome."

"Great," Hendricks said. "We'll come back in a couple of hours." He looked to Kat and Brooks, then jerked his head toward the front door.

Zach stretched back in his chair and clasped his hands behind his head. "Well, it looks like we have a couple of hours. What do you want to do?"

I watched Ethan and the VIGs as they huddled once Hendricks had left. They were talking animatedly. I was relieved that Hendricks hadn't seemed too eager to ask them to leave. Asking them to stay gave me hope that their presence wasn't the problem he had dreamed it up to be. Did we need to open our gates and let tourist vamps in? No, but Ethan's team and other VIGs... What was the harm in that?

"Abby..." Zach sing-songed my name. "Hello... Earth to Abby." He waved his hand in front of my face.

"What?" I grabbed it and pulled it down from my view. "I wasn't paying attention."

"I noticed."

"What did you say?" I vaguely recalled something about going somewhere.

"I said, what should *we* do? Since we have a couple of hours."

"Oh, I don't know. Maybe we should just hang out here."

"Why? You never want to hang out here."

"Yeah, well, we have to be back in a little while anyway, so..."

He leaned into me then, pressing his nose against my temple as he whispered conspiratorially in my ear, "Are you afraid to leave them alone in your hotel?"

"What? No!" I looked at him like he was insane. "Not at all." I scowled.

The vampires had heard Zach's comment, my suspicion confirmed by Ethan's hardened gaze and Sylis's laughter.

"Actually, you know what? You're probably right, Zach." I turned my head slightly toward Zach but kept my eyes on the vampires. "One of them is a lush, and I probably wouldn't have any booze left if I left them here alone."

Sylis dropped his mouth open and pressed his hand to his chest in mock horror as the others laughed.

"What the hell are you talking about?" Zach was confused.

I snorted. "Nothing. Give me a few minutes, okay?" I patted his leg and walked over to Ethan before he could argue with me.

Sylis had a sly smile on his face as I approached. "We aren't going to take anything that doesn't belong to us."

"But you'll drink all the booze?"

"Nobody's perfect, Abby."

"That's not what you said this morning."

"See! That's exactly my point. But I think I'll go tell Zach that the property is safe." He raised his brow and looked at Zach.

"Sylis," Ethan chided.

"Ethan," Sylis taunted as he backed up a few steps, then spun on the balls of his feet and meandered toward the back of the room, where Zach still sat at the table.

"It's hard to believe he is the oldest of us all," Pike huffed.

He and Seivor walked to the bar, where Malik and Josh were animated in conversation.

"Looks like you're stuck with me a while longer." I tugged lightly on the front of Ethan's shirt.

"I can think of a lot of places I'd like to be stuck with you," he whispered in my ear, his cool breath spilling down my neck and giving me chills. He pressed a light kiss just below my temple.

"So subtle."

He chuckled. "They're coming back in to get us. Hopefully, our invitation extends."

Hendricks walked in and hollered at him. "Ethan, would you and your team come with us?"

"Of course." He winked at me.

Then they left, and I was without him for the first time in a week.

Chapter Twelve

The afternoon hours passed quickly, and before I knew it, it was time to head back to the O.

Zach and I had left after Hendricks and the VIGs had gone to have their private meeting. There'd been no point in staying after that, and Zach was right—I never wanted to hang out there if I didn't have to. The only reason I'd been this last week was that the VIGs were basically trapped there. If not, we would have gone anywhere else, at least some of the time.

It hadn't taken long for us to decide what to do, and soon we were at Zach's shop/garage/upstairs apartment, so he could check in on his "baby".

Zach did auto-mechanic work when he wasn't out on rotation with the guard. He was part of the team that kept the vanguard fleet up and running, also partially responsible for all the vehicles' exterior protection upgrades. All the crazy ideas people came up with, including his own outrageous concepts, Zach and several of the others put into action. They were constantly trying new ways to fortify the vehicles or turn them into better weapons. Zach was particularly proud of the "grinder"—the bus that had the blades welded to the wheels' discs.

He also spent a lot of his time tinkering with what I referred to as "the love of his life". His treasure was a 1970 Boss 302 Mustang named Sally, which was in reference to some ancient song, apparently. It was a fully loaded, tricked-out muscle car with one-of-a-kind accessories. The paint was a blood orange that looked 3D in the sunlight and conversely had black racing stripes so dark it didn't reflect the sunshine at all. The windows were tinted the darkest shade possible, and you could barely see out of them during the day and not at all at night.

Over the years, he'd had several hobby cars, but this one was like finding a pot of gold at the end of a double rainbow. He. Loved. This. Car. Personally, I didn't get it. It was a nice-looking ride, but it was just a car. It was as old as dirt, so I got the excitement there, though. Finding it in as good of a condition as it was in was something of a miracle. Even so, it was still *just* a car.

Not to Zach. He treated this thing better than he treated himself half the time, always washing and waxing, polishing, or buffing inside and out. He constantly and meticulously checked all the working parts—lubing and oiling, filling or replacing fluids, rotating tires, measuring brakes, and adjusting the alignment. The list was endless. It was weird how much energy he put into this hunk of metal, and even more so that he never got bored or tired of it. For me, it'd become a sort of a meditative space where I could let my mind wander while I helped clean it. There was something mesmeric about the process that I found relaxing. However, I would never seek this distraction on my own, but it was something he loved, and I loved him, so ... I indulged.

He took the cover off, and once he was satisfied that the car was sufficiently wiped down, greased up, and ready for the road, he insisted we take it out for a spin to "get the juices flowing after sitting for so long". So, we drove around town for a while, back and forth across the main street, up and down the side streets. Eventually, we went to the O for our meeting, where Sally had its very own parking spot—that wasn't a parking spot at all. He just pulled it on the grass and under the shade of a big sycamore tree.

We had been back for about fifteen minutes when Hendricks came in through the front door of the O alone. He didn't have to announce himself; we had all been waiting for his arrival. By the conversations I'd heard around me the general tenor of the room, everyone here was ready to fight and defend our home—and any others—from this new threat. While Hendricks paced and drummed his pointer finger against his lips, everyone took their seats and waited for his final command on the subject.

He came to a stop in the middle of the room to face us, placing his hands behind his back. "Based on the new information we received from the VIGs today, we've asked them to stay." He squared his shoulders and straightened his spine as he looked over us.

I was so relieved with the news that my shoulders dropped and relaxed.

"What do you mean, stay?" Zach all but sneered out the question.

"I mean" —Hendricks snarled back at him with a "sit down and shut up" look— "that since we don't know what we are up against while they have been tracking it for some time now and have a better idea of what we're dealing with, we can use their help. I also think we can help them, and they agreed. So, we've asked them to stay, and they accepted."

"In town?" Zach's problem was he didn't know when to shut up sometimes.

"Yes, in town." Hendricks's words rolled out of his mouth heavy with annoyance.

"Here at the O?"

"Yes, Zach, in town, here at the O. Do you have any other stupid-ass questions, or may I continue?"

"Sorry," he balked.

I snorted once at the exchange but literally bit my lips together when Hendricks looked at me. My eyes widened, and I cringed a little shrug as a "sorry" gesture. Sometimes, it was hard being the boss's daughter.

He squinted his eyes at me, looked back at the room, and continued. "As I was saying, they will stick around with us for a while. Maybe indefinitely. I have no idea. I know it goes against everything I've ever said about Thompson Falls being vamp-free, but from the way it sounds and the pattern this thing is traveling, it could end up here and on our front step next. I would rather all of us be safe than sorry. Even if that means breaking my own damn rules and accepting help from vampires." He scratched over his hair like he wasn't completely sure of his decision either. Or maybe he was but was conflicted about how it would affect the town and its people.

"Does this mean I have to keep the O closed?" I asked.

It was a valid question. I didn't think he'd keep us closed and them in hiding, but I'd learned a long time ago to never assume anything with Hendricks.

"No. I've asked them to stay, and that means they are our guests and will have the same freedoms as anyone else. I will make an announcement tomorrow night at the tribute social so the town will know of their presence."

"Where are they now?"

"They left. They had some business or arrangements that needed to be made on their end. I don't know, but when they are done, they'll come back here and bunk at the O as agreed."

"And what about what they eat?" Zach was practically fuming.

I hadn't known until today that he had such an aversion to vampires, and I wondered when it had started. I'd never known him to be intolerant of anyone but *spyders*. Everyone else, he always gave the benefit of the doubt.

"They won't get their nutritional requirements from anyone in town. That was made very clear," Hendricks stressed.

"What about the people who don't like vampires? Or the ones who came here because this was a vampire-free town? What are we supposed to tell them?" someone asked.

"Send them to me," Hendricks said. "This is my town, and it was my rule. If I want to change it, I'm going to change it. Especially if it means keeping this town and its people safe. I don't like it any more than you do, but until we know what is going on out there" —he jabbed his finger toward the main gate— "we will do whatever we have to, to make sure it doesn't affect us in here."

There were a few more questions but not many. Hendricks was the boss, so even if they didn't agree, there wasn't much to be done about it.

"You're comfortable with this?" Zach's voice was still hard and clearly annoyed after the meeting.

We were alone in the O, which shouldn't have been strange after being cooped up here for the last week, but it was since the place was empty. Neither of us had said anything to the other while everyone had filtered out.

"Yes, absolutely."

"I don't like it." He stood from his chair to pace back and forth in front of me. "It doesn't feel right."

"What are you talking about?"

"It's weird, Abby!"

"Why? They have been nothing but helpful since we met them."

"They're vampires!"

"Yeah, and if it wasn't for those *vampires*, you might be attending a memorial gathering for more than just Evan, Clay, and Dave," I hollered back at him. He was being a jerk, and I was sick of it. "Both Hendricks and I could have easily been added to that list, Zach. They saved us." More than once. They'd helped us. They are good people.

"And for that, I'm forever grateful." His voice softened.

"You don't sound very grateful."

"I just don't understand why we have to host them. They can help and stay out of town, do what the rest of us do when we travel—make camp. It makes more sense for them to watch our borders than be inside these walls, anyway."

"They're not animals!" I was really offended by him and his words now. "They deserve respect, and I will not listen to you bad-mouth and bash them. You don't know them—I do. You're judging them on a bullshit opinion and prejudice I didn't know you had. You're being rude, and I don't appreciate it. You need to give them a chance."

"I don't like it." He smashed his finger against my mouth when I started to argue with him more. "But for you, I will try."

I swatted his hand away from my face. "Better than nothing."

"No promises, though."

"You're such a stubborn ass."

"Well, that's high praise coming from you." He brought me in for a one-armed hug and kissed the top of my head. "Now, what should we do for the rest of the day?"

We spent the rest of the day and the next afternoon together, like we always had in the past. Catching each other up on what we'd missed, I told him the news from around our small town, all the gossip, and my recent trip to Glacier with the VIGs. He was not impressed.

Zach told me how they'd fared on their long trip, the downfalls and successes, and if he would ever do it again. Other than the lack of sleep and warm showers, he said he would, even though it was dangerous at times. Though he often felt homesick, it was also freeing. Seeing more of the world than he had ever before, he seemed excited about the possibility of future adventures. He shared with me all the things he'd seen as they traveled—good and bad, the landscape, the abandoned towns and cities, the abundance of animals in areas that were too cold for *kooks*. That made me a little jealous and reminded me of the bears Ethan and I had watched on the river. I pulled myself back from the memory, though, so I could focus on Zach and his stories.

He described a town called Revelstoke and how similar it was to Thompson Falls. They'd built a wall around their compound too, and it was next to a river, tucked against mountains and trees. It was the place that had made him miss home the most, and he was glad when they'd left because it meant he was that much closer to coming back.

He shared how creepy it had been to pass by all the underwater cities that were once filled with scores of people. He likened most of Vancouver, BC and its surrounding cities to how Seattle was—flooded and covered with water, the tops of the highest buildings surrounded by sea. Zach assured me it was just as unsettling when the buildings there came to life at dark, as they did here. The solar panels still funneled energy through the walls, rooms, and hallways. When the sun set, the windows would light up around the tops and somehow still power a few below. The reflection on calm water was a ghost of what it used to be.

We changed the subject after that, and when we both got hungry, we went back to the O for lunch. After, he helped me with the work I had neglected. We picked from the garden, cleaned, and chopped vegetables. I did laundry, picked up what little mess was in the restaurant, and checked the rooms, delivering fresh towels and toiletries to each of the guests. When we finished, it was time for dinner, so I warmed up some leftover quinoa and made tacos. We ate on the back patio and enjoyed the quiet night. Zach had a couple of beers, and I enjoyed a glass of iced tea.

When it was late enough to justify going to bed, I walked him out, locked up, and went to my room. The Honor group had long ago come back and were in their rooms, and if the VIGs returned, they each had a key to use on the side doors.

The following day was much the same. Before I knew it, the morning and afternoon had slipped by and it was time for the tribute social to begin. Zach and I went together down main street, where the gathering would be held. We easily fell back into a rhythm we were both used to and comfortable with since we'd been doing it for so many years.

Thompson Falls' tradition was to have a gathering when we lost someone. Sometimes they were big, a lot of times they were small, but if anyone had been lost out in the *Morgue*, it became a town affair and everyone was welcome. We honored their story and spent the evening remembering them while trying not to focus on their death. It was sad, of course, and there were tears and shared sorrow, but we celebrated the life they'd lived, the time we'd spent with them, and loved on the ones they left behind.

Tables and chairs were set up, lights strung along with garland and flowers. There was more food than anyone could eat or drink, plus treats and cake. We'd quietly piped music around the area, but that eventually gave way to those who played an instrument, so we always made space for dancing. A stage was set up, where people could share their stories with everyone and as a place for the band to play. It was more akin to a wedding reception or birthday party than a memorial service, which was exactly the point.

Evan and Dave had been the youngest of the three men who passed away. Evan had been in his early twenties, and Dave had just finished high school the year before. Neither man had a significant other to speak of, but they'd still each had both of their parents, who were in the front row receiving people's condolences.

Clay had been the oldest of the three. He'd had a wife and a young daughter his unfortunate death had left behind. His wife was younger than him, maybe only a few years older than me. They'd met here in Thompson Falls. It hadn't been long after they dated that they were married and were expecting their first child. His wife had a small but consistent group huddled around her, each taking turns playing with the clueless and happy three-year-old girl.

We snaked through the crowd of people, first over to Clay's wife to give her our condolences and offer help if she needed any, then we moved on to Evan's and Dave's parents to do the same. I couldn't do much as far as helping them—it was really just a gesture—but there was always a cooked meal at the O, and I offered to deliver to them if that was better.

We left the receiving line, giving others a chance to speak to the families, and found my mother and Hendricks off to the side of the stage. Hendricks usually said a few words first before he turned it over to the people. Just like when they'd come to this town, he wanted their family and friends to know he cared and that they weren't just another cog in the machine. He felt their loss—we all did—and it was important to him they knew that. That they knew their loved one had been seen and would be missed.

"Hi, Zach." My mother beamed when we came into sight.

He jogged the short distance between them, bent down, and swooped her up into a big hug.

"How are you, my boy? I'm so glad you're home!"

"Thanks, Ma. I'm good." He sat her back down on her feet, but not before she planted a kiss on his cheek.

Zach had been calling my mother "Ma" for years. So long, in fact, that it would be weird to hear him call her anything else. After we'd lost everyone and it was just us three, she'd become the only parent he had. From that day on, he was her son.

"I'm sorry I haven't been able to see you until now," she said to him apologetically. "But the haul your group brought back has kept us so busy at the care center I've barely had time to eat. Well done!" she cheered.

"I'm glad it was worth it. Abby's been keeping me company." He bumped into me.

"Well, we're glad to have you back. We missed you around here." She reached up and patted his cheek again. "You need to eat, though."

"That's all I've been doing!" He slapped his stomach. "Every chance she gets, she's shoving food down my throat."

"Oh, good." She winked at me.

"Alright. I'm going to get this thing started." Hendricks pulled in a deep breath, squared his shoulders, and bounced up the stairs.

"We'll catch up more later," my mom whispered to Zach, then turned around to face the stage as Hendricks cleared his throat and called for attention.

He didn't say too much in opening, just let everyone know they would have a chance to speak when he was finished, and thanked everyone for coming as they found a seat and stopped talking to listen.

"It's never easy to lose someone you love or care about, but it always seems worse when it happens outside of these gates," he began. Pausing, Hendricks rubbed his hand across his forehead, and when he spoke again, his pitch was off and a little rough. "Clay was a good friend of mine, and I knew him for a long time. We met each other out on the road, along with some of his buddies." He nodded toward the group of men standing at the back, and they raised their bottles in recognition. "They followed me here that day and stayed as some of the first members of this town. Clay became a close confidant and a sounding board for me. He was always so level-headed and a damn good soldier. I know he'd want you and that little girl of his taken care of, Rachael. So, if you ever need anything—anything at all—you come to me."

The young woman, who held her sleeping child against her like she needed something to hang on to, mustered up what I could only describe as a sad smile. Her eyes were red-rimmed from crying. She was surrounded by good people, who would help her. Her daughter would grow up and rely on their stories as the only way to know her father.

"Evan was a bright boy with a lot of potential and one helluva right hook." Hendricks looked over to Evan's parents, and the crowd chuckled at the inside joke. "Funny too. That boy had a wicked sense of humor, and he drew people in with his easy-going nature. It made the nights out there that much more bearable when he was around."

I had never worked with Evan before the other night, but I knew of him from some of the others' stories. There was a workout facility we used to train and exercise in, and in one of the bigger rooms was a large mat he'd used as a boxing ring. I'd been told Evan was always ready to spar with anyone who wanted to go a few rounds, willing to teach those who wanted to learn the skill.

"Dave." Hendricks paused. "Dave was a great kid, taken from this world far too soon. Even though he was only with the vanguard for a short time, he more than pulled his weight, and you should be proud of your boy. He was brave and strong, and will truly be missed," Hendricks said to his parents. "You should all be proud. Not one of these guys can be replaced, and they sure as hell won't be forgotten." His voice boomed out over the crowd. "All of us will be forever grateful for their service and the sacrifice they made for this town. I don't take it lightly, and neither should any of you. The world isn't fair, and it certainly isn't just. But Clay, Evan, and Dave tried to make it a little better. Although we might not see their impact now, generations to come undoubtedly will." Hendricks grabbed the bottle he had and raised it high in the air.

The crowd followed, saluting and toasting our fallen friends.

Then, he asked for a moment of silence before he ruefully changed the subject. "I need to switch gears here for a minute." He set his bottle down on the podium and rolled his shoulders. "I normally wouldn't make announcements at a tribute ceremony, and I am deeply sorry that I have to, but it has everything to do with why we are here in the first place. As most of you now know, the Honor camp and all of its people—except for the survivors we have here—were lost," he announced, then waited for those in the crowd who didn't know to get over their surprise and quiet back down. "It would seem there is a new threat, a new mutated version of the dead."

He stressed the next part as the crowd unsettled. “Now, Thompson Falls is still the safest place to be, but these new breeds are smarter and stronger. Like nothing we’ve ever seen before. So, we need to be ready; we need to take precautions. We met some new allies in Honor. They helped us escape, and if they hadn’t been there, we would have without a doubt lost more of our people. Maybe every single one of us.”

He paused and scanned the entire crowd. “I’ve asked these new allies for their help. They saved our lives that day and have proven repeatedly that they are trustworthy. They know the enemy better than anyone else out there. They know their habits, what to look for. They’ve been tracking them for longer than we’ve even known they existed. As this town’s leader, I promised to keep Thompson Falls and all its residents safe as best as I am able. Safe by whatever means necessary, and I intend to keep that promise by accepting help from an outside source. I know some of you may not agree with my decision, and that’s fine, but I am asking you to keep an open mind.”

By now, the crowd was restless and the chatter was a low hum around the area. People were guessing and speculating on what Hendricks was talking about, and I could tell that a few of the town blowhards had figured it out as they puffed their chests and tensed with anger.

Hendricks, ignoring the crowd and the growing agitation, looked over to where my mother, Zach, and I were standing, and jerked his head in a “come here” motion.

I looked behind me to see who he was seeking in the shadows. Ethan and the rest of the VIGs—the ones I knew and a few more that I didn’t—had been standing behind us the entire time. They didn’t react, just walked up the stairs to stand next to Hendricks center stage.

The few town guffs who had gotten jumpy did not disappoint. As soon as the VIGs were on the stage, they spouted off at the mouth about everything, from this being a set-up or a trap to becoming dinner on a plate. In addition, a long list of insults, and species and racial slurs were spewed from some of the brave mouthpieces who didn't know how to control their noise holes.

None of the vampires, nor Hendricks, reacted to the barracking. Instead, they all stood stoically, waiting for them to quiet and calm down.

Hendricks's presence was commanding, and as he stood stone-faced and looked at the people in his town, it didn't take long for them to notice the displeasure under his powerful gaze. When the crowd fell silent, he remained still and continued to castigate them with his disapproval.

"As I said before, some of you may not agree with my decision, but I ask you to keep an open mind." His voice boomed over the speakers. "These are VIG members. They are not tourist vamps here for a warm meal. They are soldiers, fighting in this war as much as we are. They are why I am standing in front of you today."

"They started this war!" someone yelled.

"What about the children?" yipped a hysterical woman. I couldn't help the eye roll at her ignorance. She'd obviously been watching too many ancient movies.

"This town is supposed to be vamp-free!" another cried.

"Enough!" Hendricks barked and slammed his fist down. "This is not a debate, and I am not asking for your permission! Or your opinions! They are our guests, here to help us. Better yet, they are here to continue to help us! They've agreed to follow all the same rules this town requires you to abide by *and* more!" He banged his fist on the podium again. "Each of us, human and vampire, started this war all those years ago." He pointedly looked at the man who'd shouted out from the crowd. Hendricks must have been channeling his mother when he said this, because these were words she had used on him. "The children have never been safer than they are now." He looked down at the dramatic woman.

She shrunk down in her seat and ducked her face, turning beet-red.

"And this town is what I say it is." He looked at the other man. "*I* built Thompson Falls. *I* say who is and isn't welcome here. My responsibility to this town is to keep you all safe, and I will do that however I choose and by *any* means necessary. Every one of you is welcome here, but if you don't like how things run here, there's the door." He jabbed his finger toward the main gate.

Not a single person moved or said another word while they waited for Hendricks to speak again. It was so still I could hear the small flames crackle under the warming trays keeping the food hot at the buffet. Or maybe it was just the leaves rustling in the trees or the static of the speakers combined, but either way, the gathering was soundless otherwise.

"Now, if there are any reasonable questions, I will answer them."

"Where will they be staying?" An elderly man from the front stood up with the help of a cane.

"They will stay at the O," Hendricks deflated at the easy question. His shoulders dropped a little, and he relaxed his arms and clasped them behind him.

"Are they accepting visitors?" the gentleman asked.

Hendricks pinched his lips in a turned-down smirk, then turned to the VIGs for an answer.

A couple of them looked at each other, obviously confused, and then nodded to Hendricks.

"I guess they are, yes," he told the man.

"Oh, good!" The old man smiled. "Very good. I ran with some vampires when I was a young buck. Back when they were still a big secret to the world. Do I ever have some stories for you." He sat down again, nearly as giddy as a kid with candy.

Some chuckled at the old man's delight, and I couldn't help but laugh too. Actually, I was a little curious myself now and didn't want to miss that conversation.

"What will they eat?" someone asked, no accusation in their tone, only concern.

"They will eat food at the O or any of the other places in town, the same as all of you. Their other sustenance needs will be provided to them by their own donors outside of Thompson Falls."

That one answer noticeably relaxed the entire crowd, and the palpable tension dissipated. People weren't necessarily scared of vampires—they were just terrified of being consumed, in any form or fashion. There were only a few questions after that, simple curiosities and extended appreciation for their help, confirming that their presence mostly wasn't an issue. The town just wanted to know they were safe.

Hendricks introduced the VIGs to the group, each by name, a few of them saying a few words of thanks for the hospitality. Sylis, of course, had the most to say and encouraged the elderly man to seek him out. He seemed nearly as excited to hear the man's stories. Hendricks took over after that and closed the topic, thanking the crowd for their understanding and then directing their attention back to the memorial service.

The VIGs all left the stage. No longer hiding, they weaved through the crowd, stopped to talk to people, or moved to the side to observe. Some people avoided them while others waited their turn to shake their hands. All things considered, it was the best reception to their presence we could have hoped for.

Family and friends of the fallen took turns sharing their memories, and before I knew it, the band was assembling to play. People mingled, went through the buffet line to load up plates of food, and generally enjoyed this celebration of life.

My mother, Zach, and I had just sat down to eat when Hendricks pulled out a seat next to my mom and sat down with his own plate of food.

"That went pretty well," I said to him sincerely.

He grunted as he picked up an ear of corn and crunched through the juicy kernels. "I suppose," he mumbled through a full mouth.

"Everyone will get along fine," my mom said as though she were trying to convince herself. She was pushing around a chunk of potato from her potato salad. "I don't think we have anything to worry about."

"We definitely have nothing to worry about, Mom. You and Kat need to chill."

"You can never be too cautious, Abby." She lifted her brow at me.

"I set Ethan's new people up in rooms already, so you don't need to worry about that." Hendricks dropped his cob on his plate and wiped his hands on a napkin.

"Oh, okay. Thanks." I'd figured I'd have to do that later, but I was glad he had so they didn't have to wait for me.

"I'm going to assign some guards to the O for a couple of days too."

"What? Why?"

"Not because I don't trust them." He flared his eyes at me. "Because you're opening up again with them there. I don't expect any issues, and we all know they're more than capable of taking care of themselves. I just want to drive home that I'm not fucking around. I won't tolerate any problems, and having vanguard at the O will further get that message across."

"Oh, okay. I won't be a brat about it, then."

Zach snorted. "Yeah, right. You're always a brat."

I elbowed him in response.

"I'll walk you home," Zach told me after I'd said goodnight to my mom and Hendricks.

The gathering had wound down. After eating, dancing, and visiting people for the last several hours, I was wiped out and ready for bed.

"Maybe I should stay at the O for a while," he said when we were away from the crowd.

"Why?" I garbled through a yawn.

"Why do you think?" He gave me a side glance, then threw his arm around my shoulders and pulled me into him, pretending to bite my ear again.

"Will you stop?" I tried to shove him away, which worked about as well as pushing against a wall.

"I'm serious, Abby." He wrapped his arm around me tighter. "I agree with some of the others, and I'm worried about you."

"Worried about what? I told you they have been nothing but helpful and kind. Which is more than I can say about you right now."

"I believe you. I can still worry. Besides..." He paused. "Don't get mad. But you don't exactly see people objectively."

"What the hell does that mean?" I pushed away from him, and this time, he let me go.

We stopped in the middle of the street, next to the O.

"I said *don't* get mad."

"Zach."

He held up his hand to me. "You give people the benefit of the doubt and often ignore it when they take advantage."

"No, I don't." My defense was as weak as my voice.

"Yeah. Holden's been a real peach to you lately. I heard he came in the other night, belligerent again, to yell at you."

"That doesn't count." I started walking.

"It never does."

I sneered at him over my shoulder. "Where did all this prejudice come from?"

"I don't know." He sounded confused. "I suppose when I got back and they were in our town. You know what goes on out there; you've heard the stories."

"You can't hold an entire species accountable for a handful of backsliders. Humans are worse. I told you earlier I wasn't going to listen to you bad-mouthing them. You don't know them; your opinion doesn't count."

He stopped me again and put himself in front of me. "I don't want to fight with you. I just worry about you, that's all."

"Well, don't. Not about this, and I will not repeat myself, Zach. Stop with the shit-talking. I don't want to hear it."

"Fine," he whined and threw his arm over my shoulders again. "You're so defensive."

"You have nothing to worry about."

"Hmph." His throaty disapproval rumbled in my ear. "Where's *Walter*?"

"Seriously?" I pulled back to look up at him.

He raised his brows at me expectantly. "I didn't *say* anything."

"You're ridiculous. In my nightstand. Like always."

"Good." He turned us toward the O again and didn't say anything else until we were standing at the front door. "I'm going back to help them tear down the stage. Unless you want me to stay?"

"Good. Night. Zach."

He jogged away, and I pushed through the heavy entrance door with a ding from the entrance bell.

"Abby!" Sylis cheered when he saw me.

I didn't know what I'd been expecting, but seeing him and Pike kicked back at the bar by themselves with three bottles of booze in front of them was not it.

"You're going to owe me more chores."

"I will help with the cooking anytime." Pike lifted his glass at me. "I'm rather good at it, and I enjoy it."

"And I'm pretty to look at." Sylis winked at me.

"Don't forget to shut off the lights when you're done." I left them to their drinking. Rounding the corner to my room, I found Ethan casually leaning against the wall by my door. "Hello, stranger." My cheeks lifted.

He wrapped his hands around my face and kissed me. "Hi."

I unlocked the door and pulled him in with me. "From what I gather, Hendricks gave you all an open-ended invitation to stay." I kicked off my shoes, clicked on a lamp, and flopped on the couch.

He sat next to me and kicked his shoes off under the coffee table. "He did." Lifting my hand to his mouth, he kissed my knuckles. "And we plan to take advantage of it, which is why I have extra VIGs here and another team on their way. We had a lot to talk about, actually. You were right—he is more reasonable than Kat and your mother. He's a stubborn hardass, for sure, but I understand why this town's been so successful with him at the helm."

"Compliments make him uncomfortable, so if you're going to say nice things to him, let me know so I can be there."

He hummed and pulled me into his lap. "Do compliments make you uncomfortable?"

I squinted my eyes at him. "Sometimes, and it depends on what kind."

"I overheard your conversation with Zach as he walked you home. Thank you for speaking up for us."

"You don't have to thank me. Zach's being a jackass, and I don't know why. He's not like that. Not normally, anyway. I'm embarrassed you overheard him."

"*You* may not understand why he's acting how he is, but I do. I agree he is a jackass, though."

"You have to be nice too." I tapped his chest with my finger, punctuating each word with a gentle nudge.

"I don't care one way or the other about his opinion. Neither would the others, so don't be embarrassed on our account. However" —he lowered his mouth to mine— "I enjoyed hearing you defend us so passionately." He swept his tongue into my mouth, then smiled against my lips as he teased. "So feisty," he mumbled. "You know what else I enjoyed tonight?"

"What?" I wrapped my arms around his neck.

"This dress." He slid his hand up my thigh, under the flowy white cotton dress I was wearing.

It was one of my favorites—long but lightweight, with a wide split up the middle to mid-thigh. A deep V went down the front and back, and it had sleeves that opened at my shoulders and tied at my wrists.

"It was hard to concentrate on anything but getting my hands on you and up this flimsy thing." His voice was low, heady, and his words were unrushed.

He pressed his palm flat on my hip and circled around to grab my backside. Hooking his fingers around my panties, he slid them off a lot easier than he should have been able to considering I was sitting on his lap.

"I pictured all the things I could do to you while you were wearing it." He pulled at my bottom lip before sucking us back together as he trailed his fingers up my leg after tossing my lacy undergarment to the floor.

Ethan snaked his hand under the bottom of my dress again and up my inner thigh, pushing my leg open, spreading me as I let out a whimper. He drew circles with the tips of his fingers, inching higher and higher. My pulse quickened as liquid heat pooled at my core, and the higher he went, the more I ached for his touch.

"I kept thinking about how soft and warm you are," Ethan whispered along my lips, his hot breath like a punctuation of his remark.

When his hand met the juncture between my thighs, he languorously swept his thumb up the middle of me. The wide pad of his thumb gently pushed into my heated skin, slipping between my folds as it moved up to circle around my sensitive nub. My moan was a heavy exhale of warm breath that he matched with a deep hum before bending down to dart his searing tongue into my mouth. He tasted like fire; it was so hot.

"I imagined how wet you would be."

I exhaled noisily when he slipped his first two fingers into my core and curled them around to pull against me. As he moved, he kept swirling his thumb over the sensitive top, caressing me attentively, coaxing me steadily.

Releasing my mouth, he dropped his forehead to mine. "You're so fucking wet."

He groaned, low and husky, his breaths resonant with each exhale, coupling with my pitched sighs. I fisted his shirt and bit my bottom lip, wanting his mouth back on me but too entranced to move.

When his focused attention sped up, so did my sounded panting. I writhed against him as he pushed me to orgasm with his fingers, and when his fervent touch tipped me over the edge, he jerked his hips against me with a groan at my release.

"So beautiful." He peppered my face with kisses, moaning with me into my mouth and against my heated flesh, riding out my release. Easing me down, he stroked me gently, slowly, until I shuddered from his touch.

I sat up and crushed his mouth to mine, fisting his hair as he circled his arms around me in a tight hold. Ethan stood us up from the couch without breaking our connection, and I wrapped my legs around his waist as he walked. I'd expected the soft, pillowy mattress, but he set me down on my kitchen table instead. The cool, hard wood wasn't unpleasant, and the edge gave me something to hold on to. Ethan leaned into me, kissing me until I was flat against the surface. He broke our contact when I was prone and on display, to look down at me and further tease me with his words.

"I kept imagining all the ways I could take you over a table." His face was hungry and his voice rough as he undid his pants, pushing up my dress. When his pants were split open, he dropped to his knees to claim me with his mouth instead of releasing his hard length from where it was straining in his jeans.

I was still overwhelmed and sensitive from before, and the sudden capture of my tender flesh between his lips made me cry out. There were no teasing or languid movements. He seized me and focused all his attention on my bundle of nerves, sucking, flicking, and pulling me until I surged against him again. It only took moments, and in the midst of another climax, he stood and thrust himself into me, finishing me off with burgeoning movements.

Ethan threw himself into me repeatedly and without hesitation, hard and fast, pulling me by my hips as he slammed into me with perfect timing. The muscles at my core were still spasming and tight, and I had barely recovered when he orgasmed. His groans were loud and guttural, and when he came, his voice cracked with the strain.

When he finished, he kept himself locked against me as we panted, then he pulled me up to him, crushing my chest to his. "I fucking love this dress," he growled and sealed his mouth to mine again.

Chapter Thirteen

I woke up with him next to me for the second time, and it felt ... normal. We showered, got dressed, and readied ourselves for the day together.

It was too easy. Too "this is how it should be". Waking up with him wrapped around me felt natural. It made my heart sing, and I knew I wasn't falling for him hard—I was nose-diving.

Showers were a lot more fun now too. After the couch and once prone on the table, Ethan flipped me over and pounded into me again, the wood legs screeching across the floor. From my small kitchenette, he took me to bed where we shared another long, satisfying night together before eventually passing out in each other's arms, completely spent.

He'd warned me about how possessive and insatiable he was, but experiencing it was so much more than I'd thought. I'd never been with someone who had the stamina he did, and his ability to keep going even after a climax was new.

Vampires were so different from humans in many ways. I was truly enjoying *this*, though. I'd always had a voracious sexual appetite; having met my match and then exceeded libido was fantastic.

My muscles and other parts were sore when I woke, and I knew I'd be reminded of him all day just by walking. We'd lathered up and were slipping around each other before rinsing off, touching and playing with the soap on our bodies.

I was under the spray, smoothing out the shampoo from my hair, when I opened my eyes to find him leaning against the wall, staring.

"Are you watching me?"

"You're the most beautiful thing I've ever seen. Of course I'm watching you."

My cheeks reddened instantly. "You're making me blush."

He stepped under the spray, pulled me to him, and crushed his mouth to mine.

"But am I making you wet?" he purred as his hand slipped between my legs from behind.

My answer was to pull him tighter to me by circling my arms around his neck. He took us out of the spray, and when he lifted me to him, I wrapped my legs around his waist. He eased himself into me gradually. I was swollen from our busy night and the water was thinning my silk, so he took his time sinking into me, which was tortuously enjoyable in its own right.

He went slowly, holding me with one arm around my waist and the other braced against the wall, next to my shoulders. It was nearly overwhelming. I was so tender, and I couldn't control my voice. He rolled himself into me languidly, mindful of my sensitivity as he found a rousing pace.

"You're so fucking tight," he groaned and curled into me, stroking himself slowly with my body.

My response was to claw at him with a moan and tighten my fingers at the root of his hair. The intensity was quickly pushing me to a peak, the aching pleasure and snug grip around him all-consuming. I knew I wouldn't last long, and I didn't.

"Ethan," I whimpered and clenched my limbs at my release. My core pulsed hard around him, pulling him with me as rhythmic spasms milked his hardness.

"Oh ... *shit*..." he groaned and exhaled with a loud sigh.

He tightened his hold on me, resting his face against mine as his whole body bucked, but he held his steady pace instead of throwing himself into me with heavy thrusts, like he normally did. When he stopped moving, both our bodies jerked and shuddered. We wrapped our arms around each other and he held me tight, kissing and licking up my neck before locking his mouth with mine.

When he removed himself from me, he did so gently, then set me down. My feet were flat on the tile as he kept me against him and never once released my mouth.

"Mmm, that's the best shower I've ever had," he mumbled.

"Ever?"

"Ever." He crushed himself to me again.

"Me too," I told him when he released me for air.

When we left my room, he went to change his clothes. I went to the restaurant and busied myself to prepare for the day.

With the O officially reopened to the public and the VIGs no longer a secret, it was busier than ever. Breakfast was steady all morning. Nearly every table was full, the orders were backed up, and some people waiting to be seated just ended up leaving because it was taking so long. Even with almost full staff, we were having a hard time keeping up. I didn't doubt that they missed Gigi's cooking, but most of the diners were only here hoping to catch a glimpse of the vampires. Their craning necks every time someone came through the door or was seated were proof of that.

When breakfast was over, it slowed down significantly. Either word that the VIGs weren't at the O had gotten out, or people just weren't interested in our regular simple lunch of veggie sandwiches and chips.

Now that the vampires were officially here on business, the relaxing morning and afternoon hours of day drinking and bar games had been quickly put to a halt. Hendricks had wasted no time involving the VIGs in his business. I fully expected them to be occupied and gone all day, and every day following. Meaning, my days would go back to normal as well. I was only a foot soldier, so they didn't involve me with the day-to-day and decision-making, and as such, I would be here. Which was *totally* fine with me.

When the afternoon staff switched out with the morning crew, I grabbed a sack lunch and got some fresh air. I didn't realize that I had missed my routine until I was in the middle of doing it again, but I was happy for the break and took full advantage. The lunch menu would be the only thing served for the next several hours and they wouldn't need my help, so I took a long, leisurely walk along the trails behind the O.

I found a soft patch of grass on a small slope facing the wall, with a sliver view of the water at the base of a mountain on the opposite side of the river. The sky was clear and the temperature warm, but a small breeze ruffled my hair. I took refuge in the shade of a cottonless cottonwood tree and ate my lunch. I didn't know how long I was there, but when a small patch of clouds cut across the sky, I figured I had better go.

"There you are! Where have you been?" Zach ranted as soon as I was through the door. He was the only one in the O, sitting at the bar.

"Down at the trails. Why?" I walked past him to put my brown lunch sack in the compost bin.

"I've been waiting here for an hour. The VIGs got word that another settlement was attacked."

"What? Where?"

"I don't know." He shrugged. "Hendricks has all the team leaders and the vampires in a meeting right now. We're all supposed to meet up in an hour."

"In an hour? Then why are you so agitated?" He'd been acting like we were running late because of me.

His brow furrowed. "It's nothing. I'm just—"

"In a bad mood?"

"I didn't sleep well last night."

"Well, maybe you should have a nap then and not a beer." I reached across the counter and took his empty bottle, then grabbed two glasses and filled them with ice water, sliding one to him.

"Hey, Abs?"

"Yeah?" I pulled the dirty tub out and set it on the counter to take it to the dishwasher.

"Can we talk later, after the meeting?"

"Talk now. We have time." I looked at the clock.

"No. Not here."

"What's wrong with here? We're alone. Mostly." Which was super weird considering how busy it had been earlier, and I hadn't counted the staff in the back.

"No. We can stop by my place after the meeting."

"If this has anything to do with the VIGs or your misplaced concern, I don't want to hear it."

His face dropped in exasperation. "No, it doesn't. Not everything is about them."

At the high school, Zach and I fell in line as we all filed into the gym, and everyone was seated. Hendricks didn't waste time and told us what they knew.

Henry Stampede Park in old Idaho was a small island housing around a hundred people. Nothing in or around the area would make living there comfortable or secure, so its attraction suited only those content with camp-style and rugged outdoorsy living. The only way on or off the island was by boat since the higher water level had swallowed up its connection to the mainland. This was thought of as their defensive perimeter, and no other precautions had been taken aside from personal gear.

The park was a favored and frequented pit-stop for tourist vamps. The settlers there welcomed them, and the open invitation was always accepted. At any given time, you could find at least a handful of vampires on the island. The vampires' needs were taken care of, and in turn, they would bring the islanders various things: food, clothing, weapons, medicine, etcetera. It was a decent arrangement for both groups.

So the attack on this little town was startling and disturbing news in multiple ways. One, there was nothing left and no survivors again.

"When you say nothing..." someone asked.

"We mean nothing." Hendricks's voice was vacant. "There were no bodies—human, vampire, or *kook*. Nothing."

"Except for blood," Pike said, and the room stayed quiet. "There was a lot of blood."

Two, this was another vampire-protected outpost, and it had been overrun.

"How did they do it?" Another question from the bleachers.

"We don't know."

Three, an attack on Henry Stampede Park meant that our new enemy was capable of swimming long distances or clever enough to use and operate machinery. Either way, not good.

"How was it discovered?" Malik asked. "I mean, if there were no survivors and no bodies."

"A citizen came across it and reported it. From there, a team was dispatched and confirmed their findings to VIG headquarters. The information was then relayed to us," Ethan answered.

"Citizen?" Zach's voice was tight as he prompted for further explanation. If this was him trying to be nice, he'd need to work on it.

Ethan's jaw tensed at the sneer in his voice.

"Tourist vamp. Isn't that what you call them?" Sylis mocked the slang term and Zach at the same time. Zach had made this a game for him, and I knew he was going to be relentless.

Zach glared at Sylis, then clamped his jaw tight. Sylis caught my eye, winked, then looked back out at the bleachers. I held my chuckle in and bit my lips to keep my smile in check. I didn't have any hope my reaction had gone unnoticed, though.

Pike didn't look at me, but he smirked. They obviously took about as much offense to the slang term "tourist vamps" as I did to "spyders". We each had our dregs of society.

Hendricks continued with the briefing and informed us that he, the team leaders, and the VIGs had agreed that further weapons training for the vanguard and any townspeople who wanted to learn would be a good idea. Their years of experience and skill with a blade would be a valuable and practical technique to learn. With virtually no skill, someone could defend themselves easier than they could with a gun, but with training, they could potentially save their life or someone else's. Swordsmanship was also a quieter defensive method and meant less upkeep. Bullets out in the *Morgue* were hard to find, so when you ran out, you were out. Melee weapons, on the other hand, required no additional resources to use. Training would start first thing in the morning for the vanguard and would be open to the public after.

Hendricks had officially put the town on high alert after hearing about Henry Stampede Park. The perimeter watch along the wall was increased, and teams were sent out to posts further around the town. They informed the townspeople of the new threat and security measures. All non-essential jobs and businesses would temporarily stop and close. There was no need to build homes or cut hair while on high alert. Some regular *Morgue* runs would stop too, and they had reassigned those teams to the town. Any teams that could be reached were called back, and all vanguard were on duty until further notice.

After the meeting had ended and our team leaders had given us our assignments, Zach and I were walking to the Safe to get in our gear.

"Where are you assigned?"

"East outpost on the exit road," he answered. "You?"

"West."

"Figures." We both knew Hendricks still separated us when he could.

Near the Safe's entrance, we found Hendricks and Ethan facing off against each other in what appeared to be a heated debate while the rest of the VIGs and some vanguard stood off to the side, backing their leader and standing on opposite sides of an imaginary line. They'd only been working together for a day and were already at each other's throats, so this was going well.

"What's going on?" Zach's voice dropped and dipped into anger.

Holden, resting his weight on one hip with his arms crossed, looked over at us with a toothpick hanging out of his mouth. "Abby's boyfriend is trying to tell the commander how to do his job."

"He's not her damn boyfriend," Zach clipped, then clenched his jaw.

"Coulda fooled me." Holden's smirk spread wide into a full smile. He straightened and bounced once as he tugged on the waist of his pants, ready to pull at the line of bait Zach had bitten on.

I ignored them both and kept walking.

"Abby." Sylis darted to my side and stopped me from going any further.

"What's the problem?"

"Just a minor disagreement. Nothing to worry about." He grinned, then looked over my shoulder. "Hi there, Zach. How are ya?"

"Better ten minutes ago." Zach's voice was low and rude.

I turned on him. "You're not even trying to try."

He didn't say anything. Instead, his giant blue eyes bored into mine, and if I didn't know him like the back of my hand, the intensity of his gaze might have frightened me. Zach was a big guy, tall and thick. His neck was as wide as my thigh, and when he was angry, his veins bulged on corded muscle. If I were anyone else and he was anyone else, the look he gave me would have had me backing away. His normally sky-blue eyes had darkened like deep seawater, and his brows pulled down tight over the lids.

"This *is* me trying. It's harder than it looks, and I still don't like it," he growled.

"And water is wet," Sylis smarted off, making a goofy face to Pike and Seivor standing nearby.

"Excuse me?" Zach snapped his attention from me to Sylis.

"Calm down, friend. I'm just joking around."

"Well, I don't think you're funny," Zach snarled. "And I'm not your damn friend. In fact, I don't even like you."

"Get a load of Captain Obvious here."

"I'll show you Captain Obvious—"

"Alright. That's enough." I put a hand on his chest.

"What does that even mean?" Sylis needled him, completely ignoring my attempt to defuse the situation.

"Put your people wherever the hell you want. Just don't tell me where to put mine in the future," Hendricks said loud enough to hear him over Zach and Sylis's bickering.

"Great," Ethan clapped back.

"Zach, is there a problem here?" Hendricks yelled.

Ethan appeared next to me before Hendricks had finished the question, and suddenly, I was in the middle of three *very* large males. Two of which couldn't stand each other, and one who was hell-bent on making it worse by taunting and telling bad wisecracks.

"No, sir." Sylis gave Hendricks a thumbs-up. "Just a misunderstanding. Zach doesn't get my jokes; he told me I wasn't funny. Which actually hurt my feelings."

"How 'bout we save it for the enemy then, shall we?"

"For sure," Sylis agreed with Hendricks. "What do you say, Zach? Can we be friends?"

"Abby, let's get you in your gear so we can go," Ethan said to me, ignoring Sylis and Zach.

"She isn't going anywhere with you!" Zach roared.

"It isn't up to you."

"I told you to stay away from her."

"Excuse me?" My mouth fell open. But no one was paying attention to me. I would have had better luck getting answers as an invisible wallflower.

"That isn't up to you either," Ethan seethed.

"I told you to back off!" Zach took a step toward Ethan around me, and then just like that, I was out from in the middle of them and next to Sylis, who'd tucked me into his side and put his arm around my shoulders.

"So, how are you?" he asked conversationally.

"Confused and growing angrier by the second."

"What the hell is going on?" Hendricks shouted at them. Which was exactly what I wanted to know.

"I don't want this bloodsucker around, Abby."

"Zach!" I yelled, but I may as well have been talking to a rusty bucket.

"Are you being serious right now, Zach?" Hendricks put his hands on his hips.

"I don't trust him!"

"This has nothing to do with trust." Ethan's voice took on a snide tone.

"Oh, for fuck's sake! We don't have time for a cockfight. Zach, pull your head out of your ass, get in your gear, and get to work. Abby, you too," Hendricks hollered.

"I'm going with Abby," Zach said to Hendricks.

"God damn it, Zach. No, you're not!" Hendricks shouted at him.

"Well, she ain't—"

"Commander!" Kat belted. "We have an emergency. Burke Canyon is under attack!" The urgency in her voice shut Zach up mid-sentence and grabbed all our attention.

The warning bell sounded, and we all ran to get ready.

"They radioed a few minutes ago," Kat explained loudly over the sound of the bell. "A group of *kooks* triggered their defensive perimeters on both ends of ID-4. They killed off some of them, and called St. Marie's and us for help before the connection went dead. They said they were being overrun."

"What about Wallace?" Hendricks asked as we rounded the corner. Wallace was a small town next to the even smaller town they were talking about.

"Don't know. They didn't have time to say, but I swear I heard explosions before the line went dead," Kat told him in between panting breaths.

Kat was a little overweight. Not from lack of exercise—we all had plenty of that—but from a medical condition I wasn't privy to. She had a small wet spot on her back, and her short spiky black hair was sparkling in the sun from sweat, but she kept up her pace and finished telling Hendricks what she knew.

At the Safe, other members of the vanguard filtered in. The alarm was a signal to all vanguard to report to the main gate, get suited up, and wait for their team leader for further instructions. Because we were all being assigned to perimeter duty, the room filled up fast since we were already on our way.

"What rigs are ready to go?" Hendricks asked both Zach and Jeff since they were responsible for keeping our vehicles running.

"Everything but the bus." Jeff zipped up his leather jumpsuit. "It hasn't been cleaned."

"We need something to transport the survivors. What about the other one?"

"We can't rely on it." Zach was tying his boots and yanking on the laces so hard I was sure they would snap.

I ignored him and got dressed. When I had my cut-proof underwear on, I pulled my jumpsuit up to my waist, then sat down on the bench and shoved my feet into socks. Lauren, my teammate, offered to braid my hair and as she did, I laced up my boots. When she finished, I zipped up my suit, and added pieces of protective gear and weapons to my ensemble.

"When you're dressed and armed, find your team leaders. We're taking whatever vehicles are lined up first to go," Hendricks told us as we walked toward the exit door. "Sylis!"

"Yo." Sylis poked his head around the outside of the door.

"You want to drive that bus again?"

"The meat grinder? Hell yeah!"

"It's a total mess!" Jeff warned.

"We need something, so it'll have to do."

"It's cool. I've smelt worse. I've bunked with Pike." Sylis hooted at himself then dodged whatever was flung at him, clanking loudly against the building.

"Rude." Sylis disappeared around the corner again, and I heard a scuffle.

"Let's move, people!" Hendricks yelled over his shoulder.

"Damn," I cursed quietly as my hand landed on the space that *Walter* should be occupying.

"What's wrong?" Ethan asked from behind me.

I jumped and squealed. "You're not supposed to do that," I complained, but all he did was chuckle at me. "I just don't have *Walter* with me."

"Walter?"

"My gun."

"The one you pointed at me?"

"The very same." I smiled. "He's my good luck charm. I always take him with me to the *Morgue*."

"You don't need luck. You have me."

"Does that mean I can strap you to my hip?"

His answer was a deep rumble in his chest and a lingering gaze at my lips.

"Let's go!" Zach growled when he walked past us.

"Piss off, Zach. I don't want to hear another word out of your mouth unless it's an explanation."

He ignored me and stomped away.

"I don't suppose you'll tell me what that was all about?" I asked Ethan as we walked out of the building.

"I think you should talk to Zach." He gave me a small smile, and that was the end of that.

I found Brooks and my team standing next to a big beefy truck and helped them load it. We threw the extra gear, weapons, and emergency supplies in the back. Each team did the same. It didn't take long before we were ready to go, less than fifteen minutes since the alarm had sounded.

Hendricks stood with a megaphone on top of his GILA and waited for everyone to quiet down after he'd squealed it to get everyone's attention. "My group and the VIGs are taking the lead. The rest of you fall in line. Our focus is the old mine. They went there to take cover, and that's where we will look. We don't know what we are up against or what we are walking into, so we get in and out. If there is no sign of life, we blow up what's left, leave, and figure it out from there. We will not lose more people today! Do I make myself clear?"

Everyone nodded and shouted a sound of agreement in unison.

"The St. Marie's guard is coming in from the opposite direction, so keep your eyes peeled for uniforms, but if it looks dead or something close to it, shoot it. We are not taking chances today. Keep your masks close. We will use mercury and fire to clear the town. Stay with your team, your vehicle, and keep on the road. I don't want anybody going off-grid here. At the first sign of danger, we clear out, and I need you all to stay in a smooth, straight line as we do it. No heroics today, people." He jumped down from the GILA and landed on the ground with a thud. "Let's move out."

Burke Canyon had been an ancient mining town way back in the day and then a ghost town until the outbreak. The people who'd moved there blocked up the streets going in and out, and put up a barrier around the tiny space. They lived in parts of the mine that hadn't collapsed and around the small town.

Only about fifty or so people lived there, no vampires at last count. The group was reclusive. They traded with us and were nice enough, but they weren't quick to trust. Hendricks had worked hard to gain their confidence, though.

The two-lane highway ran straight through their territory, and although we could have gone around them when we traveled, it'd been easier to make them allies so we could pass safely through. Plus, they were our closest neighbors and weren't nearly as prepared as we were. Hendricks thought that since we were so close, they were somehow his responsibility.

From Thompson Falls, it was just over a hundred miles away and if the roads were clear, we could usually get there in about an hour's time. Once we were out of the gates, it didn't take us long to pick up speed as we headed for the mountain. The road was mostly straight, so it was easy to travel fast.

The closer we came to the town, the more smoke we could see off in the distance, and it wasn't clear if it was from Wallace, the town next to them, or if it was Burke on fire. Whichever it was, hopefully it would burn out fast. A forest fire was not something that could be controlled or put out, and it would also draw unwanted attention—from both the living and the dead. We already had enough to deal with, so fingers crossed it wouldn't spread.

The road barrier to the town was still in place and could only be opened from the inside. When we came to a stop, Sylis and Pike left the bus and jumped the fence. I thought they meant to open the gate, but they were only on the other side for a few quick seconds before coming back over. They ran halfway back to the bus when they stopped in the middle of the street and threw two bombs each before they hurried back onto the bus.

The first two bombs didn't blow up the gate and released mercury smoke instead. The second two exploded moments later, the small concussive force from the blasts rumbling the ground and gently rattling the truck we sat in.

The metal frame of the barrier gate had blown open on one side, and when the dust settled, it gave us our first view of Burke. Inside was a small horde of *kooks*—maybe fifteen—in a mass of bubbling and smoking flesh. The mercury bombs had ravaged them just as they were meant to and had dissolved them from being a threat. Past them, further in town, was another small group making their way toward the gate, presumably drawn in by the commotion. If we waited, the mercury would take care of them too. Then we could move in, finish them, and focus on rescue. The only danger remaining would be the mercury, but even that was slim since it was busy attacking the dead and would become inert—as it was designed to—once the tissue it was attached to became necrotic.

When the second group of *kooks* stumbled into the slurry of the first, Hendricks radioed for Jimmy's team to pull around and clear a path for the rest of us. I watched nervously as Zach drove past the line, in the only truck that had a plow in our group, and inched into the fire and smoke. Past the blown-apart gate, the plow lowered and scraped loudly against the pavement until it hit the heap and pushed the bloody mass of not-all-the-way-dead bodies out of the way. The truck steadily moved the mess until it was off the main road and onto the side of the street. Inside the truck, the team members had put their masks on and were firing out of the windows.

After what felt like forever, we finally drove forward. Dawsen was in the driver's seat, but when it was time, he positioned himself out of the side window and released control of the pedals and steering wheel to me. From my middle seat position, I drove the truck behind the bus until we came to a stop, everyone else in the truck shooting at the dead through their windows.

We continued forward, past the mess of dead at the gate, until we were in front of the old mine the townspeople used as their main shelter. We parked close together and as near to the door as we could get, making a large half-circle with our vehicles. As we exited the cabs of our trucks, we did the same with our bodies. Hendricks's team and the VIGs would go into the mine to search and rescue any Burke residents while the rest of us stayed to cover.

The doors to the mine were locked, and the electronic keypad next to the handle had been destroyed. The surveillance cameras hanging around the area were also knocked down and broken, or damaged and hanging at odd angles.

There was no other way in. The entrance had no windows, only a single door and a large rolling door with a security barrier down over it. Hendricks pounded on the entrance and yelled, then waited for a response. The sound of his fist beating against the metal was so hollow you could almost hear the echo as it bounced around inside, down through the hallway, and into the shaft. When it was clear there would be no response, they broke in, trying to bust the lock with a tire iron, and when that didn't work, they used a large crowbar. Pike jammed the flattened end in between the door and frame. With Ethan's help, he bent the door open enough for Sylis to grab and bend the top back so Seivor could place a grenade between the two sections. We all took cover before they let go of their hold on the door and weapon. When we were at a safe distance, Seivor pulled the pin, and all four VIGs blurred away to take cover too.

The explosion didn't open the door, but it dislodged it from the frame enough that it pried and bent open, which allowed Seivor to slip inside, unlatch the steel slide lock, and kick it open the rest of the way.

"We'll be right back." Hendricks switched on his headlamp.

When the group disappeared into the dark entry, Dawsen, Brooks, and Blaise took up a three-pronged position in front of the door and aimed inside, just in case something that wasn't alive tried to come out. Pike stayed back with our group and positioned himself behind the three men, in such a way that he could defend them from either the front or the back if need be. The rest of us assumed our previous positions and faced the town with our guns at the ready.

It was quiet in Burke Canyon—eerie, even. It didn't feel natural. Like all of nature and the trees had been threatened into silence. No wind or air movement of any kind blew through branches or shuffled the leaves. Birds—if there were any—were mute, as were any other living things in the forest. Even the creek seemed dimmed of sound as if trying to pass by unnoticed. The muffled vibration from the motors on our vehicles was loud in comparison—that, and our breaths.

We kept watch for a few minutes. Zach moved around from his position to stand next to me. We didn't say anything to each other—it wasn't the time for that—but when we were out in the *Morgue* together, he always made his way next to me on the field when he could. Which was exactly why Hendricks didn't let us work together.

Normally I didn't mind, but today it bugged me. I didn't react to his nearness, though, and ignored my petty desire to move away from him. Which also annoyed me because this distracted me from focusing on my job as I should be.

I forced myself to compartmentalize that situation—whatever it was—and what we were doing now. There was no room for error out here, so my curiosity would have to wait to be unpacked later, when it was safe for us to talk about it.

A loud explosion helped—followed in rapid succession by two more— and my focal point became the location the sound had come from. Everyone around me tensed and raised their weapons a little higher. The blasts weren't close to us—they were off in the distance toward Wallace—but the detonations confirmed what we hadn't been sure about before. We weren't alone.

"What the hell was that?" Hendricks yelled over the radio.

"Not us. It sounded like it came from Wallace," Brooks replied.

"*Get back, get back, get back!*" a distorted, garbled voice said over the radio as Brooks released the mic button.

"*They're coming this way!*"

"*Circle back!*"

"What is going on up there?" Hendricks yelled.

"We're fine; it's not us!" Brooks answered. "We must be picking up someone else's signal!"

"*Get back to your trucks!*"

"*Mack, where are you guys?*"

"*Stuck in the storage building! We're surrounded!*"

"*Stay put. We're on our way!*"

"*No! It's too dangerous! We're dropping Hg-80 all around us!*"

"*Hank, there's a group headed your way!*"

"—rooks!" Hendricks was in the middle of shouting when his signal broke through the interference.

"I hear you!"

"Get a team down there and help them. That's Mack from St. Marie's!"

"Copy that." Brooks started pointing at our group. "Dan, Jimmy—your teams are with me. Blaise, you take over. Pike, you're with us," he ordered, and we all moved at his direction.

"Stay close to me when we get there, Abby," Zach yelled at me as he ran for his truck.

"He sure is bossy," Lauren chafed as we climbed into the truck—me in the middle front and her in the middle back, like when we had arrived.

I glared at Zach's disappearing back. "Yep." I popped the P.

"It's not like you don't do this all the time without him."

"Right?" I agreed. "So irritating!"

"It's a guy thing," Pike said through the back window of the cab. He had jumped into the bed of our truck as we loaded up. "We like to be the protectors. It makes us feel strong and useful."

"And important," Dawsen agreed as he put the truck in gear. "We want to be number one in your eyes all the time."

"It's annoying," Lauren told them. "Sometimes," she amended, and the men laughed.

"We don't mean to act like dumb cave-dwellers; we just are," Pike teased. "Vampires are much worse than humans too. It's almost psychotic."

"I'll try to remember that." I smirked at him over my shoulder.

"What do you mean 'psychotic'?" Lauren balked.

"Obsessive, possessive, demanding, controlling." I felt like I was getting a lesson. "It can be intense."

"That sounds healthy." Lauren scrunched her face.

"It's not like that all the time. We're not actually insane. It can just seem like it when someone you care about is in danger, or perceived danger. But when there isn't anything threatening harm, all that intensity gets focused elsewhere. Everything that vampires do in comparison to humans is heightened. You know that. Our senses, our strength, all that. Emotions aren't any different. Humans evolved and tamped down their intense primitive behaviors, but vampires just learned to recognize them and try to control them. It doesn't always work. Some of your human stories portrayed aspects of our species correctly. How we love, for example."

"Well, this is a weird conversation to have right now." Brooks shook his head.

"You mean, like fated mates or that whole 'bonding' thing?" Lauren mocked.

"Yeah, actually. It's not that bizarre of a concept. There are tons of examples in the animal kingdom that experience the same intuition and mate for life. Humans, believe it or not, have the instinct too. It's just not universally accepted or recognized in your species—another one of your senses buried deep down in your psyche, thanks to centuries of indoctrination and denial. I don't know the bonding firsthand, but it happens with vampires all the time. We live long lives. It makes sense that there would be a biological or chemical attraction that anchors deep love forever. Or we'd all be a bunch of cousin-fuckers."

The whole truck shook with laughter, which was a good way to end that conversation since we'd reached our destination.

Wallace was just a short distance from Burke, but as we approached, we realized all the commotion wasn't coming from the town itself but a stretch of abandoned housing just outside the city border. Trucks cluttered the street. Old houses and buildings were on fire or blown up, and debris littered the entire area.

A small group of St. Marie's guard members were firing on some *kooks* as they tried to rescue their trapped team from inside of the building. In front of a two-story brick structure, a bubbling mass of the dead was blocking the exit doors. They had obviously used an Hg-80 and inadvertently trapped themselves. They were trying to escape out of a broken side window while their team members protected them from the *kooks* still coming at them. Two guys stood on top of a truck, shooting at the dead, and one at the base of the window, helping the ones trapped inside.

We came to a stop and had just exited our vehicles to go help when a bright flash of light blasted us, followed by another loud explosion that knocked us off our feet and threw us back several yards. I landed hard on the ground and bounced around before I came to a stop. My ears were ringing, and my eyes were readjusting around the black spots in my vision after the flash of light. Fresh smoke and dust filled the air. I coughed several times, then pulled up my neck buff to keep the dust and debris from my lungs.

Someone grabbed my arm and tugged me up from the ground. Pike put his face in front of mine and mouthed words I couldn't understand. I realized he was talking, not miming. He wrapped his large hands around the sides of my face, making me focus on him as he continued to look and speak at me intently.

"Abby," he mouthed.

I covered my mouth and coughed, then nodded between the pressure of his hands.

"Abby!" he hollered again, and I could hear him a little.

"I'm okay." My throat was raw from coughing.

"You sure?"

"Yeah. I'm good."

He let my face go but kept by my side.

It took what felt like forever before my hearing adjusted. Everyone around me was getting up slowly, dusting themselves off, and a few had already pulled out their weapons, covering those of us who were slower to our feet.

The truck the two St. Marie's men had been standing on was flipped over and burning from the explosion. The roof was crunched in, and the windshield had popped out and broken. The men who had stood on top of it were nowhere to be seen, and the ones who had tried to escape from the building were dead from the blast, their fresh blood splattering the brick on the building. Those who had made it to the ground had also been killed, either from the explosion or the impact of landing.

None of us understood what had gone wrong. Everything had happened so fast, but we needed to continue, so we moved forward. We stayed knit together as we went through the street, huddled close as a group. I walked with Pike on one side and Zach on the other, like my personal guards. As we moved further into the old neighborhood, there were a few *stragglers*—loners that had been burned by various blasts, staggering around after light exposure to the mercury bombs, their movements faulting as it slowly ate away at their flesh. There were no St. Marie's guards, humans, or anything else alive that we could see.

We moved past the building, where the dead soldiers' bodies had painted the brick, and the turned-over truck now only smoking and no longer on fire. Continuing forward, we heard screams then another detonation from down the road. We stayed in formation but went faster toward the commotion and pressed ourselves up against a building to not draw attention to ourselves.

Brooks was at the front of our line, followed by Pike, and when he peeked around the corner, the look on his face became a mix of confusion and concern. Pike switched places with Brooks, and his face pinched similarly too. They whispered to each other, and I thought we might turn around and go back, but then Brooks motioned to us to move forward again. Once around the corner, I could see what they had seen. I knew why they had the troubled look on their faces. I found myself likewise confused, then concerned.

In the middle of the street, between one demolished building and another one burning, was a row of tall, round posts, like the kind used for outdated electrical wires, but these were shorter and closer together. They were old—really old—but still sturdy. The poles looked as if they had been stuck right through the asphalt and lined up in the middle of the street a long time ago. The pavement where the poles punctured the ground had patchy concrete around the base of the beams, as if to reinforce the paving that had been broken in order to hold the poles up straight. That wasn't what was most concerning. It was odd, for sure, but not any stranger than other things we'd seen across old states.

The cause for alarm was the woman lassoed around the neck and hanging from the furthest pole on the right. She was alive, struggling to stay upright as she teetered precariously on her tiptoes. The rubber of her soles found purchase against the blacktop, so she'd push herself up by a fraction of an inch and held still long enough to catch a quick breath. Her hands were free, and she tried to push her fingers in between the rope and her throat, but the noose was tight with no wiggle room in the tether, so all she could do was pinch around the binding at her neck to pull it away from choking her.

Next to the dangling female were six others, each hanging from a pole. Their struggle was over, and the woman would be next if we didn't act fast. My first instinct was to run to her aid and free her from her hanging, but as I moved forward to do just that, I was stopped—not only by both Zach and Pike but by the woman herself. She held up a shaky hand in our direction and shook her head with the slightest movement she could spare.

She choked out a mouthful of indiscernible words. "Nnnnn ... tttttr ... ppp." She spat and stuttered, her face turning redder as she struggled, but she seemed determined and kept trying. "Nnn ... ooooo..." Gasping, she brought her outstretched hand back up to the rope around her throat and frantically pulled at the twine as she fought for breath.

"Hold on!" I told her and looked at Brooks for direction.

"I can get her," Pike said.

"No," Brooks ordered. "Something's not right." He scanned the smoke-filled space.

"It'll be quick."

"I said no!" Brooks yelled at Pike. "Look around. Something is off."

"I can't see through smoke any better than you. What am I looking for?" Pike argued with Brooks.

The woman had slipped off her toes, struggling so much to hold the rope away from her throat that her feet weren't finding their previous grip on the pavement.

"We can't let her die!" Pike yelled at Brooks.

"We're not going to, but we can't—"

I aimed at the woman and shot off three rounds. I'd missed the first time, but the last two had loosened up the rope and given the woman enough slack to find her footing to catch her breath.

"Dammit, Abby!" Brooks shouted at me.

"You said we weren't going to let her die." I re-aimed my weapon to take the last shot when a discharge went off next to me and the rope snapped.

The woman dropped to her knees with a heavy thud and a thwack as the rope fell next to her. Zach lowered his weapon after taking the last shot.

"You should have waited!" Zach yelled at me.

"Brooks said we were going to help, and she needed it now. Not in ten minutes!"

"I didn't want to draw attention to ourselves. It doesn't matter now. Focus!" Brooks growled. "Get over here!" He took a small step forward and hollered at the woman.

She was free and breathing, and although that was a positive, the attention I had just brought to us was a huge negative. I'd reacted without fully thinking, trusting that Brooks had a plan.

The woman struggled to get up from the ground, weakened because of the lack of oxygen. She would stand halfway, balance her weight on one leg, but when she pushed herself up to stand on the other, she'd collapse and fall again. With each turn and subsequent fall, she would land hard, cough, and grab at her neck as if still choking and gasping for air.

"Come on, lady!" Holden yelled at the woman.

"I can get her," Pike pressed.

"No," Brooks snapped.

Pike balled up his free hand but didn't argue, staying where he was.

The woman fell again and nearly dry-heaved as she fought to control her hacking.

"Crawl if you have to!" I urged.

She tugged the heavy twine from around her neck and tossed it to the ground. When she pulled in air, it was a loud, deep gasp. She started toward us on all fours, slowly at first, but then picked up her speed.

Around me, my teammates took shots at *kooks* that had filtered in through the smoky streets, and in the distance, we could hear more of them, their hungry cries loud in the eerie haze, smoke, and ash from the fires. The gnarl and grouse from the dead bounced around the otherwise calm space and echoed off the walls of the still-standing buildings. The smoke that seemed to settle around us like a heavy fog muted everything but their gnashing and howls, capturing the errant sounds like fresh snow absorbing timbre. The tranquility of the stillness was marred only by the looming clamor of death as it rambled toward us.

The woman had crawled only a few feet when she stopped to stand up—motive anew—with the danger of death so close. Her foot slipped on her first attempt, but she recovered quickly and was up on her feet in no time, taking her first steps in our direction. She looked frantic and panicked but ran after an unstable and shaky launch, then her head violently wrenched back and her feet kicked out from under her.

One moment she was running toward safety, and the next she was dangling in the air again—her head held up high like a prize by a fistful of dark blonde hair while her decapitated body fell and spilled against the ground.

Chapter Fourteen

The keening, wicked laugh that escaped the creature's lips would haunt my dreams for years, and the sight of the woman's head as it dangled like an ornament on a solstice tree—her features frozen in shock and pain—would be forever burned into my memory.

The creature before us was grotesque and unsanitary, sickly and ghoulish, all the while somehow appearing lucid, comely, robust, and oddly familiar. He was tall and muscular, and his pitch-black hair was slicked back and shiny. His skin was a chalky gray, his lips purplish, and dark rings circled under his eyes. Clearly in some form of death, he was different from regular *kooks*—not alive but not entirely dead, the intelligence in his eyes a clear distinction from the rest.

He disregarded the woman's head with a simple toss, then disappeared into the ashen smoke just as quickly and quietly as he had appeared. It was surreal, and if it weren't for the woman's disparaged remains in front of us, I would consider what just happened a *folie à deux*—a shared delusion.

Baffled into silence, no one moved for a short time, shocked still. When we did, we looked at each other in a daze.

"What the hell was that?" someone whispered.

The murky haze swirled with movement as *kooks* emerged from the smutted cloud and pulled us from our quiet stupor. We found ourselves surrounded by death as zombies materialized out of the carbon smoke, one by one, and stalked toward us.

We had all been hypnotized by surprise, even Pike. I could only describe the look on his face as horrified, and if it were possible for his almond skin, he even looked pale.

Collectively pulling ourselves together, a barrage of gunfire lit up the smog as we defended ourselves. We had been in a nearly straight line as we faced the hanging poles, but we now grouped together in a half-circle formation to face off against the oncoming swarm. Walking back through the streets, we retreated and ducked around the corner of a building, using it as cover to shift our positions and keep moving.

In a sort of oval shape, we moved as a group back to our vehicles, but when we reached the turned-over truck, we had to stop and find another way around it. The truck had caught fire again; whatever spilled from the engine had taken flame and set the building on fire, which blocked our easiest path of escape.

The other vehicles the St. Marie team had brought with them were jig-sawed together near the bed of the truck, and they cut off our straight path. We would have to maneuver one or two at a time through the maze of hastily parked vehicles to get to the other side of the street.

Half of us had made it around the metal labyrinth when a swarm of *kooks* came at us from near the burning building, merging with the dead that were still chasing us from the gallows on the street.

"Go, Abby. You too, Zach!" Brooks yelled at us.

"I'll be right behind you," Pike swore to me.

I stopped shooting and rested my finger next to the trigger of my gun. Turning, I hugged the rifle close to my body and made my way through the path as quickly as I could, with Zach right on my heels. When Zach was through, Brooks followed next, and Pike was last.

I cleared the truck maze and readjusted my rifle.

The air stalled again, and for a second there was no sound, only stillness.

Then a *boom*.

The crack was so violent and piercing that I covered my ears and dropped to the ground on instinct.

The disturbance echoed through the forest like a clap of thunder in the dead of night. The too-loud sound confused me more when nothing else happened.

There was no explosion. No fire. No obvious location it had come from or what caused it. The only thing it had accomplished was to stop and disorient us, and it had worked.

The result was devastating and chaotic.

Like an ocean wave rolling in during a storm, row upon row of *kooks* staggered and stomped toward us on the side of the burning building we had just escaped to. They moved together, neatly lined up, like synchronized soldiers marching into war. Organized and deadly, with the beast that had killed the woman leading the way—Pike in tow.

The creature somehow had power over him and steered him by a fistful of hair. The thing was taller than Pike, larger, bulkier, and obviously stronger.

Pike struggled and fought back against his hold, but it did nothing except make it harder for him to walk. His right arm hung loosely against his side, swaying with their movement, but otherwise seemed useless. Dislocated. His left hand raised high above his head, balled into a fist, and beat against the arm that held him, but the creature didn't seem to notice, utterly unfazed by Pike's attempt to break free as he held him out at arm's length to marshal him forward.

Pike was clearly angry and in pain. He limped between stumbled steps, grimacing every time his loose arm would bang against his thigh. His face was bloody, his clothes covered in soot, and his neck strained back from the tight hold on his hair.

The *boom* that had distracted us was the only thing that could explain how Pike had become a hostage. He was otherwise too strong, too fast, too aware of his surroundings to lose. It still didn't explain, however, how this creature continued to overpower him. The dead weren't strong, just opportunistic. But they also didn't keep their victims alive and show them off as bait.

Ethan, Sylis, and Seivor appeared in front of us.

With Pike being used as a shield, we had all stopped firing at the herd but were at the ready, though all a bit baffled and unsure of what to do. There was a lot of muttering and questioned whispers on how to proceed between our people, but when no one had an answer, our solution was to hold our ground and wait.

No one could get a clear shot of the beast. Pike was too close and in the way. It was frustrating, and my chest clenched with pain and anxiety at the sight.

The *kooks* and their leader came to an abrupt stop at the appearance of the VIGs, and the creature laughed in response at the sight of them. That same cruel cackle he had belted right before decapitating the woman peeled through the air around us. It sent chills down my spine; it was so unnatural.

"Let him go!" Ethan seethed. He took a step forward but stopped hard in his tracks, as if his anger had propelled him to move but his uncertainty held him back. His face was ice cold, his jaw like stone.

Sylis and Seivor looked equally dangerous and enraged.

The monstrosity chortled in an eerie, deep way that sounded as if it had come from his chest and rumbled up through his throat.

Ethan advanced again but stopped abruptly when he said his name.

"Ethan," the beast cawed huskily. He drew out the syllables in a menacing wheeze as if speaking wasn't something he was used to, like he didn't have full command over the movements required for speech.

Astonishment hung thick in the air as the creature spoke, my team's surprise evident on their faces.

The beast's legion of *kooks* stepped forward in slow motion as if on a silent order. Everything happened so quickly but at an exaggerated rate, like my synapses were firing so fast that everything else seemed slow.

The creature smiled, his dirty face drawing up into a snide smirk that exposed sallow fangs, which seemed to glint with a razor's edge even through the rottenness. He wrenched his arm back and yanked Pike against his torso, jerking his head to the side, then he snickered before clamping down hard on the strained muscles of Pike's neck. The demon ripped his teeth down through Pike's flesh, tearing past his muscle and into his jugular.

Pike howled, then choked on the pain and blood, going limp with silence when the monster snapped his neck.

The wails that left Ethan, Sylis, and Seivor were so piercing, the sound reverberated around us, echoing in my soul. I shrunk back and covered my ears, rage filling me as my heart broke with them.

The monster laughed as Pike's blood dripped from his fangs and his body hung dead in his hand.

The three vampires moved as one and charged after the fiend, but fear didn't seem to register for the creature. He simply turned his back on the three livid, viciously dangerous vampires charging after him. The savage picked up Pike's body, flung it over its shoulder, and disappeared into the sea of dead, the horde swallowing him as they covered his retreat.

They came at us then. No longer moving in an orderly fashion, their control had been released, and they reverted once more to their primal state. *Kooks* and *evos* charged forward, their only common goal blood and devouring need.

These were monsters we recognized, creatures we knew how to deal with.

In an attempt to go after the murderer of their friend, the VIGs killed the entire front line before any of us had thought to move. We tried to help, shooting at the dead when we could get a clear view, but it was chaos and there were so many of them. Our close combat weapons—mostly hunting and combat knives—weren't enough. Minutes piled up as time stacked against us.

The *kooks'* numbers seemed to grow as our ammo shrunk, and the dead bodies piled up as our energy drained. We reloaded over and over, again and again, switching back and forth between gun and melee, but with each turn, each time, it became increasingly more dangerous for us to be here.

"Fall back!" Hendricks ordered.

We were in a losing battle, and it was time to go. My team was panting from exertion, covered in black blood, and defending themselves more frantically and less skillfully. The surrounding bodies had become hazardous in their own right, and my team members tripped over them several times, which turned into its own problem and an unsafe distraction. Two people became preoccupied with the complication—the one who had fallen, and the one who covered them so something didn't maul them to death.

"Go, now!" Hendricks reiterated.

"Get back to the trucks!" Brooks's deep voice boomed over the mayhem. His order was more like a code word.

The drivers were our most important means of escape, aside from the vehicles themselves. The rest of us would only stop our attack once the drivers were safely behind the wheel, in gear and ready to go.

The designated drivers quit their attack and left for the vehicles. Spread out over a large area and almost completely surrounded by *kooks*, moving out was a process. The more we tightened our ranks for our team to flee, the more the horde seemed to grow, but half had already loaded, so we worked faster until it was safe to abandon the fight altogether.

"Abby, go!" Zach yelled when there was little more than a handful of us left.

Hendricks snapped his head in my direction. "Now!"

I shot off a couple more rounds and put down a few of the dead that were already too close. Lowering my weapon, I hugged it to my body to run, heading for the truck my team had driven here in. All the vehicles had turned around and were facing our escape route. Staggered across the road, they weren't exactly in a line nor exactly in a row, just ready to go. When the last of us were loaded, we would blow up as many *kooks* as possible on our way out.

I could see the truck ahead from my position, but to get there wasn't a straight run—I had to maneuver my way around the rear tailgate of the large truck to get to the passenger side. All our *Morgue* vehicles were massive, and this truck was no different. The top of the tailgate sat taller than my head and blocked my view of the other sides. So when I rounded the bumper, I nearly ran into the *kook* monster with fangs.

His eyes were like fire, the red irises as bright as a warning light flashing in the dark. The pupils seemed hollow, somehow so black. Tiny blood vessels webbed across the sclerae, crimson over gray and altogether sinister.

The monster squinted at me and cocked his head oddly, another minute display of his inhumanity. It looked like rubber, pallid and worn. He was dead, had been dead, or was dying—the terminology didn't matter; the creature was death incarnate, and it showed.

He leaned into me so fast I didn't have time to flinch. We were less than a foot apart, but the movement put him within inches of touching me. A flash of fear hit me as my adrenaline spiked when the monster smelled the air around me. My knees shook. The fiend took in one long pull through his nose and sniffed me, starting at the base of my neck, up the length of my throat, along my carotid artery, then stopped at the corner of my jaw. The air wheezed in his nose as he pulled in my scent, and his exhale stunk of rot and death. I would have gagged if I hadn't been so terrified.

I tried to be subtle, stealthy, and move unnoticed, but the sound of metal as I shifted my gun drew his attention. He cocked his head again. I was prepared to shoot him, repositioning to do just that, when an intense force punched into my stomach.

The pain didn't register immediately, only that the creature's left hand had somehow moved to the top of my shoulder. His hold pulled at me, which made me realize I had been thrust back ever so slightly. I swayed on my feet, and the fiend squeezed my shoulder until I stood still again. He left his hand where it rested against me, like a friend offering a comforting touch. The agony didn't come until the demon twisted whatever weapon he had planted into my stomach. I felt no discomfort until he turned it, contorting my insides.

I stared at the monster, into his burning dead eyes, and mine widened at the surge of pain. The demon watched me intently as I choked and spit up blood when the first wave of torment hit. As if enough damage hadn't already been done, he then slowly withdrew the sharp object, tilting it up when he pulled it out. The retraction stung as it sliced through unbroken skin and split my flesh in two. I coughed and choked as my mouth filled with blood.

I dropped my weapon—it was suddenly too heavy to hold—placing both my hands over my stomach. Thick, warm liquid gushed from my body. It coated my hands and laced through my fingers, tickling the sensitive space between them, then slipped past and fell through the air in a stream until it hit the ground. My palms filled until blood overflowed at the top, covering them. The hot, tacky warmth ran out of the wound like water from a drain, and when it hit the pavement, I heard the *drip, drip* as it splashed and pooled at my feet. It was as annoying as it was alarming.

When I choked again, I sputtered blood. The movement tensed my stomach muscles, sending pain through my body like lightning through the sky. I felt cold, my hands warm, and my stomach hot. My nerves lit up from the torture like fingers of fire.

Frozen in place—either from shock or fear—I watched in horror as the beast tasted the blade that ran tacky red with my blood. He extended his sickly black tongue and moved it up the length of the flat surface as he sampled the hemorrhage. When he swallowed the cruor—my blood bright and shiny as it rolled into his dark and dirty mouth—he stared at me with creepy eyes, a low hum grumbling from his chest.

He licked the steel clean, the stain ruby on his lips. The savage let the overflow drip down his chin to mix with Pike's blood as he swept his tongue across his chapped mouth. When he finished, he leered at me and flashed his pink-stained fangs, then exhaled the smell of death over my face.

The attack was so clear, so vivid, I noticed everything around me. My senses heightened like never before. I felt everything, smelt everything, and my vision was clearer, picking up even the most minute details from my peripheral.

Time moved differently, and I became more aware of everything in life as I bled to death. It had all happened so fast it could have only been a matter of seconds, but it felt like an unending stretch of time.

My hearing was the only thing denied heightened sensitivity, due to the earlier explosion, but the ringing in my ears grew louder as it further dimmed the commotion. The gunfire that blasted and lit up the smoke-filled sky was barely a muffled vibration of sound. The colors from the explosions and bullets flashed and faded from bright to dark against the haze. The accompanying voices were like murmurs through a wall, the words dragged and slow—a non-distinguishable string of sounds and syllables. The shift of movement from my team was exaggerated and leaden as if they moved in slow motion.

Something throaty mumbled through the monster's lips, but I couldn't make it out or understand the words. I only noticed his mouth move. The proteins had congealed, so when it opened and closed its lips—my blood still between them—they held together like strands of connective tissue. The stringy threads shrunk and stretched with the separation and movement.

Little splatters of blood dotted his chin as they found their way over onto mine. I coughed again, and the action brought up more of my internal bleeding. It sputtered out of my mouth and speckled the face in front of me—each of us now trading bloody sialoquent.

His eyes moved past mine briefly then returned to recapture my gaze for a moment, before the monster disappeared in a black blur. The sudden removal of his hand on my shoulder jerked me slightly, and I took a step as if to catch myself from falling in reaction. The movement shifted my body, so when I caught sight of Zach out of the corner of my eye, I instinctively shuffled the rest of the way around. Still holding myself together, confused and unsure of what to do while I continued to bleed out, I turned to him in desperation.

I had left him only a few moments ago, but I could guess how my face looked. The burgundy pool at my boots I all but sloshed through was proof enough of my pallor, and I had spewed blood from my mouth several times, the sticky heat oozing from the corners of my lips.

Zach's features contorted upon seeing me. "Abby?" he mouthed in slow motion.

I couldn't hear him, but I was sure he'd yelled.

He dropped his gun to his side and ran toward me, his face stressed and his muscles strained.

My legs finally gave out on me, and I dropped to my knees. The crack as they contacted the pavement jolted up through my body, thudding in my muddled ears. The impact jostled my hold, but I pressed my hands harder against the weeping trauma at my midsection as another wave of pain raked through my body, casting up more blood for me to choke on.

My eyes unfocused during the hard landing, and so when I looked up, I had to search for Zach again, but he was too far away to help break my fall.

The world tilted as my view spun, and my body toppled toward the ground. My side hit first, my shoulder next, and then my head jerked toward the blacktop from the force, but I couldn't stop myself or brace for the impact. I just expected it.

Ethan blurred into sight, his hand extended as a buffer before the pavement and I could make our acquaintance. He pressed his other hand against the opposite side of my face and cradled my head, then gingerly rested it against the hard surface, rolling me over onto my back. As soon as I was flat against the ground, he ripped open my suit.

Starting at the top and pulling at my collar along the zipper, he tore open both sleeves and peeled the front away from the back along the seam. I heard the dull pop as the threads released their hold without much of a fight. He lifted my hands, pulled at my shredded suit, and pressed my palms back against my stomach. I wouldn't have noticed, but the reapplied pressure had triggered a fresh ripple of agony up into my chest and through my spine.

I wheezed and disgorged another mouthful of blood.

Zach was next to me then, opposite Ethan, and smoothed his hands down my face.

"You're okay," he said.

I heard him as if through a wall.

"You're going to be okay." His eyes were frantic and wide as he wiped at the blood on my mouth.

All around us, the commotion was nonstop. They fired shots, bombs blew up, and commands were yelled from person to person.

Ethan yelled something I couldn't hear, then looked down at me. "Abby, I'm going to move you now."

Time caught back up with me, and everything narrowed again into acute focus. "O-kay." I gurgled the word in the back of my throat.

"Brooks!" Hendricks yelled as if right next to me. "Get to the bus!"

"I've got her!" Zach shoved his arms under my neck and legs.

"*No*!" Ethan pushed him, the force wrenching Zach out from under me and sending him flying back.

Zach hissed something, but I couldn't hear it over my yowl of pain at the sudden movement.

Ethan pressed a bunched cloth against my stomach, pushing my hands down on top, and put his face in my line of vision. "Hold this tight against you. Don't move it."

I tried to nod, but my face went slack instead.

"Abby!" Ethan yelled.

I blinked and pressed against myself as best as I could, but I was weak and knew I must barely have any hold.

He slid one arm under my knees, the other around my neck, and lifted me. I barely felt a thing, just the whoosh of air across my exposed flesh.

A loud keening pierced my ears, and then I was on a hard surface again.

The bus. The domed metal and rivets were a dead giveaway. The last four seats were gone from the space I now occupied. It felt cold.

Brooks knelt beside me after Ethan had released my legs and rested my head against the bus floor.

"I'm going to look." Brooks peered down at me.

I didn't respond, just blinked and swallowed against the lump in my throat.

My hands were lifted, the cloth pressed against me removed, and then the space filled with a surge that ran warmly down both of my sides.

"Shit." He pushed it back down, harder and with more pressure than I thought I could handle.

The lump I had swallowed against filled my mouth, and my breathing became even more labored. I coughed up blood with the compression, and my face and neck slicked wet as a frame of shadow dimmed the light around my eyes.

"There isn't time." Ethan's voice was hard.

"She needs my blood." He took off his jacket and threw it.

"No!" I recognized Zach yell. I hadn't seen or heard from him since when we were outside.

I must be losing time...

"Just let me think!" Hendricks hollered next.

"She's dying!" Ethan roared.

I felt the boom of his voice in my chest. The metal of the bus seemed to shudder under me.

"I'm not asking for permission!"

My eyes were on him. Whatever time I was losing wasn't affecting my sight. Not yet, anyway.

He pulled back his upper lip, exposed his fangs, and bit down hard on his wrist as he scooped up my head with his other hand. Bringing his bleeding puncture to my mouth, he pressed his wrist against my lips, splitting them open in the process.

"*No*!" Zach yelled again, and then I heard a struggle. "Let me go!" he raged.

Whatever he said was lost in a scuffle.

"Brooks?" Hendricks demanded over the furious commotion.

The world was fuzzy. Dark spots clouded my sight where once there'd been light, and I knew I was slipping in and out of consciousness, no longer just losing time. I was zoning out—one minute here, the next there, not remembering anything in between.

"There's nothing we can..." Brooks' voice was strained and a little muffled, but I guessed that was just my hearing again. "...carved into. Not just stabbed..."

"Drink." Ethan put his face in front of mine and pressed his vein harder against my mouth. "Drink!" he commanded and jostled my head.

I thought I was drinking...

Both my hands fell heavily to my sides. My feet were cold, which was strange since the rest of my body felt nothing but numb. Except for my abdomen. The warmth there was always present, but the pain was gone again. I was glad about that.

My vision narrowed, but I watched as Ethan moved his arm away from me and bit down into it again. It horrified me as he buried his teeth deeper into his flesh and then ripped at the tissue.

He shoved his forearm into my mouth and yelled at me again. "Drink, Abby! Now!"

His blood filled my mouth ... and then poured over the sides. I could only feel a cool trickle down my throat while the rest of the liquid swam in my mouth. I tried again, but I couldn't—aware of the thought, but my body wouldn't comply. Then my awareness was failing me too. Swallowing seemed to be an impossible task.

"Drink Abby!" It was Brooks who yelled at me this time. "Do someth..."

I tried to focus as I clung to consciousness.

"She's not breathing." Ethan moved his arm from my bloody mouth. Something was wrong with his face.

What's wrong with his face?

He tipped my head back, grabbed my neck, and the blood in my mouth slipped down my throat, followed by a cold rush of air that filled my lungs.

I could hear Zach and Hendricks in the distance. Not what they said, just the familiarity of their voices.

Darkness crept in around my eyes, and my mouth was again full for a moment. Then, another cold rush of air.

"... compressions."

My head rocked back and forth on the floor of the bus. Back and forth. Back and forth.

It was kind of annoying.

Back and forth.

Mouth full. Cold air.

I lost all focus, but I don't think my eyes shut.

I never felt so relaxed, and there was no more tension in my body. No more pain. It was nice not having any more pain.

I nearly felt nothing. Just nothingness occupying a limited amount of space.

Mouth full. Cold air.

The loud ringing in my ears had finally gone quiet now. I no longer heard a thing. It was actually kind of peaceful. Relaxing.

Mouth full. Cold air. Repeat.

Nothing.

Chapter Fifteen

My eyes flew open with a sudden sting of cold and a throb.

"She's awake."

"Hold her."

"Do it."

Hot, searing pain ripped through my abdomen once again. My sight was almost in focus as I watched Ethan push down on his forearm, draining his blood out of a wound and over my stomach held open by Sylis's hands.

A scream tore through my throat; the strain ripped it raw, then cut it off.

My head lolled to the side in defeat.

"... stopped again."

"Then start compressions!"

The cracking was loud in my ear with each jerk on my body.

"Let me help. You don't have enough blood to give"

"Then she'll take it all."

Cold air.

Darkness.

I woke up in a dim room, quiet besides the *beep ... beep ... beep* near my ear. I felt cold, stiff and too heavy to move. My eyes might have opened. If they did, it was too dark to see.

I was so tired, somewhere between half asleep and trying to wake. I felt sleep-drunk, like after a long hard day that left you physically and mentally exhausted. Then, when you finally fell asleep, you'd wake again too soon. Your brain would feel heavy and slow, your surroundings wouldn't seem real, and the only thing you could think about was getting back to sleep. Feeling even more exhausted by being awake, to the point where it almost hurt, like a fog in your head weighing down everything but the most basic functions. If your life depended on it, you probably couldn't make being awake work long enough to save yourself, an almost physical pressure crushing your consciousness into submission until you relented.

It was euphoric to let go and slip back into the ether of darkness.

Once, I'd stayed awake for over forty-six hours. I'd been so tired it was hard to fall asleep, and when I did, it was like blinking out of existence for a while. Like a light being shut off. I hadn't moved. I hadn't dreamt. The sleep had been so deep, so sound, it was a surprise to finally wake up.

In normal sleep, you still seemed to be aware of the passage of time. That had felt like time travel. I knew I had slept and that time had passed, feeling rested upon waking. But it had all happened in an instant—one minute here, the next there.

Waking up now felt much the same. Only surreal. It took a few blurry moments once I opened my eyes, but then was wide awake, more alert and focused than I had ever been. Once the sleep fog had lifted, everything was acutely clear.

I sat up to get out of bed and then remembered why I was in the care center. Frantically, I pushed away the blanket and pulled up my gown, surprised by the near lack of pain and what I saw.

My stomach was almost perfectly smooth. No bandages. No wound. Just a faint, soft, irregular pink line that ran up my stomach, from navel to breastbone. I ran my finger over the scar with a shaky hand, scared to touch it as if it might break open. It was sensitive to the touch. Not painful, just annoying, like my nerve was exposed to the drag. The skin around the scar was tender when I pushed against it, and my stomach muscles flexed in response. I flinched from the pang.

The images of what had happened were very clear in my mind, so I couldn't have been dreaming. I worried about how much time had passed. How could I be nearly healed already? It felt as though it had happened only a few moments ago.

I checked myself over. I wasn't hooked up to any machines, but that only furthered my concern—I remembered hearing the beeping from the heart monitor, the cold in my arm from a saline drip, and the sting from the IV tape and tube. None of which were present now.

It was light outside, but from the way the sun was shining in through the curtained window, it was evening. The ticking of the clock on the wall confirmed my suspicion.

I moved the blankets and stood easily from the bed before padding over to the window. It was dusk, and Thompson Falls was quieting down for the night. Porch lights were coming on, people were going home, and stores and shops were closed. Night guards traded places with their daytime counterparts and evening patrols began as I stood at the window, watching the progression of life go on around me.

The door creaked open, then a cast of fluorescent light flooded the dark room.

"You're awake!" Zach said in a muted tone, then rushed over to pull me gently against him. "How are you feeling? Are you in pain? Why are you up? You should be in bed." He gingerly grabbed me around my shoulders and pushed me back toward the bed.

"I'm fine," I croaked hoarsely, sitting down on the bed, and he pulled at the tangled sheets to cover my legs. "Really, it's okay."

He shifted and tucked me in, continuing to fuss. "I'm so relieved you're awake and not in pain, but maybe you could take it slow? Wait for someone to check you over before you go getting out of bed again."

"Seriously, I feel fine."

"Do you want anything?" He cautiously sat on the edge of my bed. "Another blanket or a pillow?" Taking my wrist to check my pulse, he placed his other hand over my forehead as if to gauge my temperature.

I didn't know what he thought he was doing. He wasn't a doctor or anything near it, and he had—at best—basic first aid knowledge.

"I don't think so." I wrinkled my brow at him as he moved his hand all around my face. "Will you stop? You're being ridiculous," I snickered and finally brushed his hand away.

His face grew serious as he ran his palms down my arms. "You died. You scared the shit out of me. To you, I probably seem crazy, but I can't help it."

I squeezed his hands, my face going soft. "I'm okay."

He swallowed hard, then kissed my forehead, letting his lips linger against me for a moment before pulling away. "Are you hungry?" Pulling the rolling tray closer, he handed me a cup of water.

My stomach growled at the mention of food. "Oh, maybe." I placed a hand on my empty stomach, registering for the first time the hollow pit. "Starving, actually."

"I'm on it. I'll be right back." He ran out of the door before I could tell him what I wanted.

Although, I didn't care, now that I was aware of it. I didn't know that I'd ever felt this hungry before. It was kind of painful even, and my mouth salivated at the mere thought of food. Any food. *All* the food. I didn't want to chew on my lip, so I drank down the entire cup of water instead.

Zach was back a few minutes later with the largest mug I'd ever seen. When he handed it to me, I gulped it down, insanely glad he'd brought me a refill since the little glass I had was gone. I felt the icy liquid flow down my throat and coat the inside of my entire belly. It was so cold that it hurt and sent a chill through my body, but it tasted good, so I kept drinking until I was full.

"They are bringing something up," Zach said when I set the mug down. "These will hold you over, hopefully." He held his hand out and chuckled when I tore into the crackers, then shoved a whole saltine in my mouth.

My stomach grumbled and cheered as the substance made its way to the empty space. I crammed another one in and mumbled, "'hank 'u," around the dry paste coating my mouth, then grabbed the water again, swishing it around to clear some of the stickiness.

"You're welcome." He laughed and brushed away the crumbs on the blanket. "Your mom and Hendricks are on their way. They should be here soon."

I wanted to ask about Ethan, but he was the wrong person.

Swallowing, I broke open a third pack of the tiny crackers before taking another drink to loosen the gluey coating in my mouth. He was watching me like a caged animal, and I laughed at his expression when I realized I must look insane stuffing the crackers in my mouth like I was.

"Sorry. I don't know if I've ever been this hungry." I covered my mouth. It was kind of embarrassing.

"I'm just glad you're okay. And look, you're totally normal," he taunted.

"Very funny," I mumbled as flakes of cracker spit and puffed out of my mouth to make a mess on the bed again. "Is this all you brought?" I pouted when the last packet was empty.

He handed me a couple more packets. "Obviously not."

I clapped in excitement like a little kid, took the saltines from him, and sat up in the bed a little higher to eat them over the tray. I didn't feel like a ravenous animal anymore, so I thought I could at least eat with what little dignity I had left.

"So, what happened?" I tore open another of the small packages.

"You were gutted and almost died." He was perched on the edge of a chair and had pulled it closer to me. "What do you remember?"

I mostly remembered everything from the attack. Somehow. I also knew I would hear recounts of it repeatedly for some time—from my mom and Hendricks, my team, Zach, and anyone else who had been there and seen what happened.

War stories and battle wounds were always conversational pieces. Like, how moms compared their labor and deliveries or when dads caught a big fish that one time. I wasn't really interested in visiting the topic of my near-death experience right now. I was fine—more than fine, actually.

"That's not what I'm talking about." I crunched another small bite. "What did you say to Ethan?"

"Abby—"

"Zach, just tell me," I cut him off before he could give me some excuse why it wasn't the right time for this.

He dropped his shoulders, released a deep breath through tense lips, and rubbed his palms on the front of his jeans. I imagined he had hoped I'd forgotten about the fight that happened before we were pulled away to Burke, or at the very least, thought I'd wait a while before bringing it up again. I had almost died, after all.

"Zach." I put the cracker down and chided as he stalled.

"I love you," he said.

"I love you too." I crossed my arms over my chest.

"No, Abby." He looked away for a moment, then refocused on my eyes. "I'm in love with you."

My throat tightened and dried instantly. I swallowed hard as if I could push down whatever had blocked the passage, but that did nothing since there was nothing there. I blinked at him, then grabbed the water and took a couple of sips. Still, the lump in my throat persisted.

I nodded, then shook my head, which turned into a mix of a nod-shake. "No, you're not." He had to be joking.

"I'm in love with you, and I have been for a while."

"No, you're not." I shook my head in disbelief.

"Abby."

"I almost died. You're coming down from that."

"No, Abby."

"Things get confused during a crisis."

"This isn't that."

"Zach—"

"I know you don't feel the same way." He rubbed his hands over his face. "I kept waiting for a sign from you, thinking that if I gave you time, you'd finally see me." Standing from his chair, he paced around the room as he continued to speak. "I was going to tell you before I left on that medical run, and then I thought, 'Maybe time away from me will change how she feels.' So, I didn't say anything. I just left. And while I was gone, I imagined how things could be between us. How it would be different when I came back. I convinced myself that your feelings would change while I was gone, that the time away would make you finally get to where I was and have been. I promised myself that even if you didn't realize it, I would tell you when I came back, and then you would see it for yourself."

"Zach," I whispered, but he just kept talking.

"I hoped you would miss me, *really* miss me. The same way I missed you." He laughed humorlessly. "Then, when I finally made it home, full of hope and courage and excitement, we heard about Honor and the attacks. That we were hosting vampires. I couldn't believe it. My hopes were a little dashed then. I knew you needed me, but I didn't want to push anything during a tragedy. That wasn't right or fair. I planned to give you time and wait until after the memorial." He flopped back down into the chair he'd been in a few moments ago. "And then I walked into the O, and things were the exact opposite of what I'd expected, what I'd wished. I saw you wrapped around one of them in a hug and ... all the courage, hope, and excitement I had built up over weeks and weeks in the *Morgue* just ... vanished."

"But, Zach, you never—"

"So I didn't say anything. I was caught off guard. We fell back into our normal rhythm, and it was so nice to be home and clean, and around you again that I decided to wait. But the longer I waited, the more I noticed how you and Ethan looked at each other. How you interacted with each other. Your secret smiles and inside jokes. You were so familiar with each other, and *I* was the outsider. Before I knew it, my disappointment turned into annoyance and then anger. Not toward you. I could never be mad at you. You had no idea; you were just living your life. But I was convinced he was toying with you. Using you. So my anger turned into hatred, and I spun a different kind of fantasy. He was always there. Always around. Making demands where you were concerned. I didn't like it."

"Zach," I tried again when he paused for breath.

"Just let me finish." He put his hand up. "I ran into him one night. Now, keep in mind that I had been villainizing him for days at this point and falling for you for years, and here this son of a bitch waltzes into my town and sweeps my girl off her feet. I was hurt and pissed off." He huffed to himself.

I didn't bristle at his term for me. It had always been that way and not as possessive as it sounded.

"So, I see him, and without thinking, I march up to him and tell him to back off. I told him we had been in a relationship before I left and he was getting in the way. He was a vampire and you were a human, and it would never work. You were never leaving Thompson Falls, and he would never be welcomed or happy here. When he argued, I cut him off and used every example of our closeness that he might have seen. Things I knew someone on the outside would easily misconstrue as intimate. I made sure to be around you as often as I could. He hated me at that moment as much as I hated him. We didn't like each other before, for sure, but after that, it exploded. He didn't believe me, not even for a second. He told me there were dozens of reasons off the top of his head that he knew I was lying. But he only gave me one. He told me you never would have returned his affection if you and I had been involved. That it wasn't you or your character and it was insulting to imply otherwise. He made me feel stupid, like I didn't know you at all—he was absolutely right. We both knew he caught me, but I dug my heels in. We argued. But he didn't taunt me, not when he caught me in my lie. Not after. Not even once. Which actually pissed me off more." He huffed and shook his head. "I would have taunted him if our roles were reversed."

"Zach," I scolded.

"I know." He dropped his head in shame. "I almost got you killed because of it. I'm so damn stupid!"

"What? No, you didn't."

"If my lies had worked and he backed off—or worse, if they left... He wouldn't have been there."

"You didn't do this to me."

"No. But he's why you're alive. And I put that in jeopardy. If he hadn't been there with us ... he wouldn't have been there to save your life."

"That's a hyperbole."

"It doesn't matter. We still don't like each other and probably never will, but I misjudged him," he said out loud, maybe to me, but mostly to himself. "He never gave up. Not once. Not when you bled out on the floor. Not when your heart stopped beating. Not when you quit drawing breath. Not even when you were dead... He never gave up. He didn't stop, and he saved your life." His eyes were the sincerest I had ever seen. "I owe him everything for that."

"So do I," I whispered.

"It's not the same. You wouldn't have had to live without you."

My eyes swam. "But I get to live."

"Yes, you do." He reached out and took my hand. "I'm so sorry, Abby. He already knew, but I admitted everything anyway, what I just admitted to you. Being honest with you both—and myself, really—was the least I could do." He scooted his chair closer. "I'll back off too, do whatever you want me to. If you need time to forgive me, take as much as you need. If you need space, I'll give it to you. You're the most important person in my life, and almost losing you was the scariest and most sobering experience I've ever had. I don't want to lose you because of this."

"You won't."

"Really?"

"You won't," I promised.

"Can you ever forgive me?"

"Of course, I forgive you," I told him sincerely. "I don't want to lose you either, Zach. You're my best friend. We'll figure this out."

"It won't be weird. I promise you. Everything I said was true, but this whole experience has changed me and put things into perspective for me. I swear to you that nothing will be different between us. I'll never bring it up again. We'll never talk about it again. Like it didn't even happen."

"It'll be fine, Zach. Everything will be just fine."

I didn't really believe him. I wouldn't say that to him, though. It was embarrassing enough for him, regardless of whether what he'd said was true or not, and I certainly didn't want to discredit his feelings one way or the other. Everyone's emotions were running high, and things had been crazy for a while. We all just needed to take a breath, get some perspective, and let things work themselves out.

Besides, being out in the M*orgue* did strange things to a person. I'd be lying if I said I hadn't had confusing thoughts and feelings about people myself. Sometimes lines got blurred, and feelings and thoughts got crossed. It didn't mean they were real. Humans were complex animals, and we acted without thinking—that's where we ran into trouble. We were still learning. I would never hold what Zach had said against him, even if it turned out to be true. I hoped the same courtesy would be extended to me if I spoke too soon and ended up with my foot in my mouth.

There was a quiet knock on the door.

"Yeah?" Zach turned his head toward the sound.

My mother and Hendricks came in, and my stomach flipped at the sight of the tray of food she was holding.

"Oh, perfect timing, Ma!" Zach grabbed the food from her.

"Finally." My mouth swam with anticipation. "I'm so hungry," I moaned as Zach sat the tray on the bed table that hovered across my lap.

He removed the tray lid and revealed mashed potatoes and gravy, green beans, two dinner rolls, fresh fruit, and what I guessed was supposed to be some sort of meatloaf of mushrooms, wild grains, and quinoa. Whatever it was didn't matter. It was warm and delicious, and filled my empty stomach. I had never been so grateful for a meal in my life.

While I shoveled food into my mouth, the three of them carried on a conversation about what had been going on around town. I was so surprised to discover I had been here and in a medically induced sleep recovery for five days that I even choked on my potatoes and had to swallow them down with some water.

"Five days?" I balked.

"You didn't tell her?" Hendricks looked at Zach.

"We didn't get that far." Zach gave me a small smile.

"No wonder I'm so hungry." I grinned and continued with the shoveling, prompting them with my fork to continue, like a conductor with a baton.

Halfway through my meal, I felt better enough to slow down my greedy consumption and actually enjoy the food. This also allowed me to ask questions between bites.

"So, what did you find out?" I didn't need to ask specific details. They all understood shorthand.

My mother fidgeted in her chair, which prompted Hendricks to reach over and take her hand, but otherwise, she didn't object to the conversation I was asking for.

"I don't know what you remember about your attacker," Hendricks explained. "But evidently, vampires are now just as susceptible to the virus as humans. Maybe they always were. We just didn't know it until now."

"So I wasn't imagining that, then? They can be turned? That thing was a vampire?"

"It would appear so," Hendricks confirmed.

"But they don't turn into mindless *kooks*," I stated.

"No. No, they do not," Hendricks said. "Everything we witnessed suggests higher reasoning. A *kook* has never commanded an army."

"Or attacked with a weapon." Zach reached out to squeeze my hand again.

"Or that." Hendricks solemnly nodded in agreement.

"Or killed out of spite and taunted it." My throat felt tight thinking about Pike.

"No. That is cruelty." Hendricks ground his teeth. "We've never seen that level of organization before either. Ethan confirmed they, too, have never witnessed anything remotely close to what we'd encountered at

Burke. He said that it made sense with how the other attacked towns and outposts had been left. This is all brand new and unfamiliar territory."

"So what are we doing, then?"

"Everything we can for now." Hendricks lifted his shoulders.

"Speaking of..." Zach stood from his chair. "My shift starts soon."

"Your shift?" I questioned.

"We've added extra patrols and posts outside the gates, and inside the walls to walk the perimeter and the town around the clock," Hendricks said. "We sent up a large crew a few days ago to clean up Burke of anything left behind. There were some *kooks*, but not as many as we imagined. We don't know where they went. They could come this way, or they could be with their leader. Either way, we need to be prepared. We've also armed everyone in town who was willing and able to carry. Sent word to our allies and friends. Relayed everything to VIG headquarters."

"Wow." I was surprised.

"We have to be on high alert and extra cautious now. We know what they are and what they are capable of."

What we had witnessed in Honor and again in Burke, I couldn't imagine here. I didn't want to, anyway. We had to expect the worst now. It was the only way to keep the town and the residents safe.

"I'll walk you home tomorrow after my shift." Zach bent down and kissed my forehead before he turned to leave. "Get some rest." He looked at me one last time, then pulled the door closed behind him.

I waited until he was out of the door, then I sat up higher and turned to my parents. "I feel fine—better than fine, actually. I don't want to stay another night."

"I told you." My mother nudged Hendricks.

"Yes, you were right." He chuckled.

"Right about what?"

"You, silly." Mom said. "I'd like to check you over again before you go, though."

"Really, I can go?" I had thought I'd have to fight them. "Look. I'm fine; it's like it never happened." I moved my food tray, pushed down the blanket, and lifted my gown to expose my stomach. "There's barely anything there. Is that normal?"

Mom came around the bed.

Hendricks rolled the stool he was sitting on forward. "I guess so."

"Remarkable. Lie back." She pushed on my shoulder softly and stepped on the paddle at the floor to lay the bed back. "When I examined you yesterday, there were still a few sutures and thick scar tissue. The sutures are completely gone now." She ran her hand over the smooth surface of my abdomen. "And the scar is so much smaller."

"May I?" Hendricks looked at me in question.

I nodded.

He reached out, pushed on my stomach, and pressed along the scar. "Does this hurt?"

"It's tender, but I wouldn't say it hurts."

"Scale of one to ten, ten being the worst?"

"Four."

"Here?" He moved his hands out, away from the scar.

"No."

"And this?"

"Nothing."

He was pressing along my ribs now, where the scar ended.

"It's crazy, but I feel great."

"It's amazing," Mom marveled and sat down in the chair Zach had been in. "I've never before seen that much damage healed so quickly. I can't wrap my head around it."

Hendricks pulled my robe back down, covered me with the blanket, and sat away from the bed.

"What's wrong?" I worried that he was changing his mind. "I promise, I'm good."

"You died," he deadpanned. "More than once. And here you sit in near perfect condition. I'll never be able to repay him for that."

"I remember he gave me his blood."

"He did more than that, Abby. He never gave up. Not once," he repeated the same things Zach had said earlier. His voice took on a kind of reverence as he relayed the story to me. "He did everything in his power to save your life, and even when the rest of us thought it hopeless, he kept fighting and gave you everything he had to give. He tried to ... feed you and you weren't swallowing, but somehow, he was able to get it down your throat."

I listened intently as he recounted. I was curious, after all.

"When that wasn't working and your heart kept stopping... I remember watching in horror when he removed the bandages from your gut. I even yelled at him. And then I nearly lost my mind when Sylis reopened your wound. It's a good thing others were around to hold back Zach and me from stopping him," he described darkly. "He ripped open his entire forearm and literally poured his blood inside you. I thought he might bleed to death himself." He shook his head at the memory. "It baffles me how far he was willing to go, and at that point, I stopped fighting whoever was holding me back. I gave up trying to resist and watched. I couldn't believe the lengths he went, and I knew at that moment that he wasn't doing anything to hurt you." He choked back tears as he continued, "He was saving you." He looked at me then. "At any moment, he could have turned you to save your life."

I'd never thought that a possibility until he said the words.

"Sylis told him to. He kept telling him you were gone and to turn you before it was too late. But he wouldn't do it. He just kept breathing for you, giving you his blood and CPR. It would have been so much easier to turn you," he said seriously. "Never even considered it, as far as I can tell." He gave me a crooked smile and wiped at his eyes. "He didn't leave your side for three days. I don't know if I'm supposed to tell anyone this, but he fed from Sylis and Seivor so he didn't have to leave you, in case something happened. After giving you so much of his blood, he needed to replenish himself, but he refused to leave, so that's when they offered him their veins. I was willing to break another rule for him and let him take blood from anyone willing, but he refused." Hendricks shook his head. "He's more honorable than I could have imagined. More than anyone else I've ever met—human or vampire."

"Where is he? I want to thank him."

"We've all done that more times than we can count." My mom wiped away her tears.

"As soon as he knew you were no longer in danger and was certain you wouldn't need any more blood, they left to see if they could catch up with the *kooks*. We received information of a large horde. They radioed that they found something and were going to follow and find the revenant," Hendricks told me. "That didn't stop him from filling a couple of blood bags for you just in case, though." He shook his head again in wonderment.

"The revenant?" I was confused about the term he used.

"It's what we're calling that thing." He glanced at my mother, and his voice grew dark. "It isn't a *kook* or an *evo*, not like we're used to. Revenant seemed to be the most fitting term to describe what it is. Of course, it was Grady who came up with it, and immediately Sylis agreed. It stuck after that."

"Have they checked in or found anything more?" I was worried now. They were hunting the thing that had killed Pike without so much as a struggle.

"It's been more complicated than I think they thought it would be. They went after it but doubled back when they lost the trail to the water." He pinched his face in deep thought. "They picked it up again near an extinct town, called Murray. They radioed for help, thinking they'd caught a break, so we sent down Brooks, your guys, and Rick's team to check it out, but they lost it again by the time they arrived. They checked in just before we came here and said they were headed back this way. He knows you're awake." He smiled at me. "You'll be able to talk to him as soon as they get here."

I nodded in relief that they were coming back. "Murray? That's really close." I remembered seeing that town name on our maps. It was in our territory and only about an hour away.

"Which is why we didn't send an arsenal when they asked for help. If there had been trouble they couldn't handle, we're in radio contact and could have had guys ready to go at a moment's notice. But since it is so close, we needed to protect the town."

"I agree, and it's all the more reason for me to get out of here."

"Listen, Abby." He sat up. "I know you feel like new—and surprisingly, you look and act as if nothing is wrong—and we're willing to let you get out of here tonight." He wafted his hand between himself and my mother. "But there's no way in hell you're gearing up to work or even walk the wall for a while. You're not going out to meet your team. You're not doing any patrols. You're not even going to sit at a desk as a radio operator. You can go home, and that's it." He swiped his hands across his lap, one over the other. "Paige is the only one still staying at the O, aside from the VIGs, and I'm sure she'd feel better with someone else in the building with her. But you're not going back on duty for a while. At all. End of story. Not until I say otherwise," he told me with finality in his voice.

"But I feel fine. I can help." I still needed to try, though I knew it was a lost cause.

"It's non-negotiable. The answer is no."

"For how long?" I whined.

"Honey, you almost died." My mom reached out and took my hand. "Can you please just take a little time off? Let your body fully heal. Let me have some time with my daughter, and be grateful that you're alive."

"That's blackmail."

"I don't care what you call it," she asserted. "You need time."

"You need to be cleared by Aemen, anyway," Hendricks threw in like a side note.

"What? Why?"

Aemen was the vanguard counselor. We had regular sessions with him as part of our job already, so I wasn't expecting this.

"Abby, like your mom just said, you almost died. You've been through a traumatic experience. You were attacked and nearly killed. I know you're strong, but you could have some latent PTSD. Besides, it's protocol, and you have to follow the same rules and guidelines as everyone else." He raised his brows at me.

"So, then, not tomorrow?"

"No." He laughed at me. "Not tomorrow."

"But as soon as I'm cleared..."

"You'll be back on active duty," he vowed.

I sighed in relief.

"Are you ready to go, then?" My mom retrieved the bag of clothes she'd brought with her and jangled it in her hand.

"Oh yes, please." I threw off my blanket and got up to get dressed.

Chapter Sixteen

"Abby!" Charlie and Harper ran to me as soon as my mother and I walked through the front door of the O.

Hendricks had left the care center room so I could get dressed and had gone to wait for Ethan, the other VIGs, and the vanguard teams at the gate. He wanted to get their report firsthand, and they should have almost been back to town by now.

"Hi!" I laughed as they smothered me, hugging them back as best I could but since they pinned me, it was difficult. "What are you guys doing here?"

"We saw Zach on his way to work, and he said you were awake," Harper said.

"So, naturally, we came here because we knew you wouldn't be staying another night there," Charlie bragged.

"Even though Zach told us you weren't coming home until tomorrow."

They both laughed together.

"Oh, poor Zach. When will he ever learn?" I smiled.

"I think he may have been hoping she would stay more than he actually believed it." My mom winked at them.

"Yes, he's a dreamer." Charlie exaggeratedly blinked her eyes.

"I'm so glad you're okay!" Harper hugged me again. "You had us all really worried."

"Yeah. Don't do that."

"I'll try to remember for next time."

"There will not be a next time," my mother said, unamused.

"So, fill me in," I told my two friends.

We talked for a short time, next to the check-in counter since the O had already been shut down for the night. They didn't stay very long but promised to be back in the morning to help Gigi open. We'd catch up more then.

With the town on high alert, the O wouldn't be open for recreation, but cooking and taking food to everyone on duty was something the O normally did for the vanguard. We always made grab-and-go things—sandwiches, granola bars, power and protein balls, etcetera—and we helped stock the decon zone's fridge too. With all the extra security and duty shifts scheduled around the clock, we would be cooking extra and delivering often. We'd still be busy here, even without all the patrons.

When they left, my mother stared at me for a few seconds.

"What's the matter?" I asked her.

"I'm just so happy you are okay." Her voice broke, and she teared up. "You had me worried. I don't know what I would do if I ever lost you."

"I love you." I wrapped her up in a tight hug and cried with her. It had been scary for me too, but I could only imagine what it must have been like for her.

"Okay. I'm done." She mopped at her face with a tissue, cleared her throat, and smoothed her hair. "You're alive. You're here, and you're healthy. I have everything to be happy and grateful for. No more tears."

"I'm so sorry I scared you." I wiped at my face. "I'm mostly sorry that it's part of the job."

"You don't need to apologize to me." Her voice quivered. "I try my best to keep a positive outlook. I know what you do, and I know you don't want to be in danger. But it still scares me."

"I know." I hugged her again.

"I love you, Abby," she whispered into my hair. "Alright. I'm going to grab a few things from Lane's, and then we'll both be back here to stay."

"I'm going to my room. Unless you want me to wait until you get back?"

"No, don't be silly. We'll come by and check on you when we get back. But you need to get some rest."

"Okay. See you soon."

I left the lamp by the door on for her and the VIGs but clicked off the other lights as I walked down the hall to the guest rooms. Going in the opposite direction of my room first, I knocked on Paige's door. I wanted to check in with her and make sure she was okay since she was the only guest still here from the Honor group. I wanted her to know that I was back and that she wasn't alone.

When she didn't answer after my second attempt, I figured she was asleep and went to my room. I'd check on her in the morning.

My room was one of only two down the small corridor on the opposite side of the building. They had once been four double rooms, two on each side of the hallway, but had been converted into two living spaces—one for my mom and one for myself.

The door to my room was ajar, and a dim light was coming through the open crack, the soft glow casting a warm hue in a line against the dark carpet.

Reaching for my gun on instinct, I remembered I didn't have it because I was in pajamas right out of the care center. I thought about going to the kitchen for a knife or heading out to find someone to help me. But then I thought maybe Harper or Charlie had opened my door and turned the lights on for me, and I might be overreacting. This was the PTSD I needed to get cleared of. So I pushed open the door, peered around the barrier, and stepped in.

"Hello?" I called out because that's what you did when you walked into a room you weren't sure was empty.

Standing in front of the window, facing away from me, was a tall, dark figure. The lamp on my bedside table was on and illuminated just enough of the room to cast shadows, but not bright enough to get a clear view of the person, just their silhouette.

"Ethan?" I moved further into the room. "When did you get here?"

I was excited and relieved he was back, so I walked faster past the bathroom to the end of the small wall that opened to the rest of the space ... and regretted it instantly.

I had ignored my gut. I should have run to the kitchen to get a knife or run outside to get help, scream, or call for an army.

Paige was standing near the foot of my bed, shoulders hunched over and arms dangling loosely to her sides. Her hands and fingers twitched spastically, and her body swayed oddly as her head jerked up to look at me. Bloody hair stuck matted to her neck and face, clumps of it swung—sticky and hard—while the rest lay plastered down against her scalp, smooth and shiny with wetness. Beads of dark liquid dripped from the ends and landed on her red-stained clothes, the clean, light-colored carpet now a drip cloth to catch her leaky death. Her pallor was ashen. Hollow, sunken, and black eyes that once held whiteness in the sclerae, were now bloodshot and dull yellow. Her pupils were cloudy, the vibrant blue now muted and gray, and a sound like congested breath wheezed through her skewed and gaping mouth.

"Paige?" My voice trembled in question.

Her head jerked and twisted at the sound, crazed eyes darting around in the sockets, absent and unfocused.

"I didn't know what would happen once I fed off her," a familiar voice said as another turned around to face me.

"Pike?" My heart jumped in my chest, my voice barely a whisper.

"I'd hoped she would be more like me. Alas, she woke a mindless drone." He sounded bored as he walked from the window over to Paige, picking up a twisted lock of her matted hair. "Rather disappointing, actually." His voice was laced with contempt. He dropped the hair he held and rubbed the red wetness between his forefinger and thumb before licking it off. "She follows directions, though. That's something."

He looked at me as she stumbled a few steps away from him, raised her arms, and dragged her feet toward me. I was sure it was a demonstration on his part meant to scare me.

It worked.

"He killed you. I watched you die." I backed up each step she took toward me.

Pike didn't answer me. He pulled his arms behind his back like I had seen him do many times while he'd been alive. Unblinking, he watched as Paige continued forward, never taking his eyes from mine—his now the same sinister red as the revenant's, who had killed him.

"Why?" I asked through broken breath. The fear and sadness laced heavily in my words, and as I flinched away from Paige's proximity, my heart broke at the sight of her face.

The stranger before was someone I'd grown to know as my friend. Now, he was just as deadly and beastly as the creature who had turned him.

"Why what?" he sneered. "Why have I come? Why did I turn her? Why am I doing this?" He took a few steps closer to me, and Paige came to a sudden halt. "All good questions, Abby." His voice changed as if detached from the sound. All the warmth and kindness he'd once had were no longer there, and in their place was something sinister and cold.

"I did this." He pointed at Paige as if she were a thing. "To see what would happen. Of course, I was hungry. I'm always hungry now. But mostly, I was just curious. Poor girl, in the wrong place at the wrong time," he said dismissively of her and what he had done. "I thought she was you."

"This isn't you. This is not who you are."

"It is now. Blood and power; power and blood. It's all that consumes me now, Abby. I want more. I need more. And I'll do anything to get it." His voice was dead as he stalked toward me like a cat hunting prey, his admission a serious threat.

"What do you want?" I shrunk away from him and his approach, terrified and all alone. To think I had survived death just long enough to be killed by its neophyte.

"I came for Ethan. Where is he?" His voice twisted into a baleful curiosity.

"I don't know." My voice broke on the lie, so I tried again. "I don't know." I took another step back but was stopped by the wall behind me.

Pike stood in front of me now, less than a foot away, the smell of death on his tongue like the breath of whiskey on a drunk.

"I can smell him on you," he breathed. "In you ... coursing through your veins," he nearly whispered as he raised a hand, slowly bringing it to my face.

I wanted to recoil but was scared stiff, too afraid to move.

He pressed a frigid finger against my neck, ran it down the carotid artery, and asked again, "Where's Ethan?"

The words caught in my throat, and my lips trembled. I shook my head, answering his question.

"Liar," he seethed.

Pike reached up with his hand, wrapped his stony fingers around my chin, and grabbed me tightly. The pressure was so great I knew I must be instantly bruised. He jerked my head to the side and held me in place as he inhaled my scent from the base of my throat up my neck. A deep, throaty rumble vibrated through his chest, the sound somewhere between a growl and a purr.

"I wonder what you taste like mixed with all his blood swimming inside of you," he mused in my ear. Pike dropped his head to my collarbone and pressed his tongue to my throat, then licked up the length of my neck. "I always knew you'd taste good. I imagined what it would feel like to wrap my mouth around you and sink my teeth into your soft flesh. So elegant and enticing. Tender and pliable. Such a unique flavor coursing through your pretty little veins. So rare. You're probably so *sweet.* But now, I bet you're utterly delectable." He flattened his tongue under my ear and rolled it up to suck in the lobe.

Then he tightened his grip around my face and slammed my head into the wall.

Chapter Seventeen

The air was rancid. That's what woke me—the stench of death so strong it felt heavy and thick, like humid summer air next to a warm ocean. I could feel it around me like a fog, coating my nasal passages with each inhale, clinging to the delicate skin, and sticking to the tiny hairs. I was careful not to open my mouth, afraid to taste the particles in the air.

My wrists hurt from the binding around them, and my shoulders screamed out in pain. They were stretched beyond a comfortable limit, pulled behind me, wrapped around a pole, and secured with something rigid and hard. My legs had been left free and unbound, but they were so cold from the concrete that my bones ached and my joints throbbed. The back of my head pounded, the sore spot thrumming to the beat of my heart, each pulse a twinge and an ache as it hammered through my head.

I opened my eyes, but my sight didn't reveal any additional information. It was so dark.

But I wasn't alone. All around me was a chorus of wheezing, groaning, and gurgling breaths that stirred and polluted the air with death. There was movement; the distinct sound of shuffling, shoed feet over a surface and teeth as they clanked, grounding together with the impact of an empty jaw.

My legs were stiff and numb, my feet like ice. I bent my knees and pulled my calves against my thighs, ignoring the pain as I pressed my weight into my heels and inched my way up the pole until I was standing.

My thighs burned from exertion, my spine was sore from the pressure of the hard surface, and my skin felt on fire from the friction. Blood rushed through my legs and feet now that the circulation was no longer cut off, and the numbness was replaced with a needling tingle that traveled from the bottoms of my feet up into my hips. Even my arms prickled and pinned with the returning nerve sensation.

Now that I was upright and standing, the room didn't seem as dark. Either my eyes were adjusting to the blackness, or I was somewhere where light could filter in from the oncoming daybreak.

With runty steps, I inched my way around the pole to get a better view of the room and assess my situation. I clenched my teeth, ignoring the skin burns as the thin sheath around my wrists stretched and rubbed off with the movement.

As I crept around, the dimmest glow lightened the panes of glass in the windows. I couldn't be sure because it was still so dark, but I thought it might have been an industrial space. Other pillars like the one I was shackled to were in the room, but I couldn't see them clearly, just columns of dark against the muted light. The room was otherwise empty besides the shadowy figures responsible for the smell and noise.

I stopped when I saw them, only a quarter of the way around the post. My heart rate jumped, blood swooshing in my ears, and my breathing spiked as I shook. My heightened anxiety seemed to agitate the creatures, and their mindless shifting intensified in response. So did their groans of hunger.

"Care-ful," a gnarly voice graveled from a distance. The strangled growl—a deep bass that filled the room with dread—carried over the clamor of the dead. The *kooks* in the room stirred, their own deadly chatter whirring with a buzz.

I whimpered. The sound of his voice set off every alarm in my body, but there was nothing I could do. I couldn't move. I couldn't protect myself. All I had with me was my voice, and that was worthless right now.

Panic spread through my body. I knew that rasp. My body recognized it as it clenched in fear, my stomach aching with remembered pain. I'd heard it only once before, but it frightened me to the marrow in my bones.

"You remember me," he crooned in my ear, the deep bass quaking through my startled body.

I hadn't heard his approach. His cold breath stung my flesh and sent shivers down my spine. The space around him seemed to cool as he hovered—breathing, tainting, and chilling the air. His respiration was dark and hollow.

My breath was shallow and fast, each inhale of his exhale as frigid as winter and as putrid as death. I fruitlessly pushed myself further against the pole and shrank away from the monster, but we were locked in place together—me unwillingly, and him menacingly.

For the longest time, he didn't move or speak. He just stood there in front of me, existing in *finis*. Abruptly, he turned away, and a loud growl ripped through his chest.

The fury was so great it hurt my ears, and I flinched away. Something moved near me. The drag and shuffle of feet drew my attention and gave me a fresh worry. Panic shot through me, and I realized the revenant didn't have full control over the creatures that loomed in the room. Not like Pike had seemed to have over Paige.

Frantically, I worked the binding on my wrists, pulling at the material to stretch it so I could get free, but I only made things worse. I broke open my skin. Whatever was holding my wrists together seemed to have found purchase in the soft flesh and sawed through me at the hint of movement.

Another roar escaped the revenant's lips, then the crack of a skull splitting and a body hitting the floor locked me into place.

A hard hand wrapped around my throat and squeezed. "Don't ... move," he seethed.

I didn't. I couldn't even if I wanted to.

The scuffle of dead slowed after a moment, and so did their avid cries. Their agitation seemed to simmer second by second until they were once again a mindless drone of surround sound. The light in the room shifted from dark to a blue hue, and I could see everything around me in the muted lambency. The creatures were no longer just shadowy figures, and the revenant's face was as clear as a bell, his red eyes almost aglow now that they were catching the light.

I tried to stay still, to calm and gather myself and my thoughts, but even my struggled breath around the revenant's firm grasp caused the tie around my wrists to slash deeper into my flesh.

The fiend panted noxiously in my face and groaned in time with the newest cut of my skin as the warmth slipped from the gash, grabbing his attention. The hand he had pressed firmly against my throat tightened a fraction more, then the revenant shifted, moving his arm to swipe at my bound hands behind the pole. His icy finger swept the trickle of blood that rolled down my hand, and with a deep rumble from his chest, he brought a dirty hand to his mouth to lap at his fingers.

"Vampire," he mewed at the taste of Ethan's blood in my system.

He pushed on my stomach with a cold, hard fist and nearly knocked the wind out of me. The sudden and quick pressure forced all the air from my lungs, and the pain felt like a dulled version of the knife wound the revenant had given me.

"Get ... away," I panted. "Get ... away ... from ... me."

He grabbed my face then, the same way Pike had, hitting the bruises and sore spots along my jaw and neck. Twisting my face one way, then the other, he jerked me side to side as if to get a closer look.

"Appy," he mispronounced my name, but the word was clear—deliberate.

My heart pounded in my chest. "Abby," I corrected through clenched teeth. It didn't make sense why. I didn't know what had made me do it.

"Happy ... Abby." The creature grinned.

The words sent a fresh wave of chills down my spine. Adrenaline flooded my system as I panicked. My breath was quick, my heart rate jumped, and my muscles shook. I needed to leave and escape this room, this nightmare, more than ever before.

I tried to jerk my face away and move my body, but the revenant's grip was so solid I didn't budge.

"No," I yelled and tried to rip my face from his hold.

"Happy ... Abby." He lowered himself to look directly into my eyes and repeated the words.

"*No*!" I yelled, my chest constricting. A crushing, invisible weight pressed down on me as my mind reeled.

"Appy."

"No." My jaw quivered.

"Are you ... my Appy ... girl?" the wicked creature asked, using a nickname only my father knew.

"No." My voice was smaller than I'd meant it to be. "Get away from me."

The sound broke as my face ran hot with tears, and the dead around me stirred.

It wasn't him. It *couldn't* be him. My father was dead. He died a long time ago. It couldn't be him.

"You... remember... me," the revenant stammered in his drawn-out way. "Don't ... you ... Appy?" He cocked his head to the side like I had seen him do only once, right before he stabbed me.

The *kooks* in the room stirred again, unchecked, their moans louder and their teeth clanking together with growing anticipation. The revenant was focused on me instead of the room, reminding me again of the multiple reasons to fear this place.

"Get away from me!" I seethed, my breath hitching on the words. "Get away!" I wailed as my eyes and throat burned.

I wanted him away from me, but I needed him to control his flock.

The door kicked open with a bang, and a wash of light splayed through the room. "Release her," Pike demanded, his voice like acid.

Around me, the *kooks* simmered instantly into a calm compliance. Where they had once swayed and shifted around the room under the revenant's control, they now stood stock still and nearly motionless, appearing as dead as they should be.

The revenant released his stranglehold around my neck, and I gasped for breath. The influx painfully stretched my throat open where it had been closed off for too long, and the air stanched the burn in my lungs. I coughed as I tried to regain control of my breathing and swallowed against the lump in my throat.

"Get away from her," Pike ordered.

"She's ... my," the revenant's baritone voice boomed in defiance.

"Your daughter. Yes, I know." Pike looked at me expectantly. Though the words were bored, his interest in my reaction was not.

"Blood and power; power and blood."

He wanted this power over me, wanted me to react.

The devastation consumed me, and I knew it was true.

I clenched my teeth and sucked in a quick breath to hold in my sob. My eyes, however, were not under my control, and tears blurred my vision as they spilled down my face. Anger flared through me, so much so that my face flushed. I knew he wanted to watch me fall apart. I could see it in his eyes, on his face, so instead, I spit at his feet.

"Did your parents not teach you any manners?" He marched over and backhanded me.

The impact dimmed my sight and confused my senses, and I was sure I'd pulled a muscle in my neck. My lip split open and my mouth filled with blood, but I barely felt the sting. It was just another stacked brick on an already full load.

"No!" The revenant turned on Pike. His voice was cold and deadly. "Mine."

"And you'll have her forever when we're finished using her," Pike sneered.

The revenant hummed with glee, deep within his chest.

It was decided then. I wasn't getting out of this alive. Not as I was. Not that I'd expected it. Even in death, the need to procreate one's species was at its core, and I was the daughter of death itself.

With Pike's confirmation, the revenant backed away to disappear into the sea of the dead. I didn't want to believe that thing was my father, but somehow, I knew it to be true. I felt it. Perhaps, deep down, I knew from the first moment I saw his face.

I tried to remember him, to remember what he had looked like when I was a child, but just like before, I couldn't get a clear picture of him in my mind. The memories were distorted and fuzzed, fragments and pieces the most I could see. Fleeting and blurry moments, but never anything concrete.

Confused and heartbroken, I was convinced that none of this would ever make any sense, and worse, I would never get answers. I'd never know.

Because I wouldn't leave here as anything but undead.

Chapter Eighteen

Grasping my shoulders in his vise-like grip, Pike stepped into my view.

"Comfortable?" he said in a snide tone. Knowing it would hurt me, he spun me around the pole, slowly.

My skin burned with the friction against the metal, and the binding at my wrists dug deeper into my flesh. It stung with each new cut and slit. I yelped once but bit down on my cries when my pain made him smile.

He pushed against me as he spun me around, my spine grating against the hard surface. My arms threatened to pull free from the sockets with the movement. When I was where he wanted me to be, he stepped back, crossed his arms over his chest, and glared at me.

"Why does he listen to you?" I asked when the pain ebbed enough that I could speak without my voice cracking.

"I'm cognizant and more powerful," he boasted. "Another evolution of the virus. I'm older. My blood is stronger, purer." He paced as he theorized, offering more information than I had asked for. "He's not as sentient or aware as I am. I remember everything, where he seemed to only remember fragments over a long period of time. Then he learned, gained knowledge and power along the way. Whereas I am exactly as I was before, only better."

"You are *not* better," I snarled.

"You know nothing."

"He knew you and Ethan," I stated to keep him talking.

"Yes."

"How?"

"Ask Ethan." He smirked.

"How will I do that when you intend to kill me?" I fumed.

"Kill you? No." He chortled. "I'm not going to kill you, sweet blood."

"You're going to let him turn me into what you did to Paige?"

"Don't be daft, Abby. I'm not going to make you a mindless poppet. I'm going to turn you into a vampire and then make you like me."

My sharp inhale lit up his face.

"You can't," I whispered.

"I can," he thrilled. "And I will. You'll still be mine to control but not a disgusting savage slowly rotting away," he said with disdain as if his minions were truly beneath him.

"You failed with Paige." My voice was shaking now.

Pike came to stand in front of me again. "I tried and failed, yes. I won't make that mistake again." He ran his finger down the side of my throat.

"How, then?"

"I have the vampires from Henry Park," he gloated. "Well, one of them. The others were too delicious not to kill, and there was virtually nothing left to reanimate once I was finished. But that was when I had just woken." He wrapped his hand around my jaw again, forcing me to look at him. "Don't worry, I'm in control now."

"You're holding a vampire hostage?" Icy fear gripped me as blood ran cold in my veins, my skin crawling with disgust at how insidious he truly was.

"I'm holding you hostage. Why is the other surprising?"

"Why are you doing this? You remember what it was like to be alive; you said so yourself. You remember the fear and the need to get rid of these ... creatures."

"Yes," he said matter-of-factly. "But now, I no longer care. It appears I'm not burdened with morality. I told you, Abby—blood and power. It's all I want now."

He wasn't lying. What he'd done to Paige... The Pike I knew would have never been like this. He would have never said these things, never done what he'd done.

He tightened his hold around my jaw, squeezing the bruises he'd left the first time, as he wrenched my head from side to side.

"What are you doing?" I asked through clenched teeth.

"I can't have you turning dead before becoming a vampire. Especially before Ethan gets here." He pulled my face back to look at him. "What fun would that be?" He sneered, then smoothed down my hair and pushed the wayward strands from my face.

"What do you mean, before Ethan gets here?"

"I'm sure he's on his way now." He stepped back and looked around the room, bored.

"How will he find us?"

"I left him a note."

"A note?"

"Paige."

"She can't speak!" I yelled at him, angry at him for killing her, for not caring that he had.

"Of course not." Tsking, he ran his thumb across my bottom lip. "But he'll get the message." He sauntered out of the room through the same door he came in.

Fear latched onto me. I scanned around, sure his drones would activate and come for me now that he was out of sight. When they didn't, I still couldn't relax, and my back hurt from the tension. I wanted to break free but was afraid the smell of fresh blood would set them off, so I didn't dare move. I couldn't scream or call for help. There was no one around who could assist me. I was stuck—literally.

As I waited for death to return for me, the room lightened from blue to light gray. My feet hurt from standing for so long in one place, cold and numb again. My shoulders were throbbing from the awkward position

I was trapped in, and my neck hurt from where Pike had wrenched it. I probably had a concussion—my head was still throbbing too.

I wondered where Pike had gone, how much time I had left. Pike's plan—to use the captured vampire to turn me and then make me into whatever he was—was horrifying. I wasn't resigned to my fate, but there was nothing I could do about it either. Instead, I stressed how his actions and decisions were not a prize for himself but some sort of victory over Ethan. It seemed he was obsessed with hurting him and was using me to accomplish his goal. Everything Pike had been, he was now a complete opposite of in his death.

Suddenly, Pike was in the room again. Putting himself in front of me, he faced the door and weirdly cocked his head, all in one fluid motion. He turned an ear toward the opening and his eyes down to the floor. A low chuckle rumbled through his chest before he swept his eyes at me with a satisfied leer.

Two *kooks* flanked my sides as Pike stepped back and nearly pressed himself against me. The two dead turned to face me, and brought their faces so close to mine that the whisper of air washed over me from their movement. The stench of fetid decay choked me, and I gasped out in fear when their teeth chomped together in reaction.

The door banged open, stopping short when it hit the wall hard enough to lodge the knob into the surface.

"You got my note," Pike crowed.

"Where is she?!"

"Ethan!" I yelped.

Pike shot out his hand behind him and had his vise grip around my throat in an instant, cutting off my voice and most of the air. "Don't. Or I'll snap her neck."

I could barely see Ethan around Pike, but Pike's threat had stopped him from removing his sword from its sheath.

He released his grip on the hilt of the blade and held his hands up in surrender. "Pike. Let her go."

"Why would I do that?"

"You don't need her. You have me now."

"I knew you'd come for her," Pike taunted smugly. "So predictable."

"Let her go."

"No. She's still useful. She'll be your first meal after I turn you," he revealed another version of his ever-changing plan.

"*No*!" I screamed through his chokehold.

Pike tightened his grip around my throat, severing the sound completely. I tried to twist my head free from his grasp, but his fingers only dug deeper in response.

His eyes were full of hate. "Stop moving. Unless you want your mother to join this family reunion," he spat at me.

I stopped struggling. Not because I thought he would keep his word and leave my mother alone, but because I couldn't take the risk on the off chance that he might.

"Get your hand off of her!" Ethan yelled at his old friend.

"Or what? You cannot stop me, and I no longer take orders from you, *my liege*," Pike roared like a madman. "You have no idea what I have become, what I am now! The power. The freedom. I rule an army! I will sample this tasty little morsel you claimed for yourself, and I'll make you watch. Then, I will turn you and watch as you have what is left. I will be your master, and you will serve me!" He was confident. Overly confident, just like a narcissist. Blood and power.

And then it hit me.

"Or you will serve him." I barely got the words out around the tight hold on my neck. My voice was a rough whisper, and my throat burned from the scratch of enunciation.

"What?" Pike whipped his head around, his eyes slant and the red of his irises pulsing with angry intrigue.

"He will take over your rule, just as you took over your maker's." It was difficult to speak. Painful. His large hand covered my entire neck, and his fingers easily wrapped around to the back with a firm grip as he squeezed and pushed against my larynx.

Blood was not equal to the power he craved. If it were, we would all be dead already. His bloodlust was second and didn't rule him as entirely as it did his subjects. His tell was obvious in this game once you realized it.

He knew Thompson Falls well enough to try to overthrow it. He knew its vulnerabilities. Its protocols. Its people and their abilities. He knew the VIGs' tactics and could surmise our combined response to any threat.

Power was what he wanted. Power was what this was about. Power over *Ethan*.

Pike looked at me with fiery eyes, but he didn't contradict me, and in his silence, I could see it—the realization that I was right as it flitted across his features. He hadn't considered it. True to his narcissistic state, he thought no one could beat him. That he was at the top and no one could take that from him.

It was almost too easy to play into his fears, so I continued with the distraction. "You were stronger than your maker; you said it yourself. Evolution. Blood strength." I choked as the pressure increased with his tightened hold. "Ethan is older than you. His blood is purer. He's stronger than you in every way. He was your leader once, and he will be again. He was your better in every way in life, and he will be again in death." My whispered promise was strained now. I didn't know if what I was saying was true, but by Pike's reaction to it, some of it must have been.

He was furious and his brows furrowed, but with his attention split as I brought his fears to light, Ethan was able to slip out his sword.

"You will serve him," I strained over his clenched hand, my throat raw. "And he will take all your power."

A shot rang out, and the *kook* to my left dropped.

Pike roared, released his chokehold on me, and turned to defend himself, just as Ethan swiped his sword down through the air. The dead in the room snapped out of their mind-controlled stupor, and all at once, they stirred the room with chaos. Pike released his pets from his command, and I was little more than a skewered meal in mortal danger of being eaten.

The *kook* my right didn't take but a few moments to resume its natural state. It lifted its rotted hands, grabbed my shoulder, and dug its fingers into my flesh with surprising strength for something so putrefied.

Instinctively, I jerked away and pulled my arm free of its grasp, dislocating my left shoulder in the process. My scream was almost as loud as the pop it had made, the pain was only masked by the imminent threat of death.

"No, no, no, no, no!" I prattled fruitlessly and watched in horror as the dead brought his face closer to the meaty bicep of my arm. I had barely an inch more of leeway now that my arm was free of the socket.

The pain was nearly too much to bear as I moved around to evade the set of teeth, but I couldn't gain enough space or stop what was to happen. I moved my body around the poll, sidestepping in inches to gain feet, but the creature latched on to me in tow.

"Abby!" Ethan yelled out, his voice pained and angry, but no rescue came. He was stuck to fight for his own life against Pike.

The *kook* was a near breath away from its first bite when its head violently wrenched back, its neck bones snapping with a loud crack as it twisted unnaturally. His head ripped from the rest of its body, like a cap twisted free from a bottle and pulled off. The skin stretched and ripped, followed by the tear of muscle.

The revenant held the *kook's* head in his hands as the spine tentatively hung onto the cavity. He crushed its skull like a watermelon, the sound a hollow pop, and it squished together as the two solid sides smashed into the soft tissue. Pulling at the pulverized head and kicking the body at the same time, he severed its connection to vertebrae, then tossed it aside like disregarded waste. A disgruntled roar escaped his lips in what I assumed was a defense and claim of me—the prey. Then he killed the other *kooks* nearest us. When he finished, he shook the blood, brains, and guts from his hands, and looked at me with determined eyes as he stepped closer and reached out.

I shrunk away from him automatically, my shoulder exploding again in agony. My breath caught, and tears sprung to my eyes. If I had felt my feet, I was sure my toes would have curled with the pain.

The revenant stepped behind me and the bindings shifted at my wrist, when two more figures blurred in through the door. The windows around the walls shattered with a *rat-a-tat-tat* as a spray of bullets ripped through the room and into the dead.

Everything was chaotic in an instant, and it was hard to track it all around me.

The revenant stopped untying me at the sight of Sylis and Seivor, and instead left me prisoner to disappear again into the throng of the dead. The two VIGs split off once inside, darting out of sight so fast I couldn't keep track of them or their movements.

Ethan and Pike were locked in a battle against each other, fighting around the *kook* threat in the room while taking turns blocking the other's path to get to me. The ear-splitting metal against metal as their swords collided chorused with the gunfire and destructive mayhem in the room, and I was stuck to agonizingly watch on in horror.

Abruptly, I was sprung free and fell heavily to the ground. My freedom was an unexpected and painful surprise, which left me unprepared to catch myself. The concrete came at me fast, hard and unforgiving, but I didn't fall face-first. Instead, I lobbed off the side of the pole and landed on my ass. My dislocated arm jostled around and was an excruciating reminder of my limited ability to help. But I gritted my teeth and forced myself from the floor before I became something's meal.

I stood, grabbed my arm, and spun in a circle around the room to catch my bearings, unsure what to do. The exits were blocked; *kooks* surrounded me, and I didn't have a weapon. I was still wearing the pajamas, and although being out in the *Morgue* in these clothes wasn't any better than being naked, I felt lucky today and used it as an advantage.

Sucking in a breath, I clenched my teeth and pulled my useless right arm across my body, shoving the hand down the waist of my pants to secure it in place. The waist was elastic and had a tie that I cinched as tight as I could for it to hold my arm. If I had been wearing my vanguard suit, I couldn't have done that. With my hand snug against my stomach, my arm didn't move around as much with each shift and turn of my body, so the pain was more manageable as I moved to duck behind the pole that had once been my prison.

"Here." Sylis appeared at my side and pressed a weapon into my hand.

I looked down at *Walter*.

"Defend yourself." He shoved two magazines in my front pockets and then disappeared again.

I was preferably right-handed, but that wasn't an option. I'd practiced shooting with my left hand before, and even though it wasn't great, it was better than nothing.

Aiming with *Walter*, I stepped around the pole and fired. Now that I was free to see all around me more clearly, I recognized the room and put together what Pike had meant about leaving a note for Ethan.

We were in Honor. Paige had been the message. The building we were in was one from the small town. I wasn't part of the team that had cleared this building, but I recognized the devastated town outside the windows.

The room looked like a war zone. Dead bodies lay all around in various degrees of decay, and the smell only seemed to get worse each time a bullet or sword ripped through a carcass to release fresh gases from decomposition into the air.

I aimed and shot at whichever *kook* was closest to me, and when I'd emptied my first clip, I bent down to the ground to reload. With only one working hand, it took longer than expected, and I struggled more than I was used to. Loading a weapon with one hand hadn't been on my list of practice skills, but it would go to the top if I were lucky enough to get out of here alive.

"Abby, behind you!" Seivor yelled as I stood up.

I spun and elbowed the *kook* in the temple just as it lunged at me, which knocked it off balance enough for me to swing my gun around and shoot it in the head. Before it hit the ground, another came at me in its place, but I waited for it to get closer before I put it down. My shots weren't exactly accurate using my left hand, and Sylis and the revenant had moved in my line of sight as they fought, right behind my target. I was afraid to miss and hit Sylis.

I held my ground and counted my breaths as it continued toward me, all too aware that while I waited for this one, more moved closer. The way it came at me confirmed my earlier suspicion—we weren't just dealing with the regular dead anymore. This one, along with the one I had killed before him, was an *evo.* The determination behind its eyes looked a lot like awareness, and its steady and deliberate movements spiked a fresh wave of fear in my chest. Fighting off *evos* could be done. But if there were even as half of them as there were regular *munchers*, the five of us in this room wouldn't survive. They were just fast enough and just smart enough to make it too dangerous to take on in large groups, and we were in their den. Even with the help of the vanguard, it was too risky.

With the new threat and unpredictability of the revenant, and now Pike, we had no idea what we could be dealing with. The *kooks* and *evos* could have evolved further too, and we didn't know how many more were like Pike and the revenant. Everything was new again, and there was no way to know what we were up against. Most importantly, though, Pike had set this trap and he was certainly no fool.

When the *kook* I was aiming at was close enough to reach out and touch me, I stopped it with a single bullet between the eyes.

"We have to go!" I screamed out to the others as another *evo* put itself in my path from an adjacent door, with more to follow.

The revenant roared like a beast and grabbed Sylis's sword with both hands as it descended on him, clapping the blade between his palms. He shoved at Sylis, pushing him backward, and threw him through the air and out of a window. Then he stomped in my direction, his long, heavy strides pounding against the floor.

"No ... mine!" he roared again.

I raised my gun at him, and with each step he took, I pulled the trigger. I couldn't think about what I was doing or whom I was shooting. If this creature was truly and technically my long-dead father, it didn't matter right now. It didn't matter at all. He was a monster coming after me, and I had to defend myself or die trying.

I didn't want to miss, but I did. The use of my left hand, along with my fear, messed with my coordination. The first bullet landed in his shoulder but did nothing to slow him down, barely jolting him with the impact. The second and third pull both missed and instead planted in the plastered wall behind him. I hit him with the last five bullets, but nowhere critical enough to slow him down. If there even was such a thing. Four in the torso, and one that grazed the side of his face. His body jerked with the slugs to his chest, but his advance never faltered.

I dropped to my knees again to reload, but I knew I wouldn't make it in time, though I had to try. Impending death marched brazenly toward me as images flashed through my mind and blurred my vision.

Fear took over; it seized my focus and held me hostage, my muscles shaking. If he reached me, it would be over. If he took me away from here, I'd never survive, and although it should have done the opposite, the idea of living a gruesome existence in death nearly paralyzed me.

I tried, so hard, but I couldn't reload my weapon in time.

The revenant grabbed me by the hair and pulled me to stand. "My … Appy."

Walter clattered to the floor, and my good hand reflexively went to my hair to break free. It was no use, though. The revenant towered over me; I was nothing but a branch at the mercy of a mighty tree. He was stronger than I could have imagined, with combined brute force and merciless determination. He let go of my hair once I was on my feet, only to wrap his iron fist around my upper arm to steer me.

"No!" Pike bellowed from across the room.

The sound was so pained it stopped the revenant in place and drew his attention away from the retreat. The anguished, murderous glare on Pike's face as he scrambled to stand was almost tangible. I followed his gaze down to the floor, where his detached hand lay, still holding his sword.

Ethan's blade dripped dark with Pike's blood as if to punctuate what had happened. He kicked Pike's hand and the sword away from them, swinging toward Pike's head without hesitation, aiming to take it off.

Pike jumped back and narrowly missed being decapitated, then fled from the room. Ethan didn't follow him; he turned his attention to me and the revenant instead.

"Release her." He pointed his sword at the revenant, and though it was covered in black blood, the blade still glistened with a razor's edge in threat.

The revenant jerked me toward him and wrapped his forearm around my neck, trapping me against his body and using me like a shield. He laughed at Ethan but otherwise ignored him as he dragged me away.

Ethan darted after us in pursuit, and while the *kooks* ignored the revenant's attempt to escape, they appeared intent to go after Ethan to stop his advance. With every other step he took, he raised his weapon to kill as he continued forward.

I tried to pull at the revenant's arm and claw myself free with my good hand, but I wasn't strong enough, and if he at all noticed that I was fighting him, he didn't show it. With my other arm dislocated, it was nearly impossible to fight back, but I had to try, and so I did.

I wrapped a foot around his leg to trip him, but that didn't work and I lost my footing instead. I tried to punch him in the face, jab him in the eyes, pull his hair—anything to get leverage over him. I dropped my center of gravity to throw him off balance, elbowed him in whatever part I could reach. I even tried to hit him in the groin.

"Let me go!" I yelled.

We were at the door to the other room. If he pulled me through that door, it would be over. He would run, and Ethan wouldn't catch us. I had to do something, or my life would be forfeited.

I lifted with my stomach, ignoring the wince of pain deep within my injured belly, and kicked both my legs up into the air, as high as I could get them, then I threw myself forward. If he was human and I had tried any of these attempts to break free, I would have succeeded. This wasn't the same, but it was enough.

The shift of my weight and the force I had gotten with my kick forward pulled him with me and stopped us from passing through the door. The motion left me kneeling on the concrete and the revenant bent over at the waist. His arm was still wrapped around my throat when Ethan made it to us.

"Bram," he called the revenant by name. My *father's* name.

My heart pounced in my chest, my mind reeling at the implications. If there was any doubt in my mind who this creature was, it was gone now.

The revenant moved his arm and grabbed my neck again. The cold hand constricting my airway was painful but nothing compared to my heartache. Ethan had confirmed this monster was my father, but worse than that, he acknowledged he knew him.

"Let her go!" Ethan yelled.

"Stop. Or ... I kill ... my ... Appy." The revenant pulled me up from the floor by my throat until I was flat-footed and standing on the concrete, then he lifted me higher until my feet dangled in the air.

He laughed maniacally as I tried to pull myself free from his grasp. My legs swung and kicked the air, and I pounded with my good arm against the one he held me with, but after everything, my body didn't have enough fight left in it and resigned to dangle in my fate.

Ethan yelled at him again and again, but the revenant ignored us both and held his ground as my lungs burned.

Two jolts in quick succession thrust the revenant back and jerked me in the air, the delayed sound of the gunshots following as blood splattered my face. The revenant's hold on me loosened with the larger-scaled impacts, enough that I could wiggle free from his grip and drop to the floor. I scrambled away from him and threw myself at Ethan, who was just out of reach of the revenant.

He was shot three more times when Pike appeared behind him and yanked him through the door. The revenant grabbed a hold of his neck, wrapping the same hand around his throat as he had around mine, and bellowed through a gurgle of black blood. The tar-like substance spattered from his mouth and oozed through his fingers on his neck.

The revenant and Pike stared at us, anger, hatred, and disappointment unmistakable on their faces. The revenant looked torn. His eyes darted back and forth between me and the gathering vanguard that had overtaken the room. Self-preservation won the battle as he backed up further away from us.

Pike was seething. His teeth clenched, remaining hand balling into a tight fist, and his eyes glowed red as he stared Ethan down—pure evil and full of hate.

Behind them, *evos* and *kooks* filled the surrounding room.

The seconds ticked by like years of tension as the four of us faced off against each other.

Pike snarled an ear-piercing battle cry as he stepped back deeper into the room. He pulled his eyes from Ethan and stared me down as he disappeared into the shroud of death.

The hairs on the back of my neck stood in fear and warning. My skin tightened, and my blood ran cold.

He had said nothing. He didn't have to—the threat was there, written all over his face.

He wasn't giving up, and he was coming for me.

Chapter Nineteen

Ethan stepped forward as if to run after them when I grabbed him around the arm.

"Ethan! We have to go!"

The vanguard, Sylis, and Seivor were fighting off and killing *kooks* and *evos* faster than ever, but their efforts still weren't enough. The room was being overrun.

"Clear the room!" Hendricks shouted. It was the first time I had heard his voice.

"Your men go first!" Ethan yelled at him over the rapid gunfire.

"Wait! There are more hostages," I told them in a panic. We couldn't leave them here.

"They're dead," Ethan told me.

"How do you know?"

"We found them on our way up."

Hendricks waved his hand, and at the signal, the vanguard retreated through the windows and doors they had come through. "Abby, let's go!" Hendricks yelled at me as he stood next to a large window.

I turned to run to him but was stopped by a gentle tug on my good arm.

"She's with me." Ethan hollered and swept me off my feet into his arms.

I didn't protest and instead wrapped my left arm around his shoulder to hold myself steady. Sylis and Seivor circled us as we made our way through the room and killed anything brave enough to get too close. We weren't on the ground floor like I had thought, but only one story high. Ethan didn't linger, and as soon as we were on the lip of the window, he stepped out and dropped us effortlessly to the ground. The landing wasn't as soft as it could have been, but I chalked that up to the dislocated arm since even breathing was painful, so jumping from a building was to be expectedly uncomfortable.

When we hit the ground, he didn't waste time standing around and ran us away from the building, with Sylis and Seivor right on our heels. We circled back and met up with the vanguard team as they spilled out through a back door, then we all ran as a group past the security fence surrounding Honor and continued along a dirt-packed back road.

"I can run now if you put me down."

"No." Ethan tightened his hold on me and pulled me closer to his chest.

The vehicles were in sight and facing the opposite way from Honor. Most of the vanguard were running alongside us, but there were several team members around the convoy—who must have told them about this back road—including Ryan.

I was surprised to see him, considering the last time we'd been here. But maybe that's why he had been left with the vehicles outside of town this time.

"Start the engines," Hendricks ordered into the radio. I hadn't noticed him next to us and was amazed by his effortless ability to keep up with Ethan.

"Is everything in place?"

"Yes."

"Then do it," Ethan demanded.

"As soon as we are on the bus, Grady will hit the detonator."

"If you don't do it now, they will get away!"

Hendricks nodded and shouted over the radio, "Grady! Hit it!" Then he yelled at our fleeing group, "Move faster!"

The first explosion went off seconds later, followed by another, then another until I couldn't keep up the count on one blast beginning and another ending. Like dominos, once the first exploded, the others fell in line one after the other, until the town was only the aftermath of a bomb. The sky glowed orange from the fires, clouding with dust plumes of gray.

There hadn't been much left of Honor before the bombing, but I again felt the sad swell of loss at what once was. At one time, Honor had been a safe harbor for lost souls in search of a better life. Instead, it had unknowingly become the first step in their demise. The cleansing fires would wash away the stain on Earth that Honor had become, and as it raged on, I imagined the flames consuming all the pain and sadness with it.

When we reached the convoy, everyone went to their assigned vehicles and loaded up. There was no time to waste. The gray smoke wasn't only from the buildings as they burned, but mercury mixed in with it too. If Pike and the revenant had been in there, there was no way they could have survived. One thing was for certain though—all the *kooks* and *evos* we had left behind were no more, and if the two of them had escaped, they had just lost their entire army.

"Abby!" Zach ran up to me. "Oh, thank fuck."

"Zach!" Hendricks yelled at him. "Get on the damn bus!"

"Yes, sir." He smiled down at me in relief, but turned and led the way in.

Hendricks was the last to load, and as soon as he had climbed on the first step, the driver hit the gas.

"Nice job, man." Zach fist-bumped Grady as we walked by.

"They all worked this time." Grady looked back at the town with a huge smile on his face.

"Yeah, they did!" Seivor clapped him on the back.

"That's good," Hendricks agreed. "That's real good. Small victories in a large war are still victories."

We knew it wasn't over as we drove away. Pike and the revenant could still be out there, or there could be others like them that we didn't know about. We didn't know for sure, but this horde was gone and that was something.

"We need to set your arm now," Hendricks told me when we were on a smooth, paved road, off the dirt lane and far enough away from Honor. We were away from Thompson Falls, and he was worried about permanent damage if he didn't set it soon.

"Maybe she should have some pain reliever first," Zach suggested.

"I don't want to be unaware of anything for a while." The only type of pain reliever that would do anything to help would make my brain foggy or put me out. I didn't want that.

It was the first time I spoke since getting on the bus, and I heard it in my voice as it settled in—the weight of information, the sadness, the fear. More, even, that I didn't want to put words to yet.

"But you've already been through so much." Zach's voice was concerned.

"Yeah."

Zach slid forward in his seat and leaned on his elbows. "It's going to hurt like a motherfucker."

"Zach," Hendricks interrupted him. "Shut the hell up."

"Why don't you all give Abby some room since she can't have privacy." Brooks turned to the group that had crowded around me.

It was a gracious gesture, but we were all trapped in the same moving bus. Privacy wasn't an option, and more room wouldn't help with the pain. I was on a gurney at the back of the bus, Ethan next to me on my left, Zach at my feet, and Hendricks to my right, with Brooks next to him. Seivor and Sylis had both followed us to the back as well, and my team members had taken over the remaining rear bus seats. Dawsen, Joni, and Lauren had all turned themselves around to face me, with relieved and concerned smiles. Lauren and Joni medically knew what I was in for, and Dawsen had experienced it firsthand. I was glad they were all here with me. Privacy be damned.

"It's fine. Just do it already." I took a deep breath and released it.

"Okay." Hendricks's voice had dropped an octave, almost sounding somber. He put a rubber strap between my teeth and then wrapped his hands around my limp arm still tucked into my pajamas. It jostled around and had shifted out an inch or two, but had mostly stayed put.

As soon as he pulled my hand free from the elastic waist, I sucked in a breath and gritted my teeth. With my free hand, I grabbed the padded mattress, then closed my eyes.

"Ready?" Hendricks checked.

I nodded.

"On the count of three," he said. "One..."

POP! He twisted and shoved my arm back in the socket with a hefty jerk and a grunt.

I cried through clenched teeth at the searing pain and panted through until it ebbed enough that I felt myself relax. It hurt *really* bad, but it also felt better.

"Are you okay?" Hendricks wiped the hair from my forehead.

I nodded at him.

"Can I take this?" He touched the strap between my teeth.

I nodded again.

"Don't I feel like a giant baby now. I cried when they set mine," Dawsen lamented, humor in his words.

I split my eyes open a crack to see him smirk at me, so I returned the gesture. It helped a little.

"You'll need to wear a sling for a couple of months," Brooks told me.

"A couple of months?" My voice was hoarse from the pain-filled scream, and the volume of my whine was more like a ragged whisper.

"Twelve to sixteen weeks. And that's if there aren't complications and you have no fractures."

"Well, this is bullshit." I was annoyed. "I can't sit around for twelve to sixteen weeks, twiddling my thumbs."

"Oh yes, you can." Hendricks's authority boomed as he unwrapped an ace bandage.

"No way."

"Yes way. You'll be staying safely tucked away behind the walls of Thompson Falls for as long as I can reasonably keep you there too."

"What?!" I tried to screech, but it came out as a squawk.

"You heard me."

"Why?"

"Because I said so, that's why..."

"Alright, that's enough." Brooks took the ace bandage from him and interrupted our bickering. "We can talk about this later." He indicated to the spectator section behind him.

I poked my head around Brooks's large body and watched as everyone on the bus awkwardly hid their smiles, held in their laughter, and turned around in their seats. Hendricks treated everyone like this, but it was especially funny to the rest of the team when he did it to me. The Commander parenting me was, evidently, *hilarious*.

"You'll probably only need to wear it for a couple of days, and any complications or fractures will heal quickly in that time. You still have my blood in your system." Ethan sounded reserved, his voice tight.

I didn't turn to look at him. I couldn't.

"That's right." Brooks agreed. "I forgot about that. We'll take it day by day, then. Okay?"

"Okay." I could do a couple of days, even a week if I had to, but weeks? I would go crazy.

"Were you hurt anywhere else?" Brooks asked. "Other than your lip." He dabbed the cut with gauze and then added a layer of petroleum jelly.

It was deep. I knew that when it had happened. But it felt better too, and now that I remembered I had Ethan's blood, it made sense.

"My wrist from the binding and I might have a concussion, but nothing else. I didn't get scratched or bitten." If I were infected, there would be clear signs by now. But saying it out loud still relieved some tension in the room.

Zach's shoulders even dropped a little. My team's faces relaxed, and I swear I heard sighs of released breath.

Brooks cleaned and bandaged my wrist, then tipped my head down and leaned forward so he could look at the back of it. He moved my hair around, and I winced.

"We'll do tests back home, but based on the bruising, I think you're probably right."

"How did you find me so fast?" I took some pain reliever from him, then laid back against the gurney and shivered when Hendricks draped a blanket over me. I was cold and suddenly exhausted.

"We barely missed you." Ethan squatted down next to me, his voice low and guarded. "As soon as I walked in the building, I knew something was wrong, that someone had died there."

Images flashed through my eyes as he spoke.

The shadowed silhouette of someone standing in front of my window.

Paige hunched over, hair matted and dripping with blood.

"I knew it wasn't you. I know all too well what your blood smells like. But I recognized Pike's scent. Even though it had changed, I knew it was his."

Pike's face and his red eyes. His apathetic expression and the sneer of his voice.

"I went to your room and found Paige."

Tears snuck out the sides of my eyes at the memory of her.

Pike's hand wrapped around my face.

"I knew instantly that he had taken you, and I understood his message."

My head smashed into a wall.

Hendricks took my hand and squeezed it. "We figured out the time he had on us after we were on the road. He only had a twenty-eight-minute head start. I still don't understand how he made it to Honor as fast as he did." Hendricks's face was grim.

"Do you remember anything?"

"No." I shook my head, then winced.

"We don't know a lot more," Ethan added. "You know everything else."

Ethan calling the revenant by my father's name.

"Not everything, but I know enough." I stared at him.

His eyes flashed.

I looked away and let sleep overtake me.

My mom led me to the shower room, where she cut off my shirt and bra, undressed me, and helped me under the spray. I held my arm against me while she washed my hair and looked me over to make sure I had no bites or scratches. She dressed me in fresh clothes, gently put my arm in a sling, and escorted me into the medical bay so I could take the blood test. When it came back negative and they cleared me to leave the decon-zone, we drove to the O, where everyone else was already waiting.

"We'll be staying here tonight and for the foreseeable future," Mom told me.

We were in the restaurant, sitting around a large table. Everyone else had gotten something to eat. I wasn't hungry, so I'd opted for water.

I didn't respond to her, just stared at the water in my glass and spun it in circles between my thumb and fingers on my left hand.

"I'll stay home unless you want me to stay here too? In which case, I'd be more than happy to," Zach suggested.

They waited.

I didn't respond.

"We'll be here too," Ethan said of the VIGs, and Seivor and Sylis both agreed.

I watched as the light caught the liquid swirl in my glass.

"I'll have extra guards outside too," Hendricks added.

It was so quiet when they weren't talking. Piercing, but quiet.

"Abby, honey, please say something." My mom's voice was low and thick. Her hand lifted and wiped across her face.

They all shifted around uncomfortably as I spun through my thoughts—a blinking, mute statue with a twitchy hand. The scrape of the glass as I spun it on the table abrased the silence.

Ethan was next to me. Next to him were Sylis and Seivor. Zach was on my other side, my mom beside him, and then Hendricks.

Ethan put his hand on my leg. He had reached out to me on and off for the last couple of hours. I didn't acknowledge it. I couldn't.

"You're going to be safe now, Abs." Zach squeezed my hand. "You don't have to worry."

I blinked at the table and kept my breathing steady.

"We know how far they'll go now, peanut. We will not let anything like that happen ever again." Hendricks leaned forward on the table. "I promise." His voice cracked.

I stared at my water, but I could see them from my peripheral. When I didn't answer or comment, they'd look around at each other and someone else would say something and try again.

"Additional VIGs are coming too," Ethan tried. It must have been his turn. "We're not taking any chances with them out there. Not anymore."

I huffed, then spun my glass again.

My reaction startled the table.

"Them?" My voice was so flat I didn't recognize the sound. "You mean Pike and Bram."

If the room had been quiet before, it was dead silent now. Ethan's hand tensed on my leg. My mom jerked and sat up straighter. Seivor and Sylis, for their part, folded their arms over their chests. Hendricks dropped his chin and scratched his head.

Zach looked around the room, confused, then over at me. "What are you talking about?"

"You didn't know?" I looked at him.

His face was drawn down into a scowl, and his eyes shifted back and forth between mine for answers. "Know what?" His voice sounded confused.

"That Bram was a vampire." I was impressed with how even my voice stayed as I said the words out loud for the first time.

Zach shook his head in small, quick movements, his brow furrowed. "No. I don't understand what's happening. I didn't know. What are you talking about?"

I looked at Hendricks. "You knew."

"Yes." He didn't bother denying it.

"Abby..." My mom's voice trembled when she said my name.

"I won't bother asking you. I already know the answer." I looked at Ethan.

His face showed ... concern? Regret? Sadness? Anger? I didn't recognize the look on his face. I didn't know what it meant. Maybe I never knew.

"Abby..." He moved closer to me.

"You lied to me." My breath hitched.

"Abby..." My mom tried to get my attention again.

"Please let me explain." Ethan shifted in his chair.

"And you two knew each other?" I was already staring at him, so I turned to look at her.

"Yes." She was quiet. "But..."

"This entire time" —I was talking to her— "you two knew each other. And you shared a secret."

Her eyes moved to Ethan, then back at me. "Abby..."

"How?" I faced Ethan.

"I turned him."

I laughed with no humor as tears fell from my eyes. Then more clicked into place. "When?"

"Before you were born."

"Hold the fuck up. Bram was a vampire, and you are the one that turned him? Then he isn't..." Zach was pissed as he asked my mother for answers

"He is her father," she said.

"She's not a vampire!" Zach yelled and pointed his finger at me. "That doesn't make any sense!"

"It can happen." Ethan's tone was stiff. "Bram was human. I turned him to save his life. Half-breed children can take after either parent."

"Half-breed?" I repeated the word incredulously. Another insult, another blow, as if I hadn't been hit enough.

"No. No, that's not what I meant! *No.* I don't know why it came out like that." Ethan was pleading, his voice growing stronger. "That's not what I meant, Abby. Please. I didn't mean to say that."

"You knew who I was."

Ethan clenched his teeth and swallowed hard.

I didn't need to hear his answer. Laughing again, I covered my good hand over my face and wiped once angrily as I stood from the chair.

Ethan begged, "Please listen to me. Let me explain. I wanted to tell you. I wanted to tell you everything."

"I told him not to. I made him. I was trying to protect you." My mom stood up too.

"From what?" I was so calm it surprised me. "Protect me from what? My identity? The truth? *What* I am?"

Zach was glaring at Ethan. "When you met her in Honor, you knew who she was, didn't you?"

Ethan's eyes locked on mine, his face tense.

I took a step back. His soundless admission was painful.

"I wasn't certain until I saw Olivia."

"That was the first day you were here!" I raised my voice a little, even as a hole punched through my chest. "You knew the whole time? Were you just using me?" My eyes swam again.

"No." His answer was immediate and hard, the denial calm and increased in intensity as he repeated it. "No. *No*. It was *not* like that. It was *never* like that. I never used you. I would never do that. This is real. Everything we have is real, Abby. What we have has nothing to do with them."

"All this time, you were worried about him hurting me." I shook my head at my Mom. "And here you were, doing it at the same time."

"I'm sorry. He wanted to tell you. I—"

"You told me Bram was dead."

"I thought he was." Her words were barely audible now.

We were both crying; she was sobbing, and my face was just a never-ending stream of tears down my cheeks.

She brought her hands up to cover her mouth. "I'm so sorry."

"Whoa, wait. What do you mean you *thought* he was dead?" Zach looked at me. "How did you find out about this?"

"Bram told me."

My mom and Ethan sucked in a breath as Zach's eyes widened.

"How..."

"He's the revenant."

Hendricks folded his arms across his chest and was looking down at the floor. Sylis and Seivor stepped away but not out of the room. Just away. Ethan's hands twitched, clenching and unclenching, lifting and dropping heavily by his sides. Zach was beside me, his face red and his fists balled.

"You knew it was him. Didn't you?" Zach sneered.

I wiped at my face. "What?"

He looked down at me with big eyes, then he turned back to the three of them. "The revenant. You knew it was Bram, and you didn't say anything."

Ethan, Hendricks, and my mom didn't say a word.

"You knew?" I swayed on my feet.

"We didn't think..." Ethan inched forward and then stopped.

"You didn't think that we would find out." Zach laughed. He came to stand next to me. "So it wasn't just that you lied about Bram being a vampire. Or that she's a *half-breed*. Or that he was alive. Or that you turned him. Or that you all knew each other and kept it a big secret. You knew Bram was the revenant too."

"We didn't know it was him until he killed Pike in Burke," Ethan fumed. "Don't exaggerate the facts and make this worse than it already is!"

"I'm making it worse?" Zach barked out a dark laugh. "You are fucking unbelievable! How is this not information we all should have known?" He looked at Hendricks when he asked the question.

"We made a judgment call." Hendricks owned the decision.

"You could have gotten away with that one." Zach shook his head in frustration. "If she'd known everything, you could have played off that you didn't say anything because you only just found out yourselves. But you weren't ever going to say anything because if you did, the rest of your lies would have unraveled."

None of them denied it.

"He tried to kill me." I felt sick, and my breathing sped up again. "No, he *did* kill me. And you saved my life, Ethan, just to turn around and break my heart." My voice quivered. I felt like I was dying all over again. But this ... hurt worse.

"Abby, no, please. Please ... *please* let me explain."

My eyes were blurry, and my breath hitched on the words. "I can't believe anything you say now."

My statement was as if I'd slapped him. Ethan was a vampire of integrity. Not being trustworthy was a stain on his character. A contradiction to who he was.

"It's not his fault," Mom defended him.

"You're right, it's not just his fault." I swiped at my face. "You all lied to me."

"To protect you," Hendricks pleaded. His face was blotchy, and his eyes were glassy too.

"You keep saying that, but you haven't explained why. Protect me from what, exactly? What was the point of hiding it all?" My chest heaved. "He was going to make me like him."

My mom brought her hands up to her face.

"They were going to turn me into a vampire. Kill me. Then make me one of them."

Ethan clenched his jaw.

None of them knew what Bram and Pike had said to me. I hadn't told them before now.

"Knowing the truth wouldn't have changed that, but at least I would have known!" I sucked in a breath. "My entire life is a lie. My relationships with each one of you were built on a lie. Everything you've *ever* said to me is founded on a lie."

"I'm so sorry," my mom cried. "I'm so, so sorry."

I wiped my face again. "So am I."

Zach wrapped his arm around my shoulders.

"Where are you going?" Mom's voice rose in panic.

"You're all staying here, and I don't want to be around any of you. So I'm leaving."

"Abby, wait." Ethan followed behind, and when I didn't stop, he put himself in front of me. "Please don't go. Talk to me." His eyes darted around my face, and his voice was pleading.

"Now, you want to talk?" I shuddered with a fresh wave of tears. "Now's too late, Ethan. *Now*, I don't want to hear anything you have to say."

His face crumbled.

My head was pounding, and my cheeks were hot. Throat raw and sore, my mouth felt thick and full of cotton.

"You should have told me. I would have listened. I would have let you explain. If you had respected me enough to try." When my diaphragm started to spasm, I hid my face to catch my breath.

"No, no, no." Ethan reached for my hands. "Please don't cry. I'm sorry. I'm so sorry. Please stay. Let me explain. We can talk this through."

My world was crashing around me, my heart taking the brunt of it.

Cracking.

I wiped my face and looked at him. "This isn't a fight, Ethan. This is the end."

Breaking.

His face blanched. "No, Abby, please ... please don't do this."

Shattering.

I swiped my tears and sucked in a breath. “I didn’t do this. You did.”

EPILOGUE

"I'm taking Sally out for a spin. I can drop you off if you don't want to walk today." Zach said from his tiny kitchen, then downed the rest of the chocolatey protein shake in his glass.

"Sure," I grunted as I bent over to tie my shoes.

I just got back the night before after being out on rotation for the last two weeks, and I was going back to the O this morning to help with breakfast. It was the first time I'd been on vanguard duty since my arm healed, and I was relieved to get away from town for a while.

For all of Hendricks's threats to keep me sealed behind the walls of Thompson Falls, when it came down to it, he hadn't held me back. Maybe it was guilt, or maybe he just came to his senses. Whatever it was, I didn't care. I was glad to be working.

My team had gone on a supply run, and we hit the jackpot with our find. We had discovered an old company warehouse full of breakfast-related food items. The intact building had remained sealed, along with everything in it, and it was all still good and usable, which was amazing.

Once it had been cleared for entry into the town, Gigi was told first and, of course, planned to take full advantage of it. She had put out the word that there would be a vast assortment of muffins, scones, pancakes, waffles, biscuits, and gravy with eggs the entire week. The last time she announced a huge feast like this, we could barely keep up and asked some diners to help serve other people when they were done eating. I had been mortified but so thankful for the help. Needless to say, I expected it to be crazy and wanted to get there early.

"I'm ready when you are." I stood up from the couch when my shoes were tied.

The late spring and early summer months were long and hot here in Thompson Falls, and even though it was still morning, it was already bright and very warm. The sky was clear, and the air still smelled fresh from the springtime bloom, even though it was dry.

The town bustled with life around us as we exited the building, the familiar sounds of work equipment in the distance the bass to the chorus of squealing laughter from kids who played outside the school. Dogs barked happily, birds chirped high in the trees, and the ducks and chickens clucked and quacked as they feasted on the buffet of grasshoppers and bugs.

"Whew, it's going to be hot today. This summer's going to be hell if it keeps like this." Zach rolled down his window as soon as we pulled out of the garage. The interior temperature of the car was at least fifteen degrees warmer than it was outside, and the distinct smell of warm leather was heavy in the air.

The cool breeze through the windows combated the temperature's steady rise as we drove but did nothing about the sunshine through the windshield.

"I should have worn shorts." I rubbed the front of my legs to swipe away the burn as I looked down at my bad-decision jeans.

"You can change at the O." Zach floated his left hand out the window and steered with his right.

"If there's anything there." Most of my things were at Zach's place now. It seemed like every time I left the O, I took something else with me.

"I'm sure you can find something." He turned into the O's parking lot and went to his designated parking space. Then, he put the car in park, pulled the E-brake, and took his foot off the pedal.

"Are you staying for breakfast?"

"Yeah, right." He looked at me with a goofy grin. "I just had that huge shake."

"That's never stopped you before." I reached over and patted him on the stomach.

"Hey!" He pushed my hand away, then grabbed my arm and tickled my side.

"Stop it!" I laughed.

"You started it."

"You started it," I mocked him.

"Real mature, Abby." He chortled and shook his head at me.

His smile dropped from his face when his eyes shifted over my shoulder. He gritted his teeth, shut the car off, opened his door, and stepped out—all in one fluid motion. I didn't have to look to know why his mood had changed.

Zach sauntered around the hood of the car to the passenger side, whereas I hadn't moved. "On second thought..." He reached in through the open window and pulled the handle to open the door. "I think I will stay for breakfast."

"Zach," I chided as I stood from the seat and moved out of the way so he could shut the door.

"What?" he acted innocent. "I got hungry. That's all." He threw his arm over my shoulders and started us toward the steps.

It had been five weeks since I found out about my father, and all the secrets and lying. I haven't said more than a handful of words to any of them, other than acknowledgments or brief answers to questions that pertained to either of my jobs. The first two weeks after I found out, I had kept away from them completely. I stayed at Zach's night and day, and he would get me anything I needed, or Charlie or Harper would bring it with them when they came to visit. I didn't want to see or speak to any of them. I had nothing to say, and I wasn't interested in listening to them either. Too hurt and angry, I needed time.

After the first two weeks, however, I had gone back to work but continued to stay with Zach. Pent up and restless, I concluded that I wasn't the one who should stay away. I had nothing to be sorry for—I wasn't the one who had lied and kept secrets. Also, I'd missed my routine and was going stir-crazy, but nobody needed to know that.

I was seeing the vanguard counselor regularly too. It was mandatory for all members of the vanguard, but regularly scheduled appointments weren't part of my normal requirements, just something new. I'd been set up with additional appointments after my father had tried to kill me and Pike had kidnapped me, and I was grateful because it helped a lot. I wasn't as angry anymore; still hurt, yes, but not nearly as angry. Talking with Aemen, I came to understand the instinct to protect someone from something you knew would only hurt them.

What I struggled with was that I wasn't just anyone. I was an accomplished, self-reliant member of the vanguard who had gone through years of conditioning, not just physically but mentally too. I wasn't unprepared for the unexpected—I'd been trained for it.

All the lying didn't make sense to me, and it's what I'd struggled with the most—I didn't understand the point of it.

Feeling stupid because I hadn't known I was being lied to, I was embarrassed and ashamed. Hurt and felt betrayed, and then of course, angry. I knew I wouldn't have felt the same way had I been told about everything right away. I absolutely would have been shocked and would have probably gone through a gamut of other emotions, but not this.

I wasn't a little girl, and I certainly wouldn't have run after my not-so-dead-psychotic-vampire/*kook*-hybrid-murderer of a father in a fit of daddy issues.

My mother had more to apologize for than anyone else. The half-vampire thing hadn't thrown me off as much as one would expect. Knowing my biology my entire life would have been nice, but I had to accept it—there was literally nothing else to do. I understood now why I adapted and accepted change better than my peers. I was coined an old soul or a pushover, depending on who you talked to, when really it was just in my nature.

Now that I knew, it cleared up some things in my life. My health and testing scores made more sense—I'd never been sick, not even a cold, and I easily retained information. Nowhere near perfect recall like a full-blooded vampire, but my memory retention wasn't anything to balk at. I didn't have super senses necessarily. Nothing that would have drawn attention or made me question my biology all these years. But I'd always been more athletic than the other girls growing up. I had more stamina, which was why I liked to run so hard and long. My hearing and eyesight were perfect, but that wasn't unusual even in humans. My marksmanship was less impressive now that I wasn't a human with a skill but part vampire with an innate ability.

There were ... other things that made more sense now too. My libido, for starters. Humans were sexual creatures, absolutely—some more than others—but I'd always felt like a horny teenage boy. Now, I knew I was just a horny half-blood and my biological urges were just standard operating procedure. Vampires weren't hairless, but they didn't have coarse hair all over their bodies like humans did either. Just a fine dusting of soft delicate hair, everywhere. The rule didn't apply to facial hair and head hair, obviously, just everywhere else. Biologically, it made sense. Hair was meant to protect from the cold, and a vampire's temperature ran different than a human's. Neolithically, it helped with scenting. For humans specifically, that included attracting a mate by holding onto pheromones. But vampires had heightened senses naturally, so there was never a need for scent catching, hence the hairlessness.

My mother had always told me that my hairlessness was a hereditary anomaly I'd gotten from my dad. That was true, I guess. I had felt weird about it growing up, when all the other girls started getting hair during puberty, but then they envied me once they were tired of it. So that had balanced out, and I'd never felt self-conscious about it. Female vampires didn't hormone the same way as human females either, which explained my weird cycles growing up. Not that I'd had them for long, I had taken full advantage of medical and gotten rid of that nuisance as soon as possible. But still, it was another thing cleared up for me.

I had also accepted I had some innate personality traits that were more vampire inherent and less human, with a moderate perfectionist syndrome.

Zach had his own issues to come to terms with about the whole thing. He'd been lied to by my mother for most of his life too. Hendricks lying to us about something that affected our jobs was a major problem for him, and he already didn't like Ethan. He'd promised to give him a chance after Ethan had saved my life, but it was almost too easy for him to fall back on his word and use this as an excuse to hate him more. He'd been great to me, though, as usual. He had my back completely.

"Good morning, Abby," Ethan greeted.

He always did this. It used to piss me off, but I was not as angry anymore. I certainly wasn't going to go out of my way to be friendly, though.

"Ethan," I responded, refusing to look at him. It was petty and I knew I used it as punishment, but it was what he wanted from me, and I didn't want to give it to him.

If I was being completely honest with myself, I also did it because I was afraid. Not *of* him, but of what I still felt *for* him. I didn't want to be captive to my feelings, but I was afraid that if I looked at him, then I'd let him talk to me, and if I let him talk to me, then... I didn't know what. But I wasn't ready for it, whatever it was.

"Kick rocks, bloodsucker." Zach didn't even try to hide behind manners or pleasantries.

Ethan ignored him, which was standard. "We have news."

The three words stopped my step and froze my hand on the doorknob.

They had new information about Pike and the revenant. He wouldn't have said it like that, like it was something he knew I'd want to know. He wanted my forgiveness, so using my assumption that he was referring to this one subject and tricking me into speaking with him was not something he would do. He wasn't stupid.

I was curious, and I wanted to know what he knew so badly that my stomach hurt. I couldn't ask him, though; I couldn't bring myself to talk to him.

I wasn't ready, and I didn't know if I ever would be.

So, petty as I was, I let him know with choice words that I still wasn't over it and didn't trust him. "If that's true, then I'll talk about it with my team leader."

Then I opened the door and walked away.

Reader's Note

Thank you for reading Revenant, book one in The War of Blood and Roses Series! Your support means everything, and I look forward to sharing the rest of this world with you.

For the latest updates, news, series soundtracks, and character playlists, connect with me on social media.

Happy reading!

—R

ACKNOWLEDGEMENTS

I want to express my sincere thanks to my amazing husband, Jerry. Your constant support and encouragement mean everything and have made this writing journey possible. Your belief in me has been invaluable, and I truly couldn't be more grateful for the constant strength you've provided.

To my children: You are my greatest creation. I love you to the farthest star and all the way back—times infinity.

To Mr. Smith, for rescuing the rough draft of this book from the clutches of a different kind of virus.

To the fans, your continual support and enthusiasm for this series have been deeply appreciated and incredibly inspiring.

To the talented artists and diligent editors whose expertise has elevated the quality of this book.

I have immense gratitude for every single one of you.

Thank you,

—R

ABOUT THE AUTHOR

R. Valentine is an author with a deep appreciation for life's simple pleasures. Her immersive writing style has gained her a dedicated following of readers and won the hearts of fans worldwide, putting her books at the top of Amazon Best Seller Lists.

With a love for fantasy, paranormal, science fiction, and romance, R. Valentine's stories offer readers an escape from the mundane. In her free time, she can be found lost inside a good book, pretending to cook, neglecting her flower garden, or making memories with her family.

Follow R. Valentine for up-to-date information on The War of Blood and Roses Series, upcoming projects, and new releases.

If you enjoyed R. Valentine's writing, explore more worlds crafted under the author's other pen names.

NVREADS.COM/NVP-PENNAMES

Glossary

'I-M' — The vaccine intended to mitigate human frailty but instead turned them into the undead

PEI — Pure Energy Initiative (pronounced: pay) A global renewable energy campaign aimed at combating climate change

Morgue — Open land outside of the security walls of Thompson Falls

Kook/kooks — The original dead: zombies. Humans who perished with 'I-M' in their system and became the undead. (Grave mutants, flesh monsters, munchers)

Evo/evos — The evolved dead. Infected from the original dead. (Kid/kids, kook-spawn, ankle-biters)

Spyder/spyders — Lawless groups of humans with no moral or ethical code

Laurel — Human blood donor for vampires' sustenance

Decon-zone — Decontamination zone. These are the gated sections preceding the main entrance to Thompson Falls, including the preliminary entrance, medical bay, overflow section, death palace, and security gates

Med-bay — Medical facility within the gated section, where individuals are screened for bites and undergo blood tests to confirm absence of infection by the virus

HG-80 — Mercury hand grenades

HGB — Mercury bullets

The Safe — Facility for storing wearable gear, weapons, and defensive supplies

The Pit — Transport garage with vehicles, heavy machinery armaments, food, water, and first aid supplies

TRIGGERS AND CONTENT

MATURE AUDIENCE 18+ ADVISED

READING MATERIAL FEATURES:
STEAMY/SUGGESTIVE SCENES
SMUT/SEXUALLY GRAPHIC SCENES WITH EXPLICIT LANGUAGE & DESCRIPTION
BLOOD, GORE, & SEVERE LANGUAGE
EXCESSIVE OR GRATUITOUS VIOLENCE

READING MATERIAL WILL INCLUDE OR IMPLY:

ABORTION
ABUSE: (EMOTIONAL, MENTAL, PHYSICAL, SEXUAL, VERBAL)
BULLYING
CANNIBALISM
CHEATING/IMPLIED INFIDELITY
CHILD ABUSE/PEDOPHILIA
DEGRADATION
DRUGS/ALCOHOL & ADDICTION
FORCEFUL DEPRIVATION OF/ DISREGARD FOR PERSONAL AUTONOMY
HUMAN TRAFFICKING
INFANT/CHILD DEATH
INJURY, MILD TO EXTREME/HOSPITALIZATION
KINKS
KIDNAPPING
MENTAL ILLNESS
MISOGYNY, MISANDRY, SEXISM
MISCARRIAGE/STILLBIRTH
MURDER/DEATH
PEDOPHILIA
PREDATORY BEHAVIOR
PTSD, DEPRESSION, ANXIETY
RACIAL AND PHOBIC SLURS
RAPE & SEXUAL ASSAULT
REVENGE
SELF-INJURIOUS BEHAVIOR (EATING DISORDERS, SELF-HARM, ETC.)
SLAVERY
STALKING
SUICIDE/ASSISTED SUICIDE
TORTURE

THIS SERIES INCLUDES AND THE AUTHOR WRITES WITH INCLUSIVITY AND DIVERSITY:

LGBTQ+
BISEXUAL
GAY
LESBIAN
POLY
STRAIGHT
CHARACTERS & RELATIONSHIPS

TROPES: AMNESIA, APOCALYPSE, BONDED, CLIFFHANGER, CLIMATE FICTION, DARK SECRET, DYSTOPIA, ENEMIES TO LOVERS, FOUND FAMILY, FORCED PROXIMITY, FRIENDS TO LOVERS, INST-LOVE, LOVE TRIANGLE, MARTYR, MISSING PERSON, MULTIPLE POV, OBLIVIOUS LOVE, PANDEMIC, PARANORMAL ROMANCE, SECOND CHANCE, SECRET IDENTITY, SLOW BURN, SOULMATES, UNREQUITED LOVE

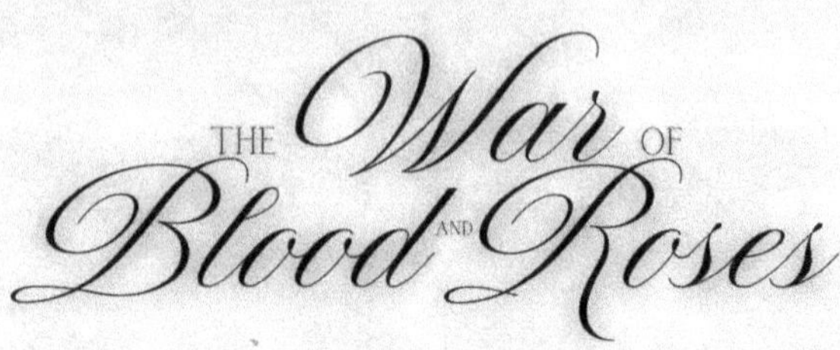

Revenant
Virulent
Evanescent
Vehement
Revivescent

THE WAR OF BLOOD

WORLD

www.ingramcontent.com/pod-product-compliance
Lightning Source LLC
LaVergne TN
LVHW010632110826
845149LV00014B/2832

* 9 7 8 1 9 6 3 3 3 6 0 0 9 *